More praise from both sides of the Atlantic for

FIRST LIGHT

"Readers may look forward to comic suspense of almost Hitch-cockian precision, to feats of inventive exuberance, and to some elements of considerable pathos."

The Times Literary Supplement (London)

"A performance of much skill and ingenuity.... [Ackroyd] is a writer of highly intelligent entertainment."

The New Republic

"[Ackroyd] can make you believe anything while you're reading him. He's a breathtaking trickster, who knows that everything is invented, and that the best human beings can do is make up stories 'in the dark.' "

The Observer

"Witty, suspenseful, inventive and above all extremely imaginative."

Boston Herald

"Ackroyd is such a master of mood, of tension, angst, foreboding, frisson, but also of tenderness and exultation, that one is drawn into his tale as by a magus.... An absorbing, mysterious, learned, beautiful, and rather awe-inspiring novel."

Sunday Telegraph

"First-class entertainment... Ackroyd neatly balances the antics of his eccentric cast with the deeper enigmas of the cosmos."

The Orlando Sentinel

"An absorbing, compulsively readable story."

The Listener

FIRST LIGHT

OTHER NOVELS BY PETER ACKROYD:

The Great Fire of London
The Last Testament of Oscar Wilde
Hawksmoor
Chatterton*
Dickens

*Published by Ballantine Books

FIRST LIGHT

PETER ACKROYD

BALLANTINE BOOKS
NEW YORK

Library of Congress Catalog Card Number: 90-93250

ISBN: 0-345-36887-7

This edition published by arrangement with Grove Weidenfeld, New York

Cover design by Bill Geller
Cover photo: The Image Bank

Manufactured in the United States of America
First Ballantine Books Edition: April 1991
10 9 8 7 6 5 4 3 2 1

PART ONE

*But if he spoke it would mean that all this world
would end now – instanto – fall down on your head.
These things are not allowed. The door is shut.*

'The Finest Story in the World'
RUDYARD KIPLING.

◆ I ◆

THE UNCERTAINTY PRINCIPLE

LET ME be drawn up into the immensity. Into the darkness, where nothing can be known. Once there were creatures of light leaping across the firmament, and the pattern of their movement filled the heavens. But the creatures soon fled and in their place appeared great spheres of crystal which turned within each other, their song vibrating through all the strings of the world. These harmonies were too lovely to last. A clock was ticking in the pale hands of God, and already it was too late. Yes. The wheels of the mechanism began to turn. What was that painting by Joseph Wright of Derby? I saw it once. Was it called 'The Experiment'? I remember how the light, glancing through a bell-jar, swerved upwards and covered the whole sky. But this too went out: the candle flame was blown away by the wind from vast furnaces, when the electrical powers swept across the firmament.

But there were always fields, fields of even time beyond the fires. Empty space reaching into the everlasting. At least I thought that as a child. Then there came a tremor of uncertainty. There was no time left. No space to float in. And everything began moving away. Nothing but waves now, their furrows tracking the path of objects which do not exist. Here is a star called Strange. Here is a star called Charmed. And after this, after this dream has passed, what then? What shape will the darkness take then? I . . . Damian Fall turned to his companion. "Of course you know what we will be observing?"

"Aldebaran."

"Yes. There." Damian pointed towards the horizon, and both men looked out at the great star. "One hundred and twenty times brighter than the sun," he said. And he put his hand above his eyes, as if shielding them from the heat. Burning star. Seeming to be red, but the colours shifting like an hallucination. In this same area of the sky they saw small cones of light, called the Hyades and believed to

3

be at a greater distance from the earth – cool red stars glowing within the clouds of gas which swirled about them. And close to them the lights known as the Pleiades, involved in a blue nebulosity which seemed to stick against each star, the strands and filaments of its blue light smeared across the endless darkness. Behind these clusters they could see the vast Crab Nebula, so far from the earth that from this distance it was no more than a mist or a cloud, a haziness in the eye like the after-image of an explosion. And yet Damian could see further. He looked up and could see. Galaxies. Nebulae. Wandering planets. Rotating discs. Glowing interstellar debris. Spirals. Strands of brightness that contained millions of suns. Darkness like thick brush-strokes across a painted surface. Pale moons. Pulses of light. All these coming from the past, ghost images wreathed in mist which confounded Damian. I am on a storm-tossed boat out at sea, the dark waves around me. This was what the earliest men saw in the skies above them – an unfathomable sea upon which they were drifting. Now we, too, talk of a universe filled with waves. We have returned to the first myth. And what if the stars are really torches, held up to light me on my way? I see what they saw in the beginning, even before the creatures of light appeared across the heavens. I can see the first human sky.

"Yes," he said. "Aldebaran. Once this region was thought to form the outline of a face in the constellation of Taurus – " He looked at the face of his companion, but he could see only a silhouette in the darkness. "But the Pleiades contains three hundred stars in no real pattern. Just burning, being destroyed, rushing outward." The last vestiges of cloud had now drifted away and the entire night sky had reappeared, so bright and so clear that Damian Fall put out his hand to it; then he turned his wrist, as if somehow he could turn the sky on a great wheel. And for a moment, as he moved his head, it did seem that the stars moved with him. "Why is it," he went on, "that we think of a circular motion as the most perfect? Is it because it has no beginning and no end?"

"Now that's a deep question."

"Like circles in stone. You know there was an ancient historian who wrote about the stone circles around us here? Even on the moor. He describes how the god was supposed to return to the island of Britain every nineteen years, the period in which the stars completed their cycle. During his visitation the god sang and danced continuously by night – on just such a night as this – from the spring equinox to the rising of the Pleiades. And of course the rising of Aldebaran with them." His young companion shifted his feet, and said nothing. "You know one thing that has always puzzled me, Alec? Why does our galaxy rotate as it does? The mass of the visible stars is not enough to account for the movement. There must be other kinds of mass. Other fields of force. Black holes. Patches of darkness. Uncertainties. I'm sorry. I'm boring you. You know all this."

"Yes. I had heard. It's my job." Alec blushed, instantly regretting his tone.

"A hundred thousand million galaxies. A hundred thousand million stars in each one."

"Serious numbers."

"I wish we could see them all, but then probably the light would blind us. Still, we do our best." He turned around and looked back at the observatory, its white dome gleaming in the starlight. "What I meant to say," he went on, more cheerfully now, "is welcome to the project. Welcome to Holblack Moor."

"Tea up." The two men were roused from the darkness, and stepped apart, as a young woman called over to them. "Almost dawn," she said. "Time for a nice cup of tea."

"Coming, Brenda. We're coming."

This star is Strange. And this is Charmed. Everything is rushing away. Damian drank his tea and, under the light issuing from immensity, he chatted with Alec and with Brenda.

He drove back by way of Pilgrin Valley and, as he turned down the small track which ran beside it, he was forced to brake suddenly in order to let a brown car pass. He looked at it curiously, and saw a man and woman sitting in the front; they were saying nothing to each other, but the woman was holding up a small mirror in order to pat her hair into place. It was already light.

◆2◆

AFTER THE FIRE

"FROM ASHES to ashes," she said. "How gorgeous."

"And you see," he went on, "where the fire died down within the ash forest? There. Over there." In his excitement he took off his green deerstalker hat and pointed with it across the valley.

"You mean all those alarming black stains?" She peered vaguely in the direction of his outstretched hat, and noticed large scorch marks which at this distance looked like shadows on the earth itself.

"The burnt trees were cleared away, after the fire. And that's when we saw it." He looked at her, his eyes still wide. "That, Miss Tupper, is when we made the discovery."

"It's the most extraordinary story I have ever heard in my *life*." On this spring afternoon, her words disturbed the vast pool of bird song around them.

Evangeline Tupper and Mark Clare were standing on a track beside the west slope of Pilgrin Valley and ahead of them, across the east slope, stretched the bright grass which sprang from the chalk of this region. It is so bright that it seems to blaze and its line of flame to follow the curve of the chalkland for many miles, sweeping across its ledges and plateaux, filling its shallows and depressions, rising with its dunes and hills. From the air it appears to be a huge river moving inland from the sea but those who walk upon it know how fragile it can be, how easily uprooted from the soil, how close to the hard bed of the chalk itself so that its brightness becomes a kind of delirium, its green a fever of imminent destruction.

From the west slope of the valley they could see how one area of the chalk grassland was still scorched and blackened after the fire but how, to both sides of it, the landscape remained as it had always been – the fields here of varying colours, as if clouds were passing overhead and turning the vivid green into darker shades of emerald

6

or of jade. Here also there were patches of juniper scrub and, dotted amongst them, dark evergreen bushes which from this distance looked almost black against the varying shades of the land. There was a ridge above the valley at this point, with a decaying plantation of beeches clustered upon it; mixed among the beeches there stood a clump of young ashes, their smooth grey bark like strips of light against the dark wood of the older trees. And there, further down, on the edge of the burnt forest, was the ancient tumulus itself.

The grass or turf which covered it was of a darker green than any in the fields beside it and although at first sight it might seem part of the natural landscape – its shape was like that of a hillock or dune – on further inspection it was clearly not in proportion with the rest of Pilgrin Valley. It was twelve feet at its highest point and some eighty or ninety feet in length, seeming to emerge from the side of the valley itself and then rising gradually before sloping abruptly downwards. This long narrow mound might have marked the sudden emergence of some creature now extinct or have represented some ancient and forgotten disease in the landscape – a large growth which had for centuries been successfully concealed beneath the covering of ash trees, but which had now at last been revealed within the blackened circles of a forest fire.

A wind started up from the east and carved strange shapes in the grass before it reached Evangeline Tupper, who gave an expressive little shiver before tying the knots of her bright red scarf more firmly under her chin. "It's all too much," she said to Mark Clare. "I'm coming out in goose pimples. Or is it goose *bumps?*"

He put out his arm, believing that she needed support, but she backed away quickly. "I think it was the wind," he said. "We're accustomed to strong winds up here."

"Something absolutely rural like that, I'm sure." It was growing cold, and her toes curled involuntarily within her brown walking shoes. "Something utterly unchanging like this—" She could not think of an appropriate word. "—this territory."

"No. It has changed." Mark had a deep voice and he took some pleasure in employing it, in reciting all he knew while Evangeline looked out mournfully over the valley as if she were some Dryad about to be turned into a tree. "It has changed," he said again. "This would all have been forest once, and some of it must have been cleared away before they built the tomb. Cleared by fire. And then the stones were brought here. This must have been a sacred place.

Perhaps they thought of it as a centre of the earth." His eyes gleamed with his own romantic vision of the past and, as the wind swept through the grass and the trees, it was as if a multitude were on the march.

His voice trailed off and Evangeline, assuming that he had finished, murmured, "I must have a Woody. Do you mind awfully?" She took a packet of Woodbines from the pocket of her tweed jacket, and stuck a cigarette into her mouth without lighting it.

"Shall we follow our ancestors?" he asked her, impatient to reach the site itself. "Shall we go down?"

"Go down where?"

"To the tomb." He hesitated, so odd a mixture of bravado and uncertainty that there were times when one person seemed to retire as another stepped forward. He had long sideburns which covered half of his cheeks, and now he began to smooth them down with his hands. He looked at Evangeline almost in defiance, as if she were about to contradict him. "We're almost sure that it must be a tomb, you see."

"I can't wait. Really can't." But it was with a noticeable reluctance that she followed Mark Clare.

"Tally ho!" he shouted, sensing her slowness, and began running down the slope, his long loosely-fitted overcoat billowing out behind him.

"Wait for me," she shouted back, in a much weaker voice. "Wait for the little fox!" The ground was still soft after a recent rainstorm, and Evangeline had some difficulty in picking her way across the flints and old stones which littered the valley; she jumped over one boulder but then skidded into a patch of mud and sat down heavily upon the damp grass. "Shit!" she shrieked, before getting up very quickly. And then she laughed, as if she had enjoyed her own fall – a loud, long laugh which echoed through Pilgrin Valley. It also startled two sheep in an adjoining field; they ran into a corner of the tall hedge and they waited there, the red brands clearly visible upon their cropped wool as they averted their faces from the wind. At the same moment two small white vans passed along the track from which Mark and Evangeline had just come; they stopped, and then moved on again into the dark foliage which grew over this stretch of the old road.

Evangeline searched in the wet grass for her cigarette, retrieved it with a flourish, and then in much better humour followed Mark

8

down to the stream which ran through the bottom of Pilgrin Valley and which was swollen now with the recent rains; here she felt it necessary to pause for a moment. Concealing from Mark the fact that she was still smiling to herself, she turned around and with a magnificent gesture waved across the valley. "And who—" she managed to say after a few seconds "—and who do we nature lovers have to thank for all this?"

"I'm sorry?"

"Who owns all this lovely scrub?"

"The ash forest and the tumulus belong to the Forestry Commission now. And the rest belongs to the local farmer. Farmer Mint. You can see his house over there." He pointed in the direction from which they had just come and there, along the track, she could see what appeared to be a collection of corrugated iron shacks.

"Ah," she said. "The good life. Nothing for miles and miles."

"Actually, Colcorum village is down there. At the other end of the valley."

"Colcorum? Let me roll it around my tongue." She took the damp cigarette from her mouth and threw it into the stream. "Colcorum. What a lovely old English name. Like sheepdog. Or muffins." All the while she was watching her Woodbine as it floated away from her on the turbid current. "And I wonder," she added, pointing dramatically at the water, "where all this comes from?" In fact no one knew. No one could tell precisely where it came from before it fled into the sea but there were a number of underground caves or fissures in the region, carved out of the soft chalk, and it was popularly believed that Pilgrin stream issued from some mighty river which flowed beneath the surface of the earth at this point where Devon and Dorset met. In the vicinity there were many springs and seepage lines, marked by damp or rushy patches, and it was no doubt from one of these that the stream emerged into the light. "And I wonder," Evangeline added, "if it would be ever so tiresome if I tried to find a wonderful little bridge?"

"There's no need." Mark brightened at the prospect of helping her. "Allow me."

He was about to take off his overcoat and drape it across some stones when Evangeline, with another laugh, jumped over the stream at its narrowest point. "Aren't we just like Lancelot and Guinevere?" she said. "We really are." In fact they were a strangely matched pair – Evangeline Tupper was in her late fifties. She was

9

short and somewhat narrow, with a thin mouth and sharp nose which made her look like a parrot onto whose face make-up had been hurled with great force, leaving it wide-eyed and bewildered. Mark Clare was tall, although his height was in part disguised by his plumpness. He was a robust red-faced man, well into middle-age, and with his broad sideburns he might have passed as a country butcher – yet his clothes were too bright, too eccentric, and there was a wariness about his eyes which suggested a man who was compelled to make an effort to conquer self-doubt. He had taken off his deerstalker now as he climbed the slope towards the mound and, in his sudden enthusiasm, he pushed back his straggling white hair with a violent gesture. Evangeline was having more difficulty with the ascent and appeared to be walking sideways, one leg crossing the other at an odd angle, and he waited for her to reach him before they walked the last few yards. "What time is—" she began to say.

She was gesturing at her wrist, but Mark was looking at the tumulus. "Thousands of years," he replied loudly. "At least four thousand years." He gave a sigh of pleasure and put out his arms towards it.

"As old as the hills! May I?" She brushed past him and, with one finger outstretched, prodded the mound with the tip of her varnished nail. "Something very ancient has entered me," she said. "Something old and precious is inside me now." She was about to lick her finger, but at the last moment she decided not to. "You *are* lucky," she added, "to be working here."

"We never would have found it, except for the fire. The ash trees had been covering it for – for I don't know how long—"

"Absolute centuries?"

"For a long time. And then when the fire destroyed them, and the ground was cleared, we saw it. No one had noticed it before. It was just another incline, just another surface feature." He had been looking at it almost in gratitude but then he swung around towards her and, in a softer voice, added, "Of course once we open it up, we destroy it. We will have to tear it apart as we excavate. In archaeology we always ruin the evidence even as we find it, but if we could just preserve it like this . . ."

"No no no." Evangeline shook her finger at him. "Don't you be naughty. The Department would kill me. And you." Evangeline was a senior civil servant in the Department of the Environment, and had travelled down from London after her immediate superior had given her Mark's report of what might be one of the most significant archaeological 'finds' in recent years. "And where," she added, "is that fascinating stone circle which you mentioned?" She put her hand to her forehead and scanned the horizon. "I don't see anything."

"I'm a fool," he cried out and, to her alarm, hit his chest with his clenched fist; he did everything on too large a scale, as if he were always trying to convince himself. "Of course you want to see the photographs. And I've left them in the car! Hang on." Before she could say anything he marched down the slope, jumped across the stream and started running up the other side of the valley towards the track where he had parked his brown Ford Cortina.

For some reason Evangeline did not welcome the prospect of being left alone beside the burial mound. She decided to turn her back upon it and then, very cautiously, she leaned against it; but it felt too damp, too soft, and the thought of falling into it – of somehow being sucked within it – appalled her. She took out another Woodbine, and with still trembling hands tried to light it. But the wind was too strong here in the exposed valley. She could hear it soughing through the branches of the ash and beech which clustered on the ridge above her but even here, in the open area beside the mound, she seemed to hear the same sound.

And yet she needed that smoke. "Desperate," she whispered to herself. "Desperate for a Woody." She looked around for some cover and noticed a small outcrop of rock a few yards further up the slope; somehow, with her peculiar sideways movement, she managed to reach it and then she crouched behind it so that only her tweed-covered rump was sticking up above the stone. But she lit her Woody and, with a small sigh of pleasure, she stood up, brushed her skirt and sat down upon the stone itself.

She glanced at the landscape around her without interest, and puffed viciously upon her cigarette. The two sheep were still huddled in a corner of the adjacent field, and she blew a smoke ring towards them. "I'd like you well cooked," she said. "I'd like you on my plate." She looked down the rest of the valley, with its trees and hedges and irregularly patterned fields, but she did not notice how patches of white chalk showed through the vivid grass like the bones beneath the flesh of some recumbent figure. Then she heard a noise behind her. She turned back to stare at the mound. Nothing moved. It must have been the wind. Now there was something crawling on her leg. And, when she bent down to examine it, she found a small green burr stuck to her nylon; it had left a definite 'run' in the stocking. "This place," she said. "This place is not very nice." She spoke out loud, as she often did, and it may have been laughter or it may have been her own echo along the ridge behind her. She turned around quickly and peered into the clusters of beech and ash above the valley; and for a moment she thought she saw something moving between the trees.

•3•

ON THE MOUND

"**M**ISS TUPPER?"

"Oh my God!" Evangeline gave a little shriek when Mark Clare touched her shoulder.

He shrieked back in sympathy. "I just wanted to show you these," he added in his confusion, and held out the photographs he had retrieved from his car.

Evangeline gave him one of her loveliest smiles. "There was no need to scream," she said. "I'm having a perfectly marvellous time. All this fresh air." She stubbed out her cigarette on the grass and crushed it with her heel but then, seeing Mark's inadvertent look of horror, she picked up the butt and placed it in her pocket. "Isn't it gorgeous," she went on, "here in the absolute wild?"

"It was much wilder once. Look." The first photograph was of the whole landscape from the air and in the upper left hand corner the tumulus could clearly be seen with the scorch marks around it; it must once have dominated the valley and, from this perspective, it resembled a single eye staring up at the heavens. The second photograph was taken from a different vantage, and showed the tumulus in the bottom left hand corner with the ridge of trees above it. "And here," Mark said, "is the old circle." With his finger he traced a line of darker soil which extended around the mound; it took not the form of a circle but that of an ellipse, and it extended into the field beyond Pilgrin Valley itself. "We come closer here," he went on, and with outstretched arm gave her the third photograph. "These are the marks of the standing stones. At least eight are buried but there are five still above the ground. You were just sitting on one of them."

"You don't have to tell me. I sensed it. I felt all Dorset beneath me. All of it going up me."

"And this was taken immediately above the mound." In the

13

fourth photograph the tumulus emerged from the side of the valley, but there was a shadow lying across it. "Everything suggests that this was an important burial place. The size of the tumulus. The stone circle. The site itself. I can see them walking in procession down the valley."

"Oh God. Where?" If there were people coming to greet her, she wanted to look her best.

Mark had not heard her. The tumulus was sacred still, because it had not changed. And it seemed to grow brighter as he watched it, with all the centuries glowing within it. A place of power. A place of ritual.

He turned around just as Evangeline was applying a fresh layer of peach-blush lipstick to her mouth. "I don't see a soul," she said, closing her pocket mirror with a definite snap.

"They're all around us," he said, stamping his feet on the ground like a child stamping in a puddle. "Everywhere."

"I could have told you that." With a dramatic flourish she untied her red scarf, and let her bleached hair slowly unwind in the air. "The ground above us," she murmured, gazing at the sky with a rapt expression, "the heavens beneath us. Now that's what I call poetry." He nodded, not wishing to point out that she had reversed the position of earth and sky. "I could stay here all day and just suck them all up."

"I could stay here all day, too." His enthusiasm had redoubled in response to her own.

"Well. Perhaps not today." He seemed to be taking her seriously, and she grew alarmed. "But very, very soon." She dabbed the side of her mouth with a paper handkerchief, and then dropped the soiled tissue into her handbag.

"I'm sure that you've seen enough." He sensed her mood, and began stamping his feet in a more weary rhythm. "I mustn't keep you." He would have been quite happy to stay, and to explain in detail the characteristics of the site which he and his team were about to excavate, but Evangeline said nothing and seemed to have resumed her quiet contemplation of the sky. "Shall we," he added, "shall we make our way back to the car?"

She sighed. "We *could* make our way back to the car. But only if you insist."

"No, not really—"

"—Of course I would like to stay here for ever. But if you *do* insist." She began fastening her scarf.

"I didn't mean—"

"And it is rather chilly, isn't it?" Quickly she walked ahead of him, her sideways motion tilting her some degrees to the left, until she reached the edge of the stream. When he reached her, she had one foot poised above it. "Was this stream always here, too?"

"Yes. I think so." He began helping her across four white stones which connected the banks. "Burial mounds were often placed beside running water."

"And nobody knows why?" He shook his head. "Of course not. Nobody ever does." With this somewhat cryptic comment she crossed the stream, and ascended the western slope towards Mark's car.

"It could have something to do with spirits," he said, once again hastening to catch up with her.

She laughed, and shouted to him over her shoulder. "That reminds me of a terribly funny story . . ." Her voice faded into the distance. The silence around the burial mound returned. Pilgrin Valley was quiet.

•4•

THE VALLEY

MARK DROVE Evangeline to Axminster Station and, as soon as she had entered her first-class compartment, he began waving – his arm held up high in the air, as if she were several hundred yards away. "Farewell," he bellowed. "Farewell, Miss Tupper!" With a sudden access of gallantry he took off his deerstalker and began waving that, too.

In her turn Evangeline was making frantic little signals in her compartment but, from her expression, it was difficult to determine whether she was in extreme high spirits or in terrible agony. With pantomimic gestures she was mouthing some words, and Mark thought that he recognised "gorgeous" when suddenly, without warning, she pulled the orange curtains across the window. The Inter-City express pulled out of the station, bearing its precious cargo back to London as she took out a Woodbine, sighed, and relapsed into her characteristically morose expression.

Mark had lived in Lyme Regis all his life but now, instead of returning home, he turned off the main Axminster to Bridport road and drove down the narrow lanes and steep tracks which would eventually take him back to Pilgrin Valley. Perhaps the tall hedges give this region its air of seclusion and even of secrecy; certainly there were no signposts to the valley itself, and there were times when even Mark was forced to slow down beside a gate, or a break in the hedge, in order to make sure of his location: he recognised the contours of the irregularly patterned fields, of the barrows, of the ancient hill-forts and embankments, and they had become his familiar guides. He was climbing higher now. The pink campion and dog violet gave way to scrub; the hedgerows became sparser and wilder; the chalk-land itself seemed to rise up towards the sky. Sometimes it occurred to Mark, when he was walking here, that he needed only to run across the curve of this chalk and then he, too, would be able to rise into the sky, borne upwards by the serene light of these high places. But then he would feel afraid of his own enthusiasm, and he would dig his heels into the grass and loam.

He was driving past the house of Farmer Mint. It was a small farmhouse of whitewashed stone, but it was surrounded by old sheds and barns which were constructed of corrugated iron sheets, wooden planks, ancient thatch, pieces of rag and a variety of other materials held together by yards of thick rope which were looped and knotted, falling like drapery across the ruined buildings. At first glance it might have been some gypsy encampment, but Mark knew that Farmer Mint had always lived here and that these ramshackle huts and sheds were a token of his being quite at home. They were temporary dwellings but only in the sense that Farmer Mint knew the valley would survive his passing, just as it had survived the deaths of those who had come before him.

He drove another few yards down the track, and then parked his Ford Cortina beside a steep bank before walking down into Pilgrin Valley. From here he could see the landscape stretching beneath him just as if it had momentarily unrolled itself at his feet, but on this cool spring day there was a mist forming at the far southern end of the valley and the fields there quivered before disappearing from sight. He walked quickly across the flinty soil and crossed the stream. When he came up to the tumulus itself, he put his hands against its grassy side; and then, more slowly, his face. He breathed in the dampness of the cold earth and, in his exhilaration, he believed that he was reaching towards unimaginable passages of lost time. He was there. With them.

He took a step back, and with an almost proprietorial manner surveyed the tumulus. Now it was as it had always been but Mark knew that, in a few days' time, it would have to be destroyed. When he and the archaeological team met on this spot to begin their work, the burial mound would be systematically stripped bare; as they worked downwards the stages of its construction would be reversed until the first secrets of its makers were finally revealed. And in that great change it would surely lose its sacredness. When he had first seen it, when he had first been brought to this spot after the forest fire had disclosed the great mound, when he had first observed the stones which surrounded it, he had been filled with an excitement which was almost like hilarity. He had retained all that excitement but now, as he glanced around the site, his mood was charged with pity – pity not only for those who might lie buried here but pity also for the tumulus itself which was about to suffer so severe a change.

Mark turned away, rubbing his face with his hands, and his movements were so sudden that they must have startled something in the copse of trees behind the mound. He thought he had seen a movement between the slender branches of the ash trees but, when he climbed up to them, there were only wreaths of small flies suspended in the air. Then he noticed how the sun threw the long shadows of the trees across the ground and he decided to keep on walking, pacing away from the shadows; he knew the land stretching beyond the west slope of the valley from the aerial photographs, for it was here in these fields that the boundaries of the stone circle were to be found, but he had never walked across it by himself. So now he passed through the trees, surmounted an outcrop of rock which marked the top ridge of the valley, reached the plateau above and then looked over the landscape. The softly undulating fields were familiar to him, but particularly he noticed a small thatched cottage which seemed almost to be hiding in a corner of one of them. It was surrounded by a tall sycamore hedge, and was partly obscured by two ancient plum trees which leaned towards its thatch, but even so Mark was intrigued by it. "Come on," he said to himself. "Come on, Mark Clare." He liked to walk, he liked what he called a 'blow', and with a smile he marched towards the cottage. He was in another time. He was a boy again.

After a few minutes he reached a white gate which opened into the garden of the cottage but, when he looked up, to his alarm he saw a dark figure moving rapidly to and fro across a window. And there was, in these quick movements across the light, some undefinable sense of fear or apprehension which affected Mark even as he stood there in the glowing field. He turned back, and retraced his steps across the valley.

·5·

SOME INHABITANTS

H E HAD come out onto the track but was so lost in his own thoughts that he almost stumbled against a line of cows being led homewards; they had the usual air of shambling defiance and thrust their heads forward as if they had recently been blinded and were still in pain, the immemorial procession of the animal kingdom towards ignominy and death. A dog barked at regular intervals and Mark could also hear the low murmur of two voices coming towards him. He stopped, and waited for Farmer Mint and Boy Mint to appear.

"Here he is, Boy," the farmer said. It was almost as if he had been expecting him.

"Yes," Mark answered, louder and more defiantly than he had intended. "Here I am."

"No. Him." Farmer Mint was pointing upwards, and Mark realised that he had been referring to a dark storm cloud which was clustering above Pilgrin Valley. "He's been biding his time." And he put his right palm upward, as if he were greeting the cloud. In turn Mark stepped forward to meet them, and he noticed that Farmer Mint was wearing his usual collection of heterogeneous garments: old dark blue walking shoes, patched brown trousers which were laced tight at the ankles, a thick black overcoat which was in turn covered by a green plastic mackintosh. He was wearing an old flat cap but nothing could disguise the amount of hair which seemed to be sprouting from all over his face and head – hair struggling to emerge from beneath the cap, hair pouring in torrents from his neck, hair writhing out of his ears, hair climbing from his eyebrows to his forehead. In contrast Boy Mint was almost completely hairless, and there was a suspicion that beneath his own flat cap he might in fact be bald; nevertheless he, too, wore blue boots, patched brown trousers, black overcoat and green plastic mackintosh so that

19

together they resembled a pair of large garden gnomes sprung suddenly to life. But Boy Mint was unlike his father in one respect: he seemed older, his manner more venerable, his replies more measured than those of Farmer Mint.

"Here he comes," Farmer Mint was saying. "Here's the first bit of him." And he held out three raindrops in the palm of his hand. "Take a lick of him, Boy, and bring your powerful mind to some conclusions."

Boy licked the proffered drops, and meditated upon them for a few moments. "It's rain," he said.

Farmer Mint was delighted. "He's hit it on the head again! Nothing gets past that boy!"

"And how long," Mark ventured to ask. "How long will it rain?" He was concerned about the start of the excavations.

"Give us a little more of your knowledge, Boy. How long will it last?"

Boy Mint contemplated the top of his father's cap for several seconds before delivering his final opinion. "He'll stop," he said. "He'll stop eventually."

"Was there ever a Boy like it?" Father and son looked at each other in admiration and then, at the same moment, pulled their caps further down their foreheads.

They were about to go forward, and already the cattle began to sway from side to side in instinctive anticipation of their move, but Mark wanted to tell them about the excavations. "We begin work next week," he said. "On the mound."

Farmer Mint laughed, showing the stumps of his decayed molars. "And what might you be expecting to find in there?"

The two Mints turned to stare into each other's eyes, and Boy Mint addressed an answer to his father. "Sheep's bones. And rabbits' teeth."

"Say it again, Boy. Linger over it."

"Sheep's bones. Rabbits' teeth. Skeletons of dead birds." Boy Mint was enjoying this litany, and smiled as he spoke. "Cow shit. Dead foxes. Moles."

"There's no stopping him now." Farmer Mint put both hands out into the rain, as if imploring it to listen. "He's the one who knows."

Mark Clare was equally sure that Boy Mint did not know the value of the tumulus, but his evident lack of interest came as something of a relief: in the past Mark had suffered from the curiosity and interference of neighbouring farmers, and he preferred to be left alone. In fact the Mints had owned the land into which the tumulus burrowed, until it had been purchased by the Forestry Commission some six years before, but their manner suggested to Mark that they were glad to be rid of it. Certainly the discovery of the burial mound, after the fire, seemed to them to be nothing more than some kind of practical joke. And yet, if this valley belonged to anyone, it belonged to the Mints.

The rain was falling heavily upon them and, in the gathering darkness, the mist swept down from the far end of the valley. For a moment the three men looked towards the tumulus in silence. "Sheep's bones," Boy Mint muttered, enjoying his joke once more. "Sheep's bones." Then the two men and their animals started moving in unison along the track. Mark watched them until they had turned into the fields and, not for the first time, considered the possibility that they had been putting on an act, that they had been performing for his benefit.

·6·

LONDON LILAC

EVANGELINE TUPPER took a taxi from Waterloo Station, but she did not direct the driver towards her own home. Instead she was to be seen arriving in quite another part of London. She turned into a white square, empty on this spring afternoon except for two or three slender and leafless poplars. A small terrace of mid-nineteenth-century houses bordered the far end of the square and it was towards these that she walked, more slowly now. A small, very elderly, man waved at her from a window; and, with a sigh, she climbed the stone steps and took out a key from her handbag to open the front door.

"You look well," he said, as she came into the narrow hallway. "You look very healthy."

"Hello, father."

"Shall I put the kettle on?"

"No. Let me." Anyone who knew Evangeline in other circumstances would have been surprised by her sudden weariness and the resigned, flat tone in which she spoke. But her father was accustomed to it.

"Your tea's ready," he said. "You do like beetroot, don't you?" He asked this anxiously – as if he might once have known and had now forgotten, or as if he no longer knew his daughter's tastes at all.

"Yes. Of course. Whatever you want."

Everything was prepared in the small front room and Evangeline glanced at her father from time to time as they ate together: in his hurried movements and gestures she could always see her own, and even in his now sunken face she recognised her own features. And yet I am so far away, she thought, so far away from him now. So far away from my origin. She realised that she had been looking at him as if he were just another old man, not her father. And it was as if she had been looking at herself as a stranger.

"How's work?" He asked her with his mouth full. He ate with the same nervous speed as his daughter.

"The usual things."

"Nothing special?"

"No. Nothing." And, at this moment, nothing did seem special to Evangeline. In any case, she did not want to talk about her life at all. "Just the same as ever."

"You should be high up in that office now. What do they call it?"

"Environment. The Department of the Environment."

"You should be at the top of the tree."

"Yes, father." She knew that she loved him, but she could not reveal her feelings for him. She ought to have gone over to him and kissed him, this frail man so close to death, and yet she was awkward and reticent with him.

And of course he realised that, too. "I'm proud of you," he said, trying to comfort her, trying to tell her that it was all right, everything was all right. "Your mother would have been proud, too."

"Yes, father. I know." She loved him more than any other man — in fact she had loved no other man — and yet she could think of nothing to say to him. If she had explained her real feelings for him, they would both have broken down beneath them. If she had started speaking, she would have spoken forever. So there was nothing whatever to say. I am so far away, she thought. So far away from myself.

"How's your friend," he was asking her.

"She's very well." Evangeline blushed, and rubbed a stain on the table cloth with her finger. "She's not really my friend," she added. "She's my assistant." She was still blushing: it was as if she were a child again, caught out in a lie. She changed the subject quickly and in her flat, neutral tone remarked, "What a cold day. Don't you think it's a cold day. For spring?" He did not reply, but looked out of the window at the deserted square. "Can I turn on the television?" she added. She could not bear any silence between them. "Is there anything good on?"

Soon it was time to go and, in unspoken compliance, he rose unsteadily to his feet and took her to the front door. "It was good to see you," he said. "It's always good to see you."

Impulsively he kissed her cheek as they stood together on the threshold, and it was only with an effort that Evangeline stopped

23

herself from flinching. But at once she felt guilty for this. "I'm always glad to be here."

"It's a long way to travel," he replied, looking at her with something like pity. "You know I could always come to your place one day."

"No." She said this too readily. "I like coming here. It makes a change."

"Goodbye love. I'll see you soon."

Now that she was about to depart, she felt a sudden freedom. "Goodbye, father. Yes. I'll see you soon."

As soon as she walked away her mood of weary resignation returned. And it occurred to her, as she left the white square, that it was because she could not reveal her true feelings to her own father that she could not disclose them to anyone else. She walked between the leafless poplars and, when a woman crossed her path, instinctively Evangeline looked away. She looked down at the ground. So I have no connection with the world, she thought. This white square might as well be in a dream.

The orange arm of a broken doll was lying in the gutter in front of her and, as she bent down to look at it, she caught the perfume of early lilac from somewhere in the street ahead. London lilac. She had known that scent all her life and, standing upright again, this small, thin woman walked uneasily away.

·7·

WAITING

THE RAINSTORM had grown worse and it was darker still by the time Mark Clare reached Lyme Regis from Pilgrin Valley, as he drove into the town the lights from his car swept across the eighteenth-century house fronts, the newsagent and chemist on either side of a Victorian archway made of red brick, the supermarket, the stone pillars of the Georgian Assembly Rooms and the car-park before he turned out of Broad Street into Crooked Alley. He switched off his engine and for a few moments he listened to the sea – noticing, as he always did, how different it sounded each evening. And if it was the repository of the hopes and dreams of humankind, as certain writers had suggested, was it possible that it also changed with them in a perpetual and tumultuous echo?

He lived in a flat above an antiques shop, in a late eighteenth-century building which despite renovations had retained its original proportions, and as he rested in his parked car he saw a light in the second-floor window. He knew that his wife had been sitting there; she would have waited until she heard the sound of his car, and now she would be standing in the hallway to greet him.

"You're tired," she said, anxiously scanning his face as he climbed the last stairs.

"Kathleen!" He ignored her remark, and held out his arms as he came up to her. "My own Kathleen!" He was smiling at her, willing her to smile too. "Sorry I'm late. I had to take Miss Tupper back to the station." He embraced her and, as he held her in his arms, he talked over her shoulder. "And then I went back to the site, just to see it one more time."

"I didn't know—" Gently she disengaged herself from him, and led him by the hand into the sitting room. "I thought something might have happened."

25

"You shouldn't worry, Kathleen. You should never worry."

"I don't. Not when you're here." She was still holding onto him as they entered the room. There was a metal brace around her withered left leg, and it was an old habit of hers to lean against him so that her pronounced limp became less noticeable.

"You always expect the worst," he was saying. "But there's no need. No need at all."

"Of course not." She held onto him more tightly for a moment, and put her face against his shoulder.

"Home again," he added.

"I know. Home again." She repeated his words as if they were a spell. She buried her face in the sleeve of his coat and then, with a definite effort of will which Mark himself could feel, she pulled herself free. She stood up, trembling slightly as she tried to right herself, and went across to the marbled mantelpiece. "Look," she said. "I was reading this before you came home."

"Let me see." He was always good-humoured with her. "Let me take a look at this." She held out towards him a copy of *New Archaeology*, and he peered at it for a moment before taking out a pair of spectacles from the jacket of his coat. He always liked reading out loud, and Kathleen always liked to hear him. Eagerly she pointed to the page, and he began:

> *There is a theory that in the late neolithic period there existed a professional order of wise men, or astronomers, who were supported by the labours of a rural population and who were able to transmit their knowledge from generation to generation by verse and by ballad. It is clearly impossible to believe that the building of such large henge structures as those outside Lyons and Cracow could be achieved without the active superintendence of a central organising power and, since these monuments seem typically to be aligned to the stars, it is probable that only trained astronomers could have worked out the precise positions of the stones and the tumuli. We are brought, then, to the over-whelming conclusion that astronomers were the leaders or at least the magi of late neolithic society – and, since there are examples of the same tumuli*

26

> *and ritual stones in many parts of Europe, all of
> them springing up at approximately the same time,
> we are further led to believe that this order of
> astronomers was an international one.*

Kathleen was watching her husband carefully as he read this. Since she had known him she had become an enthusiastic amateur archaeologist, forgetting whatever interests she had pursued before that time as if she had somehow been renewed or, perhaps, cut free from the ties which had previously bound her. She understood the significance of the discovery in Pilgrin Valley, and in fact she was as excited by it as Mark himself. And yet she never visited the site; she never allowed herself to be seen by his colleagues.

He had turned the page of the article, where he had come to

> *the evident fact that all these henge monuments fell
> into disuse at some time around 1400 BC and that a
> corpus of astronomical and mathematical theory
> was lost or abandoned in the same period. Our
> proposition is that all this knowledge vanished
> because of a change in the patterns of climate, when
> the warm, still and dry air which had allowed
> astronomical observations was displaced over a
> period of one or two centuries by mist, rain and
> almost perpetual cloud-cover.*

Mark looked up briefly at his wife. She was much younger than her husband, not quite half his age, but in the subdued light her face – framed by long black hair – seemed tired and worn.

> *Without visibility, of course, the stars became a
> less important part of communal rituals and during
> the early bronze age there is a significant change in
> religious practices. The religion connected with
> henge monuments and subterranean burial
> vanishes, and at the same time the alignments, the
> henges, the stone circles and the passage graves fall
> into disuse.*

"Where's Jude?" he asked, putting down *New Archaeology* with a sigh. Jude was the name of their small wire-haired terrier.

"He's asleep in your study. But what do you think?" Kathleen took the article from him, and eagerly looked at it. "What do you think of the theory?" She seemed to lose herself in these vistas of the remote past, as if somehow they could mitigate the life through which she moved every day.

"It's a theory," he said. He saw the look of disappointment on her face and added, more jovially, "But of course it might be true. Who knows? Shall I go and see Jude?" He walked through into his study, a small room at the back of the flat which overlooked the yard of the antiques shop beneath them. And when he saw Jude asleep on the floor, its paws tucked in and its back slightly arched, it occurred to him that this was the way that dogs had always slept; even at that time when the great stone monuments were being erected. As soon as he entered the room the animal sprang into wakefulness and, yawning, jumped onto its hind-legs and leaned its paws against Mark. "Good boy," he said. "There's a good boy." And the dog barked in return.

Mark went over to the window and looked down at the antiques in the yard below – the broken statuary, the vases covered with mould, the other scattered relics worn down by time. Their true features were not visible in the unnatural darkness of the storm, but they seemed to glow in the gathering dusk.

•8•

EARLIER TIME

ANOTHER TIME. In another time. She is a child, a crippled child. She is standing on the shore near Lyme, looking out to sea. Her parents are sitting in a beach-hut behind her, eating their sandwiches, and she turns around to make sure that they are still there. That they have not abandoned her. And then she looks back out to sea, the light from the waves playing upon her face. It is impossible to know what she is thinking. In fact she is thinking of nothing. Kathleen has merged with the sea.

He watches her. He is walking with a companion along the shore, but he watches the crippled girl. Is it pity he feels for her? No, not that. Not just pity. Rather a sense of opportunity. A sense of adventure. He would like to take her up, put her upon his shoulders and carry her to the top of the cliff where she could see more. More of the sea. More of the light. It was hard to talk to other people, but he knew that it would not be hard to talk to her. Accepted. Accepted and accepting. Mark's companion looks at the girl and says, "There is always someone left behind on the shore, isn't there?" But no one need be left behind. Not Mark. Not the crippled girl.

Another time. He knows her now. They have become friends, the girl and the man. They walk together. She seems never to be impeded by her limp. She walks forward, and all the intensity of her nature suffuses his own. New hopefulness. For, yes, she protects him too. With her he can discuss his work without hesitation or awkwardness, and in his vision of primeval time she too can lose herself. The man and the girl, meeting each week in front of the old clock in the market square, walking along the shore, walking through the foliage of the undercliffs, sitting on the highest rocks and looking out to sea. And he becomes a child again with her, a child dreaming of old stones. Old stories.

29

Another time. Later still. A cycle of the sky completed. Her mother is dead and she suffers once more the old feeling of loss, the terrible silence of abandonment. It has been with her all her life, this fear of being left behind, of being left somewhere out of the world. But she is trying to fight it back, to fight down the fear. And now he is with her. To carry her over her moods as once he had wished to carry her on his shoulders. And she, too, will never abandon him. He knows that now. Together they will conquer their fears.

Another time. She looks at him warily. She looks at him with pity. But what can she do with her leg? What must he think of her? This is the first time – the first time in all these years – that it has been mentioned. No. He tells her that he never sees it now. It is simply part of her. Her. The person whom he loves.

Present time. Time encircling her. Bereft on this stormy night before Mark returned home. He will never come back, she thinks. He has died and I am alone again. How can I live here after him? And how can I take care of Jude? This is the fate Kathleen always fears and always imagines for herself.

Past time. She had always felt destined to suffer – after she had met Mark, she was afraid of his kindness and companionship. She was afraid of her good fortune because in the end it was bound to disappear, leaving her more solitary and bewildered than before. Even after her marriage Kathleen could not keep hold of her pleasure, her joy in the feeling that she was no longer alone. It always seemed to her about to dissolve – for why else had she been crippled, except as a special mark of disfavour? Beneath the surface of her contentment there was still the same cowed and stricken figure waiting to emerge. Even when she felt loved, therefore, she felt most afraid. This was the identity by which she had first known herself and she feared that the first identity would also be the last. It would always be the one to be renewed, rediscovered. The crippled girl. Encircled. Waiting for the rebuff.

Present time. That morning she had seen the sunlight moving slowly across the room – and this movement, she thought, marks the rotation of the planet. So in small things can we recognise the great. In the same way my own life is a reflection of the movement of life itself. But I am only part of its shadow as it progresses onward. And then, oh then, the rain came, blotting out the sun. Even the shadows disappeared.

This was Kathleen as she was, and as she would always be:

brooding, melancholy, afraid. This was the meaning of her time
upon the earth.

·9·

A CHILD

KATHLEEN FOLLOWED him and leaned against the doorway of the study, watching him intently as he looked down at the broken antiques in the yard. She did not move. "I telephoned the agency," she said at last. "I spoke to someone. Mrs Lipp."

Mark was rubbing his forehead with his hand. "Are you sure you still want this?"

"Of course." Slowly she put her arms down by her side, and stood upright. "I think about it all the time. There are so many lonely children, Mark. So many unhappy children. Why can't we help?"

"All this longing for things that cannot be." There was an audible gasp of breath from her, and he turned around to face her. "I'm sorry, Kathleen. I didn't mean that. But isn't it enough that we have each other?" But, no, she needed some other reassurance; she needed some other connection with the world; she needed someone else to hold onto. There were times when he still saw her as the crippled girl upon the shore, and now he took her fingers and kissed them. "Isn't it enough?" he asked again, as he hid his face in her hands.

"How can you talk of that when you have the same – what was the word – longing? Isn't longing the same thing as belonging? And isn't that what we want? Belonging to a child?" They were both talking very quietly, both of them rocking to and fro as they held each other. "And how do we know what *cannot* be? Who is there to tell us?"

"I know." He looked up and saw his wife's stricken face. "I know. I just want to do what is best. Best for you."

"Why me?" The idea seemed to horrify Kathleen, as if she did not wish to be singled out – even by her husband – for special attention. She broke away from him gently. "We both want a child," she whispered. "You always said that you wanted a child."

32

Once more he was rubbing his forehead with his hand as she spoke, as if there were a mark there which he wanted to erase. In fact there was something about their intensity which bewildered him. In the company of others Mark was as he had always been but, when he was with Kathleen, he felt isolated, vulnerable, attentive to the darker music of the world. It was inseparable from his love for her but, still, it frightened him. "Let's eat," he said. "Is there anything to eat?" It was only at this moment he realised that Jude had been lying quietly at their feet, remaining with them in the gathering dusk.

They went into the kitchen where over dinner they discussed the possibilities of adoption and, when they eventually agreed to enter the first stage in a process of which neither could imagine the end, Kathleen clapped her hands. "I knew it!" she said. "It's all coming true!" And her thin, pale face was suffused with light.

Mark returned to his study after dinner, and sat among his books. Around him there were piles of his own papers, graphs, computer print-outs, and drawings as well as old copies of archaeological journals and volumes of archaeological research. On his shelves, too, were antiquarian studies of the area itself. For Dorset was his obsession. He believed that this place had its own sound – he had always heard a peculiarly soft quality in the bird song – and its own smells. And when he saw the sheep and cattle peacefully grazing in the fields he could feel the pressure of its beneficence, its curves and folds cradling the life which seemed to have issued from it. It possessed an almost human presence, as if the generations of those who had dwelt upon its surface had left some faint echo – as difficult to recognise as the song of a particular bird, but a subdued persistent note beneath all other sounds. Or was it a colour rather than a note – that deep green, as rich as blood, as soft as breath, forever being renewed. When he lay upon the grass of Dorset it was as if he were being borne up by the hands of all those who had come before him. They were the ground on which he rested. Yes, this was a haunted place. It contained mysteries.

He took down a volume of *Dorset Antiqua*. Even its title evoked for him the open fields, the hollows and recesses of green, the wooded horizons, the curving boundaries of the chalk, the soft earth. And once again he felt at peace. He did not want to read it, he just wanted to hold it in his hands and look at it, turning its musty and slightly damp pages and gazing once again at the engravings of the old landscape with its ancient mounds and long abandoned pathways. He stopped at one page, which contained a sketch of a tumulus somewhere in the region. It had been drawn impossibly large, no doubt by some eighteenth-century antiquary, and it dominated the rolling landscape like a Leviathan. And yet in another sense it seemed to Mark to be in true perspective, since the landscape itself had been changed beyond recognition – with his finger he traced the outline of wild trees in the engraving, their branches inked in so boldly that they seemed to be leaning in fright away from the mound, away from the ravines beneath them, away from the distant crags which contained no reassurance of any human community. All these features might have been emanations from the tumulus itself and, above them, the antiquary had depicted a livid and turbulent sky. But perhaps this was how the landscape then was. Or perhaps, after the engraving was completed, this was the way it had become. And all the time Kathleen was standing outside the closed door of the study, listening intently as if by some sudden sigh or movement she might catch an echo of his real thoughts.

Mark put down the book and went over to the window. And so we will adopt a child, he thought, we will take one human life and attach it to our own – changing all of us completely, changing our lives, changing the child's life, changing the lives of those who will come after us. It all begins now. From this time a set of relationships will be established which may endure for ever, passing down echoes of Kathleen and myself from generation to generation; a change in the human pattern and yet why is it so random, so unforeseeable, so permanent? Is everything so tenuous and yet so unassuageable as this one act?

He looked up at the sky. The rainstorm had passed and it had become a clear, calm night – on just such a night Gabriel Oak was tending his sheep on Norcombe Hill in Thomas Hardy's *Far from the Madding Crowd*, and Hardy describes how ". . . the sovereign brilliance of Sirius pierced the eye with a steely glitter, the star called Capella was yellow, Aldebaran and Betelgeux shone with a fiery red" for this was a night when "the twinkling of all the stars seemed to be but throbs of one body, timed by a common pulse". But the stars are not pulsating in quite that manner. They are rushing away from an unknown point of origin, and this planet is rushing away with them, driven on by the force of some event that created time in the same unimaginable moment as it created space.

Mark Clare was not thinking of this. He looked up at the heavens and for him the constellations were transformed into the faces of Farmer Mint, Evangeline Tupper, his own wife. This was the story written across the sky. And then these faces faded, and he began to see the outline of an unknown child's face. "A child," he said. "Our own child."

Kathleen could not make out his words but she had heard the strange tone in his voice; she knocked softly and entered the room, seeing only his silhouette against the sky. Then she heard the collection of antique clocks chiming the hour in the shop beneath them – all of them, great and small, sounding together. "It's so dark in here, Mark," she said. "Put on the light. You should put on the light."

AT THE SITE

"**T**HIS WILL be a kind of inquest. And yet it will be one in which the dead will speak to us, if we know how to listen. You have all seen how much equipment we need to use, but there are other kinds of signals as well. There are signals which come from the people who are buried beneath my feet, and it is these which we must really learn how to decode." Mark Clare was standing on top of the tumulus, with the other members of the archaeological team gathered around him. He stopped for a moment, enjoying the rhythm of his words, and they could hear the swollen stream running through the sedge and the dripping bracken before disappearing once more beneath Pilgrin Valley. It had been raining once more – until just after dawn, a thick and steady rain that had seemed to hover in the air or, rather, to rise up from the earth and fall backwards into the sky. Yet the sky itself was now a pale translucent blue, brighter than the earth which in its dankness still seemed to be shaking off the night. And above the noises of the stream the wind brought to them the bellowing of a cow, whose calf had been taken from her under cover of darkness by Farmer Mint.

"Our first task is to walk the whole area, to survey it and then to map it." Mark was gesticulating like a public speaker, pointing urgently towards the distant fields as if something of himself had been left there. "And this will require intense observation of every single feature in the landscape. The circle of stones around this site emphasises how important it must once have been, but we must also look for peripheral burials further out in the valley. And we must try to find traces of the settlement, if any, from which these people came. Quiet though it is today, many hundreds of them may once have lived and worked here. So look out for the smallest things. A broken flint or a sliver of stone may be the relic of an activity or even a gesture that will help us to understand this forgotten world. One of

36

the builders here may have dropped a flint in anger, or spoiled one of his tools as he worked, and that brief moment has lain dormant here until we came to revive it. A few seconds of human activity may have been preserved for the last five thousand years, and it is our task to restore them." Some members of the team knew Mark well, but were still surprised by the fluency and energy with which he always spoke; it was as if he became inspired.

The wind was blowing strongly now, and Mark raised his voice so that his words might be properly understood. "All of you must keep records of everything you see. Drawings. Notes. You know all about systems theory, don't you?" Some of them nodded, others looked at each other uneasily. "Keep everything in sequence. Nothing must be lost, since all the data we collect here will pass through high level computer analysis. Our goals include total recovery, objective interpretation and comprehensive explanation. We are creating an electronic archive, because only then will we understand the real nature of this site." From this vantage Mark could see down the valley, and for a moment he looked across at the adjoining field where a line of sheep seemed to be forming into a circle, then breaking apart, and then reforming, driven by the impulse of some private energy. "But we also have to understand the events which are missing from here. Sometimes the silences, the gaps, tell us more than anything else. Why is it, for example, that the tumulus was constructed by the side of the valley rather than in the open grassland—"

"Arseland!" A high voice came from somewhere behind him, and Mark turned in surprise towards the charred remnants of the old ash forest.

"Hey, mister! Mind out for the old one! You're standing on the old one!"

"Don't go waking *him* up!" Two small children ran across the burnt clearing and then down towards the stream, laughing as they went and disturbing a flock of starlings which rose up and made small patterns in the sky.

The archaeologists laughed, too, and Mark smiled as he rubbed one eye with the palm of his hand. "Well," he said, "there are all sorts of theories. Even the children have their own stories, as you can see. That's why . . ." And he faltered here. "That's why it is so important to discover the truth. Before it's too late."

"Too late? What on earth does he mean, too late?" Owen Chard,

37

site surveyor, turned with a scowl to the colleague on his left.

"You know dear Mark. Sometimes he doesn't mean anything at all." Martha Temple, 'finds' supervisor, said this in her most pleasant voice as if she were paying him the greatest compliment in the world. She was a large woman with a deceptively jolly manner, and her plump beaming face would have led almost anyone to trust her. "Quite likely," she went on, very agreeably, "that he hasn't a clue. Oh look, here's Julian very late indeed. Do you think he could have been told the wrong time?" And she gave a girlish little wave to Julian Hill, the site environmentalist, who came panting up the slope towards them.

These three stood apart now as Mark continued to address the band of voluntary helpers who, otherwise unemployed, felt themselves to be taken up in a great adventure. There were twenty of them – most of them young, but there were two or three middle-aged men among them who had gone to the local archaeological unit with a kind of desperation. Now they were working again and, just as importantly, working their way into a past which belonged to them as much as to anyone else. They no longer felt excluded, and they were listening intently to Mark.

"We are very lucky here," he was saying. "The tumulus had never been seen before fire destroyed the ash forest, so it has remained untouched, unvisited. My guess is that this is a burial site from the late neolithic period, and that when we enter it we will find evidence of a period which has remained undisturbed for almost five thousand years—"

"He hopes," murmured Owen Chard. "Amazing how certain people will jump to conclusions."

"Do let's give him the benefit of the doubt." As Martha spoke, she was smiling and nodding towards Mark. "Someone has to."

"I don't want to blow my own trumpet—" Julian Hill was still sweating after his late arrival, and stood just behind them as he wiped his forehead. He was a young man – sturdy, self-confident, but with a strange wild look as if he were always watching something in the far distance. He had unkempt red hair which, absent-mindedly, he now pushed back as he spoke. "I don't want to boast—"

"Well, don't then." Owen took a pipe from his top pocket and clenched it between his teeth; in this attitude, with his grey hair, firm mouth and imperturbably serious features, he resembled a solicitor or headmaster. He was well known for the sharpness of his remarks but, if someone had explained to him how often he seemed unkind, he would genuinely have been astonished. He had no idea of his effect. He merely said what he thought.

"It may be very important," Julian Hill went on, not at all discomfited.

"Yes. Do let Julian continue, Owen. We all have our little contribution to make, don't we? You of all people should know that."

"Has Mark mentioned my idea about significant clustering?"

"Oh Julian dear." Martha could not have been more concerned. "Not as far as anyone can tell."

"Not even my very important point about the multi-dimensional factors here?"

"It must have slipped his—" She gave a delicate little cough. "His mind."

"Oh well. Oh well." Julian shook his head impatiently. "I *am* right, anyway." He smiled to himself. "Of course you know my theory—"

"I'm sure there's a lot to be said on both sides." Martha had put out her hand to stop Julian talking about himself once again. "But I think we ought to make an effort to listen to Mark for a little while, don't you? He tries so hard, after all."

In fact Mark was coming to the end of his prepared remarks. "So we will excavate down to the forecourt." He walked onto the western end of the tumulus, which opened out into the rough shape of a wedge. "And if this is a chamber grave, as we all expect, we are likely to find the entrance here. Then we will work in from the entrance itself, towards the eastern end of the tomb." He gestured towards the point where the tumulus tapered to a point which seemed to vanish into the side of the valley itself. "But, remember, this will be a slow process. We must never dig too hastily or too deeply. As we excavate the mound we have to keep in phase with each other, working downwards together so that all the recognisable events of each period can be exposed at once. We have to follow the layers. We have to follow the traces of the soil. We have to listen to its secrets before we discover what, if anything, is still inside the mound." Mark stopped abruptly, as if he wanted to catch the echo of his own eloquence.

At this moment Martha Temple nudged Julian Hill and

whispered, perhaps a fraction too loudly, "So he didn't bother to mention you, after all." Then she began to applaud Mark with excited little claps.

◆ *II* ◆

FIELD WALKING

WALKING ACROSS the grass, leaving the planet
step by step and then returning; walking upright but
with head bowed, freedom and submission as the
conditions of being on the earth. Field walking. They
are searching for traces of their ancestors, who had once walked with
the same posture. Heads bowed. Looking for seeds and roots. And, if
it was the same posture, was it not also with the same sense of the
world and of the sky above it? Had there been any essential change
from the time when the stones were used as arrow heads until this
time, now, when the stones are being assembled once again?

Walking over the grass in unison, seven of them in a line across
Pilgrim Valley, feeling the pressure of each other's steps like small
changes in gravity around them. Others had walked this way before
them, and now they too are changing the surface, eroding it, leaving
their own traces which in turn will be found. And this was why the
walkers resembled dancers, when the dance is always the same while
the dancers change and change about.

Walking over the ridge of the valley into the fields of the plateau
beyond, tracing the curve of the chalk, keeping in time with a
common purpose, stepping across the rabbit burrows, examining
the old tracks which run like white threads through the grass,
looking for flints, for particles of bone, for seeds, for snail shells.
Walking over the grass which is always the same, always renewed, so
that even beneath their steps it is itself the past for which they are
searching.

And yet there will be other evidence too. Evidence for these field
walkers who know that, since fossils still emerge from the coastlines
of this region, belemnites and ammonites thrust from the rocks by
spillage or by sudden fissure, it is likely that the inland region will
also disgorge the evidence of its former inhabitants. Traces found

41

suddenly, as if they had sprung up overnight.

Martha Temple cries out in alarm: a black creature has emerged from one of the burrows and fled towards the small whitewashed cottage in the corner of the field. It had the shapelessness of something she might have seen out of the corner of her eye. It must have been a cat. Yes, a cat. And she looks across at the cottage, taking a step forward when she thinks she sees a figure crossing in front of the window. Then crossing again. But this must have been a cloud passing across the sun, or the shadow of a branch falling across the window. And she returns to her field walking. Walking in silence in unison with the silent earth; the silence of dust, the silence of soil, the silence of trace elements, the silence of phosphates, the silence of those who are now guiding her steps across the silent fields.

Now the silence is broken as Julian Hill and a young woman call out readings to each other. Placing the valley within a framework of Euclidean geometry as the various gradations and contours of the site are mapped. Replacing Pilgrin Valley with a vision of numbers as its coordinates are plotted. Degrees. Declinations. The flow chart. The matrix. Just another vision as the numbers are called out beneath the sky.

At the same time Mark Clare is supervising the digging of a trial trench, some fifty yards away from the tumulus, so that he can expose a section of the ground. The immediate surface of loam and clay contains minute particles of chalk but the excavators go deeper and deeper until they touch the soft weathered chalk beneath the clay and the loam. Deeper still until they reach the harder chalk which is the shape of the land itself. And in these layers of chalk and soil they hope to discover the layers of human settlement also. Clusterings. Hypothetical time.

Mark Clare and Owen Chard are now working around the tumulus itself: Mark is driving terminals into the ground, while Owen watches a small black box and makes notes. It is clear from their expressions that they have come across something entirely unexpected: the fluctuations of magnetic noise suggest that there is a semi-circular pattern of holes within the forecourt of the unex-cavated tomb. Why should they be here? They can only assume that they were designed to support large wooden poles. All may be resolved in time. Real time.

They have also registered differences in the levels of electrical activity – for even chalky soil has less resistance than stone walls or floors – and the data suggests to them that there is some kind of stone construction within the tomb itself. But perhaps this is optimistic guesswork: most of the signals from within the mound are so faint, and so complex, that they cannot yet be analysed. There will be another phase. The process continues. Hypothetical time. Real time. Curving towards each other. Like the field walking which spreads out from the tomb and then returns to it; tracing and retracing the old steps; understanding how the dead do surround the living. Everything is touching everything else.

◆ *12* ◆

AN ARGUMENT

"AT THE time of the vernal equinox, the tomb was in direct alignment with the Pleiades. My theory still stands. I was right all along." Julian Hill was triumphant, and his voice became shrill as they sat together in the Portakabin on the site.

"So now you can go ahead and write your nice article." Martha Temple could not have been more supportive. "Don't forget to mention our names. We exist too, you know."

"What a stroke of luck for me. And for us, of course."

"Of course." Martha was being very sweet. "So you think this is a shrine . . ." As she prompted Julian, she directed a brief but significant look at Owen Chard.

"Yes. This is the burial place of someone who understood the stars. In the late neolithic period, the astronomers were kings. They were the communal spokesmen. They were the interpreters. And I'm the first person to—"

"It's a lovely theory, Julian." Martha had interrupted in the nicest possible way. "And I'm sure you're right. I just can't imagine why no one has found any evidence to confirm it, can you?" And once again she darted a significant look at Owen.

"You're very good at telling stories," Owen said now. It was almost as if he had been prompted by her. "You should get an award for fiction."

Julian laughed, a high-pitched laugh with no amusement in it. "People would have assembled here, in this sacred place. There is no doubt about that." He made an effort to control his voice. "And I wouldn't be surprised, *I*, at least, would not be at all surprised, if there are other astronomers interred here. Buried over the centuries."

Owen had put his head in his hands and was murmuring, "Oh

44

dear, oh dear, oh dear.''

"What was that, Owen? Did you say something?" Martha seemed genuinely anxious to know if he agreed with Julian.

"We haven't even opened the grave yet and here he is, telling us what we can expect to find in it. Could we have a few facts, please?"

Julian glared at him. "I wish you would explain to me what you mean by a *fact*."

"And I wish you two wouldn't argue." Martha seemed to have forgotten that she had instigated the confrontation. "You know how I hate any kind of disagreement. Any kind of unpleasantness." She waited eagerly for them to continue, however, but they fell silent.

Mark Clare had been listening to the conversation; he had been leaning forward in his chair, almost doubled up, restraining his impulse to break in. But now, his eyes bright, he felt impelled to speak. "Someone was talking about stories," he said. "I have a story. Or perhaps it was a vision. I don't know. I was much younger then."

Martha, ready to leave now that the argument had subsided, was tying the strings of a plastic yellow rain-cap underneath her plump chin; but she found time to arrange her face into an open and enthusiastic expression. "Do tell," she said.

At first Mark said nothing, merely clearing his throat. Then he got up, thrust his hands deep into his pockets, and began swaying from side to side. This was how he usually prepared to address the others, but Martha could not resist giving a wide conspiratorial smile to them. It faded when she realised that Owen and Julian were paying no attention to her. Instead they were looking at Mark as he began his story.

·*13*·

A VISION

I WAS ON a field-trip in Peru. Beyond the rain forest, they said, was an Inca settlement. A morning's journey through the forest, they said, would take us there. And so we set off at dawn.

It was like entering a dream. Everything was too large – the stumps of dead trees covered by moss, the creepers which trailed down like the strings of huge kites, the plants which seemed to grow both upward and downward so that there was no room for us to pass between, the slender trunks of trees which seemed to rise for ever, the fronds opening out in front of us – and everything was too green, too vivid. It was as if we had wandered into the drawing of a forest in a story-book, and at any moment giants were going to part the leaves and peer at us. You know how in an English forest you can feel the peacefulness of its age? How centuries of quiet have entered it like a mist? There was nothing of that in the rain forest. It was so vivid that it might just have sprung into life, and you could see as you walked that it would never change, never grow old. It would always be too bright. And the smell – the smell was not soothing, not the smell of decay, but the rank smell of things newly born. And the continual noise, the noise of insects, the constant noise of chattering birds, the screeching of howler monkeys, the noises of other animals, was like some perpetual carnival, some perpetual celebration. And I thought, how could ancient ruins exist in such a place? Of course I was wrong.

We had been walking all morning, with the guide ahead of us clearing a path through the undergrowth. It was not rough terrain but it was treacherous – and the dampness, the dampness weighed down all of us. Our faces streamed with it. It was as if we were perpetually in tears. Yet in fact there was something about this sweet clotted atmosphere which exhilarated us; we were almost hurrying

46

in our eagerness to find the ruins, and then when I looked down I saw that we had not really touched the ground because were were walking across a carpet of dead insects and the small light skeletons of forest creatures. They had given us the momentum in our steps. And yet, when I look back upon that day, I realise that I might have been mistaken: the foliage was so thick above our heads that we had been walking all the time in a perpetual green twilight, and I must have seen very little. The forest acted as a canopy, and we were continually in shadow.

But then I began to feel flickers of sunlight upon my face, the ground became firmer, some ferns brushed across my face and quite suddenly I found myself in a clearing. The dazzling light seemed to be all around me, as if I were in a cloud, and I had to fight to get my breath.

When at last I could see, I found that we had reached an open space, a kind of plateau, which seemed literally to vanish into thin air since the only thing in front of us was the sky – a shimmering, iridescent sky with nothing in it. Nothing. No clouds. No birds. Just this vast empty bowl above my head. The guide told me to step forward, and so I crossed the clearing towards him. He was standing on the edge, just at the beginning of the sky, and as I approached him he pointed with his left arm. I came up to him and, as I followed his outstretched finger, I realised that we were standing on a crest above a huge valley. I could see beneath me ridge upon ridge of dark green trees stretching down towards a wide river which flowed along the bottom of the valley; and the river was such a deep blue I could not tell whether this colour came from its water or the reflection of the sky within it. Then I looked across, in the direction the guide was pointing, and I could see a wide plateau of rock upon the other side of the valley. There were no trees here, just flat stone with its own intricate pattern of ridges and rocky outcrop.

"Do you see them now?" he asked me and, as my eyes grew accustomed to this dark grey expanse, I saw tall standing stones behind the plateau. They were in a circle and there, in the centre, I could see an earthwork. It might have been a tumulus like the one in our valley but it was bigger, much bigger, and the summit of it had been flattened as if by some giant hand. I couldn't speak, and I simply stared at the stones and at the mound. The guide came up to me and put his hand upon my shoulder. "You see there," he said. "You see clearly now?" He pointed at the great earth mound, "This is the place. Here it was that in the sacred times men used to fly." I asked him what he meant. "I thought," he said, "that you saw it clearly." Then he chuckled. "They would fly from the great hill. They would fly from out of the circle into the sky."

And, you know, it was a circle just like this one. Just like the circle in Pilgrin Valley.

•14•

THE VISION FADES

THAT EVENING Kathleen Clare clung to Mark on his return from Pilgrin Valley. "Did you have a good day?" she asked him. "I hope you had a good day."

"Good? I suppose so." The memory of his journey to the ruins through the rain forest was still with him.

She broke away from him, as if she were half-expecting some rebuff. "What are you thinking about?"

"I wasn't thinking. I was miles away. I'm sorry." And then, knowing how easily hurt she still was, he went on with "I was telling the others the story about Peru. Do you remember, how there were once men who flew?"

"Tell me," she said, clapping her hands.

"But you know the story." It was one of the first things he had told her about his past life.

"Tell me again." She crossed the room, holding onto the back of a chair to steady herself. "Why won't you tell me?"

"Not now. Not now."

"Did they really fly away?"

"No one knows. No one ever knows." He wanted, for Kathleen's sake, to change the subject. "Come on. Tell me all about your day. I'm sure you had a much more exciting time than I did." He was able to regain his usual tone of enthusiasm. "Did you visit the adoption agency?"

"I went this morning, and they sent me to a social worker. From the way they talk, you would think it was *me* who was being adopted." With strangers she was always very conscious of her limp, and Mark could imagine how difficult this interview had been for her. "He was very nice. He asked me all about you. About *us*." Her face brightened. "He said he would be writing. And you know," she went on, making her own connection, "I had a dream about us last

49

night." Again she emphasised the pronoun, as if her real identity depended on it.

There was a small scream from the street outside, and Mark went over to the window. He looked down and could see the owner of the antiques shop dancing on the pavement, in front of him the shattered remains of a plaster head; he had dropped it while bringing it from his car into the shop, and now he stooped down to pick up a piece of eye and forehead. Then he saw Mark in the window above, waved the white fragment in the air, smiled and shrugged his shoulders. "Goddess Nelly is all in bits," he shouted up at him.

"What did you dream?" Mark asked her as he turned away from the window.

Jude had started to bark at the sudden noise; Kathleen picked him up and, as she talked, she was stroking his fur, all the time stroking it. "I dreamt that we were walking along a dusty road, towards some large town. It was a very hot day – did you know you could feel the warmth in dreams – and the white road was baking in the heat. Yet there was something comforting about it. Something comforting about the smell of the dust." She did not mention to him that, in her dream, she could walk without impediment; but this was her clearest memory. "And then a horse-and-cart stopped beside us. There was a little square window at the back of it, and when I looked through I could see the silhouettes of some old women talking. And then the dream faded."

"It sounds," said Mark, "like the beginning of an interesting story."

"I know." She hesitated. "What was that noise outside?"

"Augustine dropped a statue."

"Not again." She laughed at this, but it was clear that she was thinking of something else. "You're right," she went on. "It was like a story. It was like entering the plot of a novel. And when I was young, did I ever tell you, I always wanted to get inside a book and never come out again? I loved reading so much I wanted to be a part of it, and there were some books I could have stayed in for ever." Mark looked at her with something like alarm. "Not now of course," she added. "We're happy now, aren't we? This was ages ago." Quickly she put down Jude and went across to the window, her back turned to Mark.

Now that she had talked of books, he remembered one incident in the early months of their marriage. They were visiting London and had been taken on a guided tour of the British Museum, and when she had seen the books beneath the great dome, with the volumes curving away from her, she had started to cry. She had never explained this, but now Mark understood her sadness. These had been alternative worlds in which she might lose herself, imaginary landscapes in which she might walk freely for the first time, but she would never be able to enter them. She was in a sense locked out.

"Come and look," she said. "Augustine is putting back the pieces." He stood beside her and watched as, on the pavement beneath them, the antiques dealer was carefully fitting together the fragments of the whitened head. "It looks so easy from here," she said. "But it won't be the same. It never is the same."

·15·

THE EXCAVATION

THEY BEGAN work in Pilgrin Valley the next morning. Over succeeding days the ancient site was stripped of all its natural characteristics and an area around the tumulus itself, stretching as far as the ring of stones, was systematically cleared. The top soil was lifted off and placed in separate heaps away from the excavation itself, leaving "the natural" or sub-soil behind. As the earth was unrolled it became steadily darker; it was like stripping the skin from an animal while it was still alive.

And when Mark Clare first cut into the surface of the tumulus itself, it was almost with reluctance: this was a beginning for him, but an ending for those other workmen who had preceded him thousands of years before. He could feel their sense of loss as he and the others, in driving rain, began to remove the covering of the tomb; in the grey light they cut away the turf and stacked it, grass face to grass face, in another part of the site. And so the wound spread.

"The capstone—"

"Capstone? Don't tell me you've found their teeth already. I can't bear it."

"I'm sorry." For some reason Mark was apologising to Evangeline Tupper for her own mistake, and he started to laugh. "The capstone is the roof. I was going to say that the stone roof is about three feet below the surface."

"There are no words." Gingerly Evangeline stuck the toe of her brown shoe into the damp soil. "No words for something so divine."

"Oh there are words. You just have to choose the right ones." Nevertheless he was grateful for her evident enthusiasm; he clapped his hands together, although it was not cold. "And we've already found traces of the period," he said. "There are tiny flecks of charcoal in the turf stack, which suggests that the area must have been cleared by fire before the mound was constructed."

"It makes me feel very quiet and humble."

"Oh dear no." Martha Temple had joined them as they stood in the rain beside the mound. "I don't believe that for a minute, Mrs Tupper."

"*Miss* Tupper, in actual fact."

"You're far too important. We are the ones who feel humble." If there was a note of asperity in Martha's voice, it was well disguised.

"Too kind of you to say so." Evangeline had taken an immediate dislike to this plump woman, with her confiding and even cosy manner. "And what precisely is it that you do?"

"I look after the finds."

"I suppose someone has to do it. Did you say fines?"

"Finds. Pins. Beads. Pottery. Objects from the site." Martha was talking very slowly, as if it were just conceivable that Evangeline might have some difficulty in following her.

"Now I understand. You mean old things. Broken things. Like bones."

Martha, smiling sweetly, was examining Evangeline's dark tweed suit with an almost professional interest. "I can see you understand our work," she said. "But bones are not really in my department."

"Oh no?"

"Owen Chard looks after the bones. We have quite a complex stratification system, you see. Bones and other organic material are not classified as finds. Not as such. They are part of a different matrix. But I'm boring you. Archaeology is very dull for outsiders." She said this so gently and so lightly that no reproach could possibly have been intended.

"I'm not in the least bored." In fact Evangeline had been poking her fingers around her handbag, looking for a cigarette and humming a little tune as she did so. "But don't we have to fly?"

She addressed the last question to Mark Clare, who seemed to be exhilarated by it. He laughed out loud. "Fly? Fly where?"

"To meet your friends, the Flints. Are they old? I love old men." She remembered her father for a moment, and put the unlit Woodbine between her lips.

"Of course. The Mints." Evangeline had once expressed a fleeting interest in seeing Farmer Mint in order to thank him for his cooperation and, to her dismay, Mark had taken her seriously enough to arrange this meeting. It was one of the reasons she had travelled from London. "Yes," he went on. "They're expecting us. They're probably waiting for us now."

"Under the greenwood tree?"

"What was that?" Mark was smiling, but only because Evangeline smiled.

"I think," Martha Temple said, "that Mrs Tupper—"

"Miss. Or Ms."

"That Miss Tupper was making a joke."

"That's right. One of my ghastly little jokes. Think nothing of it." But she put back her head and roared with laughter – causing all those who were working on the site to pause for a moment and glance up at her. She looked around and then added, in a whisper, "I don't suppose one ought to laugh beside a tomb, ought one?"

"Oh don't think of it like that," Martha said gaily. "Think of it as a place of entertainment. We don't mind."

Her tone was so pleasant that Evangeline might just have believed her but now, shutting her handbag, she turned to Mark. "This has been a perfect visit. But perfect things do come to an end." She took a few steps down the slope but then paused, turned, and smiled at Martha. "My dogs like bones, too, by the way. Au revoir." And she gave another loud laugh which echoed down the Pilgrin Valley.

She and Mark had hardly reached the other side when Owen started moaning. "This is it," he was saying. "I've had enough. I give up."

"What is the matter, Owen dear?" Martha eagerly rushed over to him, anticipating some minor disaster. "I'm the one who had to put up with that Tupper woman, after all."

"Another spade has gone. I put it down a minute ago. And now it's gone. Vanished." And indeed, when Martha looked over this corner of the site, she could see only the damp exposed soil. The spade had disappeared.

VISITORS

FARMER MINT had seen them coming down the track, and was waiting for them on the threshold; he was wearing a dark donkey-jacket on top of an even darker overcoat and, as he stood with arms hanging loosely by his side, Evangeline considered the possibility that a scarecrow had been placed in front of the door. So she gave a momentary but visible start when Farmer Mint grinned and said, "I'm waiting for the cows."

"Well," she replied, apparently regaining her composure. "Here we are at last."

Farmer Mint nodded, very slowly. "I know about you," he said. "You're expected, too. Along with Mr Clare here." He rocked back and forth in his old wellington boots, preparing himself for sudden movement. "Boy Mint's inside," he added, as if his son were the real object of their visit. "Waiting with his powerful brain."

"This is too exciting." Evangeline was already hurrying down the narrow path as Farmer Mint turned into the house. She had expected a small passageway – some alcove, at least, where she might pause for a moment and pat her hair into shape – and it came as something of a shock to find herself stepping at once into a large room. Boy Mint was looming against a wide fireplace, in exactly the same scarecrow posture as his father, and he took off his flat cap when Evangeline entered. "Boy." He announced himself gravely and yet with a certain cautious pride.

"Miss," she replied, equally gravely. Then she stepped back and gave a little scream. "Aren't you gorgeous?" she said. "Just look at you! You're gorgeous!"

She turned around towards Mark for confirmation of this sentiment and, to her alarm, found Farmer Mint standing right behind her. But he seemed to share Evangeline's emotion. "That's a good boy, that is." And then he added, more confidentially, "He can milk a cow as soon as look at her.''

"And cows, too. This is incredible. Do you get many of them in the country?"

Boy Mint reflected on this question, as if he would have preferred to have been given notice of it. "A lot of cows," he said at last. "Yes. And sheep. And chickens. And rats."

"Oh, we have those in London." She smiled, trying not to laugh. "But we don't have you. We would love to have you."

"They all love the brain in this boy." Farmer Mint was eager to join the conversation. "That brain would rise anywhere. But it don't want to leave this spot. This spot is it."

"Of course it is. No one would ever willingly leave Dorset." Mark Clare had spoken for the first time, and Evangeline looked at him with some surprise. It was only for a moment, but time enough for her attention to wander from the enthralling subject of Boy Mint's cerebellum. Now she was looking around the large room, her mouth half-open. "I don't believe it," she said. "I really don't believe it. Am I going potty or am I in the Arabian Nights?"

And in fact the room was filled with miscellaneous objects which looked as if they might just have been conjured into existence – candles in various stages of decay, old lanterns, a pair of warming pans, one wooden chest filled with boots, two broken stools, bulky glass jars containing torn pieces of newspaper and, in one corner, a brass bucket filled with dried grass. On the wall above this bucket a clock, constructed out of heavy ebony, had come to a halt many years before; and, beneath its motionless face, there was affixed a metal plaque bearing an advertisement for Bourneville's Cocoa. The hearth of the wide fireplace was filled by a cast-iron range with two separate ovens; perched on top of one was an ancient black kettle and, on the other, a conch shell with some straws sticking out of it. Against the side of the range had been propped a broom, made out of twigs and bound together with a wand of hazel; beside it had been tossed a hinged metal box, a spade and a pair of bellows. But the most notable feature of this room could be seen above the fireplace; the heavily patterned wallpaper here was covered with row upon row of photographs, medallions, miniatures and drawings, all of them bearing images of men and women in profile or in full face.

"Pinch me, somebody," Evangeline muttered. "I must be dreaming." Boy Mint, who had a somewhat literal understanding, stepped forward to oblige her; Evangeline quickly moved out of his way by picking up the broom and brandishing it in front of her. "An early form of flight?" she asked.

"No," he replied. "That's a broom."

"Really?" She seemed nonplussed and turned to Mark for assistance, but he was looking out of the main window; from here, he could see the tumulus very clearly. "All this is ecstasy," she went on. "Sheer ecstasy. I insist that you leave it to the nation."

Farmer Mint considered her offer and then shook his head. "They can't be parted from us now," he said. "The valley wants them. Isn't that right, Boy?"

He looked at his father and then at Evangeline, deliberating which one should receive the full benefit of his next remark. "The valley needs them," he said triumphantly.

Farmer Mint chuckled and took off his flat cap in homage to his son's sagacity. "You don't get a thought like that every day, do you?"

"Not in London, no." Evangeline started desperately to examine the portraits, drawings and miniatures which were hanging above the mantelpiece. "What lovely old faces," she said. "They all look so rural, don't they? But I suppose that can't really be helped." Father and son stared at her, whenever they had nothing to say, they lapsed into what Evangeline was later to call a "primeval stillness". But for the moment she was disturbed by their silence and turned around again to face the dead rather than the living. "And who," she asked, pointing to a faded brown photograph, "are this gorgeous old couple who look like something out of Holbein?"

Farmer Mint came up and lightly touched the photograph with his finger. "That," he said. "That is the aged pair." An old man and woman were standing outside the closed door of a cottage, its thatch just a few inches above their heads. The woman was wearing a white bonnet with its ribbons hanging around her neck; her hands were folded in front of her over her white apron. The old man was wearing a dark smock and was leaning forward on a stick, apparently staring into the eyes of the photographer. "They're that Boy's great-grandparents. That's what they are."

"Never," Evangeline replied. "I have never been more astonished in my *life*." She shook her head with a delightful look of perplexity and interest but, if she had looked at the photograph more carefully, she would have noticed that the old couple were standing outside the Mints' farmhouse – and she would have noticed also that, with its broken path, with its whitewashed stone, and with its cracked green door, the house had not changed at all. It might have stood like this for centuries.

"They're all his," Farmer Mint was saying. "Boy Mint's ancestors. He goes back a long way." And in fact these pictures and photographs, which seemed to mark a continuous line of at least three centuries, displayed a succession of faces which bore a striking resemblance to those of the present Mints. "He stretches right back."

"Don't tell me." And, for once, she meant what she said. She thought of her own parents, and their parents before them; they were strangers to her. But somehow worse than strangers. Somehow they were her enemies.

Mark was still looking out of the window, distracted: he thought he had seen a figure standing on top of the tumulus, waving its arms, and, although the impression had lasted only a moment, he was still wondering who it could have been when Evangeline came up to him. "It's a marvellous view from here," he said eagerly. "But you know I could have sworn I saw something . . ." No one seemed very interested, and he began again. "Miss Tupper—"

"Evangeline. I'm always Evangeline in the country."

"Evangeline wanted to come and thank you both for being so helpful to us. We're making steady progress now." Farmer and Boy Mint did not seem to understand what he meant. "You know," he said. "With the passage grave. The great mound."

"Pretty as an absolute picture," Evangeline added.

Farmer Mint had moved across the room and was staring at the photographs and miniatures of his ancestors. He seemed to be paying no attention to this conversation but now he broke in with, "I wouldn't know anything about that." He turned around and faced Mark. "There's no good," he said, "in raking over dead soil. You won't find much in that." Mark had heard all this before, and simply shook his head. "Tell him what he *will* find, Boy. Let your mind wander along that question."

For once Boy Mint did not need several minutes to collect his thoughts. "Sheep's bones," he said at once. "Rabbits' teeth. Skeletons of dead birds." It was as if he had memorised this litany. "Cow shit."

Evangeline put up her hand and interrupted him. "I don't think that I have ever spent a nicer or more informative afternoon." Boy was continuing with his list under his breath as she continued. "I'm positively stuffed with rustic lore."

Farmer Mint approved of this. "That's right," he said. "He'll stuff you with it. He won't stop."

"And neither must we." This seemed to Evangeline a very graceful farewell and, smiling triumphantly at Mark, she walked towards the door, opened it and stepped out on the path. Three hens, who had been peacefully browsing amongst some ancient straw, started a chorus of protest and scuttled into the hedge. "I wonder," she asked the Mints as they followed her down the path. "If you fed them chicken, would they become savages?" She did not wait for their answer. "Goodbye. You Mints just keep on being adorable. Like your delightful ancestors. Goodbye."

PART TWO

Creation began when you were born. It will end on the day you die.

Oscar Wilde.

•17•

ON THE BEACH

THE OLD man in the straw hat and pink blazer was
sitting on an outcrop of dark grey rock, singing softly to
himself:
Only to see the old cottage again!
How my poor heart would rejoice,
  To see the old faces I loved
And to hear my poor mother's voice . . .
His voice trailed off, and he started humming instead, when an
elderly woman with difficulty crossed the stony beach to join him.
"Honest, Joey," she said. "Never again. Not for all the money in
China."

"Tea, dear."

"I don't care what it is. It's still my poor feet." She was wearing
pink, too, this rather dried-up little old woman with her white hair
carefully crafted into bunches of tight white curls; and her voice was
husky, as if she had a permanently sore throat.

"But, Floey, don't you enjoy your morning promenade? In a
lovely spot like this?" He smiled and tipped his straw hat at a
conventionally jaunty angle, although his face retained its somewhat
lugubrious expression.

She looked behind him at the slate-grey cliffs of St Gabriel's Shore,
broken down from landslips, disrupted by the underground springs
which leaked from the cliff-face, the ancient strata of the region
fashioned here into blocks of subsided limestone and sloping banks
of clay. Small streams of water, gravel and clay ran down the cliffs
and, beside them, lay the tumbled boulders and broken rocks which
reached down to the edge of the beach. "It's a mute point," she said.

"Moot."

"It's debatable." She put out her hand and helped him up from

63

the rock. "We have no call to be here in the first place. On a wild duck chase."

He laughed. "Do you remember that old song, Floey. 'For the sake of the days gone by'?"

"Sung in a mysterious way?"

"That's the one." They were now walking arm in arm along the strand, the reflected light from the sea making the stones shine in front of them. "I'm here for the sake of *my* days gone by. I'm a thing of the past, old dear."

"Don't go on about it, Joey."

"I just want to know what my past is. Or was." He stopped and looked out at the sea. It was at low tide, and stretching down towards it from the exposed shore were flat outcrops of dark slate. From this distance they seemed smooth, as if they had been polished by the endless movement of water, but when Joey Hanover came closer he saw how they were marked with small holes and grooves. He was a large and apparently ungainly man, but with a sudden graceful gesture he leapt onto the surface of the slate and began to walk across it to the sea.

"Joey! Break a leg!" Floey laughed at the silhouette of her husband, in straw hat and pink blazer, nonchalantly standing in front of the bright waves. In response he kicked one leg in the air, tried to make a twirl, slipped, and fell upon the slate; but he could not have been seriously hurt, since immediately his attention was drawn to something lying upon the rock beside him. He picked it up, waved it above his head and shouted something; but the sound of the slowly advancing sea drowned his words.

"I've got something here," he said when he returned, slightly breathless, "which is thousands of years old."

"One of your jokes?"

"Don't mock, Floey. Take a look."

He held a piece of rock towards her and, wrinkling her nose in apparent disgust, she examined the spiral shape of a snail-like creature embedded in the stone. "Is it dead then?"

"Of course it's dead. Things that old don't come to life again."

"Don't you be so sure." The shape of this thing, curled in its last primeval sleep, reminded her of the image of a star, its various gases spiralling around a tiny central core. "It's one of them mammonites," she said at last.

"Is that the right word? Mammonite?" Joey was accustomed to

his wife's little mistakes with the language.

She gave him a look of utter contempt. "Of course I'm sure. I read about them."

"So," he said. "That's solved that, then. They're all digging for mammonites!" The Hanovers had been puzzled by the presence on St Gabriel's Shore of five or six people, clutching buckets and small hammers, who had been clambering along the cliff-face. In fact this coastal region was famous for the wealth and variety of its ammonite fossils which, after a period of long rain, were often dislodged from the crumbling clay and limestone or washed down onto the beach itself. So portions of the fossil-bearing beds sometimes lay among the debris and the fallen rock at the base of the cliffs, remnants of the delicate creatures which had moved across the surface of this place 140 million years before.

The Hanovers walked further along the shore, Floey hanging back for a few moments while she placed the ammonite in her bright yellow handbag. When she caught up with him, she resumed the theme of their previous conversation. "And what good does it do to come back," she asked him, "after all these years? The past is past and buried. Why go digging it up again?"

"I have to know the truth. Before I die." She was about to interrupt him, but he held up his hand to stop her. "I mean it, Flo. Before I die."

"Joey "

"How would you feel? You would want to know, wouldn't you? You would want to find out. All these years I've been thinking about it, wondering, making plans . . ." Then he began to laugh at his own earnestness and, taking off his straw hat, put it to his chest with a theatrical gesture. "Oh, Floey, I can't forget the days when I was young."

"And grief too keen to talk about was thine?" She knew the song.

"The Lyceum, Wolverhampton, 1946."

"Sung with immense success?"

"That's right! We were a success, weren't we?" Joey sighed. They carried on walking, hand in hand, and once more he returned to the subject which had never left his mind. "I know it was somewhere near here. As soon as we came here, I remembered. There was a cottage with a garden. I remember purple flowers. And there were faces, too. White faces like the faces of angels. It's a dream. Do you know what I mean? Except that this dream is somewhere close to hand. And I have a feeling, Flo. I have a feeling that I'm just about to find it."

A mist had gathered above the cliffs and, now that the wind had dropped, it began to curl downwards in wreaths towards the debris of the fossil beds. Someone had lit a fire on the strand, and its smoke rose into the mist until it became a part of it. The sea was quiet and, for a moment, Joey Hanover felt afraid. "Come on," he said. He took his wife's arm and, as they returned to their car, he began to sing out in a loud voice

> Oh I do like to be beside the seaside,
> Oh I do like to be beside the sea . . .

•18•

THE FAMOUS MAN

IT WAS late morning when the Hanovers returned to Lyme Regis, and Joey smiled placidly as they drove up Broad Street before turning left into the Cobb Road; it was the smile of someone who is accustomed to being observed. "There are more old fossils here," he murmured, "than there are on the beach." He looked with barely suppressed satisfaction at an elderly woman who was crossing in front of them. "All I need is a hammer and a bucket."

Floey parked a few yards from Crogg Lane, where they had rented a house for three months. "You great goose," she said. "Have we got time for just the one?"

"*Just* the one."

They left their Rover 2000 and began walking downhill to The Hungry Donkey. The public house was some distance, but Joey retained his smile – even when a small boy came up to him, looked at his face, opened his mouth in astonishment and then skipped past him. The boy then ran quickly down a side street, doubled back, turned the corner and, with a look of wonderful blitheness, slowly came walking towards him again. Joey was amused by this and, when the boy passed him once more, he whispered, "Does yer Mother know yer out?" This was a well-known 'Joeyism'. The boy screamed with laughter, and started walking backwards so that he could keep abreast of the Hanovers as they made their way – all the time contemplating Joey's lugubrious features. This attracted some attention and, from the other side of the street, a young man shouted "'Ow's yer poor feet?" This was another of Joey's famous catch-phrases, but he did not look around; he smiled, waved his hand vaguely in greeting, and walked on.

The Hungry Donkey was perched beside the Cobb, the ancient fortification which protected the town from the depredations of the sea; they could hear the waves breaking against the old stone wall as Joey pretended to kick the boy in the seat of his pants and murmured, "Fly away, care."

Floey had already scurried into the saloon bar and was trying to catch the attention of a middle-aged barmaid who was, at that moment, plucking a hair from her nose. "Two port and lemons," she was saying. "Easy on the lemon."

Joey came up beside her. "The wife's a bit particular, you see."

There was something about his voice which attracted the barmaid's attention and, very slowly, she turned to face the elderly pair. "I know you," she said to Joey. "I know you very well." She was shaking her head from side to side, as if she were reprimanding him for some minor offence. "Joey. Joey Hanover."

"That's my name and that's my nature."

In fact everybody knew Joey. Immediately after the Second World War he had started work as a stand-up comic in variety and in working men's clubs, and had quickly acquired a reputation for his 'patter'. While on tour in 1948 he had met Floey at the Gaiety Theatre in Huddersfield; she was in the chorus there, but had given up her own career as Joey became more popular. He had followed the natural route from the clubs to radio and television, with occasional seasons of pantomime to renew his acquaintance with the stage, until he had become by the Sixties one of the most popular of modern comedians. But his comedy was of an especial sort: although his career coincided with the extinction of the music-hall he was still associated with that particular kind of theatre and, despite the fact that he was a 'star' of television, he still seemed to carry with him the garish and sentimental aura of the halls. His persona was close to that of Dan Leno or Max Miller: Joey Hanover, too, was the lugubrious Cockney, downtrodden but not down-hearted, bent but not broken, an object both of pity and of laughter. His repartee was often coarse, but he seemed quite innocent of all the innuendoes which entertained his audience. He was sometimes merry, sometimes in tears, but he always made them laugh. His features were unmistakable even when he played the dame in pantomime; and, with his wide mouth, his pendulous nose, his large hands, there were some who saw in him the lineaments of such clowns as Mathews or Grimaldi. He was also famous for his 'Joeyisms' or malapropisms, which in fact he stole from his wife's ordinary conversation.

The barmaid was so busy looking at him that she seemed to be in no hurry to provide them with their drinks. So Joey, nudged by his wife, put his chin upon his hands and leaned over the bar in a confidential manner. "I bet the port and lemon—"

"Easy on the lemon," Floey added quickly.

"I bet the port and lemon will come in a glass. Don't you agree?"

The barmaid giggled, seemed to shake herself awake, and prepared the drinks – all the time looking slyly across to Joey Hanover to make sure that he was watching her. "A bit more lemon, Joey?"

"Anything, darling. Anything so long as it's wet."

A middle-aged man was sitting on a stool along the bar and now looked sideways at him. "Excuse me," he said. "Excusez-moi." The man was resting a straw hat on his knee and now he picked it up and twirled it around, at the same time looking at Joey's own headgear. "Snap," he said. "Snapette." With his free hand he picked up his glass. "Your health."

"Bad on Fridays. Not so bad on weekends."

"Fraicheur, sir."

"I love fresh air."

"Don't be a scream," the man replied. "That's my name. Augustine Fraicheur. It's in big black letters all over town."

"Undertaker?"

"No, but you're very warm. Antiques. Clocks the spécialité de la maison."

Joey Hanover was beginning to like this man with rheumy eyes, who was now brushing down his bright orange cravat. It was set off by a pale striped shirt and tweed jacket that might have seen service in colonial India. "Hanover," Joey replied. "As in Germany."

"Oh, I know *you*. Everybody knows *you*."

"And that's my wife. In the red corner." Floey had scuttled off with her port and lemon and now, apparently taking no further interest in the proceedings, was sitting beneath a darts-board.

"I was in the profession once," Augustine was saying. "Another G and T, Betty dear." He was signalling for another drink. "And something for Mr Hanover." There was the sudden flurry of a pink cotton dress, as Floey miraculously appeared at the bar. "And of course his lovely lady."

"Proust!" she said, taking the refilled glass and going back to her secluded spot.

"Yes, I was in the business. But that was during the War."

"Entertaining the troops, were we?"

Augustine shrieked with laughter. "I don't know what you mean! I was only at the back! Kicking my legs up like there was no tomorrow." He sighed. "I had lovely legs in those days. Lovely gams."

Joey was used to similar nostalgia from the people whom he met, and he had a series of prepared remarks for the occasion. "They had real theatres then," he said, looking his most mournful. "Real acts. Tennyson and O'Gorman. The Tiny Websters. Clapham and Dwyer. Murgatroyd and Winterbottom . . ."

"Gladys Cooper's sister."

"Gladys Cooper's sister?"

"That's right. Gladys Cooper's sister."

There was a silence between them, and Floey looked tentatively at the bar to see if any more drinks were being offered. Then she cleared her throat very loudly, reminding Joey of her presence. "My wife was a danseuse, too, you know. Oh yes. Another one for you, my darling?" He took across a large drink and, when she gave him a baleful stare, whispered, "He may know something. He may be able to help us."

"I'm still an old thespian at heart," Augustine was saying when Joey returned to the bar. "I can't help it. Put me near a stage and I yearn for tights. I run this little amateur company, you know." Suddenly he looked at Joey Hanover with additional interest. "We're doing *The Family Reunion* this season. For the summer trade. I wonder—"

Joey forestalled him. "T.S. Eliot? Am I right?"

"Frightfully highbrow, I suppose. Especially for Lyme Regis." Augustine took a large swallow of his drink. "But I think it ought to be played as comedy, don't you? These tragedy queens aren't in my line at all." He looked across at Joey, and said again. "I wonder—"

Joey adopted his most lugubrious expression. "No. Of course not. Of course you wouldn't."

"I'm in retirement." Joey said. "Close the shutter, Joey's dead."

"Silly me. Slap slap." And Augustine did indeed slap both sides of his face; since he was now rather drunk, he hit himself harder than he had intended and he winced. "But I do hope you'll come and see us."

Throughout this conversation the barmaid had been staring at Joey's features; she was now quite red in the face and was wobbling slightly, as if the effort of trying to restrain her amusement had become too much for her. Now something within her stirred and quite abruptly she came out with, "It's all very well, Mr Pell, but you can't sleep here." This had been another of Joey's catchphrases, but the barmaid laughed so loudly that she might have just invented it herself.

Joey was used to being quoted. "No roof above our weary heads," he replied. "Born to wander, that's what we are."

Augustine was not sober enough to follow this turn in the conversation. "I thought you were summer visitors."

"Actually," Joey said. "We're looking for something. We're looking for a cottage."

"How clever of you to come to the country. We have plenty of cottages here. We're quite famous for them."

"No. We want something very particular." He glanced over at Floey, but she was swirling the last of her port and lemon around in the glass. "Now follow me closely, will you? This is rather intricate." Even when talking seriously, instinctively he reverted to the lines of his old act. "We – me and her – are looking for a cottage. It's got to be a special cottage. It must be in a valley. It's got to have a wood near it. And I think it's got to have purple flowers in the garden."

"Flowers are *very* common too. Thank you, darling." Another gin had been placed in front of him, and at once he became more intimate. "As for valleys, my dear, they are everywhere. There's no stopping them. Up and down. Up and down. Too ghastly for words."

"But I remember—" Here Joey broke off for a moment, and swallowed the rest of his drink. "Sorry. The mouth went all queer for a moment. I mean to say that we're looking for a very secluded valley. Very quiet."

Augustine pursed his lips. "I'm afraid the country tends to be very noisy. If you want tranquillity, you should try London."

"It's quiet up your way, Gussy." The barmaid was taking this conversation seriously. "Too quiet."

"You haven't heard me in the kitchen, dear. I go wild. In the country, you know," he went on, looking at Joey, "there's a very thin line between us and absolute savagery."

Joey was more anxious to pick up information of a geographical kind. "Where *do* you live?"

"I'm in Colcorum. Just a common-or-garden village nestling in the Pilgrin Valley—"

"—That's what I mean," the barmaid interrupted. "That valley is ever so quiet. And there used to be cottages there."

"Derelict now, dear. Very much a case of the time that land forgot. Or is it the other way around?"

Joey began singing under his breath as he took out a small notebook. "Is that Pilgrim as in to be one?"

"No. Pil*grin*. Pill. Grin."

The barmaid leaned towards Joey, watching eagerly as he wrote down the name with a pencil. "I love them old songs," she said. "Give us another."

"Let me refresh Madame Sin first."

He took another drink over to Floey, who grabbed it and muttered, "I suppose you're making a fool of yourself."

"I'm just being agreeable, Floey. And if that makes me a fool, then so be it." He stood up now and, with his back against the darts-board, stretched out his arms toward the barmaid. "Listen," he said. "This'll do you good." And then in a quiet voice began to sing

> In the twi-twi-twilight
> Out in the beautiful twilight
> We all go out for a walk, walk, walk
> A quiet old spoon and a talk, talk, talk
> That's the time we long for
> Just before the night—

It was an old song and it brought back to the barmaid memories of her earlier life, memories of her childhood. Past time. Another time. And she began to cry as Joey carried on singing

> In the twi-twi-twilight
> Out in the beautiful twilight . . .

•*19*•

GRANNY'S TEETH

AS THEY left The Hungry Donkey somebody passed across them, brushing against Floey Hanover; since by this time she was a little unsteady on her feet she staggered back, and was about to shout out something when Joey checked her. It was a crippled woman. She had not seen them because she had been reading a letter and now, apparently staring at something far out across the water, she hurried forward towards the Cobb. It was clear that she did not know, or care, where she was going; she was simply advancing towards the sea, with the letter in her hand, and now she began to mount the narrow stairs which are cut into the Cobb and which are known as 'Granny's Teeth'. But she was limping badly; suddenly she slipped and, unable to hold her balance, she fell sideways onto the ground beside the harbour.

Joey Hanover, clutching his straw hat to his head, rushed to help her. "That was a nice tumble," he said. "I wish I could fall like that." She did not seem to be injured, and gently he helped her to her feet.

"The letter," was all she managed to say. "My letter." She had stretched out her hand as she fell, and the letter had been blown against the Cobb.

But the same small boy who had accompanied Joey down the street now ran up to her, clutching it. "Here it is," he said. "I got it." He winked at Joey, as if he had known him all his life, and quite by instinct Joey winked back.

The shock of the fall had clearly unnerved the crippled woman, and she was still shaking. "I'm sorry," she said. "I'm sorry. I don't normally slip." She started to cry.

"We all slip once in a while, don't we?" Joey was addressing the boy, who nodded benignly. "There's no reason to be sorry."

"I don't normally fall."

73

"Of course you don't." He put his arm around her and led her away from the Cobb. "Don't worry," he said. "Just like the ivy I'll cling to you." The boy smiled, saluted Joey, put his hands in his trouser-pockets and strolled away. "Show me the way to go home," Joey was saying. "And I'll take you back."

For the first time she looked up at him; she knew his face but she was so shaken that it seemed to her to be the relic from some powerful dream she must once have had. "I'm fine. Really. It was only—"

"We insist." Floey came up to her and took her arm. The young woman bowed her head for a moment, and Floey bent down slightly so that she might see her face. "Here we are," she said very gently. "Nothing the matter at all." The three of them walked slowly towards the car, the Hanovers on either side of the crippled woman. She told them that she lived in Crooked Alley. She tried to laugh and held onto the letter more tightly. "That's a fine name," Joey said. "An old name." He ran his hand along the Rover 2000 now that they had reached it. "I'm Joey. This is Floey."

"Kathleen. Kathleen Clare." She bowed her head again as she said this; it was as if the name did not really belong to her, as if it belonged to no one in particular.

Floey helped her into the back seat and moved in beside her. "Show us where to go," she said. "We're the ones who need help around here."

And so Joey drove back through Lyme Regis as Kathleen directed him through the maze of small streets which cluster by the sea and around the narrow river which runs through the town. "You've got to get under," he was singing softly to himself. "Get out and get under." They reached Crooked Alley, and at once he noticed the sign "Antiques. Augustine Fraicheur". He smiled and wound down the window, hearing the sound of the encroaching sea which was only two streets away. "I know him," he said. "I like him."

Kathleen got out of the car, and turned to thank them. Her hands were still trembling and there was so much intensity in her manner that Floey pitied her. "Go and have a nice cup of tea," Floey said. "The cup that moves."

"Soothes, dear."

Kathleen thanked them and turned away; but not before Joey noticed that once more she was crying. He watched her as she opened a door by the side of the antiques shop, and slowly began climbing some dark stairs. Then he sat over the steering wheel for a while, with head bowed. "Floey," he said eventually. "Shall we take a step inside?"

They got out of the car and walked into the shop. A young man, his long red hair tied back into a sort of pigtail, came from behind a grandfather clock. "Gussie's out," he said, flatly. He had a strong Belfast accent.

"I know," Joey smiled. "I was just with him in a public house. Someone may have to show him the way to go home." The Irishman said nothing and, a little disappointed that his joke had met no response, Joey took his wife's arm and began to look over the objects collected here, gathered on tables, hidden in corners of the dusty room, placed high up on shelves so that they were difficult to see – there were general items but, pre-eminently, there were clocks. Sand glasses with their metal bases stained or worn, chronometers, deck-watches, pocket watches, alarm clocks, clock watches, table clocks, grandfather clocks, an orrery made from the thinnest and most glittering brass, a marine timekeeper with a mechanism so intricate that it seemed to be in perpetual nervous motion – all of them measuring time with weights and balances, springs and wires. And as they stood in silence within the shop the Hanovers could hear the sounds of time being measured and despatched, with the scraping of tin cylinders against each other, the rustling of gears as thin as wafers, the winding and unwinding of delicate springs, the more familiar tick as the seconds were checked one by one. No other sound could move Joey half as much as this and, as he stood with his fingers lightly touching a dial made out of ivory, he felt himself being carried away on the stream of time.

Augustine had come in. "When the cat's away . . ." he said to his assistant and, even from a few feet, Joey could smell the drink on his breath. Then Augustine turned and, suddenly seeing Floey in the half-light, gave a little cry of recognition. "This is unexpected," he said. "Did you come for anything particular? An astrolabe? A nice Victorian travelling clock?"

"No thank you." Floey looked around for her husband. "We were doing that thing people do with books."

"Burning?"

"No." The word came out triumphantly as she prepared herself to leave. "We were browsing." Joey could smell the dust all around him but, when she suddenly opened the door, he felt the stream of fresh air and a sudden access of light as if someone else had entered the room. And he thought of the crippled woman, who lived above this place where the ancient clocks were gathered.

◆20◆

IN THE TWILIGHT

WHEN MARK CLARE returned home that evening from Pilgrin Valley he hoped that Kathleen, as usual, would be waiting to greet him. But she was sitting in a chair beneath the window, her profile against the darkening sky. "Hello," he said gently. But he sensed that something was wrong and he called out, more enthusiastically, "Hello there. No light? Shall I switch on a lamp?"

"No, Mark. Not yet. Please." It was as if she wanted to disappear with the disappearing light, to fade and so cease to be herself.

"What's the matter?" He said this hesitantly, almost apologetically. "Is there anything the matter?"

She handed him the letter without replying, and he stood behind her so that he could read it by the waning light from the window. It had come from the adoption agency and explained, very carefully, that since Mrs Clare was registered as a disabled person further inquiries would have to be instituted before any preliminary steps for adopting a child could be taken. There were circumstances in which a disabled person could be considered eligible as a parent, but unfortunately there were also circumstances in which no such decision could be made. Matters were proceeding.

"This doesn't mean anything," he said. For some reason he was trying to swallow. "This is just routine stuff." But, as soon as he put his arm around Kathleen's shoulder, he felt her despair and helplessly began to enter it. He let the letter fall to the floor. Although he had not wanted to expect it, he knew that it would come; and he had tried to prepare himself for the moment. "It's just routine," he said again. "A routine precaution."

"A precaution?" She turned around to look at him. "A precaution against what?" Her voice had sounded shrill and, moving away from Mark's embrace, she put her hand upon her neck.

"They just have to be sure," he said. "As soon as they've seen us, they'll know. People like us . . ." It was the very starkness of this "people like us" which made it sound piteous – it was as if he were seeing Kathleen and himself from the outside, as if they were not unique but somehow so marked by loss or incapacity that they had become representative, as if they had ceased to be fully real to each other. He knelt down beside her and took her hand.

"I was beginning to forget about it," she said very softly. "But now that's what I am again. That's what I've always been." She touched her leg. "It weighs so heavily upon me."

"I know." He wanted to help, but once again he felt himself being overtaken by her own sorrow. If someone had entered the room suddenly Mark would at once, as if by instinct, have become the genial and enthusiastic person whom all his friends recognised; but, with Kathleen, his own secret self emerged. He was always surprised by its promptings and now his work, his investigations into the past, his reconstruction of the abodes of the dead, were not of the slightest importance when compared with his wife's despair. It was one that other people had suffered through the centuries – "people like us" – and yet it was always fresh, always renewed, always the first pain.

"Perhaps they're right," Kathleen was saying. "Perhaps it was all a mistake." —

And as she spoke he realised how fragile was her hold upon her apparent good spirits and optimism; how little she had changed. He tasted his own fear, like metal in the mouth. "Try and be angry," he said. "Don't direct it all into yourself. Direct it outward."

"But you don't know what it's like to be trapped. And to know that nothing will ever be different. Some things change," she said. "But the important things remain the same."

"It's not important." He was not sure what he was saying. "Try and see beyond this."

"And then what will I see? The sky? The earth? They will go their own way without me."

Mark could hear in her voice the intensity, the withdrawn low sound, which he had sensed when he had first met her. And now he knew that he was being excluded from her suffering. This dialogue with herself was one she had conducted since infancy and although once he had heard it, faintly, it had soon been drowned out by their life together. Now Kathleen's intensity was so real that it seemed to annul all the years between; she was what she had always been, and was it possible that being crippled was the only real meaning to her life? But no, that could not be true, not now. "We have each other," he said. "Don't forget. You're not alone."

"And you have to carry me like a burden. Is that what it is?"

"You're no burden. You are my life." He had never seen such pain in her eyes and he watched fascinated, as if in front of him she was being transformed.

"Yes," she said. "I know." Both of them were holding each other, rocking to and fro in the twilight.

GOING DEEPER

OWEN CHARD watched the young man working beside him and noticed with some pleasure that his movements were getting slower and slower. Perhaps it was the warmth of the late spring morning that was affecting him, but from time to time he sighed and passed his hands across his eyes. "Well well well," Owen said eventually. "Tired already. Where's the fibre?"

"Not tired exactly." The young man had been kneeling on a piece of black plastic sheeting, in an attitude which from a distance might have resembled that of someone praying to the ground, but now he stood up to ease his legs and aching back; as he did so, he looked at the dark exposed surface of the earth all around him. "I don't know what it is."

"Don't worry about it." Owen was unusually cheerful. "Everyone gets it once in a while. We call it Stone Age gloom." He tapped the earth with his trowel. "It just seems to seep up from here. Coming up for air."

"Like a disease?"

"No. Like gloom."

"Now what are you two boys talking about?" Martha Temple came up to them, wagging her finger in the most delightful way. "I heard a horrible word, and I don't like it. Let me hear a happy word. Like gingerbread. Or doughnut."

"I was just telling him about Stone Age gloom," Owen said. "I presume you remember what that is."

"I don't want to know." Gaily she put her hands up to her ears, and walked away. But she knew already. She knew the cold sweat which gathered on the forehead, the sense of futility like an ache in the limbs, the strange sensation of being watched. It had affected her once severely, but she was very cheerful now. "Julian," she called out. "Julian Hill, what *are* you doing?" She was so playful that she could not possibly have been drawing attention to the fact that Julian, as usual, was doing very little to help the excavation. He was standing at the eastern end of the tomb, where the tumulus seemed to emerge from the side of the valley; his head was thrown back, and he held his arms in the air. "I have a theory about the midsummer sunrise. One of my best theories as a matter of fact—"

"And you're the expert, as everyone has been told. Why don't you write a very interesting paper for *New Archaeology*? Isn't that how people get promotion?"

"That's a thought." Julian had taken her suggestion quite seriously. "I wonder how much they would pay for a really good piece?" It was a peculiarity of Julian's temperament that he assumed everyone would agree with his own estimate of himself. "I could work up my lecture, too." Julian Hill's lecture, which he had never yet delivered, concerned the future of archaeology. He had a vision of a time when there would be no cause for excavation at all, when soil-sounding devices would be able both to detect all the objects buried underneath the earth and to reconstruct them in three-dimensional form. The subterranean world need never be disturbed, since these three-dimensional images could then be reproduced as holograms: in the museum of the future, passage graves and underground chambers would float in light upon the exhibition floor, perfect simulacra of objects that remained concealed within the close-packed earth. The stone of these neolithic monuments would seem as real as the stone of the museum in which they had been created, decayed bones and pottery as solid as if they had just risen out of the earth, all the evidence of prehistory resurrected in glowing form. And nothing would actually have been touched: there would be two worlds, therefore, one buried forever in darkness and one filled with light. Julian Hill saw himself in the light, also; he saw himself far away from the detritus of digging, away from the sphere of his own body, away from all his colleagues, away in that distance towards which his eyes always seemed to be fixed.

Martha Temple watched as he pressed some numbers into his pocket calculator. "It is lucky," she said in her most charming fashion, "that one of us doesn't have to do any actual digging. You can stand back and get an overall picture, can't you?"

"That's what I do best."

This was not quite the answer she expected, and there was a

81

certain disappointment in her voice. "I mustn't keep you," she said. "I have to get back to some real work now."

At this moment her own work was to be found in the contents of a wooden tray, which she had left on her desk in the Portakabin attached to the site. Here were the objects which had been discovered during this morning's excavations – two flints, both of them in an advanced stage of decay but bearing enough traces of their original shape to suggest that one had been much broader and flatter than the other. The precise location of these finds had been noted and, although there were several hundred years' difference in the date of their manufacture, they had in fact been discovered very close to each other. There was also a piece of pottery. It was no more than two inches in width but, when Martha bent over to touch it with her fine brush, she noticed at once that there was a groove within it which had the appearance of cord – in another time, someone must have pressed a rope against the clay when it was not yet solid, leaving this faint trace of decoration. In another time. But the dating was again curious; the grooved ware came from a period which suggested that the site was still in use many hundreds of years after its construction.

Carefully she placed the fragment in a polythene bag, which she then sealed and tagged. She heard the door open behind her and she said, as if to herself but in her most engaging manner, "This is all very strange." No one replied. "It may just be silly little me." There was still no response, and she turned around sharply to see Owen Chard taking out his pipe. "I didn't hear you come in," she said with a delightful little laugh. "What must you think of me, talking to myself like that?"

"I wasn't listening." He knocked the pipe-bowl against the side of the computer. "You thought I was Mark, didn't you?"

"I didn't think it was anyone." Again the delightful laugh but, since Owen was paying no attention, she added rather more acidly, "Where is he anyway?" She went to the door of the cabin and called out, "Mark? Mark? Has anyone seen Mark?" – thus drawing attention to the fact that he had not yet arrived. "I hope," she added to herself, trying to suppress a slight smile, "that nothing terrible has happened."

In fact Mark did not arrive until later in the day. The others were so accustomed to his enthusiasm that no one, except Owen, noticed how forced and strained he seemed. But Mark said nothing and all of them worked through the day, slowly removing the chalky earth which pressed down upon the chamber tomb within the mound. Their backs ached as they knelt over the ground; their knees were grazed and bruised even though they tried to kneel upon the black plastic sheeting; they developed painful cramps in the neck as they examined the soil which they loosened with trowel and scapula; their fingers were scraped by the sharp stones; their wrists ached with the effort of sifting the earth and placing it in plastic bags for later analysis.

They worked on until the light began to fade, and the setting sun cast long shadows of the boundary stones across the flat site. The tumulus itself, although now some eighteen inches lower than its original position, cast a pool of darkness on the side of the valley. A wind had started up in the early afternoon and it had blown particles of dust and chalk into the eyes of the excavators, entering their mouths and streaking their hair. But the wind had dropped and the first faint vestiges of mist were succeeded now by a heavier veil which hovered over the beech and ash trees on the crest of the valley – so deep did it become that the trees were like pencil drawings upon the mist itself, and seemed ready to dissolve within it.

"Over here!" It was the voice of the young man who had suffered the Stone Age gloom. "Come over here!" Mark and Owen walked across the site towards him, and looked down as he pointed with his trowel at a shape embedded in the earth. It was twelve inches in length, and curved. "Some sort of bone?" he asked, embarrassed now in case his discovery was of no real importance.

"Oh yes, it's bone." At first glance, Mark knew what it was. "But not human bone."

"No," Owen added. "This is the scapula of an ox. Shaped to form a shovel. Do you see?" He bent down and traced the outline with his finger, making sure that he did not touch the object.

Mark took a step back. "That's right," he said. "That's what it is. We're getting close to them now."

♦*22*♦

INVADERS

SOMETHING HAD happened during the night. Owen was the first on the site the following morning and, when Martha arrived, she found him shaking his head and smiling grimly to himself. "Now," he said. "Now. I wonder who did this." As soon as the excavation had begun, this section of Pilgrin Valley – including the stone circle and of course the tumulus itself – had been cordoned off with lengths of bright green rope attached to wooden posts. But overnight the rope had been cut on all four sides, and the ends trailed upon the freshly dug earth.

"Could it have been some sheep?" Martha asked, innocent as ever. "Sheep can bite, after all, and I can't imagine anyone wanting to harm the site. Not even . . ." Her voice trailed off, principally because she could think of no one in particular to accuse.

"Sheep? Oh yes. Sheep could have done all this. Of course." Owen pointed to the area around the mound itself, where a series of planks or walkways had been placed to protect the newly exposed ground. Now these planks had been removed – some of them broken in half and thrown beyond the area of the site, while others had been stacked together and left in a pile beside the Portakabin. It was at this point both of them suddenly realised that the door of the office itself had been opened. Martha ran ahead, eager to be the first to see any possible damage, and she allowed herself the luxury of a little scream when she entered the office. All the orange plastic chairs had been turned over or ripped, the screen of the computer had been smashed and several files had been scattered across the floor. Now in genuine alarm, she went across to her small desk where the "finds" were examined before being despatched to the laboratory of Exeter Museum. And, curiously enough, the objects assembled yesterday had not been harmed: the flints, the section of grooved ware, the seeds, the shells and the fragments of animal bone were intact. And

84

yet there was something missing . . .

She waited until Owen had entered the Portakabin before putting her hand up to her mouth and exclaiming, "The scapula! The scapula has gone!" She had placed the shovel carved from ox-bone, found the previous evening, in a sealed plastic container; but the container had disappeared. "I don't believe it," she said. She picked up one of the chairs, dusted it down with her hand and sat upon it very deliberately. "I *won't* believe that anyone from this site could cause so much damage." Owen had not really considered the possibility that one of their colleagues had done this, and he looked at her in bewilderment. "I may be wrong. I may place too much stock in human nature. But I don't believe it." She sounded delighted.

Mark rushed in, taking off his jacket as if he were late for work. "What is it?" he asked. "What's been going on?"

"Someone doesn't like us." Owen was very grim.

Martha's mood changed as soon as Mark entered the little cabin. "Oh don't say that, Owen. It may all be just some awful mistake. Some accident. Even though," she added, looking slyly at Mark as he bent to pick up a file, "it may take us weeks if not months to get over it."

He stood up and wiped his hand across his face. "What exactly has happened here?"

This was the question which the others debated throughout the day. Owen Chard had decided that the site was under concentrated attack, and spent most of his time telling everyone what everyone already knew. Julian Hill arrived immediately at the theory that this invasion corresponded to their own spoliation of the neolithic grave, and became so strongly convinced that the whole "experience" needed to be "internalised" that he paid no attention to the damage which had been caused. Martha Temple was angelically good-tempered, almost breezy; but, in her lovely attempts to "keep up the spirits" of "the team", she managed inadvertently to cast the lightest possible suspicion on practically all of its members.

Only Mark himself was able properly to deal with the situation: at this moment he seemed positively to enjoy creating order out of disorder as if, in some way, he were trying to free himself. He itemised the damage and took immediate steps to rectify it, while all the time considering the significance of this strange incursion into the area of the site. The actual event was clear: someone had destroyed much of the equipment belonging to the archaeological team but, curiously enough, had damaged neither the tumulus itself nor any of the objects retrieved from it. Even though the planks had been forcibly removed from the area, the ground beneath them had not been touched; there were no footprints here, no fresh stains upon the ancient earth. Only the ox-bone shovel had been stolen.

Mark at first assumed that the culprits were local children, perhaps even the small boys who so many weeks before had interrupted him with their laughter. But would children have shown such curious reverence for, or fear of, the site itself? And why would they have stolen the shovel while leaving behind everything else? But, if children were not responsible, who would have cared to disrupt the excavation? It seemed to be a kind of warning, but there was no one living in Pilgrin Valley who would feel the need to offer such an omen. Then he remembered the old cottage beyond the ridge of the valley; and he remembered, too, the shape which he had seen walking backwards and forwards in the lighted room. But he said nothing to the others and, meanwhile, he telephoned Evangeline Tupper to explain the events of the night.

·23·

TWO LADIES

"HOW UTTERLY grotesque. How terribly reminiscent of the French Revolution. Did you say an ox-bone? I hear the tumbrils already." Evangeline Tupper was reacting to Mark's news but now she put her hand over the mouthpiece of the telephone and whispered, "This will only take a minute, Baby Doll."

The recipient of her confidence was Hermione Crisp, an elderly lady who this afternoon was wearing a black suit with white shirt and loosely knotted blue tie; her grey hair was cropped close to her head so that, from a distance, she resembled a company director with a crewcut.

"I have never heard anything so ghastly in my life." Evangeline had turned her attention back to Mark's account of the damage. "I shan't sleep a wink tonight." She smiled at Hermione. "Sickening." She stifled a yawn while continuing to listen. "Tragedy, absolutely classical tragedy. Of course. Horrid. Ugh." And then, finally, "I'm coming to you." She put down the receiver with a flourish, and turned to her companion. "What a boring man."

"Don't say things like that." Hermione had a soft and melodious voice; it might have conflicted with her somewhat stark appearance but, in fact, it seemed strangely to complement it. "You know you don't mean it, so why say it?"

The two ladies had lived together, for the last twenty years, in a mansion block close to the Albert Hall; somehow during that time, despite all evidence to the contrary, Evangeline had fostered the belief that Hermione was the essence of femininity. "Whatever's got into your pretty little head?" she asked her companion. "Be sweet to your Evangeline. Think pink."

"I didn't know that I was supposed to think at all."

But Evangeline had not heard her; she had walked over to the window and was now looking across the street at the Albert Memorial. "I'm going down to Dorset," she said. "I want to talk to him. Man to man." Just as Hermione was treated by her as the incarnation of womanhood, so Evangeline seemed to cherish the illusion that she herself was a byword for masculinity. "I'm going to muck in. Get my hands dirty."

Hermione looked at her in amusement. "By doing what?"

"It's not Esher, you silly girl. It's rough out there. All those cocks." She shuddered slightly. "And oxen."

"That reminds me. Your father called."

"What did he want?"

"I just took his message. I know that you don't like me talking to him for too long." And this was true: even after twenty years Evangeline could not speak to her father about her relationship with Hermione, whom she always described as her "assistant". Their world, it seemed, had to remain a private one.

"I'll call him when I get back," she said, reluctantly.

"Why don't you treat him a little better?" Hermione asked her. "He is very old now. Just make an effort to be nice. For once."

"I *am* nice. I'm nice to you, aren't I?" Clearly she did not want to talk about it; in fact she rarely wanted to talk seriously at all, and Hermione suspected that the roles they played were a way of evading reality. The whole of Evangeline's personality was, in that sense, a denial of true feeling. But Hermione had grown accustomed to this and, in fact, there were even times when she enjoyed it. "Would you like to come down with me?" Evangeline was clearly embarrassed by her own dismissal of her father, and was trying instead to placate her companion. "Just the two of us? It would be nice to have a woman around."

"I thought there were women on the site."

"Naturally they work there, Baby Doll. This is the twentieth century." Evangeline knelt down beside her and playfully pinched the creases in her dark trousers. "But there's no one really feminine down there. Do you know what I mean? No one as girlish as you. Although how someone so fluffy and adorable is going to survive in the country . . ."

"Shall we bring the dogs?" The ladies owned two female French poodles, named George and Harry.

"With all those cows around? I think not. We may only be there for a day or two." Evangeline brushed a piece of thread from the lapel of Hermione's suit. "But do bring a party frock in case of emergencies. Baby Doll always looks her best in something frilly." They both knew that Hermione had nothing of the kind in her wardrobe, but now she straightened her tie as if in instinctive preparation for the journey. Evangeline looked at her in admiration. "I may be rough," she said. "I may be a rough tough old thing. But she bewitches me."

•24•

THE LADIES MAKE A VISIT

TWO DAYS later the bewitching creature, wearing a tweed shooting jacket with matching cap, was to be seen walking down the platform of Axminster Station. Evangeline Tupper followed some distance behind, encumbered by the two large brown suitcases which she insisted on carrying, and was quite out of breath by the time she reached Mark Clare. "Delightful," she said, putting down the cases and swiftly rearranging herself into an attitude of authority. "Always gorgeous to see you." Her companion was gazing down at a plastic replica of an orphan, advertising Dr Barnardo's Homes, and Evangeline beckoned her over. "I don't think," she said, "that you've met Hermione Crisp? My *assistant*? Invaluable really."

Hermione extended her hand. "Delighted," she said. Mark, alarmed by her appearance, expected a vice-like grip and was surprised by how soft her fingers seemed, how gentle her handshake.

Meanwhile Evangeline had advanced into the ticket office, as if to avoid watching this encounter, and now she inhaled very deeply. "Country air," she said. "There is absolutely nothing like it. I feel as if I belong here already."

Mark managed to manouevre both ladies past the wondering passengers and into the station car-park, all the time smiling and nodding at nothing in particular. He picked up the cases with a sigh, since their contents proved to be very heavy but, when Hermione moved forward to help him, Evangeline hustled her into the back seat of Mark's car. So it was with some difficulty that he placed the suitcases in the boot before they drove away in the direction of Pilgrin Valley.

And, as they drove, he dramatically described the damage which had been inflicted upon the site. "I don't understand it," he was saying. "Who would want to wreck the excavations? Who would want to divert us from our work?"

Evangeline had been gazing comfortably out at the passing landscape, and volunteered no reply. "What a nice car," she said, as if they had been talking about nothing in particular. "I feel as if I'm in a golden chariot."

"Chariots," he replied, "don't have automatic fuel injection. But I like the image. Its a nice image for an ancient landscape." He took his hands off the steering wheel for a moment, in a gesture either of triumph or supplication.

Hermione leaned forward. "How many miles do you get to the gallon," she asked Mark. But, before he could answer, Evangeline shook her head in a delightfully perplexed fashion. "My assistant," she said, "knows absolutely nothing about cars."

"Oh yes she does." Hermione glared at her. "I'd like to take a look under his bonnet."

"Do you see what I mean, Mr Clare?" Evangeline looked back somewhat sternly at Hermione, as if to suggest that her adorable feminine contributions might not be welcome at this moment. "Cars don't have bonnets, Hermione. Bonnets are for women. Women like you and me." She turned to Mark. "Do go on," she said. "About the tragedy."

"I don't suspect anyone in particular," Mark said. "Of course there were some children, but I don't think children would have been so careful. The site itself wasn't damaged. Some planks were ripped up and the computer was smashed, but the actual mound wasn't touched. Even the turf stacked at the side was left as it was. It was as if, as if someone were trying to warn us. Or trying to make us leave the valley. But who could that be?"

"I don't think it could have been children." Hermione was much more intrigued than her companion by this conversation but, as soon as she tried to speak, Evangeline turned around and put a finger up to her lips in order to curb her coquettish enthusiasms.

"My assistant," she said, almost as an apology, "is very interested in your work, Mr Clare. As you can see."

The three of them lapsed into silence during the last stages of the journey, a silence broken only by Evangeline's delighted exclamations whenever she passed anything remotely recognisable as belonging to the Dorset countryside. "Look," she said to Hermione. "Cows! Hedges! And look at those squelchy big things over there!"

"I think," Mark said, "that they may be pigs."

"You and your country lore. It is too staggering."

They arrived in Pilgrin Valley; they left the car, and were slowly making their way down the west slope towards the tumulus on the other side of the stream when Martha Temple came forward to greet them. "Miss Tupper," she said. "How charming. I'm surprised that you can be spared from your desk."

"The Department is always good in emergencies."

"So you are a sort of – what is that word beginning with trouble?"

"Shooter?" She opened up her handbag in order to take out a cigarette, and Martha took a step backward. Hermione was listening to this exchange with some amusement and Evangeline went on, with a slight frown, "May I introduce Hermione Crisp? My *assistant*?"

Martha had not quite caught the name and, in any case, her glasses were suspended on a thin silver chain around her neck. She screwed up her eyes at the phenomenon in the tweed jacket. "Delighted to meet you, Mr Crisp."

"Miss."

Baby Doll laughed out loud at the mistake, but Evangeline did not seem so amused by it. "It's a pity," she said viciously, "that you can't meet George and Harry."

"Not your husbands, I suppose?" Martha was very calm and sweet. "No. Of course not."

"No," Evangeline replied. "Just two bitches," Martha was puzzled. "Two dogs. We had to leave them behind. In case they went wild in the country."

"That was very wise," Martha said. "I'm told that city bitches often do."

Evangeline Tupper stared at her, and then started talking in a loud voice to Mark. "I am sure," she said, glancing towards Martha, "that there were murders committed here. Don't you feel it, too?"

"I feel so many things," he said, looking around at the landscape and smiling, "but I don't—"

"And do you think there were women involved?" She was directing her voice towards Martha.

"I honestly don't know."

"And mutilation, too, perhaps? What do we know of primitive mutilation?"

"It's impossible to say."

"Not impossible, surely? Nothing is impossible." He merely shook

92

his head.

"Well, never mind. Everyone has their own horror story. Talking of which—"

So Evangeline was shown the damage but, as they toured the site together, Mark was invaded by a feeling of futility. In the face of the now disordered excavations, the landscape itself seemed to shrink and to lose its colours. Here were the remains of a culture which no one professed to understand, relics of that expanse of time which was a 'period' only in the sense that a story must have a beginning as well as a middle and an end. The disruption of the site confirmed Mark's sense that the secrets of the tumulus would remain secrets, reminders of the larger mystery from which they had so unexpectedly been rescued. They might help to refine the story, but it was a story being told in the dark. The chaos which had descended on them was a reminder of that darkness.

"This is like a film," Evangeline told him at the end of her tour of inspection. "Just like a film. We may have been attacked." She lit her cigarette, and puffed upon it eagerly. "We may have been attacked by something awfully vengeful and ancient. Coming from the abysm of time and so forth."

Martha heard this and looked around at the others in mock bewilderment. "The only ancient creatures in this valley, Miss Tupper, are the Mints."

"The Mints! I love the Mints! Aren't they adorable?" She seemed to have forgotten her own horrid warnings. "I really do think of them as an absolutely national treasure."

"There is the old cottage as well," Mark said, half to himself. "There is someone living there."

"And I saw someone there, too." Martha had a pack mentality, and was in any case happy to create another object of suspicion. "Someone walking up and down."

"Exactly what I have been saying!" Evangeline was delighted to have her vision of horror confirmed. "It is my belief," she said in her most authoritative voice, "that someone has been playing with fire. But I will say no more. Not yet. Not till I have investigated this." She prided herself upon being 'good in a crisis', and now she stood up and threw her cigarette dangerously close to the mounds of stacked turf. "Action this day," she added. "Any volunteers?"

Eventually it was agreed that Mark and Evangeline herself should visit the cottage in order to question its owner – or, rather, to question the figure whom Mark had seen in the lighted room. So together they climbed up to the ridge, passed the copse of beech and ash, and then made their way across the adjoining field. In late May the dips and hollows of that field were filled with daisies and with buttercups and, as they walked, the yellow pollen clung to the edges of their shoes so that they seemed to be treading in light. Mark looked back and glimpsed the dark trail which their footsteps had left but, when he turned again a few moments later, the trail had vanished.

They could see the cottage in the corner of the field, its thatched roof and upper windows just visible above the tall sycamore hedge. "Divine," Evangeline murmured as they approached it, but then inadvertently she started when she saw a dark figure behind one of the windows. Now that they were so close they could hear voices coming from the cottage – not precisely voices, but murmurings or whisperings. They advanced towards the white wooden gate and, as Mark put his hand upon it, something sprang out of the hedge and raced into the field. Evangeline gave a little scream and clung to Mark's arm. "Only a cat," he said. "Only a black cat."

"It was monstrous," she said. "Pure 'X' certificate."

The voices, or murmurings, were growing steadily louder. Mark opened the gate and both of them walked down a cracked stone path. As they approached the old cottage the whisperings became audible, and they could hear now

> Solemn before us
> Veiled the dark portal
> Goal of all mortals . . .

They looked at each other for a moment, and then Evangeline dramatically turned her eyes towards two white masks on either side of the lintel – the white plaster masks of two young faces, perhaps not death masks but sombre and still nonetheless. "Do you think," she said, "that we have found Hansel and Gretel?" Then with some force she knocked upon the door.

•25•

THE WHITE FACES

THE MURMURINGS stopped. Evangeline knocked again, and after a few moments the door swung open. "I hope that you don't mind Schoenberg." A man's voice, hesitant and even nervous, came from behind the door. "Was it too loud?" He appeared suddenly in front of them – a man in his forties, his dark hair already turning to grey and his face so thin, so hollowed out, that it was one which seemed to anticipate the very look of death. "I'm sorry. Please come in."

"I thought I recognised it!" Evangeline crossed the threshold, her hand outstretched. "I am Evangeline Tupper. And this—" She waited as Mark came into the room behind her. "This is Mr Clare. You may have seen us both in Pigskin Valley."

"Pilgrin," Mark murmured.

"Wherever."

He looked at them for a moment, with a baffled and even defeated air. He had seen them once before, he had seen them in a brown car on his way back from the observatory, but he said nothing about that now. "Fall," he answered softly. "Damian Fall." He went over to his compact-disc player, turned down the volume, hesitated, and then switched off the machine. Mark noticed that he had a slight stoop. This came from no physical cause but rather a moral one: he wanted, as far as he could, to placate other people. He did not want to cause offence. "Did you have a chance to admire the garden?" Damian asked, still with his back to them.

His sombre formality had even affected Mark, who replied in a low voice. "We were only passing through."

"You must come back in summer time. Pinks. Meadow-saffrons. And so on and so forth." He was speaking reluctantly, as if he were already afraid of boring them.

"What a wonderful cottage!" Mark, eager to dispel the atmo-

95

sphere of gloom, rubbed his hands gleefully. He might have discovered the place himself. "Seventeenth century?"

"I don't know." Damian said this slowly, as if it were one more failure of many.

"Good sturdy workmanship," Mark added, banging one wall with his fist. "Thick. Meant to last. Great stuff."

There was a silence now, which Evangeline broke by advancing into the centre of the room. "And were these," she said, "all done by hand? I can't believe it." She was staring upwards in apparent ecstasy, at a number of white plaster faces which had been carved or fixed upon the high ceiling. They looked down upon the occupants of the room, their eyes rolled back.

At last Damian turned around, and looked upwards. "I imagine it's a long story, but I don't know it. You will have to ask the Mints who own all this. I'm sorry." He might have been apologising all his life. Now he glanced from one to the other, curious about the purpose of their visit but clearly unwilling to broach the subject.

Evangeline was not about to help. "So you know the Mints, too? Aren't they the most rural creatures you have *ever* seen? I feel like taking a pitchfork and just piling hay on them. Do you know what I mean?"

Damian Fall smiled nervously. It was already evident to Mark Clare that he had no connection with the events in Pilgrin Valley, but Mark had no idea how to conclude what was becoming a fruitless and embarrassing encounter. "Are you," he said, carefully, "on holiday?"

"Oh no." For the first time Damian seemed genuinely to respond. "I never take a break or rest." At the word "rest" a spasm passed momentarily over his left cheek, although his voice remained perfectly controlled. "I never have the time, you see. My superiors . . ." He broke off at this point.

"I suspect," Evangeline declared in a loud voice, "that you do something absolutely wonderful." But she hesitated, not immediately able to think of anything in that connection. "Are you something to do with weather forecasting?" This was the first wonderful occupation which occurred to her.

"Getting warm."

"Water diviner?"

"Well—" Damian Fall wanted her to guess accurately, to save any further embarrassment. "I'm afraid you're getting a little bit

96

colder."

Evangeline put her hands in the air. "I give up," she said. "I completely surrender."

"I'm in a profession like your own." He had turned to Mark, having already suspected that Evangeline herself was not an archaeologist. But then he turned back to her again, unwilling to offend. "And yours, of course."

"No," she said. "Don't taunt me. Spit it out. Etonnez-moi."

"Look around." He seemed to Mark to grow smaller as he talked and now, when he pointed towards the walls of the cottage, it was as if he were quite happy for his unexpected guests to forget that he was there at all.

Obediently Evangeline glanced around the room, one finger against her bottom lip in an adorably curious manner – as if she fully expected to be surprised or delighted by practically anything she saw. Against one wall there was a series of prints, mounted in narrow black frames, and with an apparently involuntary cry of excitement she scurried over to them. Here was an engraving of Galileo's chart of the Pleiades, published in *The Starry Messenger* in 1610, its dark lines carefully traced so that filaments seemed to spread out between the circles of flame; an eighteenth-century image of Ptolemy holding up a resplendent image of the sun, its rays represented by tongues of burnished metal issuing from a central sphere; a portrait of Copernicus in a long wig, his right hand resting on an astrolabe as he looked towards an opened door; an engraving of Tycho Brahe, surrounded by letters and numbers which mimicked the position of the stars; a representation of Kepler, his hand pointing towards a celestial hemisphere and beneath him the inscription, "Astronomy has two ends, to save the appearances of the heavens and to contemplate the true form of the edifice of the world"; an image of Newton, drawing back a curtain to reveal a model of the solar system floating within a lighted room; and, at the end of this sequence, a photograph of Einstein in front of a blackboard, with chalk marks scrawled across it.

"What lovely faces they had," Evangeline was saying. "In those days. Oh, look. More bliss." She went across to the other wall, where three larger prints had been hung carefully in sequence. The first engraving, its edges creased and stained, was of an old man in monk's habit who gazed up through an open window; his hands were raised, palms outward, in a gesture of supplication. Next to it was a seventeenth-century print of three men who were wearing tie-wigs and looking through long tubes; beneath this scene there was printed the inscription, *Prospectus Intra Cameram Stellatum*. The last engraving was of more recent date: it showed three Victorians, wearing stove-pipe hats and busy in a darkened dome, while in front of them a narrow beam of light descended from a large telescope. The legend beneath this was *Domus obscurata*.

"And what," Evangeline asked, "is the meaning of that gorgeous phrase?"

Damian was very still. "The darkened house," he said.

"I can't *bear* it. It's too beautiful."

Mark Clare had been looking at the drawings, too. "We have the same thing in archaeology," he said. "We call it the fogou. The house under ground."

"But my darkened house is above the ground," Damian said rapidly and nervously. "I work in the observatory on Holblack Moor. I am an astronomer. What was it you wanted with me?"

•26•

THE CONVERSATION

"YOU CAN never go back," Damian Fall was saying. "Signals sent into the past would be killed by their own echoes. You can do only one thing. You can send signals into the future. Sorry. Forgive the interruption."

In order to provide some explanation for his visit, Mark Clare had asked Damian if he had noticed unusual activity in Pilgrin Valley; now, more convincingly, he was outlining the nature of the tumulus itself. He stood in the middle of the cottage, his hands deep in the pockets of his overcoat, his eyes shining with the knowledge he wanted to impart. "The megalithic period," he was saying, "stretches back for an immensely long time. It lasts for over three thousand years. And chamber tombs like this one were being built for some two thousand years." In his excitement he went up on tiptoe, and then rolled back upon his heels.

"If only we could see it all in the absolute flesh." Evangeline was determined not to be left out of this conversation. "All those delicious animal skins. Delicious but no doubt very dirty."

Mark frowned, unwilling to enter the spirit of her playful nostalgia. "We don't know – we're not certain – but we think the tomb in Pilgrin Valley was constructed around 2500 BC. And we think that it is the grave of an astronomer."

Damian, hearing his own profession mentioned, blushed. Evangeline gave a little cry of pleasure. "What an extraordinary coincidence! I bet you felt someone walking over your own grave."

"It's difficult to be sure," he replied. "But certainly I must have felt something." Diffidently he smiled at Mark, as if he were trying to apologise in advance. "There are so many theories. Perhaps it doesn't matter which one you choose. Just more smoke in the air . . ."

"There were stone-circles all over England at the time this grave was being constructed." Mark was too eager to pursue his argument to notice how Damian seemed curiously unwilling to listen. "And all the evidence suggests that the stone circles were observatories. So it seems possible that the greatest of the tribe were those who watched the night sky and could somehow read the stars."

Damian put out his hand to stop him and then, looking at it, replaced it quickly in his pocket. "Now that you have imagined it," he said, "it has become true. I have to believe the story once it has been told, but—"

"Yes. Of course. And we also believe that these observatories came independently into existence all over the world. They have been found in Malta, Portugal, Denmark, Ireland. And now here. Here in Pilgrin Valley."

"—But I wish I had never heard it. There are too many stories."

Mark stopped, seeing for the first time the strain upon the astronomer's face, and then went on to say, speaking slowly and clearly, "Nobody knows why there should have been such a general interest in the stars during this one period. No one understands why the people of the earth began to see their meaning in the skies. It's rather like asking why it is that some creatures grew wings and became birds." He faltered and for one moment he had a vision of his wife in a darkened room, sitting in their small bedroom and looking out of the window.

"Go on," Damian said, blaming himself for the sudden silence in the room. Mark still hesitated. "Please go on. Every good story must have an ending."

"It may even be that the stone circle around our tumulus is aimed at some point in the heavens. It is of such an unusual shape that it might represent a fixed observation platform. Perhaps for the time of the vernal equinox." His enthusiasm had returned as quickly as it had subsided, and now he wrapped his arms around himself in his excitement. "But we're on our way. We will just have to dig deeper."

"Until time stands still?" For a moment Damian had caught Mark's enthusiasm as a mirror might reflect a face. "Did you know that time flows faster at the top of a building than it does in its basement?"

"Perhaps that's why the old inhabitants of this valley buried their leaders in the ground. Perhaps they understood that."

"But when they looked up, they would have seen a pattern of fixed stars. Why didn't they burn the astronomers and send them upwards? Over the moon?"

"Haven't I come across that phrase somewhere before?" Evangeline, bored with this conversation, at last heard something faintly familiar. "Does it mean the same thing as sick as a parrot? Or am I just being silly?" Both men were silent. "Here comes another silly question," she added with a certain desperation. "What precisely do you do on that gorgeous moor?"

"I study the stars," Damian said.

"But there are so many to choose from."

"Do you know the Pleiades?" Evangeline nodded vigorously. "Come closer and you have the Hyades. Closer still and you will find Aldebaran, the red giant. Do excuse me." He paused, embarrassed as much by his talk as by his silence, and he closed his eyes for a moment. "Naturally none of us believes in a fixed geometry. So by closer I mean closer in time. The Pleiades are 300 light years away from us, the Hyades 140 light years. Aldebaran is only 68 light years distant. They all seem so close to each other, but in reality they are far apart."

Evangeline put a hand up to her mouth, as if she were quite fascinated by what she had heard. "I didn't know," she said, "that astronomy could be so delightful. Quite a revelation." She managed to stifle her yawn.

"It is really only a model," Damian replied. "After all, we don't know what we don't know."

"Now you *are* teasing me. You're having a lovely little tease of Evangeline."

"Come and visit me on the moor," he said, without thinking. He looked down at the floor. "Then you can see for yourself."

"That would be utterly delicious." The invitation was in fact addressed to Mark but Evangeline, in her eagerness to be gone, accepted it with alacrity. "I don't know when I have had a more fascinating conversation." She stared at Mark, who showed no sign of preparing to leave. "And I'm sure that we'll have a great many more in the *future*."

"Of course." Damian took a step backwards from them, and then a step sideways, so that he seemed to be dancing to and fro.

Evangeline marched towards the door, Mark reluctantly following her, and Damian Fall watched them as they walked down the path and opened the gate. He did not want to stay in the cottage, not yet, so he went out into the little garden. Before their arrival he, too, had been examining the engravings of Ptolemy and of Copernicus, of Kepler and of Newton, all of them framed within images of their endless pursuit. Their own theories and inventions had lasted only for the briefest of periods but, if all knowledge was a story, what did it really signify? Perhaps there were no stars and no planets, no nebulae and no constellations; perhaps they merely came into existence in recognition of our wishes or demands. And if there came a moment when no one on earth was studying the heavens – no child looking up in wonder at the stars, no radio telescope directed towards the distant galaxies, no astronomer sitting in the observatory – what then? Was it possible that the heavens would then disappear? What if there is a void above us, like the void within me now? He leaned against the gate and looked out across the darkening fields. In the distance a solitary figure was driving some sheep across the valley and, behind him, a small fire was sending its smoke into the sky.

·27·

THE BLUE DOG

MARK AND Evangeline returned from the cottage to find Hermione sitting cross-legged on one of the desks in the Portakabin. She was smoking a Woodbine and, as they entered, she was jabbing it in the air as she addressed Martha Temple. "And then there's the Japanese strangle-hold. That's a lovely old move. Let me have your neck a moment." Martha had entered this conversation only to discover more about Evangeline Tupper, and she had become rather alarmed by the turn it had taken. She was not sure whether Hermione was really interested in displaying these wrestling holds to her. Certainly she seemed to be an insecure woman, despite her severe appearance, and it was possible that she was nervously playing a part. "Go on," Hermione was saying as she slid off the desk. "Be a sport."

"My assistant," Evangeline interrupted, stepping into the middle of the room and effectively preventing her from getting any closer to Martha, "is very fond of outdoor sports. Butterflies and so forth. Aren't you, Miss Crisp?"

Hermione merely smiled at her.

Martha could not have been more charmed, or indeed relieved, by Evangeline's sudden entrance. "Your assistant," she said, emphasising the last word, "has been telling me some fascinating things." Evangeline smiled graciously, prepared to agree about the wonders of the truly feminine mind. "She tells me that she always works at home."

"I am *blessed* in that respect."

"But don't you have a woman who comes in?"

Evangeline bristled slightly. "Comes in where?"

"A cleaning lady."

"There is someone of that sort, yes." She was eager to leave the subject of her domestic life. "Do you know," she went on, "that we have just had a most interesting conversation with the man over there." Evangeline pointed vaguely in the direction of the cottage. "Quite a little brains trust."

"And of course he had nothing to do with – with—" Mark said, in a voice he considered to be hearty enough to cover his embarrassment at the events of the afternoon.

"Oh," said Martha, very sweetly. "*I* never thought he was a suspect. Is that the right word?"

"Yes," he replied. "That's the right word."

He was about to add something else when Evangeline, now eager to be gone, asked him where they were supposed to stay for the night. "Of course." Mark was still talking too loudly. "You mean a hostelry?" He smoothed his side whiskers. "Something solid and comfortable. Something from old Dorset."

"Now let me think." Martha decided to be bright and helpful. "There is always the Blue Dog. They're very liberal there." She glanced at Hermione as she said this. "I presume you will be needing separate rooms?"

Hermione was standing with her legs apart. "Any berth will do for me. Any old hammock."

"I believe the Blue Dog is confined to beds."

Evangeline again intervened. "I'm sure," she said, "that beds will do very nicely."

They left soon after, as Mark guided them down the slope and across Pilgrin stream. The others worked on even as the sun was setting, and when Mark looked back he saw how the legs and bodies of the archaeologists were now in shadow while their heads and shoulders still caught the slanting light. The tumulus itself was in darkness, except for its very summit which gleamed in the rays of the declining sun. It was at this moment that he understood – that he saw – how there had once been a pyre upon it, a fire lit and then succeeded by other fires in the same region. He saw the pattern of flame across the countryside and, yes, it took the shape of the stars directly above the tumulus. The ancient fires imitated the star-glow of the Pleaides. Earth reflecting the sky. And it was with a certain lightness of spirit that he drove Evangeline and Hermione into Lyme Regis.

"Would you," Evangeline said as they stood outside the Blue Dog together, "like to join us for dinner? I'm sure they have some lovely country recipes."

"I would love to. But my wife—"

"She can join us too," Hermione added quickly.

"My wife is not very well." He looked down at the ground, already anticipating his wife's pain and dreading that moment when it would become his again.

"I am sorry," Evangeline murmured. "Feminine problems?"

"No, not really. Just problems."

"They can be just as bad. Do give her my fondest love. Tell her I'll be thinking of her."

"Of course." Mark was genuinely grateful for her concern.

"I feel as if I know her very well already."

"I'll tell her. Thank you."

"I'm the one who should thank you." Evangeline was already ushering Baby Doll, and the large brown suitcases, into the lobby of the hotel. "For such a charming day. Au revoir." Evangeline gave a lovely wave as Mark returned to his car, and she kept her smile in place long enough to speed him on his way back to Crooked Alley. "I thought," she said after he had turned the corner, "the bore would never go. Him and that so-called astronomer utterly exhausted me." Furiously she rung the bell on the hotel-counter. "And that's another thing," she added. "Why do you insist on embarrassing me in front of my colleagues? With all that wrestling business?"

"I was just making conversation. You do it all the time." The hotel-clerk came over, and it was not until after he had completed their bookings and they had been taken to their room that Hermione felt free to continue. "In any case," she said, "there are times when I get tired of being treated as the little woman. The brainless feminine *assistant*." She emphasised the phrase in Evangeline's manner. "I'm hardly dressed for the part, am I?"

All the unresolved pressures of their private life might have found an outlet here, but Evangeline chose not to take the opportunity. "Well," she said with a sigh as she placed her suitcase on one of the single beds. "I suppose that what Baby Doll wants, Baby Doll gets." She felt the bed with her hand. "And perhaps Baby would like to put on something pink for dinner?"

Hermione looked at her for a moment, astonished at her ability to ignore everything that had just been said, but then she laughed.

"Something very fluffy. Like this?" From her own suitcase she took out a green tweed jacket and held it out to her friend. "Something your father might wear?" Then they both laughed.

•28•

A REUNION

IN FACT, when the two ladies eventually came down to the
hotel restaurant, Baby Doll had dressed for the occasion in
her simple pin-stripe suit. Evangeline was wearing a
diaphanous blue gown – blue itself being what she called "an
old sailor's colour". "And what little delicacies does Baby want
tonight?" She waved the menu in front of her old friend. "A few little
fairy cakes?"

The waitress came hesitantly over to the table. "Steak,"
Evangeline said, at once changing her tone. "And make it very rare.
As if it's just been carved off the cow." Then she added, "There'll be
a tip in it for you." Hermione was having some difficulty in making
up her mind and Evangeline grew increasingly impatient as her old
friend traced her finger down the menu. "You like brains, don't
you?" she asked and then, without waiting for a reply, looked up at
the waitress. "I think she'll have brains tonight."

"Will they be rare, too, miss?"

"In this town, I wouldn't be at all surprised."

The waitress had not caught the joke. "How would you like them
done, miss?"

"She wants them burnt to ashes, dear. Unrecognisable. And two
bottles of house red."

"I do wish," Hermione whispered to her, "that you wouldn't
order for me. I *hate* it."

Evangeline looked at her in astonishment. "What have I done
wrong? You do like brains, don't you?"

Another couple were pretending not to watch them, from a
distance of three tables. "Look at those kikes," Floey Hanover was
saying to her husband. "Dressed like Winston Churchill."

"Dykes, dear. But you remember the old Irish melody, don't you?
Then tell me no more with a tear and a sigh, that our love will be

censured by many. All have their – something tra-la I've forgotten –
But ours is the sweetest of any.''

"It's not right," Floey said. "Not at their age." But she signalled
to him to keep quiet as she leant forward over her chicken curry,
trying to hear the conversation between the two old ladies.

"The bitches will be missing us," Hermione was saying to
Evangeline. Floey Hanover gave a significant look to her husband.

"They will be perfectly happy where they are. They always have
been." The two French poodles, George and Harry, had been left in
charge of the 'daily' – an Irish woman, known to them as Paddy, who
lived with her three sons in a council flat. "Paddy dotes on them,
darling. And they've always been good little bitches.''

A fork hung suspended between Floey's mouth and her plate.
"Did you hear them talking dirty?" she whispered to Joey. "And in
Lyme Regis too.''

Evangeline took out a Woodbine and settled back, preparing for
her meal. "What an enchanting day it has been," she said. "And so
educational. All those stars and light years. Baby Doll's pretty little
head would have been spinning.''

"'We must explore that valley tomorrow," Joey Hanover was
explaining to his wife. "What did he call it? Pilgrim?" He was
drawing circles on his empty plate with a fork. "I'm beginning to
remember a wood by the cottage. Or a forest. Trees, anyway. I
remember trees." He began to talk in a more sonorous voice. "I
knew by the smoke that so gracefully curled. Above the green trees.
That a cottage was nigh . . .''

"The Woodpecker Tapping?"

"That's the one. Sung with great feeling to the crowned heads of
Europe.''

But suddenly he was talking to himself. Floey was staring at
Hermione and Hermione was staring back at her; both women rose
from their chairs at the same time. "Tiger skin!" Floey shouted.

"Bluebell!" Hermione returned.

They approached one another in the middle of the hotel
restaurant, stuck their little fingers in their ears, revolved once and
called out in unison, "The maggots for ever!''

Evangeline, believing that this was one of her friends' 'old
flames', prepared herself to be at her most charming. Joey Hanover,
in his turn assuming that Hermione had been part of a theatrical
troupe which his wife had known in her youth, smiled broadly and

looked around at the other diners. "This is the old musical hall," he might have been saying. "Love it or hate it, you will never see its like again."

Floey turned to him. "What do you call it when two people meet by accident?"

"A crash?"

"No. Something else. Something like indifference." She gave up her unequal struggle with the language. "Tiger skin was at school with me," she went on to say. "You know, at St Muriel's?" She gazed at Baby Doll's suit, collar and tie. "You haven't changed a bit," she said.

"I should hope not, Bluebell."

"I don't think," Evangeline said from a distance of some twelve feet, "that I have had the pleasure." So introductions were made, the two parties moved to a larger table, and the school-friends reminisced about the dormitory of St Muriel's.

"Do you remember, Tiger, how you got drunk one night and started eating dog biscuits? You thought they were cereal. You poured milk on them, and ate them."

For some reason this seemed to horrify Evangeline. "How very funny," she said, managing to smile as furiously she stubbed out her Woodbine.

"It sounds to me," Joey said, "like St Trinian's. Is that the old school tie?" He pointed at the article around Baby Doll's neck. "Or is it the school of hard knocks?"

Baby Doll laughed at this. "Hole in one," she said.

As Baby Doll and Floey Hanover went over their past, Evangeline turned to Joey; she recognised him very well, from television, but she was not about to admit that fact. Not yet. It put her at too much of a disadvantage. "Isn't it lovely for them to meet again," she said. "And in such a charming spot, too." She lit another cigarette. "We see nothing in London, do we? Somehow we are all cut off." Joey seemed to agree with this. "But, as soon as we see Nature, we want her. We clasp her to our bosoms."

"That's what you remind me of," Joey said. "The Brave Old Oak. Crooned in a low voice."

This might have been a compliment, and Evangeline smiled. "I'm sure," she said, "that I have seen you on the stage."

"I was on the stage once. Yes."

"And elsewhere?"

"Elsewhere too." Joey Hanover had no vanity as such, but he was always disconcerted when he went unrecognised. It was as if, at that moment of unresponsiveness, he ceased to exist. "Television. Radio. But it's over. Over the hills and far away."

"And there," she said, "speaks a man who has retired with absolute dignity. Unspoiled." He made her a little bow. "I presume," she went on, "that's why you are here? In this gorgeous old town?"

"It could be, it could be." Joey seemed evasive. "A little of what you fancy does do you good."

"Now isn't that odd? That's always been my philosophy, too." There was a silence between them and, in desperation, Evangeline plunged towards another topic. "Talking of retirement," she said. "I have found this delightful old cemetery. But I don't mean a cemetery. Not exactly. What on earth do you call it?"

Floey was always ready to help with linguistic difficulties of this kind, and she broke off her animated conversation with Baby Doll. "Sanatorium?"

"Not exactly."

"More like crematorium?"

"That's closer." In fact she was referring to the tumulus in Pilgrin Valley. "There are some divine stones around it," she said. "Simply *all* the way round. Isn't that surprising? And it has something to do with the stars . . ."

She trailed off. Joey was looking into the distance, drumming his fingers upon his bright red waistcoat. "That reminds me of a story," he said slowly. "I remember a story. I don't know how I know it. But I know it."

Evangeline blew a smoke ring towards the restaurant ceiling. "Fire away," she said.

"Are you with me?" This was one of his famous catchphrases but he said it now very softly, as if it were the beginning of a spell. "Well—"

A STORY

ONCE UPON a time, and it was a very long time ago, there were spirits all over the earth. Spirits of the rocks; spirits of the streams; spirits of the forests. And in those days the people of Wessex worshipped them. There is a field by the shore, just beyond Lud Mouth, and in that field you can still see a piece of black stone so deeply embedded that no one has ever been able to prise it loose: this was where water and grain were left for the spirits, and it is still known as the offering-stone. But there were other spirits, evil spirits who came from beneath the earth. It was said that the noises of the people walking over the ground enraged them, and so they tried to lead the inhabitants of this region off the edge of high precipices or into the deepest pits. They wanted to destroy them so that they could sleep undisturbed.

Now these spirits could fly. They did not live in one place only but soared and skimmed through the great caverns beneath the earth – which is why, if you put your ear to the ground, you can sometimes hear a rustling as of wings. They could even fly up from the earth into the outer air, through the great portals which human beings cannot see; but, because they were hated by the spirits of the forests and of the streams, they could not hover near the surface but had to fly further up into the clouds or soar, higher yet and higher, into the firmament. There are some people who claim to see them still, whenever there is a quick movement across the heavens.

It was mid-summer long ago and, in the old stone village of St Gabriel, many of the men and women were sleeping out of doors and beneath the open sky. It was a small village but of course there were children – some say twelve, some say more. Naturally the evil spirits hated children and that night, as the villagers slept beneath the stars, they plotted together; they circled above their heads, sometimes hooting like owls and sometimes barking like foxes, as they schemed and planned. This is what they did. At the stillest hour of night, in the dead time, when all the beneficent spirits were resting within their rocks or streams or forests, they hovered for a little while and then fluttered down to earth at the spot where the children lay. One evil spirit crawled up to the first child and whispered in his ear, "Leave your parents and come with me. I will teach you to fly, and together we will explore all the bright stars which shine above your head." Then a second spirit touched the shoulder of another child and whispered, "Come with us. We are your real family because, like you, we know what it is to be free. We will take you with us into the skies, and show you the mysteries of the heavens." A third spirit wakened up a child with the tip of his wing and murmured, "Why lie down on the hard earth when you can be floating on the soft air? Leave your parents and come with us." No one knew if these children were tired of the arduous life they were forced to lead, or if they had been dreaming of the stars even as the evil spirits whispered to them, or if they were entranced by some other means; but, whatever the reason, they rose up together and were led by the evil spirits to the edge of St Gabriel's cliff. Then the spirits flew above them and, by trailing their wings, they made the sky seem more bright and glorious than the children had ever seen it before. The children clapped their hands, but softly so as not to wake their fathers and mothers, and the spirits smiled at one another secretly before they told them that they could fly, too. "You will all fly with us," they whispered. "And there is only one condition."

"Tell us what we must do," the children begged. "Tell us what we must do!"

"You must start a new life. You will leave the earth for ever and dwell among the stars, but if you set foot on earth again you will be turned to stone." Now the spirits murmured this very quickly, and it is said that some of the children never heard their warning; what they did hear was the excitement of flying upwards into the firmament, and what they saw was the wonder of the night sky. "What shall we see? What shall we see?" a little girl asked them.

"This is the greatest wonder of all," the chief spirit replied. "You will see whatever you wish for. You will see what you wish to see."

Of course the children became very excited at this, and all of them began clamouring to be taken up; so one by one the spirits lifted them upon their wings — and so light were these wicked spirits that it seemed to the children that they themselves were flying. At once they were soaring above the fields and the forests which they knew so well; higher and higher until their houses and their families were no more than grains of sand; upward and upward, until they recognised nothing which was beneath their feet. But now it began to grow very cold, and the children shivered. "Where are the stars?" one of them asked; and another called out, "Where is the sun which warmed us on the earth?"

And then one spirit replied, laughing, "You will see whatever you wish for."

And another echoed, "You will see only what you wish for."

But in truth the children had wished for nothing and had expected nothing. They had only wanted for one moment to escape, to fly away from their hard lives. In fact, some of them did not know what a wish was. And all around them now were cold, and darkness, and mist. "Let us down," the little girl cried.

"Take us back," her brother yelled.

"But you know the condition? If you touch the earth again?"

"We want to go home!" The children were now too frightened to care, and they wanted only to leave this terrible place.

"If that is your real wish, then so be it." The spirits quickly dropped through the air; lower and lower they flew so that the children put out their hands towards the familiar forests and hills, down and further down so that the children could even make out the old village of St Gabriel. They came so close that they could see the sad faces of their sleeping parents but, as soon as the evil spirits came back to St Gabriel's cliff, they tossed the children from their backs. And when they fell to the earth, they were at once turned into stone. Twelve of them, forming a circle on the margin of the sea. This was the end of the children's journey away from home.

Some say that this is a fairy story, to teach children not to roam. But there are some who say that there is a truth to it of another kind – that there was a child, an orphan who scavenged in the fields beside St Gabriel. Now this orphan was a strange child who fascinated the other children of the village. He was known as Barren. Old Barren. And Old Barren told them that he could fly; when they scoffed at him he became angry and insisted that he could teach them to fly also. It is said that he led them singing to the edge of St Gabriel's cliff, and that here he persuaded them to jump from it into the air. But of course they fell, and were smashed upon the rocks beneath. So these rocks are not the children changed by spirits, as the story tells us, but really the graves of the children who thought they could fly. And, although the tiny village has long ago gone under the earth, you can see the twelve rocks still.

Joey Hanover rubbed his eyes and looked at the others. "How did I know that story?" he said, to no one in particular. "When did I ever hear that story?"

Evangeline and Floey were asleep but now they woke up as Joey's voice died away. Floey had managed to keep one hand around the neck of the empty wine bottle, and Evangeline pointed wearily at it. "Was it a good year?" she asked her.

"I wouldn't know." Floey sounded offended. "I'm not a bibliophile."

But Hermione had been listening to Joey's story very intently, and she had been crying. Now she took a large white handkerchief from the pocket of her jacket, and blew her nose very loudly. "Sorry," she said. "I think there was ash in my eye." She tried to suck upon her cigarette but it had gone out and, in a softer voice, she asked, "Has anybody got a light?"

PART THREE

They more and more felt the contrast between their own tiny magnitudes and those among which they had recklessly plunged, till they were oppressed with the presence of a vastness they could not cope with even as an idea, and which hung about them like a nightmare.

Two on a Tower
Thomas Hardy.

·30·

PRIVATE WORLDS

IT WAS going to be a hot summer, and the sun had already
burned away the last of the dawn mist from the slopes of
Pilgrin Valley; the leaves of the trees were darker now, and
the recently sheared sheep crept noiselessly beside the narrow
stream. By the early morning the archaeologists were at work,
watering the ground around the grave; it might have seemed that
they were urging something to grow and spring from the soil, but in
fact they were moistening the freshly exposed earth in order to
preserve those visible markings which might otherwise be
obliterated by the dust and glare of the day. A swirl of darker clay
might suggest the presence of some long buried object, already
decayed, while stains on the bed of chalk could represent a scattering
of flints or axes. And so, as the day progressed, sheets of green canvas
were erected around the site to keep it in shadow.

They had gone much deeper, steadily moving downwards to the
forecourt and entrance of the chamber tomb. Already the capstones
of the roof had been uncovered – large dark stones wedged so tightly
together that the tomb seemed to be covered by one piece of flat rock,
the huge weight pressing downwards and sealing the unknown
interior. These stones were now protected by thick black plastic
sheeting but, some days before, when the residue of chalky soil had at
last been cleared away from them, when their pitted and striated
surfaces were finally revealed, Mark had eagerly climbed on top of
the mound. He wanted to be the first to touch the ancient roof. It was
as if, in that moment, he might be able to touch the life and the spirit
of the workers who had sealed the tomb some four and a half
thousand years before. Perhaps the whole landscape would then be
transformed, fading and folding like smoke until the smoke cleared –
cleared to reveal the ancient valley, just as it was when the tomb was
being constructed and its occupant carried towards it singing. He

put both hands upon the stone, and then looked around with a kind of wonder. But nothing had changed. The branches of the trees scraped together in the wind, the hedges crackled, a trowel was being dragged across some earth. The stone was cold to his touch and quickly he clambered down from the tumulus; then he turned and walked away, since he did not want the others to see his face. The present could not be escaped, after all.

There were some twelve workers on the site, sifting and digging silently through the summer morning, each one staying within a small area of marked ground; around them were scattered scapulas, knives, toothpicks, brushes, trowels, plastic beakers, spades. They had grown accustomed to each other now, and Owen Chard noticed with a certain grim satisfaction how their behaviour seemed to be changing as they came closer to the tomb. He knew it well, since it was always the same process. They were becoming more open, more distinctly themselves, less inclined to camouflage; it was as if their own protective layers were being stripped away. Only Martha Temple had not been affected. While Julian Hill formulated his theories in a loud voice, sometimes standing in the middle of the site as if it were some literal extension of himself, and while Mark Clare collated each day's evidence as if he were engaged on some assiduous and private search, Martha remained indomitably bright. She was triumphant at the discovery of each pin and pendant, each broken piece of pot or slate, quite as if she were the only person doing any work at all upon the site.

"Isn't it funny," she was saying to Owen this morning, breaking the silence with relish, "that there is always more work for us? Of course I'm sure that Mark knows what he's doing. I'm just so glad I can give him all the evidence he needs."

Owen was kneeling on the ground. He stopped what he was doing and stared down at the soil for a moment before saying, "The others are working too, aren't they? Not just you."

"They are doing their best. And I'm the first to congratulate poor Mark for trying . . . but I often wonder why none of the evidence seems to fit." Having scored what seemed to her to be a palpable hit, she went on her way.

Indeed there was a sense in which all the material, so far detected and gathered, provoked more difficulties than it solved; it came from so many different periods, and showed such unequal signs of human habitation, that the precise identity of the site was still in doubt. So all of them working here – the young assistants, the diggers, Mark Clare's closest colleagues – all of them had their own private vision of Pilgrin Valley and of this grave. And, as they worked on in silence throughout the day, some saw it fitfully, some saw it clearly. The people beneath their hands, beneath the soil, represented the beginnings of human life, but when they came to this spot they must have been celebrating death; there had taken place some unknown ritual, but because of it there was now some unspoken and unanalysable communion between the living and the dead; they were the same people as ourselves, but they were also unimaginably different. Everything the diggers had found – the pots, the pins, the beads, even the scrapings of ash from long dead fires – all these familiar details had suggested some continuity of human feeling and human community. And yet what could have been their words, what could have been their gestures, what were the expressions upon their faces? And, if this tumulus were truly in alignment with the heavens, what did they see when they looked up at the stars?

Time. In another time. Either before or after. They were not stars, but fires. They were the souls of birds. They were entries into the vast fire. They were the eyes of the dead. And in the darkness they were imprisoned by them.

"Have you found them yet?" Farmer Mint had come up behind Martha Temple, and he chuckled as she gave a little start of surprise. "Have you?"

"I'm probably being very stupid," she said, recovering herself quickly, "but I didn't understand a word you said."

"Tell her, Boy."

Boy Mint was standing beside him. "Have you found them sheep bones? Rabbit heads? Cow muck?"

Martha seemed to find some comfort in this. "Now don't you go spreading gloom and despondency." She wagged her finger at them. "Trying to pretend our work here is useless. And ridiculous." She was still smiling. "No one will ever believe you. Really. And I keep my own opinions to myself."

Farmer Mint was smiling with her now. "What came out of your mouth this morning, Boy?"

"They're making perfume out of gorse these days." Boy Mint scratched his head, and laughed out loud at the beauty of it.

"Do translate, Mr Mint. I'm far too stupid."

"There's all sorts of uses for rubbish these days. That's what *he* means."

She smiled and rubbed her hands together. "I quite agree with you," she said. "But I think you ought to tell the others." She looked around to see who was within hearing range, and shouted, "What a treat! Look who's come to see us!" Then she whispered to Farmer Mint, "Do tell them what came out of your son's mouth."

The others looked up to see the farmers standing side by side, and grinning; they were of exactly equal height, and they cast two identical shadows across the tumulus. The two men were not at all embarrassed at this attention, and looked across at the perspiring workers. "Warm, is it?" Farmer Mint asked them. Like his son, he was dressed in a thick green pullover with an old black jacket on top of it; there were layers of shirt and vest beneath this outer covering, but neither of them seemed to feel the heat. "Next thing you know you'll be seeing them things in the desert."

"Mirages," Boy Mint added, and earned a look of pride from his father. "Them mirages."

"Actually, I did see something." This was a young woman who had been working on the site from the beginning, always quiet and uncomplaining. "Something like a mirage."

"I wish I was young again," Martha whispered to Owen. "All that imagination."

"I saw a man. A naked man clambering up the valley here." She pointed towards the stream. "At least I think I did."

"Don't be silly, dear." Martha was happy to interrupt. "You must have been in the sun too long." The two farmers said nothing, but examined the girl closely.

"Perhaps it was one of us," Owen murmured. "We've got some strange ones working here. Oh yes."

"No." The girl spoke quite calmly. "He was different." The two farmers kept on staring at her. "He wasn't one of our kind. If you know what I mean."

"No. I do not know what you mean," Martha said. But she was clearly eager to hear more and came closer as the others gathered in a group around the girl.

Then another of them, a young man who had spent the whole morning brushing some soil off a piece of bone no more than four centimetres in length, spoke out. "It's funny, but I thought I heard voices the other day." He was silent for a moment. "And then I thought I saw something."

Farmer Mint put his head on one side, as Boy Mint leaned in the opposite direction. "So you seen them coming, did you?"

"Them?"

"You know. Them." Farmer Mint nudged his son. "Go on, Boy."

"Sheep. You saw the sheep coming for you." Both farmers laughed in unison. "They're terrible when roused, them sheep."

"Well, well, well." Owen seemed to find it funny, too. "The world is going quite mad. Voices. Naked men. Sheep. What about hauntings, too? I'm sure one of you has seen a ghost somewhere."

Martha gave him a playful slap on the hand. "Don't be so awful, Owen. They're only being honest. They're being very youthful and inventive. Let them have their little joke." She smiled sympathetically at the group, emphasising the fact that she was always on their side while somehow managing to ridicule them at the same time. No one knew how she did it. It was a gift.

At this moment Mark Clare came out of the Portakabin and, seeing the Mints, walked over to them. He was rubbing his hands "Is everything in order?" he asked them. "Is there anything the matter?"

"Not to speak of, Mr Clare." Farmer Mint was noticeably more formal with him than with the others. "Nothing to speak of. We've just been having a history lesson."

"History?" Mark was puzzled. He put up his hand as the Mints were about to turn away. "Actually," he said. "I was just about to come and see you. There was something I wanted to tell you. Don't be alarmed if you see lights in the valley tonight."

"Light?" This seemed momentarily to annoy Farmer Mint.

"Yes. Lights. We want to do some night photography."

"Light don't bother us, Mr Clare," Boy Mint replied, on behalf of his father. "Nor voices. Nor sheep. Nor strangers coming up the valley."

"It's just," Mark went on, "that we need another way of looking at the site. There are things here we don't even know how to see."

"So you need light, do you?"

Suddenly there was a mournful bellowing which echoed down the valley and they all turned towards the source of the sound. "That'll be Cow Number Four," Farmer Mint told them with a certain satisfaction. "She's lost her calf. She'll be moaning for a day or two yet." And each year it was the same – the same deep cry which punctuated the night and the day, the same lament for the loss of her offspring.

"I really don't want to hear it," Martha said, putting her hands up to her ears. "I just don't want to hear it."

◆*31*◆

NIGHT PHOTOGRAPHY

THEY RETURNED that night. A slender tower of metal scaffolding had been erected fifteen yards away from the tumulus, just on the edge of the ruined ash forest, and from here three high-intensity lights were to be directed upon the site. The glare would create short intense shadows – all the shallows and undulations of the surface springing up from the darkness in bold relief so that, even on such a misty night as this, the surface of the earth would become strange and unfamiliar. There was a circle of pale light around the moon, and in a neighbouring field a woman shone her torch as she called to some sheep that had strayed. "Bill," she cried. "Matilda!" Her voice rang down Pilgrin Valley, where there was no other sound.

Owen Chard and Mark Clare were sitting together at the edge of the site, waiting to judge the angle of the intense light that would soon burst from the tower. In the darkness they could hear Julian Hill saying loudly to Martha, "I'll have my article for you next week. I think you'll like it," and both men instinctively ducked behind one of the standing stones which encircled the tumulus. Mark sighed and leaned back against the stone in order to contemplate the mist and the night sky. "After I spoke to the astronomer," he said softly, "I began reading about the Pleiades. And the great star, Aldebaran." He touched the standing stone with his knuckles. "These people must have known them, too. But what exactly did they see?"

"Don't ask me," Owen replied. "Ask our friend Julian. He knows everything." But then, sensing Mark's real interest, he pointed upwards. "Andromeda," he said. "Cygnus. Altair."

"I didn't know that you followed the stars."

"I don't. I don't really understand any of it. All I see are lights in the sky. I know less than *them*." Mark looked across at him, not understanding this. "Less than the people buried here. If they are

123

here.'' There seemed to be a fluctuation in the sky but it was nothing; a tremor in the atmosphere. ''If they did come alive,'' Owen went on, ''they would know far more about the stars than you or I do. After all, the sky would be the one thing they would recognise.''

Mark was elated by this. ''But it's all coming together. Don't you feel it?''

''Yes, I feel it. I feel a pain in my arse.'' Owen got up from the damp grass, groaning, and looked towards the tumulus – of which the outline, in the darkness of the night, could hardly be seen. It was just the intimation of a shape and yet its presence was so strong that a stranger here would have been forced to walk slowly, peering into the darkness to find out what it was that so changed the feeling of this place.

He returned to Mark who was still propped against the stone, and crouched down beside him with the affection of an old companion. ''You don't like poetry, Owen.'' Mark carried on talking as if he had never gone away. ''And you pretend not to feel anything. But do you know these lines?'' He looked up, the brightness of the sky upon his face, and in a low voice began reciting . . .

> ''. . . a wondrous rocky world of cruel destiny
> Rocks piled on rocks reaching the stars, stretching from pole to pole,
> The building is Natural Religion and its altars Natural Morality,
> A building of eternal death, whose proportions are eternal despair.''

''That was Blake,'' he added. ''I learnt that by heart when I was a child.''

''You're getting like the girls around here,'' Owen replied, but not unkindly. ''Dreaming of things.''

The woman had stopped calling her lost sheep, and had switched off her torch.

''Listen.'' Mark put up his hand. The two of them heard a chorus of human voices, falling and rising. The words were indistinct but a sudden gust of wind from the edge of the valley carried ''beginning'' and ''silence'' towards them. ''It's coming from the cottage,'' Mark said. ''Damian Fall is playing his music very loudly tonight.''

''Someone's playing the fool. That's what you mean.'' But both men continued to listen as the words ascended towards the glistening stars.

And then the three high-intensity lights were switched on at full strength, momentarily blinding all those on the site. Mark got up, shielded his eyes and peered towards the metal scaffolding, "Down a bit!" he shouted. "They're too high. They're missing the ground!" So the lights were lowered, causing the brightly illuminated earth to shift and sway as if it were being rocked by a giant hand. It regained its solidity only when the lights were brought to their proper positions, and now each undulation or curve in the earth was clearly visible in the unfamiliar glare. The stars had vanished, leaving only the brightness of the ground.

Mark walked up to Julian Hill, embarrassed at having avoided him a few minutes before. "Do you see," he said, "how there is no true gradient? The curves of the land are sweeping away from the tumulus in every direction. But there is something wrong. Something missing. Or something I can't see yet." He shouted for the lights to be lowered slightly; once more the landscape quivered and changed its shape. "There is something—"

There was a sudden crack and a rushing sound as if a strong wind were blowing up the valley; the whole earth seemed to tilt as the brightness swung upward in an arc and then something fell to the ground. In the crash, the lights went out: somehow the scaffolding had collapsed, toppling back into the ruined forest. The confused shouts of the archaeological team rang down the valley and Mark called out, "Stay where you are. Don't move. Don't go near the tumulus!" And then he added, "Is anybody hurt?" Now there was silence as they peered at each other in the darkness; but they could see only silhouettes, shadows, shapes, as the bright stars once more reappeared above them.

·*32*·

AFTER THE FALL

MARK DROVE home an hour later. The fall of the scaffolding had unnerved him – not because the night photography had been abandoned just at the moment when it promised success but, rather, because he was beginning to see Pilgrin Valley as an 'unlucky' site. He had known such places before – soon after he had visited the excavations in the Peruvian rain forest, they had been abandoned as a result of accidents, misunderstandings, thefts. There had even been a death. And that site had returned to the rain forest; the standing stones were even now concealed by the green fog of vegetation; the great earth mound, from which it was said that men had once flown, was hidden from the sky by moss and creeper. And there surely must come a time when the tumulus in Pilgrin Valley would itself be concealed, perhaps by the trees which would eventually grow out of the burnt forest. His work upon it was just a brief interval in the course of its dissolution.

He opened the door of the flat very softly, hoping that Kathleen would already be asleep. But she found it difficult to rest – sometimes she even seemed unwilling to do so – and as he entered their bedroom he found her sitting by an open window, looking out at the night sky. "I didn't expect you back," she said. "Not yet."

"The scaffolding collapsed." She made no response. "But it was all right. No one was hurt."

"That's good." Until recently she had always wanted to know everything about his work; his life had seemed more important to her than her own. But now she was drawing back.

"I don't know how it happened," he was saying. "It just fell. As if it had been pushed over." He remained standing at the door, and he could see her head outlined against the dark window. She was not facing him; she was staring into the night.

"That's a pity," she said. In recent weeks Kathleen had been quiet, compliant to the point of passivity. Certainly she had lost interest in the process of adoption she had so enthusiastically begun, and had not even attempted to answer the letter from the social service department. It was as if she had been expecting that first rebuff; as if she had even positively invited it. Whenever he was with her now Mark felt afraid – afraid for her but also afraid for himself. They clung to each other, but they were taking each other down. "I was just thinking," she said, "what a happy time it was when we first bought this place. Do you remember?"

"Every time has been a happy time. You know that."

"But we always used to look forward." She turned to face him. "We never knew, did we? We never understood."

"Never understand what, love?" He took a few steps towards her, but she turned around again to the window. "Never knew what?"

At first she did not answer, but kept on looking up at the sky. "Everything has to end," she said at last. "All we're doing is waiting for the end." The wave of her misery hit him now, knocking the breath out of him. "I can look up at the stars," she said. "But they may be dead too by now. And what's the use of looking so far in any case? Where can I go?" This was how she had been before they had met. Time. Time returning. Time swirling around her. The crippled girl.

"Don't worry," he said. "Don't think about it." He was so confused by her pain that he did not know what he was saying. "It will all be the same in a hundred years."

"And we will have been forgotten then," she said. "We will have left nothing behind."

"But then—"

"Of course someone will take our place. There will always be people like us. Wasn't that what you said once? People like me."

"Come on. I'll help you to bed."

"They say that suffering is noble. But it's not. It's a mean thing. A petty thing. It crushes the meaning from you. Have you ever seen a lost dog?"

"It's late," he said gently. He put his arm around her and helped her to her feet; she seemed about to lean heavily upon him, but then with an effort she straightened herself and made her own way forward. But this was not an angry gesture; it was just that she wanted to let him walk freely.

·33·

ON THE MOOR

DAMIAN FALL had always been changed by rooms. He had known from his childhood how powerfully they had affected him: in his suburban parental home he had become cramped and dull, and only when he had gone beyond its threshold did he realise how free he could be. In the hospital ward where his mother had died, he had himself grown sick with a fever which abated when he left the building. In his first university rooms he had felt so strongly the pulse of generations of youthful ambition that he had become inspired but then, in the library of the university, he felt himself being invaded by the words of the books around him and he had fled in horror. In a lodging house he once sensed the distillation of loneliness, had bowed his head and wept. Even in places where the original rooms had been altered or destroyed, he could still sense the atmosphere issuing from them – some years before he visited a place which had been an asylum for the insane, and he heard the screaming. And there were times when it occurred to him that this strange sensitivity might account for his early ambitions – why he wanted to leave the buildings of the world and walk out beneath the stars. For, surely, the stars could not affect him. And, yes, he had wanted to be a great astronomer.

Now he looked around the walls of his cottage, at the engravings of those who had come before him. When he had first arrived here he had sensed an overwhelming mood of patience, of the peace which springs from inevitability; in those early months the cottage possessed the endurance of generations, the habitual quietness of labour undertaken and completed. But he could no longer feel such things. His own labour seemed so pointless, his endurance so much a matter of habit or folly, that the loss of his own hopes had affected the cottage itself. Even here his own awareness of failure haunted him, and now this place seemed to be no more than another part of the valley – no more than a frail covering, a hiding place. And he sensed within these walls the presence of something else, of a despair which seemed to ebb and flow. Tonight it was very strong. It was time to leave. It was time to visit the observatory.

It was a clear night without wind and, as he walked along the garden path, the perfumes of the earth seemed to rise straight upward; there was a scent, then no scent, and then scent again so that it seemed to Damian that he was walking among pillars – that he was walking on consecrated ground. He got into his car and drove quickly down a track which led away from Pilgrin Valley. The light from his headlamps swept across the valley in a sudden arc, and for a moment the landscape was startled into movement as if it had been woken from a dream. He drove due south and then, at Lud Mouth, turned east along the coastal road. He knew how close he was to the sea but it was lost in the darkness; he could see only the tall hedges on either side, the road just ahead of him whitened by his headlamps before it, too, ran into the night. He knew this route well. He fully expected to be driving along it for the rest of his life, so he paid no particular attention to it now. There was a section where the road curved before a stone bridge, and at this point Damian switched off his lights and turned left upon a rough track. He had come to Holblack Moor.

He drove across this expanse of flat land for five or six minutes; he could see nothing but a low level of thick shadow ahead of him, stretching from horizon to horizon, but he knew where to slow down and where to stop. He got out of the car and did not even glance at the large object silhouetted against the sky beside him. At first sight it might have been a giant's head emerging from the ground, with a curious upright ridge of hair running across the skull, but in the starlight Holblack Observatory gleamed slightly – the whiteness of the hemispherical dome contrasting with the dark brick of a small one-storey building attached to it. It was towards this that Damian walked.

For the first time he looked up at the stars, and then opened the door, "Good evening, Brenda."

"Oh, hello." This was her usual greeting. "And how's Mr Fall?"

"Much the same, Brenda. Much the same."

"That's good, isn't it?" Brenda was the secretary. She checked times; she made the coffee, she typed out reports. On this particular week of night duties, she had decided to streak her hair with blonde highlights – even in the observatory she tried her best to look glamorous or, as she put it, "keep the flag flying".

"Brenda's just made a smashing cup of coffee, haven't you?" This was Alec, the young Scotsman who had been Damian's assistant for some months – ever since Damian had welcomed him on the moor. "Made it with her own lily-white hands."

"Don't you go talking to me about hands." Brenda giggled.

"Had experience, have you?" Alec was very cheerful, and often very boisterous. He laughed now, and swayed to and fro in his chair.

"Oh go on. Don't be awful."

"Had a few hands, have you?"

"I don't know what you mean."

Damian took off his brown corduroy jacket and hung it behind the door as the other two watched him with something like pity: he always wore a white shirt with the same dark green tie, and he always smoothed his greying hair back over his head before turning round again. They were in a small room which contained three desks, two grey filing cabinets, a large clock, a kettle on a small electric ring, a calendar, some colour-coded clip-boards fastened to the wall. And on a cork noticeboard was pinned the message, 'We're Travelling To The Stars'. This was the office for the observatory, the muddled ante-room in which Alec and Brenda seemed quite at home but which depressed Damian Fall: it was the room to which he always had to return after watching the heavens. Returning to his own fallen state. And, when he saw the dirty coffee cups, the crumpled papers, the stained desks, he used to think that this was the kind of room in which he might die. "It's a nice night for it," Brenda said to Alec with a smile. "Don't you think it's a nice night?"

"It's a lovely night, Brenda. A lovely warm night. For it."

"Yes," Damian said and the other two became quiet. "The air is still. The viewing should be steady." That was why he had glanced up at the sky before entering the building. On a night bad for 'seeing', the stars would have eddied like candle-flame in a draught – the atmospheric turbulence might make them seem to 'twinkle' but, when magnified, they would leap and gyrate. But there was no turbulence tonight. The stars shone with a steady glow; on this good night they were still. He turned to Alec. "Shall we go through?" It was the same question he always asked. And for Damian there seemed failure in that, too – almost a tangible sense of it, like the smell of prison clothes.

"Keep on trucking," Alec said. "I'm with you, boss." He got up from his chair and did a little shuffle on the spot. Damian slid open a thick metal partition while he waited for him, and together they walked down a short corridor lined with bright yellow tiles. Then Damian unlocked another metal door, slid it across, and the two men entered the dome of Holblack Observatory.

"Bye!" Brenda called out from the other end. "Don't do anything I wouldn't do!"

The dome was not lit and, when Damian locked the second door and blocked out the neon from the corridor, the observatory was so dark and so cold that it might have become part of the moor itself. Then he extended his arm, touched a switch, and a bank of dim red lights illuminated the interior. And here it was: the 36-inch reflector telescope issuing from a circular green metal platform and sustained by a network of white girders as it rose towards the roof of the dome. It might have come from a fairground, so exotic and elaborate it seemed – except for the equipment panels attached to its base, and the knotted bundles of cables that were looped around its sides. These cables, some of them as thick as a human wrist, were curled across the black rubberised floor but then went down beneath the mounting of the telescope; the instrument itself did not stop at its metal base, but part of it descended beneath the floor of the dome as if it were literally rooted into the earth. It might have stood here for ever.

There was a circular metal stairway on the other side of the dome and Alec, whistling softly to himself, walked towards it. He patted the gleaming telescope as he passed, and blew a kiss towards it. "I'll go on down," he said. "Be seeing you." Alec monitored the spectrograph in the laboratory beneath the dome; it was into this that the light from the stars was hurled, through a panoply of lenses and mirrors which sent images spinning downwards to the photon-counting detectors and the spectrometers – through primary mirrors and secondary mirrors, the images of images, reflections of reflections, until the light itself was broken apart and diffused into the lines and bands of the stellar spectra. And, with his own special taped music coming through his head-phones, his feet tapping out the beat, Alec examined the light issuing from immensity.

Damian stood quietly in the observatory. Yes. There had been a time when he had wanted to become a great astronomer. But what of that now? He was no more than a technician, a useful adjunct to the work of others who had seen much further than he. He had been stationed here, at this minor observing post, because he had achieved nothing by himself. His superiors now told him at which part of the sky to look, and which measurements to take. But, when he saw how his contemporaries had succeeded where he had failed, he felt neither bitterness nor self-pity. He simply marvelled at them – marvelled at their ability to go through the world with such confidence. But it was too late for him. Much too late. He could only carry on with the work allotted to him, and derive from it what satisfaction he could. But nothing could take away the emptiness, the feeling of waste as day by day he grew older and less able to change. Even if someone had offered him an escape, a new life, he was no longer sure that he would have had the courage to accept it. And was this what happened to most people, this creeping across the face of the earth?

He walked over to the console by the side of the dome. Here the celestial coordinates were stored in digital form, and it took a matter of moments for Damian to confirm that the declination and axle bearing of the telescope had been correctly programmed. He sat down and pressed the controls in rapid sequence. The red lights within the observatory faded, the darkness returned, and the hemispherical roof began to open – its two halves parting so slowly that a sliver of night sky appeared in the centre, gradually increasing in size until the roof disappeared and the darkened dome was flooded with starlight.

·34·

THE OPEN DOME

THE TELESCOPE, moving fractionally to the east and then to the north, rose up out of the dome; and, as he watched its progress from the control panels, Damian imagined himself to be soaring with it in successive stages through the magnetosphere, the troposphere, the stratosphere, the mesosphere, the thermosphere, the exosphere until he had left behind the earth and had soared upwards into the heavens. Towards Aldebaran.

The radio telescope at Silverdown had reported strange fluctuations in the signals from this giant star, and Damian had been formally instructed to observe it and to report on the unknown reactions which were taking place within it. Once he would have done this eagerly enough, since it had been these recesses of the night sky which had enthralled him as a child. For it was here that he had found Aldebaran. He had first seen it low upon the northern horizon, one autumn night, and he had not dared move. It was as if the child and the star were studying one another, searching out the mystery. The difference was that then he had no name for the star; now it was quite familiar to him. Once the sight of the constellations had filled him with exaltation, but now they were merely figures, integers, part of the network. He was like a priest who had lost his belief in God.

Alec still had his faith, which was why Damian liked him and enjoyed his company. He suspected that the young man had been dispatched here eventually to take over from him – there were times when Damian's paranoia was like a sheet of ice between him and the world – but still he recognised in Alec the kind of person he had once been. He was eager, energetic and beneath the enthusiasm Damian sensed that steady faith which had once inspired him also – a belief in the stars, a belief in the progress of knowledge which was no less than a belief in life itself. It was this that made Alec sing out loud as he examined the stellar spectra.

The light from Aldebaran was being gathered and reconstructed even as Damian watched the computer; it was possible for him to understand its patterns and energies without once looking up at it and now, on the screen, he could see the pale and shuddering surface of the giant star. Its colours were forming and then fading, squares of light being dispersed and then reassembled – black, green, red, violet, blue. These were not the colours of the star itself but, rather, electronic markings; they were visible symbols to register differences in the intensity of its light. This was its surface as it had been aeons ago and this light, not decayed but rolling onward, was the only sign that the universe had existed before his birth. Everything on the earth existed with him, shared his time with him in an ever-receding present moment; everything was connected, but this network of invisible relations was a network of simultaneity. Damian had to assume that there was such a thing as the past but any evidence for it was part of the present, too. All the world had ever known was a succession of present moments. There was – there is – nothing else.

Except these images from a distant star, appearing now second by second but belonging to another time; and there was the sky itself, with traces of light which emerged thousands of millions of years ago. And yet what if these images were an illusion – what if the pictures of Aldebaran were simply constructions with no reality beyond this particular time and place, this particular observer who now looked up at the sky from the dark observatory, looked up at the vast emptiness? And there shall be beautiful things made new, he thought, beautiful things made new for the surprise of the sky-children.

"Any luck?"

It was Alec, standing beside him. Damian did not know how long he had been dreaming but his mouth felt dry, and he sensed that he had been asleep for many hours. "I'm sorry," he said. "I was miles away."

Dawn was breaking and in the pale light Alec could see how he seemed to tremble by the controls. "Any joy?" he added, more softly.

"No. No joy yet." Then he corrected himself. "Nothing can be determined yet."

A buzzer sounded and Alec walked over to the sliding door. Brenda had arrived, with three cups of coffee on a tray. "I bet you boys want something hot inside you," she said. "I know the feeling."

She put down the tray of coffee. "Shall I?"

"Of course you shall," Alec replied with a smile. "Don't give it a second's thought."

"Shall I turn on the lights? I don't like being in the dark with you two boys. There's no knowing." Alec put his arm around her waist, and with a little shriek she moved a few inches away. "Leave off," she said. "I'm getting those goose-pimples."

"You know where we Scotsmen get pimples don't you, Brenda?"

"If it's anything to do with kilts, I don't want to hear."

He gave her a little squeeze. "You wee sleekit cowrin timrous beastie."

"Don't talk dirty, Alec."

"Yes." For the moment they had forgotten Damian, and now they turned to listen to him. "Yes. It's certainly preferable to be in the light."

·35·

THE ENTRANCE

AN AFTERNOON in August, and nothing moves in the heat; everything living but not moving, everything waiting in the heat. And on this August afternoon the sounds of hammering echo through Pilgrin Valley, but then suddenly stop. It is as if someone has been knocking continually on a closed door, which has unexpectedly opened.

"Utterly primitive and wonderful!" Evangeline Tupper clapped her hands. "Just as I expected!"

"It must be so nice to have an imagination." Martha Temple was at her most pleasant. "The rest of us just plod on."

The two ladies were standing within the exposed forecourt of the tumulus; immediately in front of them Mark Clare and Owen Chard were examining a massive stone slab which had been placed against the entrance of the tomb.

"I wouldn't say you plod, Miss Temple." Evangeline was being equally charming. "We all walk on together. Banners waving and lovely band music."

"This is the limit." Owen sighed very deeply. "This is the absolute limit."

"What is it now?" Martha asked eagerly. "What else has gone wrong?"

"No. I mean this is the limit. We can't go any further in this direction. But someone—" and he looked at no one in particular – "someone should have guessed that this was a blind entrance."

Over the last few weeks they had uncovered the stone roof of the tomb, and had now descended further; they had reached down to its entrance, the four-foot high portal into the chamber itself. Only the sides of the tumulus were still concealed beneath the banks of turf so that the whole structure seemed to be rearing itself upward, trying to break free from the chains of the earth. The cleared space in front of the entrance, the forecourt, was semi-circular and they had found the five upright stones which once marked its perimeter; but they discovered that the entrance itself was blocked by a massive slab, wedged into position between the two portal stones. This was not an ordinary barrier, however, since it displayed a number of markings – rings and spirals, lines and hollows, all of them carved into the stone. At first sight it might seem that these had been created by the movement of the earth over the centuries, but they were too elaborately arranged to be the traces of subsidence or erosion. And yet if there was a pattern it was unrecognisable: these circles and lines might have been a form of handwriting but, as Mark Clare ran his own hand across them, he knew that it was one which might never be deciphered. If there was a message, of greeting or even of warning, it had died with those who had fashioned it.

And yet there were some things which Mark now understood; he was beginning, at last, to see the chamber grave clearly. Within the forecourt itself five small pits had been dug in a half-circle immediately in front of the upright stones; Owen Chard had already determined that these pits or holes contained a hard packing of broken stone around a softer filling of charcoal, and at once Mark realised how long wooden poles had been placed within them, poles at least fifteen feet high, poles which had all been burnt at the same time. Perhaps they had been designed to stand alone, in a half-circle around the tomb, but it was more likely that they had supported a wooden canopy: flecks of charcoal scattered across the site suggested that this canopy had also been burnt at the same time, its ashes floating over the whole area. This temporary structure might have been a covering for sacred ground, or it might have been a shrine in which some object or relic had been venerated. There had been a ritual conflagration, after the tomb had been sealed, when this wooden monument was put to the torch.

Mark walked away from the blind entrance and stood at the central point around which the upright stones and the poles had been erected – two half circles, one of wood and one of stone, so what was placed at this midpoint where he was now waiting? He looked down at the freshly exposed ground and saw how the warm wind seemed to lift the dust from it; there was always a wind in the valley. He shuffled his feet sideways and then, to his surprise, took three steps forward. Yes. The canopy on fire in a place where heaviness and lightness are the real qualities of being, where the heavy stone is god and the smoke of the burning wood is spirit. Yes. The flames are rising amid high rapid voices, voices mimicking the passage of the fire into the sky. Humans and animals have come here of their own accord, each understanding the call of the other. Here amid the smoke and the ashes are the two-legged creatures, moving up and away from the earth; and here are the four-legged creatures, curving towards the earth and sorrowful with it. Time. Another time.

"Almost five thousand years ago?" Evangeline Tupper had taken out a Woodbine, and was now waving it in the direction of the tomb as she talked to Martha Temple. "Are you telling me that you can date these stones because of something that happened in space? That is the most bizarre thing I ever heard in my life."

"But many bizarre things are real, Miss Tupper. As you must know."

Evangeline decided that she did not like Martha's tone. "I am not an expert," she answered very deliberately. "I don't have your wealth of experience."

"But surely you know all about radio-carbon dating? It simply means that we measure the level of radioactive carbon to determine age. Great age." She was looking at Evangeline's thin and puckered mouth as she spoke. "It comes from space. From cosmic radiation."

"I simply don't believe it. It's too – too—"

"Grotesque?" Martha was smiling.

"Something like that."

Julian Hill had been standing next to them throughout this exchange. He was eager to get Evangeline's attention, in the hope that she had some influence in the 'Department'. "I think," he said, "that you ought to read my monograph. It makes it all much clearer."

"I'm absolutely dying to." For the moment she could not remember the man's name. "I love everything you write."

Julian assumed that she was referring to the only article he had published, two months ago in *New Archaeology*. "But my monograph is on quite a different scale. I do think it's rather a success."

"Tell me this." Evangeline suddenly walked over to Mark. "How did they manage to get these enormous stones on top of one another? They must have been superhuman. Like coalminers. Vast hands." She thought of Baby Doll, and smiled.

"I can explain that very easily." And, without sensing Evangeline's growing impatience, Mark described in vivid terms how the inhabitants piled the outcrop of the area upon sledges before pulling them across the long wooden causeways which would have been laid in the valley; he then went on to explain how the tomb itself was filled with field rocks and packed earth, to support the stones as they were being levered and pushed into position. Once all the stones had been correctly placed, this interior packing of the tomb was removed.

Evangeline watched his gestures as he talked – wide expansive gestures, spreading outward from himself, pointing towards nothing in particular. And when he lowered his arms to his sides she knew that at last he had finished. "That was practically Biblical," she said. "Sheer Old Testament."

He was pleased by his performance, too. "Those are all the parameters," he said.

"Aren't they adorable?" Evangeline presumed he was referring to a feature of the landscape. "Sometimes I long to climb up them and just throw myself off."

But Mark's excited attention had already returned to the blind entrance, and he gazed at the carvings on its stone. He could smell their age even as he looked at them and, in a sense, they were just what he ought to have expected – further evidence that there were secrets within Pilgrin Valley which would not be easily resolved. For five months they had been exploring the site, but their slow descent had been constantly interrupted; there had been nothing like the havoc of late spring, when the site had been invaded and damaged, but ever since that time there had been a series of unpredictable events. Finds had been mislaid; tools had vanished overnight; petrological analyses had been torn up or thrown away; the computers had malfunctioned, and on one occasion valuable data had been lost. Perhaps it was the shock of these accidents which had affected the morale of the team: the normal mood during such excavations was one of rising excitement as the object of the quest slowly emerged from the earth but, as they had dug deeper here, they had been afflicted by lassitude and even by depression. There had been quarrels. There had been two resignations.

Mark could not account for this but now, as he looked at the carving on the blind entry, it became only one aspect of his larger bewilderment – there was something wrong, something missing. Why was this chamber grave not at the centre of the standing stones which stretched over the countryside? Why had it been placed at least one hundred yards too far west? And why had it been built into the side of the valley? All the evidence was suggesting to him that he was quite wrong about the significance of the tomb – but, in that case, what was it? What was escaping him? With an effort he turned to Owen, who was photographing the post-holes in the forecourt. "There is," he said, hesitantly, "there is a reason for the blind entry. It is not just to protect the grave. Somehow it's related to the symbolism of the thing."

"Don't talk to me about symbolism. I don't believe in that rubbish. That crap," Owen added, delicately stepping across one of the ancient holes dug in the surface of the earth.

"No. I mean that this stone is *meant* to be massive. Like the others." He looked at his colleague, uncertain whether to go on; but Owen, despite his abrupt dismissal of the theory, was clearly listening. "The thickness of the stone is the important thing. There is a kind of magic in it. But I don't understand these markings . . ."

Evangeline was still beside him, her back turned to Martha and Julian. "Isn't it exciting?" she said, taking out another Woodbine. "Do you think it has anything to do with worlds in collision?" She had read a book by Eric von Daniken, and had some confused memory of ley-lines and ring-markings. "I would love to know."

"We all would, Miss Tupper." Owen looked gravely at her.

Evangeline paid no attention to him, and turned back to Mark who still seemed lost in the stone. "So what's next?"

"I'm sorry?"

"I think, Mark," Martha had decided to intervene, "I think that Miss Tupper is getting bored with us." For some reason she seemed exhilarated by this. "She probably finds us very dull indeed."

Mark pretended not to hear this. "Did you ask what was next?" Evangeline nodded. "We will have to enter the grave through the side. Once we've stripped away the earth, there will be a gap. There has to be a gap in the stones. Otherwise nothing could get in. Or get out."

"Delicious." Evangeline shivered. "All the horrors of the tomb, and so forth. Talking of horrors—"

She looked back at Martha Temple who, after her interruption, was now walking delicately across a plank which had been placed above one of the deep trenches at the boundary of the site: it was here that Mark had hoped to find traces of early occupation but, although some charred seeds had been located, no definite traces of human habitation had been discovered. Martha had reached the other side when something inside the trench caught her attention; it was as if something had suddenly moved there, and she peered down through the millennia at the old surface of the earth. Then she fell forward and, with a shriek, tumbled into the trench. She tried to grasp the side of the plank, bringing it down with her, and she fell awkwardly upon her left arm. The others rushed over to her and, for a moment, they gazed down into the trench where she lay splayed out on the hard earth – she might have been a figure in a grave which they had just opened, and there was something startling in her sudden approximation to the long dead.

"Fuck!" Her normally charming and girlish manner had disappeared. "My arm! I can't feel it!"

Evangeline had hurried over. "I think," she said, "that the poor darling has broken her arm. We will have to be as gentle as absolute lambs."

And they were gentle: it took some time before Martha, placed upon a makeshift stretcher and covered with a blanket, was brought to the surface. "Someone pushed me," she was saying as they carried her onto the grass. "Some bastard pushed me!"

Mark turned around quickly, but there was nothing behind him except the hot and silent fields of Pilgrin Valley. "There was nobody there," he said; but then he relented. "At least I didn't see anybody. Did you see anybody?"

This was addressed to Evangeline, who shook her head sadly – quite as if this were one of poor Martha's sick delusions. "It must be the shock." She pretended to whisper, but her voice was loud enough for Martha to hear. "The shock of unbearable pain."

Martha tried to raise her head. "I felt him!" she said. "That bastard pushed me." Then she moaned and sank back on the stretcher. "Pardon my French—"

"—I don't think that was French, dear."

"But I didn't just slip into the hole."

"That all depends."

For once Martha was paying no attention to Evangeline; she was trying to remember the exact sequence of events. "I saw something." She lay back on the stretcher and closed her eyes. "Then I looked down. And then someone pushed me."

·*36*·

DECODING

TWO NIGHTS later and Mark Clare lay in bed, unable to sleep. Kathleen was beside him, clutching a pillow around her head. Each time he closed his eyes, coloured whorls and spirals crossed each other within the infinite recesses of his night vision; and, as always, these phantom shapes seemed to mimic the object of his thoughts – even as he tried to sleep he was still attempting to understand the circles and indentations which had been carved upon the large stone which sealed the tomb. Quietly he got up from the bed and tiptoed across the room; he did not want to wake his wife who, in the waning darkness before dawn, seemed invested with a kind of sacred stillness. The world was balanced between night and day, and her troubles had left her suspended in a fragile sleep. Or so it seemed to Mark. But when softly he opened the door she watched him from the bed with wide eyes; and when he had closed the door she pressed her face once more against the pillow, her eyes still open.

Mark went into his study where all his familiar objects were still shrouded in darkness; he switched on the light and in the sudden glare they sprang into vivid life, still somehow hollow from not being looked at, from not being seen in the night, and only by degrees reacquiring their substantiality as Mark walked among them. He went over to the drawer of his desk, and took out the photographs of the blind entrance which Owen had taken on the afternoon of Martha's fall. In these black and white prints he could see the worn grey surface of the stone, as well as the darker markings upon it. Then on a sudden impulse he took out a large yellow envelope, in which Owen had placed the negatives. He held one of them against the electric light, and when he saw that reverse image he understood it at once; for it was in this instant, when he examined what were now the lighter markings against their dark background, that he saw the affinity – here were white points of light, white circles like swirling clouds, white lines like tracks spreading across a black expanse. This was a map of the heavens. This was a drawing of the stars. These were the patterns of the constellations recorded in the only way possible then – they had been inscribed upon stone. And then these stars had been placed against the grave itself, enclosing the person or persons who were buried there. The tomb was sealed by brightness or, rather, by the brightness marked upon the stone. This was truly the grave of someone who had worshipped the stars. At last Mark knew what he was looking for – what was waiting for him within the tomb.

Kathleen Clare was sitting upright in the bed, her hands clasped around her knees. When she heard Mark coming out of his study she lay down upon the bed again and pretended to sleep. But he did not return to her. Filled with his excitement at the decoding of the stone, he walked past the bedroom and quietly descended the stairs. He opened the door into Crooked Alley as dawn was breaking, and went out into the light.

•37•

GUARDIAN ANGELS

"WOULD YOU like to swing on a star?" Joey Hanover sang as he looked down into Pilgrin Valley. "Carry moonbeams home in a jar?" He looked mournfully at a cow behind a hedge. "Or would you rather be a mule?"

"Stop that howling, Joey."

"I loved it when I was young, Flo. I loved it when I was young."

"That's no reason to sing it now."

"That's every reason."

In fact Floey Hanover was growing irritable; it was already the middle of August and they had spent the last weeks driving desultorily along the lanes and tracks of this region, looking for the right cottage in the right position. Now, finally, they had arrived in Pilgrin Valley; despite Augustine Fraicheur's recommendation they had left it until last, and this principally because it was the only one not properly marked upon their maps of the area. It had been difficult to find: they had been forced to turn back along the green ways, they had driven into farmyards, they had come to a halt on desolate ridges, they had driven along an appropriate route only to come out by a rocky shoreline or the brow of a hill. Now that they had found it, however, Joey felt unaccountably afraid; he started whistling to himself as they sat in the car. They were a few yards from the Mints' farmhouse, and could see across the valley to the excavations.

"That's another bad sign," his wife said. "When you make that noise."

"It's my nerves, Floey. I'm a prey to my nerves." They were silent for a moment. "Hello," he said. "What's that excrescence?"

"Don't be filthy, Joey." But she liked the sound of the word; she would employ it on the right occasion.

"No, seriously. What's that business over there?" He pointed towards the tumulus, exposed now but covered with plastic sheeting and guarded by a fence clumsily constructed out of chicken wire.

"Isn't that what my friend's friend was telling us?"

"Your friend's friend?" He enjoyed the phrase. "Who was your friend's friend?"

"Tiger's friend. You know. That woman with the funny face. Like a parrot. Evangeline. Don't you remember anything except old songs?"

"Not if I can help it." He could see, beside the tumulus, the burnt space where the old ash forest had stood. "But there is something here . . ." he said. "Something I *do* remember." He put on his mauve checked cap, opened the door of the car for Floey, and together they walked down the western slope of the valley towards the Pilgrin stream. Farmer Mint was just carrying a pail from his house; he stopped to look down at Joey in his bright blue blazer, and at Floey in her corn-yellow dress with large green straw hat. He watched them pick their way among the stones and the parched grass; then he scratched himself. Late summer. The turning point of the year.

The Hanovers stepped across the stream, now the merest ripple in its chalk bed, and climbed towards the tumulus. "Just look," he said. "Take a little look at that." He pointed towards the forecourt and its blind entry. "Pure pantomime, that is. Pure *Genie of the Lamp*." He turned around towards Floey and put out his arms. "There is a voice from the grave," he sang. "Calling me, calling me." Then he turned around and shielded his eyes from the sun, so that he might more clearly see the rise of the valley ahead. "Let's try up here," he said. "There *is* something . . ."

"Another wild duck chase," Floey whispered to herself as, reluctantly, she followed him. He avoided the excavations and worked his way up towards the copse of ash and beech trees on the crest of the valley; she stopped half way, to fan her perspiring face with her green straw hat. It was only when she had put it on again that she saw Joey standing very still on the ridge, with his arms in the air. She climbed up towards him, and still he did not move from this spot; she stood beside him, and saw that he was looking across a dry field towards a small cottage. There was a hedge around it, but Floey could see the thatched roof and two upstairs windows. "I know this place," Joey said. "I know this place very well."

He started walking across the field but he increased his pace, and then he began to run; his check cap was blown off in this progress but he seemed not to notice. He did not stop running until he had reached the white gate of the cottage, where he stood panting for breath. Then he sat down on the dry grass and bowed his head.

A few minutes later Floey came up to him, holding out his cap. "Here's part of your wardrobe," she said.

He looked up at her, not seeing the cap. "This is it, Floey."

"This is what?"

"This is the cottage I remember."

"Why don't you go in then?" She sounded unenthusiastic but, really, she was trying to calm him.

"I don't know." He was filled with the same fear he had experienced when driving into the valley. "Give me a minute." But he did not have a minute: the cottage door opened and Damian Fall, wearing his corduroy jacket, came out with a watering can. He saw the Hanovers at once, and stepped backwards. The Hanovers were alarmed, too, and Joey hastily got to his feet.

"I'm sorry." It was all Damian could think of saying. "I'm sorry."

Joey seemed puzzled. "Excuse me," he said. "But do I know you?"

This was a genuine inquiry, and it embarrassed Damian. He did not expect anyone to know him. "Not to my recollection. No." He ran his finger along the inside of his shirt collar.

"Do you know me then?"

Damian scrutinised him with apparent anxiety. "The face is familiar, but . . ."

"Joey Hanover," his wife said, flatly. "Of course he was first known as Joey Chuckles."

"Of course. Everyone knows your name."

"This is it," Joey answered. "This is the problem, you see." He took his check cap from his wife's hands, and began to dust it. "It's not my name at all."

"Would it be a stage name?"

"No. An adopted name. I was adopted. May we?" They had been talking on opposite sides of the gate, and now Damian put down his watering can in order to open it for them. Joey walked down the garden path, twisting his cap in his hands. "That's why we're here," he said. "I know this place. I think I was born here."

"Then you had better come in. Fall," he added quietly.

"Just over the threshold?" Floey was confused, remembering some of her old stage tumbles.

"No. That's *my* name. Damian Fall."

He led them into the front room and at once Joey saw the plaster casts of the faces, looking down at them from the corners of the room. "There they are," he shouted. "There are my guardian angels!" He looked with a certain wild bafflement at Damian, as if he were somehow keeping something from him. "There was a floor here," he said, gesturing above his head. "And then there was a bedroom. My bedroom."

"I think the floor must have been removed. It makes a larger space, you see," Damian added helplessly.

Joey was not really listening to him. "And these were my angels. Angels watch me as I sleep. From bad dreams my soul to keep. Someone sang it to me once." He sat down, rather heavily, upon a slender wooden chair. "This is it, Floey. This is it."

Damian watched him as he struggled for breath. He knew that something important, something significant, was happening to these people; and he did not particularly want it to take place in front of him. He did not know how to respond. "Can I get you something?" He was almost pleading with Floey, pleading with her somehow to domesticate this situation and to render it normal. "A drink?"

"Get him a brandy," she said. "And could I have a gin? Gin and a bit?"

"It. Gin and it." Joey corrected Floey automatically, as he stared straight ahead. When Damian came back into the room he was still staring in the same direction, and he carried on talking as if there had been no interruption. "When I was given away, you see, no one knew very much about me. My adopted parents thought that I came from this part of the world. And somehow I remembered this cottage. So we've been looking. But I never thought—" He looked up at his angels. "I'm just a poor orphan. With nothing but dreams. How did the song go, Floey? Was it something to do with scream? Or with ice-cream?" She shook her head.

"I think it was scream," Damian said. The two men gazed at each other, and this mutual look so bewildered them that they could not turn away – they stared at each other, discomposed, wild, haunted, lost.

"I want to find out who my parents were," Joey said at last. "I want to find out where I come from."

"Where does anybody come from?" Damian was talking quite directly to him, as if the strange look between them had removed any attempt at concealment.

"I'm not with you."

Floey had already finished her drink. "He's telling you to be philosophical about it," she said. "He's telling you not to give it another thought."

Damian seemed to shake himself awake. "I'm really only a tenant," he said. "I don't have much information."

"Where's the landlady?" Floey looked around, half-expecting to see the kind of theatrical proprietor she met on her travels so many years before.

"My landlord is Mint. He's on the other side of the valley."

"Can I look around?" Joey went from room to room, and then he stepped out into the garden. "Purple flowers!" he shouted to both of them.

Floey looked apologetically at Damian. "He really needs to find out the truth," she said. "He's got a bee in his—" She could not remember the rest of the phrase. "Where is it? Where do you keep bees when you want to know the truth?"

Damian understood what she meant. "The truth? I don't know." He put his hands through his hair and went over to the window. "I suppose I believe in cultivating my own garden." And as he said this he realised how much it was a counsel of despair, how much a confession of his failure.

"I do beg your pardon," she said, not without a hint of asperity. "We're stopping you."

"What?" He turned around, his face burning.

"We're stopping you gardening."

He was still considering his own failure. "Of course. Weeding. There is always weeding to be done."

Joey came in now, bewildered. "Tell me," he said. "Who am I? Do you know me?"

"You're Joey Hanover," Damian said. For some reason he wanted to make amends now, he wanted to be of some use to these people who needed his help.

"That's who I thought I was. Thank you very much."

"You must go and see the Mints," Damian went on. "They know everything. And they've owned this cottage for years."

"What do we do," Floey asked him. She was becoming tired of this apparently perpetual quest. "Follow the yellow brick road?"

"No. No. Come with me." He took them back out into the garden and, pointing towards Pilgrin Valley, directed them to the Mints' farmhouse. "Goodbye," he shouted as they made their way back across the field. "Good luck!"

"What did you make of that one," Floey asked her husband as soon as they were out of earshot. "That was not a happy person."

"I found it, Floey. I actually found it!" All his life Joey Hanover had been haunted by the image of some remote and tranquil past; he had known nothing definite about it, and his adopted parents had been able to tell him no more than that he had come from "somewhere between Devon and Dorset". Yet he had always nourished images of this place, of a high green hedge, of purple flowers, of a nearby wood. He could remember one time in his infancy when he had looked up at a cloudless sky, and the knowledge of that blue was somehow connected with the noise of rooks and the sight of some sheep grazing vaguely on the side of a valley – and he had believed these sheep to be clouds which had left the sky, come to linger for a while upon the surface of the earth.

After this solitary memory there was a break, a silence, and out of that darkness he emerged as the adopted child whom he knew very well. But, still, these images of an earlier life had remained within him, and they always left him calm. For this remnant of his infant life was a feeling like no other – it was a feeling of permanence, a feeling that the ordinary business of the world was of no consequence, a feeling like the warm passivity which occurs just before sleep. And this was true, too – the images of his unknown childhood helped him to sleep. And would they help him when the moment came to die? He found that he was crying. He wiped his face with his check cap, and then smiled at Floey. "Tears are blessings," he sang out in a strong voice as they descended into Pilgrin Valley. "Tears are blessings, so I let them flow." As soon as they had crossed the stream they could see the Mints' farmhouse on the road above the valley, and suddenly Joey stopped. "No." he said. "No. It's been a shock to the system. I can't take any more today."

She sensed how tired he felt now, and she took his arm. "We'll come back tomorrow," she said. "Tomorrow's another day. Isn't that what they say?"

"I don't know what they say, Floey. I don't know what they say."

They went back to the car but, just as he was about to drive away, Joey stopped. "Do you think we'll be able to find it again?" He looked around in panic, for at that moment it seemed to him that all this might be an illusion, a dream – and that they would never be able to return to Pilgrin Valley, where all his hopes rested now.

"Of course we will. We'll come back tomorrow." Both of them turned to look once again at the Mints' farmhouse; if there had been any sign of activity there, Joey would have changed his mind and gone over to it. But, since it was quite silent and apparently deserted, they drove back to Lyme Regis.

Damian Fall had gone back into the cottage. He washed the glasses which they had used and then he dusted the chair where Joey had sat, taking care to move it back to its original position. Then he sat down upon it. He had a feeling that something had passed him by – that once more he had not seen, or had been denied, something of great significance; and, with a terrible cry, he rocked to and fro.

•38•

THE PERFORMANCE

"**I**'M HAVING a little party afterwards." Augustine Fraicheur was talking to Joey Hanover outside the small theatre in Wagg Street. "The crème de la crème of Lyme." It was the evening after the visit to Pilgrin Valley, and Joey was admiring the bright scarlet posters advertising the first night of *The Family Reunion. By T.S. Eliot.* "Of course we're playing it as comedy."

"That's good. I like a nice cry."

Augustine was taken aback for a second, but then he recovered himself. "You're such a scream, Mr Hanover. Joey."

"That's what I mean. Comedy is serious. Just look at me."

At this moment Floey came out clutching two tickets; she had decided that her husband needed enlivening after the events of the day, and the lugubrious expression with which he was addressing Augustine confirmed her worst fears. "Five pounds each," she said, waving the tickets in the air. "These people would take the skin off your back." Joey began to smile, and she held up her hand. "No. Don't correct me. I'll do it myself. Skin of your teeth. *Shirt* off your back."

"It's all for charity," Augustine said. "We're just being cruel to be kind." With a little bow he walked away but then stopped, twirled around, and put one hand on his hip. "See if you can guess where the clocks come from." He hurried off, and then stopped for a second time. "Don't you two forget to laugh," he said. "I think it's going to be very camp."

Perhaps that was not, Joey thought as he watched, the right adjective. The play had actually been directed by Augustine in a robust manner; its quiet sad lines were delivered with a stridency that would have done credit to Gothic melodrama, and the somewhat boring characters were so padded and so emphatic that

151

they took on a grotesque life quite different from anything the author could have envisaged. But, as they sat in the small auditorium and the voices of the actors boomed around the theatre, the Hanovers felt quite at home. The world had been transformed into a pantomimic creation, but that did not mean that it was any the less effective or any the less moving. It had acquired a higher reality and, as soon as Joey Hanover heard the first lines with their refrain on clocks that stop in the dark, he was entranced by it. This was the kind of performance he had been giving all his life: strident, vivid, colourful, simplified beyond the range of 'character acting'. It had been part of his skill as a comic to understand that everything had its own form, an inner truth or consistency which was not revealed to those who insisted on some distinction between the real and the unreal. No one had asked Picasso to depict ordinary faces; no one asked a musician to transcribe the familiar sounds of the world; so why should not Joey Hanover himself create his own kind of truth by disciplining and reinventing reality? That was why in his own act he took on a character which was like no real Londoner but which still managed to capture the essence of London; that was why his 'patter', his mixture of songs and jokes and innuendoes which bore no relation to ordinary speech, so touched and amused all those who came to hear it. And that was why, as he sat in the small theatre in Lyme Regis, he was genuinely frightened when in the first scene the Furies appeared outside the drawing-room window. They were badly made-up, their costumes awry, their delivery awkward, but they were still effective. And yet even as they terrified him he knew that they were not real. A little later he nudged Floey when the Chorus, arms flailing wildly like scarecrows come suddenly to life, stepped forward to explain that events which take place in time are never lost but remain, echoing through the past and the future.

"Too much business," Floey whispered to him. But she let out a great sigh of pleasure.

"Ham?"

"Wall-to-wall pork. Wonderful."

Floey's attempt to divert her husband seemed to have worked, since Joey was so rapt in the performance that he had forgotten the search for his lost parents which had brought him to this place. He was the old Joey, watching every aspect of the action, appreciating the asides, noticing the sets and the props with the same avid care as if he were at that moment on the stage himself. But as Floey Hanover

watched *The Family Reunion* she worried about him and his exploration of his lost past; it was too late, she knew that, and those matters
which had been concealed for so long should remain so. If there was
some secret, it was one which could be of no possible use to Joey now.
It could only bring him grief. She shifted in her seat, and looked
sideways at him. Three rows behind, Evangeline Tupper noticed
Floey's movement, but with the same distant attention as she
watched the performance itself. The play meant nothing to her
except as the stage for her own memories and, as the characters
walked to and fro, she thought once more of her father's loneliness.
Baby Doll, sitting beside her, was remembering once more the story
which Joey had told them – the story of the children who flew. Then
she was thinking of the sea, and of the layers of blue she had glimpsed
within it that morning when the gulls flew around her. And Joey was
looking at the green slopes of Pilgrin Valley, studded now not by
rocks but by the white masks of his guardian angels. Evangeline had
put her arms around her father's neck, while Floey looked on
helplessly as her husband lay dying. Time. Past time. Future time.
Imaginary time. Other times curving around them. Each of them in
another time and yet each of them still following the performance on
stage, as if somehow the words and gestures in front of them
prompted their own feelings; as if the play had become the text which
gave those feelings form and substance. When the curtain fell at the
end it was as if they had been dreaming, and had suddenly been
awoken; and as they rose from their seats, they left their private
worlds and at once became their ordinary selves.

The Hanovers left quickly, in order to avoid Augustine and any
further mention of his party, but already Evangeline and Hermione
were scurrying ahead of them out into the night. "What was that
man complaining about?" Evangeline was asking. "All he needed
was a good slap. One hard slap. Around the face. It would all have
been quite different," she went on, "if it had been written by a
woman. You know what they say about one touch of Nature—"

Floey Hanover walked up between them and, taking Hermione's
arm, replied, "Makes the whole world sin?"

Evangeline did not seem at all pleased to see her, or her husband.
"This is gorgeous," she said in her nicest possible manner.
"Absolutely gorgeous. But not altogether a surprise." Joey looked
puzzled. "The theatrical profession," she went on, "never misses a
first night, does it?"

Joey did a brief soft-shoe shuffle on the pavement outside the theatre. "There's no business, Miss Tupper, like show business."

Floey looked on, and turned to Hermione. "At heart, you know, he's still an old lesbian."

"I think," Joey said quietly, "that you mean thespian?"

Evangeline had started laughing. "Well, darlings—" She had only met the Hanovers once before, in the dining room of the Blue Dog, but from her tone she might have known them all her life. "Well, darlings, what's the difference? We are among friends, after all."

Hermione and Floey walked ahead together, while Evangeline and Joey followed a few paces behind. "I suppose," Evangeline was saying, "that you understood the play far better than I possibly could?"

"Bits of it. Little bits of it."

"But why were they speaking in that very peculiar manner?"

"I think," Joey replied, "that it was meant to be blank verse."

"Oh, was it? That explains it. I knew it was a lot of fuss over nothing."

"We saw your famous tomb this morning," Joey said. "In that valley."

"How was it?" She might have been enquiring about a casual acquaintance. "I could sit and look at it all day, couldn't you? Well. Perhaps not all day. Perhaps until the early afternoon." Joey made no reply: the memory of Pilgrin Valley had provoked fresh anxiety about his prospective meeting with the Mints. Now that he had found the cottage, he was more uncertain than ever. Uncertain about his past, and uncertain about himself.

The more silent he became, however, the more animated Evangeline decided to be. "We're going inside it next week," she said, loudly. "And no one has a clue what we'll find. But I do hope it's something very grim and prehistoric. Something we can sink our teeth into."

The thought of Evangeline sinking her teeth into something grim, possibly Baby Doll herself, caused Joey to burst out laughing. "Don't mind me," he said. "I was just thinking of the play."

Evangeline tried to laugh, too. "Yes," she said. "There were parts that were terribly funny, weren't there? Just like a family reunion is supposed to be."

·39·

DARKNESS

LATER THAT same night and, as the Hanovers slept, as
Evangeline Tupper slept, as Augustine Fraicheur slept,
Damian Fall sat in the darkness of the observatory.
Squares of bright colour were reflected upon his face as he
plotted the light curve of Aldebaran. On another screen he called up
a model of the spectral emissions from the star, and he could see its
shell of gases as a dark revolving sphere – the ripples and undulations in the surface of that sphere like the dunes and tumuli of the
earth. But look, Damian. Look closely at the shapes being formed.
Could it be true that I know this place? Could the star have taken on
the shape of Pilgrin Valley? Yes. And, look, it is moving.

Darkness. He has fallen forward or backward. He has not been
able to hold himself against the power of gravity. And yet what is
gravity, except a wave of emptiness? It is not a 'power' at all.
Gravity is simply one aspect of a force which no one understands.
But what of this chair? This observatory? They are no more than
whorls or knots in the cosmic field, temporary patterns of energy like
the changes in brightness across the surface of Aldebaran. The world
and the visible universe are an irruption of stray matter into the vast
nothingness, a relic of that inconceivable moment when space and
time were created together; they are fossils brought together by the
stellar wind that has blown from that first moment of fortuitous and
unnecessary creation.

Darkness. And I know that matter itself is a residue, an obstacle in
the path of the perfect patterning of the cosmos, a stain upon the face
of the original nothingness. Gravity cannot exist without objects;
objects cannot exist without gravity; space is inconceivable outside
of time, and time itself is only an aspect of space. These forces are
fractured and incomplete, therefore; only the relationship between
them is significant, since in that relationship there is some faint echo

of the order which existed before the creation of the visible universe. And perhaps I hear some echo of the perfect order.

Darkness. Matter itself takes recognisable shape only when it is examined at a comparatively low energy; when it is observed at a higher energy it becomes simply a mode of instability – violent, spontaneous, unfathomable, the flashes of some much larger force. And how much simpler, and purer, if that force could exist without these spirals of space-time piercing through it? Does the universe expand because it is yearning to be free of itself?

Darkness. And yet the universe cannot escape from the relics of its origin – energy thrust into time and space and thereby "created", turned into light and heat, slowly decomposing into visible being. The cosmos can no more reverse its fall into the dimensions of space and time than the world can discard the relics of its own development. That is why those buried in the tumulus are as much a part of me as I am of them. Everything is touching everything else, expanding outwards but still mingled together. If a leaf were miraculously to disappear from a single tree the whole universe would be destroyed, because at that instant the balance of forces would be disturbed.

Darkness. And I, too, am an aspect of that order, a relic of earliest creation which space and time have now woven together: nothing can happen to me without subtly altering the shape of the visible universe. I too am moving away through limitless space; I am part of that infinite expansion which seems to me to be an infinite horror. Yet I am not my self; I am as evanescent and as shifting as every other part of the cosmos, a fortuitous arrangement of particles, a small plateau in the endless decomposition of space and time, a stasis in the struggle of forces which has turned into matter.

Darkness. And yet I am not matter; I am merely the space through which the forces of the universe pass, just as the billions of neutrinos pass through me in their journey across the cosmos. I am of the same order of being as a gas cloud, or a constellation. Everything is watching everything else and now, as Damian looked up through the open dome of the observatory, he could see the stars quivering and dancing in the turbulent air.

He wanted to flee. But where could he escape to? He could not flee to the sky. He knew that there was no sky. He knew that it was only light which had been trapped. Darkness still.

Damian, wake up.

·40·

HORSES AND FISHES

"WAKE UP, Damian." Brenda was standing beside him, and was digging her finger into his right shoulder. "Isn't that weird," she said as he opened his eyes. "I couldn't rouse you for ever such a long time. Just couldn't arouse you." He did not realise he had been asleep. "I've got a man in there." She tossed her head in the general direction of the office. "Who wants you."

"Who is it?" He was still lost in his dream, if it had been a dream. "Clare?"

"Of course. Bring him through." He had invited Mark Clare to visit the observatory and, yes, he remembered now, the archaeologist had written to him about some markings upon a stone; they had agreed to meet on this particular night.

Brenda led him into the dome. "I know *you*," she said, now that she had taken a proper look at him in the passage. "I've seen you in Lyme. With a woman on your arm." She giggled. "Who was she?"

"That was my wife," Mark said. He looked at her with something like panic; it was as if Kathleen had somehow entered the room.

Brenda remembered now that the woman had had a brace upon her leg, and she blushed in the darkness of the observatory. "Will I be wanted?" she said quickly.

Alec had come up behind her in the passage, and squeezed her waist. "Not till Birnam Wood goes to what's-its-name." He put his face over her shoulder, so that he could more easily see Damian; he had begun to notice the strangeness of his behaviour and, surreptitiously, he was observing him. Damian Fall was right about his assistant: Alec did have faith in the stars, and in the possibility of human progress. But this meant, too, that he had some trust in human nature; and that trust led to his concern for others. This was why he was worried now about Damian Fall. He admired him, and

157

he understood very well the nature of Damian's melancholy. Alec was more romantic – did he not sing whenever he thought of the heavens? – but he was also more pragmatic. He wanted to help Damian, to prove to him that his work was important, that even on Holblack Moor there was hope to be found.

Brenda gave a little wriggle as Alec playfully embraced her. "I don't know anything about woods," she said. "Or the back seats of cars, thank you very much. I'm just asking if they want me." They went back to the office together, Alec briefly looking back at Damian. "I like Shakespeare," she was saying as she closed the partition between the observatory and the passage. "I like that song about bees sucking."

The two men were left alone beneath the open dome. "Shall I turn on the light?" Damian asked.

"No," Mark replied. "Please don't. I prefer it like this." He went over to the telescope. "It reminds me," he said, "of the engraving in your cottage. What was it called? The darkened house?"

"*Domus obscurata*. Yes. But they knew much more then. They understood much more."

"But now—"

"Now we're really in the dark." Damian laughed. For a few moments he tapped some keys on the console, and the great telescope whirred into life; but it did not seem to Mark to be going in any certain direction. "Backwards and forwards," Damian said. "Backwards and forwards. All the time." Somehow, at this moment, they both experienced the same sensation of futility. It was as if the observatory itself had inspired it. It was as if they were standing on waste ground. Mark said nothing, and for a while the two men listened to the sound of the guiding mechanism as it turned and turned about.

Damian switched it off, and leaned against his chair. He had his back to Mark and, in the darkness, his natural reticence seemed to disappear. "We really know nothing, after all. We see what we want to see. In each generation the heavens become a kind of celestial map of human desires. I'm sorry. Am I boring you?"

"Of course not."

"They reflect all our recent theories about the universe, and although we no longer see the stars in the shape of gods or animals our own theories are no less fabulous." Damian pushed back his chair and looked up at the stars through the open dome. "The stars take on the shapes we choose for them, you see. They become the images of our own selves, shining down and comforting us." His voice sounded quite different to Mark; it was as if he had just emerged from deep water, and was still out of breath. "I'm not so sure that the Greeks weren't right. Perhaps there are horses and fishes floating across the sky. Perhaps we wished them into existence, centuries ago, and they've been trapped there ever since."

The silence which followed this lasted too long. "But there is science—" Mark began to say.

"Ah yes. Science. But who is to say that our science is any better than the science of the astronomer buried in Pilgrin Valley? You did tell me he was an astronomer?"

"We think so. In fact I've brought something—" He had brought an envelope containing the photographs of the tomb-markings which he wanted Damian to examine, and now he held it out.

But Damian did not notice this. "Science is like fiction, you see. We make up stories, we sketch out narratives, we try to find some pattern beneath events. We are interested observers. And we like to go on with the story, we like to advance, we like to make progress. Even though they are stories told in the dark."

"But you have your equations. Your mathematics—"

"Oh. Mathematics. Mathematics is like language. No one knows where it came from. No one really knows how it works. More horses and fishes. Horses and fishes trapped in signs."

Mark put down the envelope on a small table next to him but as he did so he brushed against a plastic cup, half-filled with coffee, which fell to the floor. "Oh my God," he said. "I am sorry."

"Don't be sorry. There's nothing to be sorry about. I chose this life." And yet Damian saw nothing but darkness ahead of him, the same weary routine, the same sense of futility, the same awareness of failure; the same loss of faith.

Mark had grown accustomed to the half-light, and the objects in the dome were bathed in the crepuscular glow of the stars. "But you have discovered so many things," he said. He was talking to the silhouette of Damian, poised and watchful, but when he walked over to him he realised that it was simply the chair with a jacket thrown across it.

Damian was behind him now, and he jumped when he touched his arm. "I'm sorry," Damian said. "I didn't mean to frighten you. I didn't mean to frighten anyone. Go on."

"You know so much more than we do. We only have a few scattered finds—"

Damian laughed at this. "Yes. We go further out. We go so far out that we can see nothing. Do you know that in quantum physics objects simply appear and disappear? And then we see objects suddenly emerging in two places at once which, as far as I remember, was always supposed to be impossible." Mark could see his face now, also glowing in the starlight. "We see an electron at one point but then somehow it is also at another, and it has reached it by travelling in all possible trajectories at once. Now this is a very strange thing. A strange thing for someone who believed in the orderly movement of the stars." He bent down to pick up the fallen plastic cup, and with his foot he was gradually spreading the spilled coffee into wider and wider circles. "And there is another thing, too. We know now that the scientist is actually controlling the reality while he observes it. The spin of a sub-atomic particle, for example, always does what the physicist expects. It always follows his random choice. Horses and fishes again."

"You mean that everything takes the shape we expect?" Mark was thinking of the tumulus; he was thinking of the world which they imagined to have once existed around the grave.

"Yes. And where does that leave me, the observer of the heavens?" In the same instant both of them looked up through the open dome at the obscure milky filaments of Ophiuchus, the Serpent-Bearer.

At this moment Kathleen Clare was sitting by the window in Crooked Alley and gazing at the same group of stars; Owen Chard could not sleep and was watching them, too. So was Joey Hanover. And all over the dark side of the planet there were multitudes looking up at the sky. The stars danced for them in the turbulent air, and their cares rose from them like mist into the freezing firmament.

But who was this lying down in Pilgrin Valley, lying down beside the tomb, lying down on the hard earth and also looking upward?

• 41 •

SERMONS IN STONES

"THERE WAS something I wanted to show you." Mark Clare picked up the photographs of the tomb markings, and held them out towards him. "You may understand it." The dome was closed now, and the red lighting which ran around the interior of the observatory had been switched on.

"Tell me the story," Damian said. He had sensed the anticipation in Mark's voice; it reminded him of Jocy Hanover's excitement when he had entered the cottage, and he was moved by it. It reminded him of Alec. It reminded him, too, of something in himself; something which had once set his life in motion but which had now been lost.

He took the photographs as Mark explained how the engraved whorls and spirals had been found on the blind entrance of the tomb, and he knew at once what Mark had discovered. "If this is a star map," he said, "then here are the Pleiades." He pointed towards seven marks, showing white upon the negative. "There is Alnath within them." He pointed towards a blurred indentation, which may have been no more than a smear across the stone. "And here are the Hyades." His index finger moved down to three smaller marks, joined by a trembling line. "And there—" his finger encircled a much larger area of white, which must have represented some deep indentation in the surface of the blind entrance "—there is Aldebaran, the great star. How odd that it should be preserved in stone like this." He put down the photographs. "Do you have a date?"

"All the evidence suggests—" Mark began to say and both men laughed at the phrase. "All the evidence suggests that the tomb was built around 2500 BC. Can you tell me anything about the vernal equinox then?"

"It will take a minute." Damian went back to the computer,

where all the information on the movement of the heavens was stored. On the screen a parallelogram revolved slowly; then all of its lines began to spin apart and a new pattern was formed. "At the time of the vernal equinox in 2500 BC," Damian said, "those particular stars were just visible upon the eastern horizon. Come and look at them." Mark went over to the console, but all he saw were small crosses shimmering upon the screen. "Your own map is more dramatic," Damian said, "But the information is the same. The same night sky has been restored to us."

"And it means," Mark said, "it means that the chamber grave was in alignment with the stars carved on its entrance. The tumulus points east, and from the crest of the valley you can see the horizon." He was now very excited, and his throat had become dry. He swallowed.

"If that is so, then you have evidence of remarkable planning. The stone must have taken some time to carve, so these people – is that what they were?"

"Yes. People."

"These people must have been able to forecast the movement of the stars as accurately as we do." He turned off the computer, and for an instant Mark could see the linear model rushing away towards the sides of the screen. "And there is a grain of comfort in that," Damian went on. He was no longer looking at Mark as he spoke. "At least I know the stars were really there, after all. Whoever these people were, at least they saw the same light."

•42•

IF YOU GO DOWN . . .

"DEEP. THAT'S the word I'm searching for. This landscape looks so deep. It looks as if it's been inhabited for thousands and thousands of years. But inhabited by who? By *whom?*" Joey Hanover stretched out the last word, in imitation of an owl's call.

"Keep your eyes on the road, Joey. I don't want to be hit by a coagulated lorry."

"Articulated."

"I don't care what it is. I don't want to be a living skeleton." The Hanovers were on their way to the Mints, and had already driven three miles along the road which leads out of Lyme Regis into the open country. Occasionally they passed the corpses of birds, foxes and other small animals which had been hit by speeding cars so that this route was like some sacred avenue marked by sacrifices. But travelling always exhilarated Joey and now he began to sing:

> Every little journey has a meaning of its own
> Every little story tells a tale . . .

He broke off when a car, travelling in the opposite lane, flashed its headlights several times. "Hang on," he said. "There's trouble ahead."

And when they turned the next bend they saw what the trouble was: six or seven cows had somehow got out from an adjacent field, and were now careering down the middle of the busy road. They were so bewildered that they had been stunned into a sort of half-life, terrified of the vehicles which swept past them. And to Joey they seemed like lost children – no, not children, stranger than children. They had left one world and had entered another, a world close to their own but one which they had never seen. It was a world which threatened them and, in their fear, they knocked against each other;

they were going in no particular direction, and one of them looked up at the sky as if this were the only thing it recognised or could remember. For they had come from some other time.

The Hanovers drove on more slowly and, when eventually they parked above Pilgrin Valley, Joey Hanover let out a deep sigh. "Begone dull care," he said, and then kissed his wife on the cheek.

They walked down the track and, when they reached the gate of the farmhouse, a dog started ferociously to bark. "Do you know what that sounds like?" Floey asked him as she took his arm. "That sounds like the Hound of the D'Urbervilles."

They walked down the path but the door was opened before they could reach it, and Farmer Mint stood on the threshold carrying a pair of wellington boots. "I hope," Joey said, "that we don't intrude?"

"If you've come about the cess-pit, Boy Mint is waiting there." Farmer Mint looked them up and down, and now seemed to notice that Joey was wearing a blue striped blazer while Floey was resplendent in a cherry-red dress. "On the other hand," he added, with a chuckle, "perhaps you haven't come about the cess-pit. I wouldn't know."

"My name is Joey. This is Floey."

"Mint. The other Mint is in the cess-pit."

Joey was disappointed that the farmer did not seem to recognise him; any assistance, at such a moment, would have been welcome. "Jo and Flo," he went on. "The couple who know." This had been one of their theatrical catchphrases.

"Mint and Mint. As hard as flint." He grinned at them. "So what can we do for you?" Even as he said this he was looking strangely at Joey and, apparently absent-mindedly, he let the boots drop from his hand onto the gravel path.

"I was born in the cottage on the other side of the valley," Joey said at once, not knowing how else to proceed. "I was told that it was yours."

"You were, were you?"

"I was."

"Do you happen to mean the cottage in the field?"

"The one with the plaster faces."

"Do you mean the one with the white gate and the rusty thatch?"

"And the purple flowers."

"And you think you were born there, do you?"

"I know I was born there. I remember it."

Farmer Mint took off his cap and searched deeply within it, as though his next thought were written somewhere on its lining. "Well well," he said at last. "You'd best come in then."

Several objects had been added to the main room of the farmhouse since Evangeline Tupper's visit at the beginning of the excavation, and now the Hanovers found themselves stepping around an empty milk-can, two neatly tied bundles of silver paper, a rake with some of its teeth missing, a length of hosepipe and an ancient vacuum cleaner balanced upon an upturned pail. But Joey noticed none of these things: he was staring at the paintings and photographs of the ancestral Mints on the wall above the fireplace. Farmer Mint looked at him for several seconds, and then he looked at the pictures; then he picked up the rake and, carrying it into the centre of the room, leaned on it for support. "Now that we're comfortable," he said, "we can get acquainted." He gestured Floey towards the milk-can, upon which obediently she perched herself, and then turned again towards Joey. "Who said you were born there?" Before Joey could answer he put down the rake and went over to the window. He seemed to be looking out for Boy Mint and then, obviously disappointed, he came back into the middle of the room. "Who told you?"

"My foster parents. They told me I was born in this area. They told me I lived here till I was about five years old. And I remember the cottage itself. I remember the faces." Joey was gazing at Farmer Mint, as if he were pleading with him as he spoke. "It's my old home."

"Hold on. Hold it there." Farmer Mint put out his hand. "My spit has dried in my mouth. I need watering." He left the room, and after a few moments the Hanovers could hear a tap running. It kept running for several minutes, but eventually Farmer Mint reappeared. His hair was very wet, and it was clear that he had put his head under the tap. "The Boy should be here," he muttered. "The Boy knows how to tell a story."

"Story?"

"I'm coming to it. I'm ambling towards it. Sit yourself down here." With a series of nervous gestures Farmer Mint cleared two broken cups, a statuette of some unrecognisable figure, and a cardboard box filled with buttons, from a small wooden chest. "Sit down there. Sit opposite the Mints." He had placed Joey in front of the pictures. "Let them take a good look at you while I get myself prepared." He glanced briefly at Joey again, shook his head and began pacing up and down. Then he stopped and spat on his hands – a ritual gesture which he observed before undertaking any activity. He went over to the pictures and, on the bottom line, he pointed out two sepia photographs which were framed in gilt. "Take the case of two brothers," he said. "Brother Herbert. My father." He tapped the first of them, and the Hanovers could see a man, of about the same age as Farmer Mint now was, standing beside a hayrick; from this distance, he seemed to them to be wearing precisely the same clothes as his son. "And Brother Samuel." Joey Hanover got up and walked over to this second photograph. It showed a young man, clearly dressed for a photographer's studio since he was wearing a herring-bone jacket and a stiff round collar. He seemed so ill at ease in these clothes Joey sensed at once that he was not used to wearing them; and there was something familiar about his face. With a feeling very much like despair, he sat down on the wooden chest and waited for Farmer Mint to continue. "This is a story," he said. "About them two brothers."

HERBERT AND SAMUEL

ONCE UPON a time there were two brothers, Herbert and Samuel Mint, and they lived together in a little house above the valley; they were very happy there, ploughing and tilling from morn until dusk, but the day came when Herbert decided that it was time to take a wife. So he packed some pigeon sandwiches and walked into the local village of Colcorum where he explained to the people how many pigs and cattle were raised on the farm, and how much work still needed to be done, and how happy he would be to bring up a son in the valley; he was a very persuasive man, being a Mint, and within a few hours Emily Trout, the daughter of the local timber-merchant, was chosen as a wife for him. They married at the mid-summer solstice, and very soon the farmhouse was filled with the laughter of a plump little wife and a plump little baby boy.

Now it was Samuel's turn. "I don't like the women of the village," he told his brother (making sure that Emily was out in the fields at the time), "I will go out into the wide world and search for my bride." So he took a knapsack and filled it with good country things, such as a rabbit for his midday meal, and off he journeyed into the wilderness. He walked and walked until he had gone at least twenty miles, and he came onto a moor not far from the treacherous sea coast. He decided to stop here for a bite of rabbit, but when he began to cook it on an open fire he heard a rustling behind him. It sounded like a fox, desperate enough to come and share Samuel's meal, but when he turned around he saw a young woman kneeling on the turf a few yards away from him and wringing her hands as if in grief.

"Help me," she called. "Oh, do."

"Who are you?" he asked.

"My name is Jenny Pocket, and I have run away from my father who is a travelling spar-maker and who beats me and who tries to sleep with me in my own bed. I ran away at daybreak and now, as you can see, I am all alone upon the terrible moor."

Samuel reflected upon this information for a while, the Mints being cautious folk, but at last he decided to share his meal with the wretched young woman. He had enough rabbit to spare, after all, and it seemed a pity to waste it. She ate ravenously, and Samuel hardly had time to reach his next decision. "How would it be, Jenny Pocket," he said, "if you and I were to wed and to live in my valley over yonder? There is always work to be done, and we could raise more Mints. My name is Samuel Mint, by the way. How do you do?"

She got up from the grass, dusted down her brown dress, and put out her hand; Samuel shook it and so, as the custom was in these parts, the decision was made. They travelled back together, and by the time they had reached the valley Jenny seemed to have forgotten all about her wicked father, the travelling spar-maker. Herbert rejoiced when his brother returned with new help for the farm, and in celebration he split open the juiciest calf. They were wed on the feast of the ram, which was a holy day in this part of the rolling English countryside, and by this time Jenny was already three months pregnant.

Now there is an old saying that two wives in a house are like two bees in a honeypot or two maggots in a carcase, and so it proved. Jenny could not abide Emily, Emily had no liking for Jenny, whom she called a changeling, and very soon the brothers decided that it was time for them to be parted. So Samuel, being the younger Mint, left the farmhouse and moved with his heavily pregnant wife to a small cottage on the other side of the valley; it was nothing but a ruin then, but in no time Samuel had filled the holes in the walls, mended the thatch, dug out a little garden and, as a final touch, carved little faces in all the corners of the cottage. These are our angels, he told Jenny as she went into labour, our guardian angels. So now in the year 1925 there were three Mints in the cottage, Samuel and Jenny and their baby son. Five years passed, five years of spinning and weaving and making soup, and by this time even the villagers of Colcorum (who were notorious gossips and scandal-mongers) agreed that at last they must be living happily ever after.

Now comes the hard part of the story: one late afternoon in the August of 1930 Samuel came back from the fields, tired and hungry after a day's reaping, and was calling "Jenny! Jenny! Where's my rabbit stew?" just as soon as he was within earshot of the cottage. But there was no sound. And when he unlatched the little white gate, and entered the little blue door, calling for his stew, there was still no reply. The cottage was empty. There was no sign of the infant Mint, either, until Samuel rushed out again into the garden. And there he was, sitting in the middle of a bed of lovely purple phlox; and the phlox were so high that it was only when the child popped up his head that his father could see him. Where was Mummy? Mummy had gone for a walk that morning, and Mummy had not come back. Where did Mummy walk? Mummy walked towards the little wood on the side of the valley, where the old stones are. What had she said? She had said, give a kiss to your Daddy for me.

And with a terrible cry Samuel ran across the fields.

Jenny was never found. One villager confirmed that he had seen her walking towards the ash forest and the old stones but, if she did, she certainly never came back. Jenny had vanished. Some say that she went back to her wicked father, the travelling spar-maker; some say that she was running in terror from something or someone, and that as she fled towards the sea she fell down the sandstone cliffs and was washed away; others say that she was murdered and still lies buried somewhere, perhaps beneath one of the old stones. In any case, she was never found.

Samuel Mint never recovered from his wife's disappearance. He refused to go out in the fields and sat all day in the cottage. "Waiting for Jenny," he used to say whenever a villager called. "Waiting for Jenny." But the strangest part is that he could no longer endure the sight of his little son. "Whenever I see that child," he said to Herbert and Emily one day when they came to visit him with a lovely mulch of lamb's brains for dinner. "Whenever I see that child, I get to thinking about Jenny. And, when I get to thinking about Jenny, I take a wrong turning in my head."

"You mean," says Herbert, raising his fork over the lamb's brains, "you mean you can't plough a straight furrow no more. Is that the size of it, Sammy Mint?"

"That's about it, brother Herbert. I can't see ahead of me far enough."

Now Herbert Mint would always remember this conversation, because it was no more than a month after when Samuel took down his old twelve-bore rifle, went into the wood where his wife had disappeared, sat down upon one of the stones there, and shot himself through the mouth. He was found laid out on the ground and, according to the old village custom, he was cremated in a secret place and his ashes strewn under the ground.

But what had become of the little child? Here, at last, is the happy ending: a month before Samuel Mint blew out the back of his head and, as it happens, the day after his conversation with Herbert and Emily over the lamb's brains, he had taken his little son to London. He had left him there with a couple who were so happy to have a child that they asked no awkward questions and, in return, they even gave Samuel Mint a bag of gold and silver. So the little boy was adopted, after all. And that boy's name was Joseph. Otherwise known as Joey.

•44•

ALL IN A SINGLE DAY

"JOEY," HE repeated, now that he had come to the end of his story. "Joey Mint." In the silence Joey Hanover reached over to take his wife's hand, looking at her all the while but saying nothing. She stared straight ahead, and began a low tuneless whistle. Farmer Mint turned away from them and straightened the photographs of Herbert and Samuel.

Then the door was suddenly opened, and Boy Mint burst in shouting, "The bull's got into the drainage ditch! He's in the drainage ditch!"

His father hurried towards him and put his hands on his shoulders. "Boy!" He was shouting, too, as if his son were yards away from him. "Boy, come and meet your Uncle Joey!" Boy stood very still, opened his mouth, looked in bewilderment around the room, and then put his cap over his face. "Yes, that's right, Boy! Don't be bashful. Here's your Uncle Joey at long last." Farmer Mint was now in a state of wild excitement and he rushed over to Joey. "And I'll tell you something else," he said, hoisting him up from the wooden chest. "You and me are cousins again!" He brushed a tear from his eye. "My spit's gone," he said. "I need some more irrigation." Hurriedly he left the room.

So the story had been told: Joey Hanover was Joey Mint after all. He had been taken from the cottage and adopted in 1930; now, so many years later, he had discovered that his parents had both died in Pilgrin Valley. He could not fully absorb this new knowledge, not now, and yet he was exhilarated by it – exhilarated not by their deaths but by his sense of origin; for the first time in his life he could feel that he belonged in the world. He could look back and see his parents with their parents before them; he was not alone. He had also found a cousin and a nephew and, as he sat with them in the farmhouse, he discovered that there were many other of his relatives

171

in the same area. The Mints had farmed this region from generation to generation. Joey had been the only one who had ever strayed.

Then he thought of his parents again. "I have to see the forest," he said. "Where it all happened."

Farmer Mint shook his head. "Tell him why he's barking up the wrong tree, Boy."

"Uncle." Boy Mint regarded him gravely. "Uncle, you can't."

"Can't?"

"In the first place there was a fire. In the second place it was burned down. And in the third place they're messing about with it—"

"It just pours out of him, doesn't it?" Farmer Mint looked at his son in wonder.

"Them excavators," Boy Mint went on, receiving the compliment with appropriate gravity, "have been digging and chipping and unearthing." He gave a loud laugh which unnerved Floey: she sat upright and started putting on her gloves as a sort of reflex response. "Not that they'll find anything." He laughed again, and Floey started taking off her gloves. "Little do they know."

Joey had been thinking about his dead parents, and had hardly been listening. "Little do they know what?"

Farmer Mint went over to his son, and put his hand on his shoulder. It might have been a warning gesture. "Not now, Boy. Don't open the floodgates of your powerful mind. Not yet. We have to wait until your uncle has been properly introduced."

The last word caught Joey's attention and he began to croon, in a low voice, "Hello, she cried and waved her lily hand."

Floey turned to him. "Black-eyed Susan!"

She was pleased that her husband was returning to himself, but now he seemed to forget that he had been singing. "Introduced to what?" he asked.

Farmer Mint chuckled. "There's going to be a celebration. Now that you're back." He spat on his hands and rubbed them together. "You can meet all the others. All the other Mints."

"And then," Boy Mint added, equally ecstatically, "then you'll know everything. You'll know as much as I do." This was clearly a great compliment but, before Joey could properly thank him for it, there was a roaring close to hand. "Damn me," the Boy said, going over to the window. "I forgot that bull. That bull's messing about in the drainage ditch!" He rushed out of the door and Farmer Mint followed him, stopping only to say, "Make yourself at home, Cousin Joey. You are at home now, after all."

Joey sat back and Floey looked at him, smiling. "You were right," she said. "It wasn't a wild fruit chase after all." She felt something crawling up her right stocking and, when she looked down, she saw an earwig moving slowly up her leg. With a little shriek she knocked it back to the floor.

Joey went over to the photograph of his father. "I want," he said, "to go down to the woods again."

"That *is* a good idea." Floey herself was happy to leave the farmhouse as quickly as possible. "Fresh air will do you good. And you can leave a note for your friends – I mean your—"

"My family." Joey could find neither pen nor paper; but there was a dusty mirror propped against a wall. He picked it up, licked his finger and wrote upon its surface, "Back later". Then he hesitated, not sure how to sign this brief message, and inscribed a small "j".

The Hanovers walked down the path and, arm in arm again, descended the west slope of Pilgrin Valley towards the excavations and the ruined ash forest. "It's hard to believe," Joey said. "After all this time." He looked at the palms of his hands, as if he might see some change in them. Then he looked straight ahead at the place where his parents had died, and almost marched towards it.

There was nothing left of the ash forest except the clumps of a few trees, some of them scorched and broken, and some of them so seared by the heat that they had ceased to grow. There were dark circles on the ground where other trees had stood, but even here wild grass and fern were beginning to creep across the blackened surface of the old forest. The rest of it had been taken over by the site; the Hanovers went over to the chicken wire which encircled the excavations, and looked out across at the tomb and its exposed forecourt. "I wish I knew," Joey said. "Where it happened. Where he shot himself."

The valley was suddenly very quiet, so that for a moment it seemed to him like a closed and shuttered room in which he must turn and turn about. But then he heard the banging of a saucepan and a series of fierce cries, echoing from the other side of the valley: the Mints were trying to scare the bull out of the drainage ditch and back into the fields. The bellows of father and son sounded to Joey identical, and so unlike their normal voices that they might have been possessed – these were the calls which Farmer Mint had learnt from his father, who had in turn received them from his father. These strange cries echoed from generation to generation across this valley, and how far back did they go?

He walked over to a ruined clump of trees. Floey looked on anxiously, but now he looked around and smiled at her. "What's that expression? Dead, dead and never called me Mother? Except, this time, it's the other way around."

"At least you've kept your sense of humour, Joey. I thought I'd lost you for a minute."

"You know what they say, Flo. Tragedy in the past, mystery in the future, but comedy in the present. Comedy in the present. Shall we go now?"

They walked away from the excavation, and in the Pilgrin Valley on this summer morning the cries of the Mints were united with the sound of Joey's voice as he sang

All in a day my 'eart grew sad,
Misfortune came my way.
I 'ad to learn the whole bitter truth
All in a single day . . .

•45•

A LETTER FROM DAMIAN

I NEED TO write to you, Alec. Or do I need to write a letter to myself? There is, of course, no reason why you should want to read this: as you know perfectly well, I am a failure. Like one of those figures at the end of a Chaplin film, I get smaller and smaller as I walk into the distance. I am working in a minor observatory. I am part of the network, receiving orders about what portion of the sky to watch – for how long, and to what purpose. And I once thought of the night sky as my home! I thought it was illimitable, and I suppose that I always sensed in its infinity my own feeling that I, too, was without limits. Without boundaries. That I could become whatever I wished to be. When I was a young man I saw in the sky the pattern of my own destiny. I doubt that you find this strange, Alec. I see in you the same ambition, the same hunger. That is why you look at the heavens with such admiration. I remember that you once admitted that you were a romantic, but are you sure that you are not just romantic about yourself?

There. Already I seem to be attacking rather than addressing you. In reality I am flinching from myself. Turning my face away because it is too hard to bear. I had wanted to be a great astronomer. A discoverer. I studied hard. I learnt everything I could. I mastered the facts. My life seemed to be a series of challenges but they were ones which I gladly accepted. In fact, I had no other conception of what life might be. Like you, I went from school to university and then became a research assistant at an observatory. I was an astronomer at last. A professional. Just as I had planned. But it was not long before I realised that this was not enough: now that I was working with others I, who had worked so much in isolation – worked for myself, you might say – I found that I could not move any further ahead. To tell you the truth, I was afraid. 'The world' became too much for me. I lacked the will to impose myself upon others, and I realised that without the power to move or to influence people there could be no progress. All sciences – even astronomy – are human sciences, after all. And so I surrendered my ambitions to others who were more forceful than myself: I watched them coming up behind me, pausing, and then overtaking me. I, who thought I had so much to say, could not speak a word. There were people who seemed to lead charmed lives – charmed in the sense that events merged with them, propelled them forward. Their direction seemed already to have been chosen. And as for me? Well. My own insignificance must have been determined already, too. I was being pushed around – literally pushed around by my own fate. And then the chill set in, as deadly as the chill of death: I began to accept this fate. I began to accept other people's opinions of my own self. All the time I was simply getting on with the work, following instructions. I was transferred from one observatory to the next – I did my work well, I have no doubt about that. But it was routine work. Observing. Notating. Checking. Cross-checking. I was doing nothing *for myself* any more – do you understand that, Alec? I was working impersonally, and all the promptings of my old dreams and ambitions gradually fell away. Everyone said that I was reliable, efficient, safe – there was a part of me that even enjoyed such praise, such scanty confirmation of my identity, but even as I heard them I realised that these compliments were also indexes of my inability to achieve my ambitions. In other words, I was a failure. And then, last year, I was sent here to Holblack Moor. Once I was too frightened to change my life – too aware of my own inadequacies to trust myself in the world – but now, I believe, I have also grown too lazy; I am still afraid, don't doubt that, but my fear has itself become a form of lethargy. I live from day to day, not looking ahead because I know there is nothing to see there. Only above. The heavens above me. Above my head. I go on tracking the stars, but now the sight of the night sky is a reminder of all that I can never achieve. Working without hope until retirement or death, making a virtue out of the dogged round – and, as always, the same fear. The fear of the future. The fear of other people. The night sky has become an image of my shrunken self.

But that is not the only reason I am writing to you; if that were all, I could leave it to your own keen observation. Keener than my own, no doubt. I am writing to you now because something else is happening to me, and I want to tell you about it before it is too late to do so. Before it becomes impossible for me. And I must leave one record of my life, isn't that right? Even if it is only a letter. Otherwise it will be as if I had never existed at all.

It began two weeks ago. I had left the cottage and was walking across the fields – nowhere in particular except that, as usual, I found myself walking along Pilgrin Valley. Just walking, for in the country I was safe. And it was at this moment of great calm that I felt I was being watched. Now. If I were a madman, I thought, I would believe that I was being observed by something inhuman. Some god or devil. And in the same instant, I had that sensation. I *was* being watched. By some alien presence. And at that moment, too, I was filled with nausea. My body knew it before I did – I was going mad. It was only a brief episode, but from that moment my fear of madness became more disturbing than the attack itself. Over the next few hours I waited – waited for another sign.

And then it happened: it was as if my consciousness had been involved in some great convulsion. It radiated pain like a wound, and I was surrounded by some inexplicable and unfathomable horror. Horror of myself. Horror of something other than myself. I cannot say how frequent, or how long, but there were successive waves of – what? Not fear. Fear is too obvious a word. And not darkness, either, because the world seemed to be filled with some unfamiliar light. I was dazzled by my own madness, like a man upon an operating table who looks up and sees the lights at the same moment as he shrieks with pain. I believed that I was Christ and looked around me fearfully, I believed that there was a conspiracy against me and that all those I knew were robots programmed to deceive me, I believed that there were microphones hidden within the cottage. There was some creature inside me. I was not of the human species. There was some presence within me, speaking through my own voice. And this was the greatest horror of all: that I was not my own self. Then I was sick upon the floor. And even as I suffered these things it occurred to me that insanity was simply the re-emergence of primeval images. I, who believed neither in God nor the devil, now realised that I was being watched by them. I knew the natural world to be apart from myself, and yet now I saw every aspect of it as connected, malign, purposeful. I had become a primitive again. One of my own ancestors. This was madness. And I realised how easy it is to slip into it, how close it always is. It was as if the oldest fantasies of fear and dissolution lay just beneath the surface, waiting to be brought forth. Waiting to be excavated.

There were times when the crisis passed, and I believed that it was gone for ever. I was able to breathe more freely and the ordinary world seemed to emerge with fresh definition – it must seem like this to a blind man who suddenly regains his sight. But then the tremors came again. I felt the soft movement beneath my skull, as if something were being enlarged. And it began. I have told you some of the things – but I have not told you all. How I knew that I was a murderer. How I believed that I would see my own double walking in the garden. How I knew that I was possessed by the devil. That I had become invisible. There were times when I wanted to tear out my eyes, bite off my own tongue. Even when I lay outside on the grass, I knew that the calls of the birds were directed against me – and the wind, oh the wind, how I trembled when it passed across me. It was my enemy, too.

I cannot say when the next crisis will come to me, but I am waiting for it now. I think, today, it will have something to do with *species*. Artificial species. Species changing their form. Of course I know that my madness will always adopt a new shape – there is always some new horror waiting to be revealed. For all these things are images of what I imagine madness must be *like*. Do you understand that, Alec? The insane take the shape of other people's fears. Madness is copied. Do you really understand that? The other night I was eagerly searching through a book – I do not remember why – and I came across a phrase. I can repeat it: ". . . that old sinking of the heart and longing after home". I looked around, startled, because I have no home. My threatened reason has nowhere to rest, nowhere to go.

No. I am not going to send you this letter. I was about to leave it somewhere, in case of my final collapse. But I do not need to send you this. I will destroy it. For who knows if you have not been responsible for all that has happened to me? Is it true that you are planning my death? And how do I know you will not use this letter as evidence against me? I fear, Alec, that you may be a devil.

PART FOUR

Then was the serpent temple form'd, image of
infinite
Shut up in finite revolutions . . .

Europe
WILLIAM BLAKE.

·46·

TORCHLIGHT

"AT LAST," Mark Clare said. "At last." Early autumn, and finally the chamber tomb was laid bare. After the forecourt had been exposed, they had begun immediately to remove the chalk and turf which covered the sides of the tumulus – only the back of the grave, which tapered off into the eastern slope of Pilgrin Valley, remained concealed. The rest now rose up from the ground like a long house, and one so perfectly preserved that it might have been just recently erected. A fine mist of water was being directed onto the stones so that they became darker and colder than anything around them – at least this was how they seemed to Mark, as he pointed out to Martha Temple a small gap in the side wall. "There it is," he said. "There is the real entrance. No one has gone through it since the grave was sealed."

"And how does it feel," Martha replied with the lightest possible laugh, "to be a grave robber?" Her arm was still encased in plaster after the accident but, from her tone, it seemed that she had nothing whatever to do with the excavations.

"I don't know." As always, he answered her seriously. "But grave robbers used to be known as resurrection men."

"Is that the same thing," she added gaily, "as daylight robbery? I hope you don't do anything you're going to regret."

Owen Chard had joined them. "If I were you, I wouldn't put it that way," he said. She gave him the briefest of smiles. "I wouldn't put it any way. I would wait to see what – if anything – is in there."

She turned to him triumphantly. "I do hope," she said, "that you're not suggesting that the tomb is empty? That all these months have been wasted?" No one had mentioned this possibility before, although some of them considered it to be likely, and her words spread a distinct gloom over the others who were standing beside them. "And please don't talk of robbery. I think it's so ghoulish."

She seemed to have forgotten that she had raised that particular topic. "Try and look on the bright side. Like me. I'm sure that it's all going to be an incredible success." But somehow she had managed to change the mood of the whole team.

Mark had already hurried over to the tumulus just as the final small stone was being cautiously removed from the entrance in the side. For a moment he could not breathe, but then in his excitement he called over to Owen. Martha shook her head and smiled before turning, with a delightful sigh, to Julian Hill. "They're just like children, aren't they?" she said. "But I wish them well. Now that we've done all the hard work, let them enjoy themselves. I'm the last person to be bitter, after all, although there are some people—" she looked around to see if the others were still listening "—who might feel a little bit left out. Just a little bit aggrieved."

Julian himself had no wish to go into the tomb; he could see all he needed from the outside, and could decode the rest on the computer. "Why don't you join them?" he asked her.

She gave him a vicious look, and raised the plaster cast. "Everyone seems to have forgotten," she said, "that I was injured by a person working on this site. I name no names. But one day it will all come out." Her voice had gone up an octave. "Not that I'm complaining, of course." She had recovered from her momentary lapse, and was once more her usual smiling self. "I'm having a perfectly lovely time. Watching Mark and Owen take all the credit."

This alarmed him. "Do you really think they will?"

"Aren't you the jealous one? Whatever makes you think a thing like that?" She patted his arm. "Don't worry, dear Julian. I *always* defend your interests. When they talk about you." This thoroughly discomfited him, and he glanced around. But no one was paying any attention. They were all looking at the tomb.

Mark was kneeling in front of the side entrance, so that his face was at a level with the opening within the stones; the cold seemed to be drawing him in, actually ingesting his breath, and for a moment he felt dizzy. He would have fallen, but he placed his hands against the ancient wall until he had recovered himself. Now there was no help for it: it was time to go forward. The space was just wide enough for him to pass through, but he only placed his head and shoulders between the stones; he did not want to walk upon the floor of the interior, not yet. He did not want to move inside the tomb. So he lay down within the entrance itself and peered into the small side chamber.

Bright sunlight outside, but pitch blackness within. There was no smell of decay but, rather, the denser and more pervasive smell of old earth and old stone. With a start he drew back his head; it was as if he had confronted some living thing, trapped in the tomb but now rushing towards him. The sudden movement backward had precipitated him out into the light but he did not glance at the others; instead he looked down at his hands and clothing, because the smell of old earth and old stone already seemed to be clinging to them. Slowly he unhooked a torch from his belt, turned it on, and once more manoeuvred himself between the stones. He shone the torch within the darkness of the chamber, and its thin ray of light touched something on the ground. For a moment Mark closed his eyes in terror; but the outline of this thing remained still even as the light played upon it, and he saw that it was a dish or basin of stone placed in the very middle of the chamber. There were no objects around it – no debris or scattered artefacts – and it occurred to him that this room might otherwise be bare. He placed the torch in his left hand, still with its ray focussing upon the bowl as if it might move or disappear if the light were not directed onto it, and with his right hand he felt the ground just inside the entrance where he lay. He had time only to sense flat stone, but this pavement was so cold that the sudden shock of it made him drop the torch; the clatter echoed through the small chamber and seemed to travel down the central passageway of the tomb, entering various rooms and recesses until quite suddenly it stopped. It was as if this echo had been muffled at some particular point.

The torch had not gone out but in the fall the beam had now shifted to expose the far wall facing Mark: there was a stone slab here which seemed to block whatever entrance the side chamber might once have possessed but, no, it was not completely blocked. The torchlight had revealed a circle of greater lightness, and he realised that this was the contour of a porthole carved in the base of the stone slab – a porthole which must lead to the central passage of the tumulus, and through which it was possible to enter or leave this small chamber. So at least he knew that, if he wished to, he could make further progress.

To test the echo he had just heard he whispered "Hello" and a murmured "Hello" was returned from the chambers beyond: he knew from his own earlier soundings just how large this tumulus was but at this moment it seemed to him to be immense, elaborate, incalculable. His whisper might travel for ever through the cold and the darkness. And so he was straddled between two worlds – the upper half of his body now within the tomb as eagerly he peered forward, the lower half still protruding in the outer world. Part of him had been swallowed up.

Martha had joined the others behind him and now she whispered to Owen. "Isn't it sweet, to see Mark's little legs waving in the air? Only a professional doesn't mind making a fool of himself."

Owen gave her a sour look. "He isn't the only one, is he?"

She was in one of her nicest moods, and at once rose to the defence of her colleagues. "If you are referring to Julian, I just don't want to hear. I'm sure he's doing the best he can." But she changed the subject quickly. "Look," she added, "Mark's little legs have disappeared."

Owen had already noticed that Mark had fully entered the tumulus. "Oh dear, oh dear." He shook his head. "He should not have done that. He really should not have done that."

"Why?" Martha knew the reasons, of course, but she repeated her question more loudly so that the others might have time to hear. "What else has dear Mark done wrong?"

"Nothing is *wrong*." Owen was embarrassed that his reaction had been drawn to the attention of the rest. "Nothing is wrong exactly. But there should have been a proper examination. Something might be destroyed."

"Did you hear that?" Martha turned to the others. "Mark may be destroying the evidence. But we have faith in our leader, don't we? We understand."

Mark had heard none of this. Even when he had lain across the entry he had been surrounded by the silence of the tomb which, like its dark and cold, supplanted everything from the outer world. But he had not decided haphazardly to enter the tomb: he had retrieved his torch and directed its light down onto the area in front of him, seeing at once that here was a flat stone floor which contained no debris of any kind and which could certainly bear his weight. So, very slowly, he moved further into the darkness – now holding the torch steadily in front of him so that its thin beam pierced the porthole of the stone before seeming to disappear into the passage beyond, to be snuffed out. He managed to slide through the entrance and slip down onto the floor of the tomb, and at once he could feel the cold ascending from the stone pavement into his body. But he welcomed that cold and he lay upon the floor of the tomb like an ice-bound traveller who knows that to freeze to death is simply to fall asleep.

Now, very hesitantly and very carefully, he tried to stand upright in the chamber; as yet he had no idea how low its roof might be. Then he felt it just above his head. Or, rather, he sensed its presence – as he had noticed in previous excavations, the human body seemed quickly to fit itself into the contours and limitations of these ancient places. He was bent over now, the ceiling some five and a half feet above the floor; he was crouching inside the tomb. He was the first to have entered this place for more than four thousand years, and with that knowledge he acquired new energy. He shuffled his feet, as if at the beginning or end of a dance. And then he put the torch beneath his chin, so that its occluded beam travelled upward and turned his face – if there had been anyone to see it – into a kind of gargoyle. Then he spoke some words into the cold air – inconsiderable words, nonsense words, but words that reclaimed this place for human occupation. "I am making a mappemunde," he said, and the phrase echoed through the tomb. And he felt pride – not pride in himself, for being there, but pride in the lineage and in the continuation. Pride in the words that issued from him but which had their origins among the long dead. In this enclosed space he sensed the closeness of worship but it was not just the worship of ancestors but, rather, the worship of time itself. The passage of time. And, yes, this was a passage grave.

·47·

IN THE PASSAGE

OVER THE next few weeks the tumulus was thoroughly explored, the archaeological team working steadily beyond the side chamber where Mark Clare had uttered "mappemunde" and moving along a central passageway. Until they reached a dry stone wall at the end of the passage, the wall against which all echoes stopped. This was not the back of the tomb but rather a barrier protecting a room beyond – a terminal chamber which was the focal point of the whole tomb, a chamber sealed, built into the slope of Pilgrin Valley, but pointing eastward to the rising sun.

And this is what they discovered during the course of their journey towards the hidden room: from the blind entrance, where the patterns of the stars had been inscribed, to the terminal chamber itself there ran a passage which was some four and a half feet wide, five feet high and seventy feet in length. This passage was constructed by means of twenty-four large orthostats, the upright stones which supported large roofing slabs; there was no mortar between these dry stones, and they were kept in position only by their own weight and by the weight of the stones around them. All the forces of the tomb were directed downward, therefore, its fabric held in place by gravity.

They had discovered two small chambers on either side of this passage. It had been in one of these that Mark had stood on first entering the tumulus and, as he had seen, each chamber was blocked by a high septal stone which for some reason was punctured by a circular porthole through which it was possible to crawl. The function of these low circular entrances was not immediately clear and, as Mark explained, it could really only be determined when the precise nature of the tomb was understood. Julian Hill had already come to the conclusion that to go through the porthole would have been tantamount to a form of rebirth, thus connecting the burial ritual with an ancillary fertility rite. He believed that he understood the formation of primitive worship, and everything he saw confirmed his hypothesis. But Mark was not so certain: he saw only a sacred entrance which took the form of a circle, and it seemed to him that these portholes might somehow be related to the circular engravings of stars which had been scored on the blind entrance of the tomb. The worshipper (if that was who it was) bowed his head in the passageway and literally entered a star.

But, when they passed through that star, what then? The two side chambers closest to the terminal room contained only an empty bowl made out of stone – it had been one of these that Mark had seen in the beam of the torchlight. But the other two chambers were filled with a bewildering variety of artefacts – bewildering not only in their profusion but in their respective ages. Here were shards of simple-rimmed undecorated cups which were typical of south-western pottery in the early neolithic period; but beside these were fragments of bowls or cups which retained impressions of twisted cord or the even more complex shapes created by 'finger-nailing' – the early inhabitants of this region using their own hands to create a web of impressions along the rims of their earthenware. The dates for all of these objects ranged from 4300 BC to 3400 BC, and yet also within the side chambers the excavators found examples of grooved ware which, as far as anyone knew, had not come into use until 2600 BC.

As far as anyone knew: this had become the problem of Pilgrin Valley, since the discovery of pottery from three widely separated periods threw all chronology into doubt. Either a whole range of disparate artefacts were in use for a period of seventeen hundred years, or the tomb itself was much older than the preliminary examinations had suggested. It was even possible that this tumulus was built upon the site of a still more ancient tomb, and that this place had been a centre of worship or ritual for many thousands of years. No one was certain of anything any more. Orthodox theories and even the most reasonable calculations seemed to decay or to dissolve in the face of these discoveries. And, as the expectations of the archaeologists wavered and changed, so did the evidence itself; the closer they came to the actual stones and relics, the more these objects retreated into a kind of unknowability. They seemed to resist explication, in the process becoming denser and darker. Nothing seemed to stand still; everything was in flux; and, since it was impossible to establish any definite relations between the various artefacts, the finds themselves began to lose their reality even as the archaeologists observed them. They were working in the dark.

And eventually it occurred to Mark, as they continued with their excavations, that everything depended upon the terminal chamber. It had been closed off with stone walling, but already the resistivity meter had shown that it was polygonal in shape and that there was some kind of hearth, or pit, or burial place, in the centre of the polygon. If the function of the tomb could be discovered when the seal of this chamber was broken, then perhaps this new light would flood across all the other objects and render them visible once more. But he had to wait patiently for this revelation; he had to wait until the rest of the tumulus had been cleared, and he had reached the dry stone wall. Only then would he know what was inside the hidden room.

·48·

SEA LILY

"TOMORROW," MARK was saying, "we go inside the terminal chamber."

"Tomorrow," Kathleen repeated this flatly, almost as if she had not properly heard it. She was sitting by the bedroom window, looking down at the yard and the dusty antiques which Augustine stored there.

"Yes. At last—" But he broke off, as he watched his wife. Their dog, Jude, was lying at her feet, its head resting on her shoes; it did not look up when Mark entered the room.

Kathleen stayed in the bedroom for much of the time now, looking out of this window. There had been a period when she liked nothing more than to sit in Mark's small study, reading his books and leafing through all the magazines which he brought home. But now she avoided his room; not because she disliked it – no, not that, for there were many occasions when she longed for the peace which it had once brought her – but rather because she wanted to lay no claim upon him. That was why she had long ago ceased to mention the prospects of adopting a child, because to her it now seemed that this would be just another way of forcing herself upon him, forcing him to accept as permanent a marriage which must be more and more distasteful to him. But everything was left unsaid. There were avenues of silence down which they walked by mutual consent; they did not wish to go down the other path, of open speech, since the destination was so uncertain.

In turn Mark blamed himself for her silence and her obvious loneliness; he had become so consumed with his work upon the site that he had not fully understood her own sense of loss and, on the occasions when he had tried to enter her life, he had been so disturbed by it that he had wanted to retreat. This was how it seemed to him, at least, and he believed that she was holding herself back out

189

of reproach. But everything was left unsaid. They were so frightened of understanding their own feelings that they spoke only about those subjects which did not reveal them.

And Kathleen sat all day by the window above the yard of the antiques shop. Sometimes she would fall asleep for a few moments, and it was then as if she had been launched into infinities of darkness. But when she woke up with a start, and saw once again the dusty bowls and broken statues, she returned to consciousness with a feeling of horror. But everything was left unsaid. They spoke only about things which could not harm them. They both felt ashamed, but to admit that shame to each other might have led to the release of everything. And that could not be endured.

"At last," Mark was saying, "we'll find the secret behind the wall."

"Is there a secret?" She turned from the window and looked up at him strangely.

"Of course. If there was no secret there would be no discovery."

"But sometimes," she replied. "Sometimes the cure is worse than the disease."

She was turning something over and over in her hands, and gently he went towards her, stilled her fingers with his touch and took it from her. "What is this?" he asked her.

She seemed almost embarrassed by it. "I bought it for you. But I wasn't sure if you would want it. If you would like it."

"What is it?"

"It's a piece of sea-lily. Look, do you see its little stalks?" He held up the fossil, and in the light he could just see the striations which were the marks of its slender threads.

"It's very lovely," he said.

"No. Not lovely. I liked it because it was so strange. It is beautiful in its way. But so dead, don't you think? So dead."

She said this with such intensity that he was afraid to look at her, and so he examined the fossil once more. "Not dead," he replied. "The strange thing is that it has survived for so long. For so many thousands of years."

She had turned back to the window. "I was thinking of that," she said. "But then I couldn't see it properly. Do you understand me? It comes from some landscape I don't understand. Once it was living and growing within some unimaginable sea. Beneath some unimaginable sky. Sometimes I think the past is so mysterious that we needn't really worry about the present at all." It sounded to Mark as if she were trying to console him, but he did not know why. "It is part of our past," she went on. "Part of ourselves. And yet it is still incomprehensible."

There was some meaning behind her words, or some yearning, which he recognised but which he could not understand. "Where shall I put it?" he asked her.

"Put it here. Put it here by the window, where you'll always be able to see it." And there was something in her voice which frightened him now. But her depression seemed to lift; it was not that she became more peaceful but there was a determination – almost a fierceness – which seemed to inspire her. She stood up and, leaning heavily against the window frame, looked beyond the antiques yard at the other houses of the town. "In a way I can see them all," she said. "Other people in other rooms. All the faces. They remind me of the filaments in the sea-lily. Moving gently under the sea."

·49·

BEHIND THE WALL

"WHAT WOULD they have been like?" A young member of the excavation team was asking Martha Temple's opinion as they waited for Mark to emerge from the tumulus.

"I'm sure they would have been very nice. Probably rather like Julian in appearance."

"Short and squat, you mean?"

"Well. Shortish. And, yes, rather squat too. Don't you agree, Owen?" He came up to them with some difficulty, since around his waist there was a wide leather belt, from which were suspended a small hammer, a torch, a file, a steel ruler, a pen-knife, a measuring clip, a thermometer and his pipe. "If we can hear you above the noise of your—" she looked at the belt "—your implements."

"If you really want my opinion—"

"Of course we do. Everybody values your opinion."

"If you *really* want my opinion." He glared at her. "Previous burial sites suggest that they were of slender build. And about five and a half feet tall. They had long narrow skulls and moderately sloping foreheads."

"What did I tell you, dear?" Martha turned to the young worker. "Just like poor Julian. Perhaps that's why," she added quickly as Julian came over to join them, "perhaps that's why he seems to understand them so well. I was just saying, Julian, how well you understand the people who worshipped here."

"I don't want to be tied down to worship. I'm in one of my exploratory phases." He had been reading a novel theory on the nature of primitive ritual. "But I'm sure I'm right about—"

Mark came out of the tomb. "I think," he said, not realising that he was interrupting, "that we can begin now."

The problem was to remove enough of the dry stone wall in front of the terminal chamber to allow entrance, without disturbing the chamber or unnecessarily damaging the wall itself: it was possible, after all, that the hidden room might contain inscriptions or signs just as elaborate as those which had been scored upon the blind entrance. A single arc-light had been brought into the passageway, and it was within its narrow beam that Mark now began gently to dislodge one of the smaller stones at the top of the wall: the mortar between the stones had already been taken away, and over the last few days this first section of masonry had been tested to ensure that the balance of weight within the tumulus was not changed by its removal. So now the forces of gravity held as Mark cautiously removed the stone; the fabric of the tomb was not disturbed. And he understood that this concealing wall was in fact designed to be removed without destroying the rest of the edifice; the terminal chamber was meant to be discovered. But had its builders seen so far forward into the prospect of future time?

There was a sudden noise as Mark took away the stone – a sound like a sigh or a murmur of wind. And this is what he had feared, since the entry of air meant that the terminal chamber had once been sealed. The stream of air might now oxidise whatever was concealed here, causing any human remains to crumble and to dissolve before he could reach them. He wanted to tear down the wall quickly but he knew that he could not do so: all the stones had to be removed and labelled before he could reach beyond them. But at least he could peer into the small space he had just made; he could look into the frame of origin. In the reflected glare of the arc-lamp the terminal chamber was pierced by a band of light; but as yet Mark could see nothing beyond that light, nothing except an expanse of stone.

Over the next two days the first layer of masonry was removed and, after the excavators had moved down two feet, they could see the upper portions of the chamber in the half-light. But the remainder of the concealing wall threw a shadow across its floor. It was only when the next level of stonework was removed, and a second arc-lamp brought into the passage, that the terminal chamber was flooded with light.

It was, as expected, polygonal in structure. The roof was constructed out of one large capstone, supported by a number of orthostats – these upright stones in turn were kept in place by footing stones but the separate pillars were fitted so precisely together that, from a short distance, they seemed like one vast expanse of unbroken stone.

But it was not the stones themselves that led Mark to bow his head and close his eyes for a moment before looking up again; he had seen something else. He had seen upon the stones row upon row of curves and spirals and lines, carved deeply into the surface and entirely covering the roof and walls of the polygonal chamber. Sometimes the flow was broken by a sharp triangular mark, representing the shape of the stone axes which must have inscribed these lines, but otherwise the elaborate patterning was consistent and continuous. He could tell at once that these signs were of the same order as those marked upon the blind entrance but, if that entry stone had been a star map, here was an entire planetarium.

And then he saw the figure crouched upon the beaten earth floor – the figure lying within a shallow square pit. But it was not so much a figure as the outline of a figure, cast in sharp relief by the glare of the arc-light. These were the contours of a human shape emerging from the ground – its brownish colour so similar to the soil around it that it might have been a sculpture made out of the earth and now slowly fading back into its native element. And then Mark realised that a white object was resting on its folded knees – for a moment he thought these might be the bones of an infant or a small animal but then he saw from its blotched and already crumbling surface that this was a chalk figurine already fading into the knees of the dead. The two figures had lain together, in this long duration, and were becoming part of each other; if they had remained undisturbed for another few thousands of years they would have reverted to their chemical elements, and then the human figure and the chalk figurine would have been reconciled. But that process of reversion had now been disturbed; the excavation of the tomb had broken the bond between this body and the earth upon which it rested. The burial ritual would never now be completed.

After all these days of work Mark's hands were cut and swollen, and the atmosphere of the tomb seemed to have entered his body so that he moved and talked more slowly. Now he was changed. He put out his hands and walked towards the crouched figure but, in his wonder, he had forgotten that only half the concealing wall had been removed and as he advanced he fell heavily against it and toppled forward into the terminal chamber. He lay upon the rough surface of the floor, but he felt no hurt. "I'm sorry," he said. "I'm sorry." He did not know whom he was addressing, and his voice echoed around the small chamber before returning into his own mouth.

The others stood quietly behind the half-demolished wall, looking down both at Mark and at the body which they had unsealed. He got up, and was about to dust his hands against the side of his trousers when he realised that even the earth now smeared across them might be of value; so he held them up towards the others – his palms seemed yellow in the light – and tried to smile. "I'm sorry," he said. "I hope I haven't disturbed anything."

He was whispering, and Owen whispered back. "I don't know that you'll be disturbing *him*." He nodded towards the crouched figure.

Mark could sense their hot breath entering the tomb like a stain, and he wanted them all to leave. He wanted to be left alone with this shape upon the floor. But that would never be possible. If he had come upon it alone, there might have been some communion with the dead; but the presence of the living was too strong. "Quickly," he said. "We must work quickly. Before he fades."

◆50◆

THE HANGED MAN

IN THE days that followed the discovery they knelt beside the figure, their mouths close to the gap where his mouth had been, their arms beside his arms, studying the dissolution into which eventually they all must run. With knives and small brushes they scraped away the earth around him, to reveal the human crust which was like a raised drawing upon the earthen floor. And, when the crust was lifted off and taken away, they touched the polished brown bones which lay beneath it. This was the ancient cage from which the bird had fled. And yet, when they had reconstructed his shape, it was a form of return. Old wings beating back the air. Here was the man, his body curved forward and his hands resting upon his knees; but his head was thrown back unnaturally.

"He reminds me of someone," Martha was saying. She was trying to revive her old joke about Julian Hill's appearance. "Doesn't he remind you of someone?"

Mark saw at once that the neck had been broken. "He's been hanged," he said, without thinking. "This is the resting place of the hanged man."

Three days later he went back into the tomb, now thoroughly cleared, and stood in the centre of the terminal chamber where the square burial pit had been. He examined the star markings; he looked around at the orthostats so cunningly fitted together; he looked up at the capstone; he looked down at the earth beneath his feet. And he considered those who had stood here in another time. Their smell had gone. Their smell had faded into the stone and into the earth. And the smell of death had been displaced, too. Time. Another time. No, they are not here. They are not allowed within this sacred place. They are along the sides of the valley. They are looking down on the tumulus. There is silence when the victim is cut down from the ash tree but, when his body is carried in triumph to the tomb, there is a murmur from the assembly which gradually grows louder and louder until it becomes a great roar which reverberates along the valley. Mark passed his hand across his face because he could still hear the echo of those voices – like the sound of running water, or of whispering, confused noises which seemed to be coming from behind the stones. Coming from behind the stones at the back of the room, coming from inside the valley against which the terminal chamber rested.

He went out into the light, parting the canvas of the bright green tent which now protected the tomb. A mist had settled into the valley and had grown steadily deeper throughout the day, so that Mark could see only the silhouette of someone coming towards him. The figure had something tied around his neck – a necklace or a chain with some kind of stone or jewel suspended from it – and he held out one hand in greeting. Mark stood very still.

"Press," the figure said. "*Western News*." As he came up, Mark could see that he was a tall, thin man with a camera slung around his neck. "Is there something unusual in there? Something interesting?" He was a rheumy-eyed, middle aged man with an irrepressible air of defeat about him. "Is there anyone here who can tell me all about it? Just for a paragraph."

"I don't know." Mark hesitated. "I suppose so." The isolation of the site had meant that they had been able to work undisturbed, away from the attentions of sightseers, but the tumulus was never meant to be a secret. And for some reason he pitied the man. "You can talk to me," he said, "if you want."

"What have you got in there? Tutankhamen?" Mark looked around, as if he had come upon the tomb quite by accident and did not know how to answer. "I shan't take a minute," the journalist went on, sensing his uncertainty. "I won't bother you. I just want a paragraph."

The man's self-effacement reminded Mark of Kathleen, and the terrible outline of his guilt rose up in front of him. "Of course," he said. "Of course. There's so much to tell you." And he took the journalist through the side entrance of the tomb, explaining as he went the significance of the star-markings and the grave of the hanged man.

Two other figures were lingering in the mist a few yards away, watching them as they bowed their heads and entered the tumulus.

"I have a funny little suspicion," Martha said, raising her plaster cast in the direction of the tomb, "that we have just seen a journalist with Mark. I wonder why." In fact she had talked to the man from the *Western Press* just after he had arrived. "Of course I may be quite wrong."

"A journalist?" Julian Hill seemed alarmed by the news. "Talking to Mark? I really think I ought to do any explaining—"

"That's why it's so strange," Martha said. "But I'm sure Mark wouldn't dream of going behind your back. Or of taking all the credit."

"No." Julian was biting his finger-nail. "Of course not."

"That makes it all the more peculiar. His refusing to introduce us."

"Did he refuse?"

"As good as. Don't you think?" She lifted up her face towards him in perfect innocence.

"I'm going in."

"Oh, do." Julian rushed off into the mist. "I'll stay here," she shouted after him. "To make sure that the coast is clear."

Somebody tapped her shoulder, and she gave a little shriek. "Well well well." It was Owen. "Making trouble again, are we?"

"I don't know what you mean." It was noticeable that, with Owen, she lost much of that charming girlish manner which endeared her to everyone else. "I'm just standing here."

"I don't mean anything. I'm just standing here, too. I've been standing here for a few minutes." He looked at her suspiciously.

"It's always the same with you, Owen. Always seeing the worst in everyone. I'm surprised you can live with yourself, I really am."

"And what do you expect, when I look around me?" He stared at Martha. "I don't see any angels. I don't think any of us can fly, do you?"

She could not help smiling. "I'm sure," she said, "that poor Julian will have a theory about that, too. He's probably explaining it now." And she burst out laughing.

"Of course," Julian was saying to the journalist at that moment. "I realised at once the significance of the carvings." The three men were in the terminal chamber, trying not to notice the interior cold. "So I knew that he had to be the astronomer." Julian had not explained Mark's part in the decoding of the stones, but Mark did not seem to have noticed; he had gone up to the end wall and put his face against it as if he were listening to something else. "So we have here," Julian went on, "what I have called a Merlin figure."

"Is that right?" The thin man was scribbling into his notepad. "Merlin?"

"No. Not Merlin. A Merlin *figure*." Julian sensed a slight disappointment in the journalist so he added quickly, "Although they may be much the same thing."

"Is that right? How do you spell Merlin?"

Julian spelled it for him. "And my name is easy to remember, too," he added, sounding as unconcerned as he could. "Julian Hill. Hill as in hill." He looked over the journalist's shoulder as he wrote the name in his notebook. "You can say that I'm writing the definitive book on this site."

The journalist closed his notebook. "This," he said, "should make a very interesting story."

"I know. My book's almost finished."

"A very interesting story."

And as they spoke Mark, with an attentive look, kept his face pressed against the stones.

·51·

THE WOOD

"I WISH IT could go on and on." Kathleen was walking in front of her husband, sometimes hardly able to keep her footing on the track but hurrying nonetheless – hurrying through the great wood just beyond Colcorum village. "I could walk for ever." Jude stayed with her, sometimes bounding ahead but then just as quickly dropping back so that he might trot beside her; and occasionally he would look up at her face before resuming his own secret inspection of the undergrowth. In his own time.

A Sunday afternoon in late autumn and after a night of heavy rain Colcorum Wood seemed to be soaked in the rich and hectic green which always precedes the first frosts of the new season, like the flush on a human face just before death. Kathleen waded through the gorse and the tall thickets of brake fern, and Mark could see the brambles sticking to her red coat as she disappeared into a darker part of the forest ahead; when he caught up with her she was standing very still, and staring upward through the tangle of branches. "You know," she said, "in the fairy tale, there are giants who part the leaves and peer at the little children. I wonder who's watching us now?" In the silence they both listened to the tapping of the branches above them, and the soft noise of rain dropping from the leaves onto the mass of vegetation beneath their feet. Behind her was an old elm, and in one of its forks a pool of water had collected. Kathleen turned around and dipped her finger into it; then she made a sign of the cross. "Prayers for the dying," she said. "The dying of the light."

Mark recognised her melancholy, and tried to keep back his own feelings of helplessness before it. He was wearing a bottle-green overcoat, and now he waved his hands in the air and stamped upon the sodden ground. "Look at me," he said, trying to make her laugh

200

at the oddness of his behaviour. "I'm the famous green man!" And then he added, staring at Jude as the dog barked at him, "I'm the famous archaeologist! The robber non pareil!"

Kathleen started walking ahead. "You know how proud I am of you," she said. He knew what she meant: after he and Julian had talked to the journalist the discovery of the tomb, and of its strange occupant, had become a newsworthy and even sensational event. "You don't need me now, do you?"

"Kathleen!" He tried to catch up with her, but the path was so narrow at this point that he still had to walk behind her. He put his hands gently upon her shoulders. "Of course I need you. Who else do I have?" He brushed a leaf away from his face. "Please don't say such things."

They walked on in silence, Kathleen still keeping ahead of him, limping over the massive moss-covered roots of oak and elm, putting up her arm to part the damp branches in front of her which had already soaked her face and hair, inhaling the green secluded light. Then suddenly she stopped. "Do you hear it?" she asked. She sounded almost anxious, as if perhaps this were some hallucination of her own. But Mark heard it, too, and through the ancient trees came the sound of someone singing. The voice was coming from somewhere close to them, and Kathleen crept forward.

There was a small clearing ahead and, when they came to the edge of it, they could see an elderly man – a tramp, a vagrant, a wayfarer – sitting upon the trunk of a fallen tree and feeding bread to the wood-pigeons which clustered around him. This bread must have been his only meal since he would eat one piece himself and then throw the next one in front of him – a calm and continuous gesture, which was broken when he sensed the presence of Mark and Kathleen. Now that he realised he was no longer alone he stopped singing, and sat very still.

"I'm sorry," Kathleen said quietly, moving out from the shelter of the trees on the margin of the clearing. "We didn't know. We didn't realise . . ."

He looked down at the brace upon her leg, and made an effort to get up to greet her. Then awkwardly he sat down again.

"Do you often feed them?" she asked him. And then she added, "Is this your home?" He said nothing. It was as if he were not used to speech. But he was smiling at her, and only the brightness of his eyes showed how much he was thinking; how much, perhaps, he could have said. Jude went up to him, his tail wagging, and the old man gave him some bread also.

Kathleen watched him for a few moments, content with the silence until Mark touched her arm and led her away. "I know about him," he said after they had left the clearing. "I've seen him before."

"Why did you never tell me? Why did I never know?" She seemed to be accusing him of something which Mark failed to understand. "Jude! Jude!" She had to call the dog, who seemed reluctant to leave the old man. And then she went on, more quietly, "Is this place his home?"

"As far as I know. They call him the woodlander. Once there were three of them." And as they carried on through the wood Mark told her the story which all the villagers knew.

·*52*·

THE WOODLANDER

ONCE UPON a time there was a young boy, Michael Hare, who had been born in a cottage beside the great wood of Colcorum; he spent all of his days in that wood and so great was his attachment to it that there were some villagers who said that he must have been conceived there. That he was a child of the place. And in truth Michael was.

Here he walked among the trees, making sure that he touched each one as he passed it, and in his wanderings he took great care not to break or damage any of the foliage which bordered the narrow overgrown paths. He was careful even with the grass beneath his feet, because instinctively he knew how everything in the world could feel pain. He knew, too, how the inhabitants of the wood could also bring him consolation: there were times, in moods of great sadness, when he would curl up beneath the ancient trees and, as he slept, the earth and boughs would take the sadness from him. For this was yet another truth he had come to understand: that the natural places of the earth are imbued with the feelings of those who enter them.

After a time the animals grew to recognise him and, when they came up to him, he gave each of them names so that there was not a fox or a deer or a rabbit which did not respond to Michael's calls. But animals have no sense of time and, when the boy returned each evening to the cottage of his parents, they grieved over his loss and greeted him the next morning as if he might have left them forever. In turn Michael protected everything that lived here. He would watch at the beginning of each season for signs of damage or decay and, guided by his own inner knowledge, he knew how to repair each burrow and how, at the time of the earliest frosts, to feed the birds who would otherwise have died among the trees. As winter came he spoke to the plants and calmed them, telling them of their eventual rebirth.

But he had not remained without human companionship; he had two friends who lived not far from his cottage, and Michael taught these boys all his knowledge of the wood. So throughout the early years it became their home, too – in fact they were known to the villagers as the three spirits of the wood, and it was said that Michael had found some secret magic within this place. There were rumours that he had taught his two friends how to call the animals down into the hollows, how to find food and medicine from the plants, how to pass through the spiders' webs strung between the trees without disturbing them, and even how to remain invisible once they had gone into the wood.

But, as always in this sublunary world, there had come changes. The two friends had grown older and, without the same love for Colcorum Wood, the time came when they wished to leave it. "I must be on my way," the first one said. "I have found a girl I wish to marry, and this is no place for her." Michael said nothing, but he knew that his real family could only exist here. He smiled at his friend, and then followed him to the edge of the forest. "Take this," he said, handing him a bough of an ancient ash. "I wish you well in the world."

It was not long after that his other friend decided to leave him. "It is time for me to go," he said to Michael. "I must find work in another village." Michael nodded and said nothing, although he knew that his own work would always be here. He accompanied his friend to the edge of the wood. "Take this," he said, handing him an ash bough. Then Michael waved as his friend walked from beneath the trees and set off into the distance.

Now he was alone. He sat down upon the roots of an old oak and cried so much that his tears entered the soil (and on that spot, it is said, there grew a sunflower). The birds came to sing above his head, and one of the foxes crept up to him and put his paws upon him for consolation. So Michael was left alone in the wood as he had been as a child and, after a few days, he was able to relive the happiness of his first years – the wood relived it with him, too, and through these nights the villagers thought that they could hear the singing of birds and, although there was no wind, the excited soughing of the branches. Now he spoke to the animals alone and alone he would wander among the trees, touching them as he went.

It was then that he vowed never to leave Colcorum Wood because he understood that, without the human spirit within it, it might grow tired and then decay. But he knew also that there would be a day when his own death must come, and so now Michael began to create a map of the entire wood, marking in with different-coloured pencils its various hollows and copses; he sketched leaves and trees and stones; in a notebook he kept a record of its changing seasons; and he listed all the names of the animals whose home this was.

Eventually his parents died, and he left the cottage by the side of the wood in order to live among the trees. He gave the cottage to an old woman who, in recompense, still brings him food; he sleeps on a bed of pine needles each night, and washes in the stream each morning. The years have passed and he is growing older; but this is of no concern to him because he knows how the wood will always return to life each spring, just as the young animals always come forward to greet him at the appointed time. This is the greatest miracle of all, and sometimes he pities his two companions who live in the outer world where they cannot see such things. He knows, too, that someone will come to take his place one day, which is why he always keeps by him his drawings and maps of the great wood – to help this stranger on his way. And so the woodlander lives here still.

·53·

SWITHIN'S COLUMN

THIS WAS the story that Mark Clare told Kathleen, and she was silent for a while as they continued through the wood. She was still walking ahead of him, and he could not see her face as she said, "So he is always alone?"

"Yes. As far as I know."

"But he seems happy, don't you think?"

"He was singing."

"Yes. The wood is his world." She remembered his eyes, and how bright they seemed. They had reached the edge of the wood now, and he came up to her side as she stopped. He was about to change the real silence which had existed between them for some months: he was about to speak freely for the first time. It may have been that she sensed this, because she broke away from him and walked out from beneath the trees. "Look," she said, "there's the haunted tower!"

She was pointing towards a circular isolated hill which stood in the middle of a wide ploughed field: it was covered by fir trees but on its summit, and rising above the tree-tops, was a tower erected in the form of a classical column. It had always been known as Swithin's Column although the origin of that name, and whatever purpose the tower itself once had served, had long ago been forgotten. It was rarely visited now, and of course it had acquired the reputation of being haunted.

"I must see it," she said. "Will you come with me?" So together Mark and Kathleen walked with Jude across the field and, when they came to the foot of the hill, they could see a small path winding up towards the edifice – a path so covered with pine needles that the ground seemed to spring up under their feet as they approached the column. It was much more massive than it had seemed from Colcorum Wood; it was a true monument and, as they stood in front of a small wooden door at its base, both of them hesitated.

206

For this was not a column but a hollow tower, and the door led to some space within. Kathleen tried the door gently and at once it gave way to her touch, revealing a flight of stone steps, covered with lichen and mossy damp, which wound out of sight and clearly led upward to the top of the tower. Shafts of dim autumn light came from narrow slits set in the circular walls, and Katherine had already impulsively set her foot on the first step of the ascent. For once, however, Jude seemed curiously unwilling to follow her; the dog lay crouched on the ground, growling towards the open door. Mark softly called her back. "I think," he said, "that someone may be living here." He pointed to a scrap of paper, apparently torn from a book, which was lodged against the bottom step.

She picked up the page but its words were obscured by a green patina of vegetable decay, and she could only make out the phrase '. . . has beyond it ghastliness.' "No," she said. "No. This has been here for a long time. The tower is deserted. I can feel it."

Once again she began her climb up the relatively smooth stone steps, winding round and round the interior of the tower, as Mark trod behind; and their footsteps had a dead echo in this enclosed space, like the sound of doors shutting somewhere in the distance They climbed steadily higher, Jude reluctantly following them, and there came a moment when Kathleen had to press herself against the wall in order to give support to her withered leg; but then she looked up, and with redoubled energy continued her ascent.

Eventually they reached the summit of Swithin's Column, and found themselves in a small circular room with bare arched windows from which all the glass had been removed and from which they could see the surrounding countryside. "I told you," she said. "No one comes here any more. This place has been forgotten for a long time." They looked around and saw only some fragments of a broken bottle, a wooden chair with a sagging seat, and a small rusted tin. But these things seemed to delight Kathleen. "This is strange," she said, almost to herself. "I feel as if I know this place already. I feel as if I have been here before."

Mark looked around again, looking for some clue to his wife's sense of recognition from the damp and moss-stained walls. "Perhaps you just read about it. Everyone knows about the haunted tower."

"No. I know it in some other way." She went over to one of the large arched windows and looked out across the field. "And it isn't haunted. You know that, too, don't you?"

"I don't know anything."

"Look," she said, leaning so far out of the window that she had not
heard him. "There's the sea." She pointed across the top of Colcorum Wood to the shoreline beyond. "Do you see the difference in
the light? Do you see it? That's Lud Mouth!" He came up beside her,
alarmed by her leaning so far out. "I remember Lud Mouth," she
went on, still looking beyond the wood. "I remember going down to
the shore there when I was a child. But I never liked beaches, you
know. I felt so exposed on them." Something about the peace and
emptiness of Swithin's Column seemed to make her want to talk, and
it occurred to Mark that she was replying to some unspoken question
of his own. "I hardly ever went to the beach, so I remember this time.
I was standing by the water and there were three other children
playing in the sea just in front of me. Of course I couldn't swim. Not
with my brace. I was standing by the water and they were throwing a
ball to one another. And I was watching them. It was just a game,
but I liked to watch it. And then I remember two people walking
across the sand, and I heard the woman saying to the man, 'There's
always one who is left alone on the shore.' I wasn't embarrassed, or
anything like that, but I did move further out towards the water. Just
to show them I wasn't afraid. When I turned I could see that they
had noticed my leg. The man was blushing. He took off his hat. I
remember that. I don't know why, but he took off his hat and held it
in his hands. Perhaps he was just frightened that the wind would
blow it away—"

Mark had been that man upon the shore. He stood very still,
hardly able to breathe. Time. All these years, and she had never
known. Another time. Time encircling him.

"—my parents were sitting close to me and they had heard the
woman's remark, too. And at the same time they came up to me, and
my mother picked me up in her arms and kissed me. But my father's
head was bowed. And then I remember we were sitting in a little
wooden hut in front of the beach – you know those huts, don't
you?—"

"Yes. I know them."

"—and we were having our tea. It was very quiet. And it was as if
they felt guilty for making me the way I was, and I felt guilty for
being the way I was. I was only a little girl, but I understood that
even then. Somehow we all pitied each other, but no one could say

anything about it. There was such a feeling of helplessness. Such sadness." Kathleen broke off and turned to Mark for the first time. "Such sadness. But why did I think of it now? Why did I think of it here?"

He thought that he understood the reason; he sensed that she was talking about their own life together, a life begun when he had looked at her on the shore of Lud Mouth. She had no idea that he was the stranger who had seen her then, that this had been the beginning, but somehow she had remembered the scene all the same. Time. Time encircling them both. He put his arm around her. "We ought to go," he said. "We ought to go before it gets dark."

PART FIVE

"I often experience a kind of fear of the sky after sitting in the observing chair a long time," he answered . . . *"That's partly what I meant by saying that magnitude, which up to a certain point has grandeur, has beyond it ghastliness."*

Two on a Tower
Thomas Hardy

•54•

CORONA

"LOVELINESS IS everywhere. Everywhere is loveliness." As they emerged from the back of an old blue-and-white van, they began clapping their hands and singing. There were seven of them, all wearing long blue robes with white headbands, and only when they came closer to the tumulus did Evangeline Tupper realise that there were five young women leading the way while two men followed a few paces behind. "Loveliness is everywhere. Everywhere is loveliness." They kept on clapping and singing until they came within a few feet of Evangeline. One of the young women came forward with her arms outstretched. "Softness is strength," she chanted. "Strength is softness."

"I thought," Evangeline said, "that was an advertisement for something."

The young woman's perfectly serene smile did not waver. "Are you the Feminine Principle?"

"I'm in charge of the site, if that's what you mean."

The young woman turned joyfully to the others. "Everything is female," she murmured. "Female is everything." They all laughed gaily, and clapped at this news.

"I would be the first to agree with you," Evangeline replied, thinking of Baby Doll. "Under normal circumstances." But these were not normal circumstances: as soon as news of the discovery had been published, a large number of visitors had converged upon Pilgrin Valley; it was only with the help of the Dorsetshire police that the site was now protected from those who had come to see the grave of "Merlin" or "the lost king of Wessex" or "the great astronomer", as it was variously interpreted. At the first sign of public enthusiasm Evangeline Tupper had hurried down from London and, with Hermione, had ensconced herself in the Blue Dog to cope with what she insisted on calling the "invasion". She also took over Mark

213

Clare's Portakabin by the site and was now, as Martha Temple took great pleasure in explaining to everyone, "Queen of all she surveyed".

"Everything is female. Female is everything." The young women had all taken up the chant and formed an excited little half-circle around Evangeline.

"It is a *lovely* thought, I know. But this particular female everything has to draw the line somewhere." They continued to smile. "You can't stop here, I'm afraid. The tomb has to be protected."

"Protected against us?" The young woman waved her hand in the direction of the others. "We are all here to worship. Presence is worship. Worship is presence."

"That's exactly what I've always said. But, to be devastatingly frank with you, we have had so many, so many—" she searched for the right word to describe the various cults which had travelled to the tomb "—so many groups that we simply can't let you in." And in fact the site was now surrounded by a high wire fence. "It was a dreadful decision. I agonised night and day until I was prostrate. But there it is, my darling." Evangeline was rather taken by this young worshipper. "What *is* your name, by the way?"

"I am called Corona." Corona had remained very serene and now with a light laugh she put out her hand to introduce the others. "This is Sagilla, this is Auriga, this is Ursa and this is Spica." Each of the young women giggled and blushed as she was introduced.

"What lovely names! And what an extraordinary coincidence that they should all end with the same letter. Although," she added, shaking her head at the foibles of the young, "I don't think I've ever read of a Saint Spica. Not in the Christian calendar, at least."

Corona joined in their happy laughter. "These are our sky names," she said. "We no longer have earth names."

"And the males?" Evangeline looked somewhat sternly at the two young men who had remained a few feet behind the others.

"Corvus and Cetus have been instructed. They have increased their feminine quotient."

"My assistant would be terribly interested in that," Evangeline replied. And then she added: "Her earth name is Hermione Crisp. But her sky name is Baby Doll."

Corona did not seem to understand this reference, and in fact it was not clear if she understood anything. "We would be happy to meet this sister."

"Actually she's not my sister. She's my – well, let's not go into that now." It was a cold winter morning, and Evangeline pretended to shiver. "You really will have to leave now, darlings. Goodbye." Her enthusiasm had vanished as quickly as it had arrived; she started walking back to her Portakabin, and gave a little wave to the group without turning around to look at them again. "Terribly sorry," she shouted into the air.

Martha Temple and Julian Hill had been watching this scene from behind the wire fence with barely disguised amusement. They were both on the 'duty roster' for this day's supervision of the site but, even on such a cold morning as this, they did not seem to mind – in fact they now enjoyed each other's company, united as they were in their firm but always unspoken hatred for Evangeline Tupper. "She handles such things so well, doesn't she?" Martha said. The cast had come off her arm, and she was her old cheerful self.

"She's a pro. A real old pro."

"Explain yourself, Julian." Martha gave him a playful tap. "I presume you mean that she gets on very well with those young women. Those pretty young girls."

"I don't know if she was right to send them away." Julian had been reading some radical sociology on the subject of primitive societies and, his eyes once again fixed on the distance as he spoke, he now happily launched into a new concept. "Many of these modern cults," he said, "would have the same beliefs as the working men who were forced to build the tomb."

"I don't think Evangeline bothers her head about little things like that. She's much more concerned with making statements to the newspapers. And the television cameras." This was a direct hit, since it was her assumption of a public role that had infuriated Julian Hill; and now with an innocent smile Martha walked over to the group of young women.

They did not seem at all displeased by their encounter with Evangeline; they had now formed a circle and, with arms raised, they were gazing at the sky at the same time as they let out a prolonged high note. Martha Temple stood near them and waited for the ululation to end. Then she exclaimed, "Let joy be unconfined!"

"The hymn is old Mother." Corona was as serene as ever. "Old Mother is the hymn."

"I hope," Martha replied, "that you weren't referring to

Evangeline." Corona made no response and it occurred to Martha that her smooth, soft face might conceivably be an index of blankness as much as anything else. "But don't pay any attention to her," she went on. "She has many personal problems which we probably wouldn't understand." Then she added, confidentially, "There is some sort of camp at the other end of the valley, by the way. There are lots of you there."

Corona clapped her hands excitedly. "Thank you," she said. "We will sing for you tonight. We will sing The Menstrual Song."

"I've always wanted to hear that."

The others also clapped their hands at the wonderful news of the evening's celebration, and then by some mute instinct they all turned together and, with their laughter tinkling like little bells, skipped down the slope of Pilgrin Valley towards their battered van.

As soon as they had gone Evangeline emerged from the Port-akabin. "Weren't they an absolute nightmare?" she said, coming up to Martha. "I hope they've crawled back to their slums."

"Actually their leader said—"

"—her name was Corona, dear. Like the fizzy drink. Isn't it a joke?"

"I think Corona said they were going to that awful camp. I don't know how they heard about it."

"I don't believe it! This is the *end*." There had already been complaints from the villagers of Colcorum about the makeshift site created in Pilgrin Valley. "I'm going to take poison," she went on. "Take absolute poison." Martha gave her an encouraging smile. "I can't have those silly bitches hanging around my neck."

"Are you sure?"

"Of course I'm sure." Evangeline was breathing very heavily, and scraped the ground with her foot. She seemed to be preparing herself for a decision. "I'm going down there," she said. "I'm going to talk to them. I'll show them what the Eternal Feminine is all about."

·55·

THE TRAVELLERS

EVANGELINE TUPPER drove almost a mile along the track until she came to the southern entrance of Pilgrin Valley, which was so narrow at this point that the camp site had spread across both slopes. It was not a large camp but, in the month since accounts of the tumulus had appeared in the newspapers, groups of various kinds had settled here until now there were almost a hundred people cooking in the open and washing in the Pilgrin stream. Amongst them were a number of travellers who lived in caravans and seemed to move on restlessly from one 'sacred' site to the next, but there were also solitary people who arrived without any apparent purpose and, in addition, there was a small troupe which called itself the Theatre of Peace.

In fact, just as Evangeline arrived, the Theatre was running through one of its performances for the benefit of the others – the young travellers to one side, Corona and her delightful bevy of sisters to the other. Several actors were linking hands, making what might have been the shape of a pentagon or of a star, while in the middle three others curled up in little balls and made moaning noises. Evangeline got out of her car and walked towards the crowd. "I do beg your pardon," she said to a young man who was part of the audience. "But what do I have the privilege of watching?"

"They represent the birth pangs of world peace."

"Of course. I thought I recognised it."

"And the star is the sign of unity through difference."

Corona had heard the last phrase and began singing joyfully, "Unity is Difference. Difference is Unity!"

"Oh hello darling." Evangeline turned to greet her. "Fancy meeting you here." She might have been at a cocktail party, despite the fact that the theatrical troupe had suddenly put on clown masks and with great ceremony were handing artificial flowers to various members of the audience. Evangeline took one. "A daffodil," she said. "My favourite. Thank you so much."

"The great thing is," the young man said, "they don't use words. They don't think much of words any more."

"I can see that."

"No." He looked across at her for the first time. "Don't make fun of them. They're not doing any harm."

"I'm so sorry." And in fact Evangeline was genuinely abashed by this rebuke. "I didn't know you were with them. I must be really out to lunch."

She thought that this phrase might endear her to the young man, but plainly it did not have the appropriate effect. "I'm not with them," he said sternly. "I just don't like to see them hurt."

In fact, as Evangeline was later to discover, he was with the travellers themselves. There were thirty of them, twelve couples still in their twenties, and six small children. Somehow they seemed rougher than the others on the camp-site, with that unmistakable air of having been raised in cities. They were all unemployed; they were poor; and, in a sense, they were desperate. It may be that they had come to Pilgrin Valley to be close to a world which was somehow different from the one which oppressed them and offered them no hope – as if the passage grave represented a reality deeper and richer than the one through which they were forced to move. Or it may have been that they had come here to propitiate the earth, to ask for help in their extremity.

"I'm not with them," he repeated. "But we're all in this together. We help each other."

"Isn't it strange," Evangeline answered. "I'm in a caring profession too. In some ways I'm the chief carer."

She may have been about to explain the nature of that profession when suddenly the members of the Theatre of Peace tore off their clown masks, jumped up on each other's shoulders to form a human pyramid and began to exclaim, "Peace not war! Peace not war!" Evangeline joined in the cry and, in the general excitement, Corona and her sisters began chanting, "Joy! Joy! Joy!"

The human pyramid was breaking up when Evangeline saw her opportunity to make a dramatic public statement. She rushed into the centre of the ring and, while there were still three members of the troupe with their backs bent to take the weight of the others, began hauling herself onto them. "Help me up," she said to the others.

"I've got a little speech to make." After a few moments, when she was being supported and precariously balanced on top of them, she began to speak in a loud voice. "Fellow carers!" she said. "And caring persons! You all know me. You know that I am looking after the tomb to which you have all come to pay your respects—" She made it sound like an unavoidable social obligation.

"No. Not our respects." This was the young man again. "We came here because there is nowhere else to go."

"Absolutely." She did not like to be interrupted.

"Peace will start here!" someone else called out.

"It *is* lovely and quiet, isn't it?" With a brief smile of sympathy, she launched upon the speech she had been preparing in the car. "But I must beg you. I beg you on my bended knees." Such was her precarious position that at this moment she could only manage a little bob, which sent tremors through the backs of those supporting her. "Please do not try and enter the site. It is very fragile. We still have much to do there." She flung out her arm, and was only saved from toppling over by the young man holding onto her right leg. "We ask for your understanding and, yes, your forgiveness too. Many of us have toiled for days and nights, laboured for nights and days. Many of us have planned and dreamed for years to bring this project to fruition. So if we have a fault. And of course we all have faults." She gave a sad smile. "If we have a fault, it is the fault of being patient and of being terribly, terribly careful. Forgive us our faults. Help us to protect the site." Evangeline, carried away by her new role as progenitor of the whole excavation, threw out both arms in the direction of her audience. "We love you all, yes, and we share your love of the tomb. But give us time. Give us space. One day it will all be yours. And, if I should ever, ever let you down, I promise you this. No mortal punishment would be too severe for me." At this she put her hands against her chest and bowed her head. Then after a pause for reflection she blew a kiss at her audience, but this sudden shift in her weight was too much for her bearers who began to break under the strain. Even as she was being applauded she slipped down between them, and was only just caught before falling heavily to the ground.

"Perhaps," someone called out, "perhaps we're connected with the tomb in any case. Perhaps there is a ley line."

"Of course." Evangeline was a little flustered by her sudden descent, but she was determined to retain her dignity. "I know all about it." She flung out her arm in the general direction of the tumulus. "There is a gorgeous line which runs all the way down the valley. I have trod upon it myself." She began ceremoniously to walk away, her mission fulfilled, when the young traveller called out after her, "Can we stay here, then?"

She did not turn back but called out, "That has nothing to do with me. You must ask the parish authorities." And, as she returned to the track above the valley, she whispered to herself, "Well, Miss Tupper, I do think that was something of a triumph."

But before she could reach her car someone put his hand upon her shoulder and, with a gasp, she glanced around. It was a middle-aged man wearing a purple open-necked shirt, despite this winter weather, with a variety of bead necklaces and bangles. "I have something of great importance to tell you," he said.

Evangeline was impatient to get back to her warm office. "I'm all ears."

"You think you're going forward. But you're not. You're going backward."

"That does sound exciting. Does it take a lot of practice?"

"You don't understand me, do you?"

"There is a definite possibility that you are too deep for me. Yes."

"There is something wrong in the valley. Something evil in the tomb. Don't you feel it?"

"At this precise moment, I don't feel anything."

He put his hand up to his face, as if he were literally brushing aside her words. "Please remember this." He spoke very slowly now. "In the beginning there is an end. In the end there is a beginning."

"You know," Evangeline said, drawing the conversation to a close. "I have been saying that *all my life*. But people just won't listen, will they? Goodbye."

She hurried back to her car, and he watched her. "Remember," he shouted. "When you find yourself in the dark."

•56•

TEA TIME

"HAVE ANOTHER cup that—what is the cup supposed to do?" Floey and Hermione were sitting in the house which the Hanovers had rented near the Cobb.

"Cheers."

"And to you, Tiger." Both women raised their cups. They now spent a great deal of time in each other's company, and were already thoroughly comfortable. "Seriously. What is it supposed to do?"

Hermione laughed. "Flo, you're game. I could go into the jungle with you."

"Let's hope it doesn't come to that, Tiger. I wouldn't know what to do with all those rum-babas."

Hermione rarely bothered to correct Floey's misappropriation of words; in fact she rather enjoyed them. "So tell me," she went on. "Why are you being so mysterious about Joey?"

As soon as Hermione arrived Floey had said, rather significantly, that her husband was "with his new relations" but so far she had refused to be drawn any further. Now the time had come, and with monumental deliberation she replaced her tea-cup in its saucer. "Well," she said. "This is between you and me and—" She could not exactly recall the other member of this triumvirate of secrecy.

"Gatepost. Of course I won't tell."

"Don't forget, Tiger. Pigs have ears, you know."

"Don't beat around the bush, Floey."

"Are you sure it's *beating* around the bush? I was always under the impression that—"

"Come on. Spit it out."

"Well." So Floey told her old school-friend about Joey's search for his origins, his recognition of the cottage, his conversation with the Mints, the discovery that his parents were dead and the revelation that he was Farmer Mint's cousin. "Family, family, family," Floey added towards the end of the story. "That's all they talk about." She glared at her tea-cup before picking it up again to inspect its cracked base. "You would think that they were despots or something interesting. Instead of farmers."

"But they're men, Floey." Hermione felt in the pocket of her tweed jacket, and took out a packet of cigarettes. "They're idealists. They're much more sensitive. Much more delicate. They haven't seen as much of the world as we have."

"I suppose not." This explanation did not altogether satisfy her. "And there's another thing. They're having some kind of family reunion in the dead of winter. Of course I haven't been invited. I'm not a precious Mint. I'm a persona no thank you."

"Non grata?"

But Floey wasn't listening. "Hush," she said. "I hear his tiny footsteps. Talk about something else." And, when Joey finally entered the room, the two women were amicably discussing the future of the coal-mining industry.

"What a lovely sight," he said. "Two old friends by the fireside." He took off his cap – he owned a flat cap now, exactly the same as Farmer Mint's – and bowed to Hermione.

She bowed in return and put out her hand. But instead of shaking it he kissed it, and then began to croon

> "Mid the smiles of bright eyed lasses—"

Here he bowed again.

> "And the sight of dear old friends—"

"He should go back into the business," Floey remarked loudly to her old school-friend. "He's wasted down here."

> "When the merry chink of glasses—"

He picked up a tea-cup and gave it a little flick with his finger.

> "In some jolly chorus blends."

He went over to his wife and kissed her on the cheek. "And I do feel jolly, girls. I feel very jolly." In fact the experiences of the last few weeks seemed to have rejuvenated him. There had been a time when, without any proper knowledge of the past, he saw ahead of him only the unfathomable and therefore unfair process of ageing; why should he have begun to die when he did not truly know who he was? But the discovery of his family had allowed him to see his life as part of some larger continuity and, just as he could now look backward with more confidence, so also could he look forward. The world, before, had been merely an index of his own ageing; but now it seemed to him to contain the possibility of change, to be always capable of renewal.

"I saw your other half just now," he said to Hermione. "She was in the old valley." This was a phrase which Farmer Mint always used, but now Joey hurried over it in case she should ask him his reasons for being there. "She was talking to some campers," he added quickly.

"Campers?"

"That sort of thing. Young people, anyway. But she wasn't just talking to them." He could not help laughing. "She was standing on a human pyramid. You know, Floey, like Boothroyd and Jones."

"Contortionists extraordinaire?"

"That's them. And then," he said, suddenly adopting his most melancholy expression, "she fell off. She fell between them."

"Was she hurt?" Both women asked the question at the same time.

"Not at all. She just carried on talking."

Hermione rubbed her hands with delight. "That's Evangeline for you," she said. "Always on the ball." The Hanovers smiled politely. It was clear to her that they were not altogether impressed by this commendation but she, at least, understood the nature of her companion's effusiveness and hysteria: Evangeline still possessed the selfish and impetuous needs of her childhood, a childhood from which she had never been rescued, and so her relations with the world came hurtling downwards, as it were, at a wrong angle. "Well," she said, picking up her fedora from the chair next to her own, "Goodbye dearies. I must leave you." She made a point of shaking hands with both of them.

"Are we to part like this?" Joey said.

"Sorry. Got to see a man about a dog."

"That woman," Joey muttered after she had gone, "is particularly charming. She makes me go all funny. All queer."

Floey made no response but, to her husband's surprise, started making a series of animal noises – those of pig, lamb, cow, and mule in quick succession. Then she stopped and, with a placid expression, asked, "How's Farmer Giles?"

Now Joey understood. "The family is very well. But it's not nice to mock, Flo. Not nice in the least."

"I'm not mocking. I'm making a point." But, when she saw his wounded look, she relented. "I'm sorry," she said. "But we've been here months now. Let's be ornithological. Let's face facts."

"But that's exactly it. I'm looking for facts. I'm still looking for my parents. I'm still trying to find out what happened to them. I can't leave it unfinished. That makes me feel unfinished."

"You'll live." But there was a trace of sympathy in her voice.

"Yes, I'll live. And then I'll die. Like them."

"Can't we go home now? Just for a few days?"

For some reason this seemed to cheer Joey, and he got up from his chair. "What's the old song, Flo? We all go the same way home. All the collection in the same direction. We all go the same way home. Shall we dance?" He went up to her and, gently lifting her to her feet, began to waltz with her around the small room as he crooned the old song. But then suddenly he stopped. "While we're on the subject of facts," he said, still holding her in the centre of the room, "there is something strange. I don't know yet. But it's something to do with the valley."

·57·

THE MEETING

"THERE MUST be a law against them. There's always a law against people like that." The speaker was a small, thin, bespectacled woman with her hair tied up in a bun. "I've lived in this village for thirty years," she added, as if this provided conclusive proof.

"I don't think this is a time to speak of laws, Miss Ford." The vicar of Colcorum had risen. "I feel sure that we should be addressing their need for faith. Think of the early church. It seems to me that we must not *judge* them." A meeting had been convened in the village hall of Colcorum – a low-ceilinged barn which was used for every activity, from bingo meeting to memorial service – and almost all of the villagers had gathered here to mount a protest against the campsite in Pilgrin Valley. Some of those concerned with the tumulus had also come: sitting on the cheap plastic chairs, among the villagers, were Evangeline Tupper and Hermione Crisp, Mark and Kathleen Clare and, standing at the back, Farmer Mint and Boy Mint. "The early church, don't you see, was such a prayerful gathering of folk. Such a lesson. It seems to me."

"What on earth is he talking about," Evangeline whispered to her friend. "Where is this early church?"

"Coffee?" Miss Chancellor's coffee was famous throughout Colcorum, and only strangers to the village seemed willing to accept it as she went amongst them with a tray.

"Haven't you got anything stronger?" Evangeline asked her as she was passed a cup of the gruel-like liquid.

"I do have some Earl Grey, dear. Would you care to partake?"

"No. I think I'll partake some other time."

"The early church, don't you see, had a lovely communal togetherness. A lovely feeling for life in all its felt complexity—"

"I'm getting quite dizzy," Evangeline muttered, in a slightly louder voice.

And the sound of Farmer Mint and Boy Mint chuckling at the back of the hall was also perfectly audible as another villager got up from his chair to address the meeting. "I say we surprise them. We surround them and then we attack."

"Now we're getting somewhere," Evangeline added to Hermione. And with a certain amusement she turned around to look at the speaker – a tall middle-aged man wearing a tweed jacket. He sounded measured and precise, but there was an undertone of panic in his voice which stirred a sense of unease throughout the room. Evangeline, however, smiled and nodded at him in encouragement.

"We could," he was saying, "set fire to their caravans. Steal up on them and put them to the torch. I'm a great believer in the scorched earth policy."

Evangeline was enjoying herself. "They are *barbaric* in the country, aren't they?" she whispered. "Nature absolutely red in tooth and claw."

"More beverage anyone? Still deliciously hot."

"No thank you, darling." Evangeline handed back her cup to Miss Chancellor. "One cup goes a long way in this parish."

"Or," the speaker was saying, "we could bring in the army—"

"Or you could eat shit!" He stopped at this interruption, although very few of the villagers bothered to turn their heads towards the old woman, dressed in a patchwork of old clothes, who had appeared at the door of the village hall. "Help me in," she added in a peremptory voice, and at once two of the younger members of the audience rushed over to her and supported her on each arm as slowly she made her way to the front of the hall. She had a strange decayed smell, a distillation of moth balls and old eau de cologne. "Sit me down." And, although in fact there seemed to be no reason why she could not perform these movements for herself, they duly put her slowly into a plastic chair. Now she turned to the villagers behind her, her expression as blind and immobile as that on a death mask.

Certainly her arrival seemed to have discomposed the last speaker and, sensing his opportunity, the vicar was once more on his feet. "Surely we are all Christian folk, part of a broad church—"

"Balls." It was the old woman, who had turned to stare fixedly at the vicar.

"If Mrs Trout will allow me to continue," he said, rather sadly. "I want to direct your attention to the plight of the young people. We owe the young a great debt, especially our friends in the valley who are so desperately seeking for faith and inspiration—"

"Fuck them." It was the old woman again.

Evangeline turned to Hermione. "Pin your ears back," she said, giggling. "This is becoming an absolute joke."

In her excitement she had spoken quite loudly and a man, wearing a white jacket and yellow cravat, turned around. "Didn't you know?" he said. "We are much more amusing in the country. Much more civilised." The old woman was just hurling the word "Wanker!" at the vicar. "And Lola Trout is such a splendid creature, isn't she?" he went on. "Even though she has never left the village, her behaviour is quite metropolitan."

"Is she always so foul-mouthed?"

"Just her natural enthusiasm. But underneath I am told she is sophistication itself."

"I don't think I want to look down that far," Evangeline replied. "Oh dear, do you want me?" This last remark was addressed at the vicar, who was smiling at her and lifting his florid eyebrows in her direction.

"Perhaps," he was saying, "one of our friends from the excavation might care to enlighten us. Give us the privilege of her thoughts, woefully in need of instruction as we all are."

Evangeline rose to her feet, and could distinctly hear the sound of the Mints' laughter as she prepared to speak. "I know," she shouted, "exactly what you are feeling. Every fibre of my body throbs with you. Because I, too, have suffered at their hands." Presumably she was referring to the group camped in Pilgrin Valley, although she did not specify the exact nature of her suffering. "But what more can I do? I have informed the Forestry Commission, who own the land. The police are guarding the excavations night and day—"

"Cunts!"

Evangeline rode over Mrs Trout's interjection. "Or so I am told by the proper authorities. And, apart from that, I am helpless. I am as nothing." She caught sight of the Mints grinning at her, and added for their benefit, "I am trussed up like a chicken." She wrapped her arms around herself, to symbolise her plight, and then sat down to murmurs of approval from the villagers at her colourful speech.

The vicar jumped up, to forestall some terrible interruption from Mrs Trout who seemed to be asking for more assistance. "May I call for a vote of thanks—" He had been calling for votes of thanks since he moved to Colcorum, and the gesture was instinctive.

But before he could call anything, Kathleen Clare brushed aside her husband's arm and stood up. She was very pale. "You are all wrong," she said. "All of you." Lola Trout became quite still. "The valley doesn't belong to you. Or to the Forestry Commission. It doesn't belong to anyone. It has got nothing to do with us." Savagely she pushed her right hand through her hair and Mark half-rose beside her. "This is a place for the dead. The living are not wanted. They're not needed yet. Can't you tell? Or perhaps you know that very well. Perhaps you've always known it." Mark stood up, put his arm around his wife and gently led her from the hall. She was limping very badly, because she knew that the others were watching her.

There was a momentary silence and then the vicar began once more. "That was a most interesting contribution, I thought, to our discussion. Quite refreshing." And the villagers murmured their agreement, happy to arrive at the conclusion that nothing, really, had happened at all. That nothing had been said.

But, also by common consent, it was time to go. Mrs Trout, supported on both sides, led the way out of the village hall but, as she passed Evangeline, she was able unaided to stick one finger in the air. Evangeline seemed about to protest but the vicar came up behind her, and said apologetically, "Testing for wind, no doubt." The Mints followed, chuckling in unison at a joke which no one else had as yet understood.

The two ladies were the last to leave and, as they walked onto the gravel path which encircled the village hall, Evangeline took out a packet of Woodbines and offered one to Hermione before herself deeply inhaling. "I thought my chicken image was very good," she said. "Wasted on them, of course." She looked anxiously around for the Clares and, when she saw their car turning the corner, she let out a deep sigh. "Thank God they've gone," she said. "Wasn't the wife a nightmare? I wouldn't be at all surprised if she were some kind of witch. I feel so sorry for poor dear Mark."

"Do you? Actually, I feel sorry for her. It can't be easy."

Evangeline seemed surprised by this. "You and your girlish sympathies," she said, rather nervously. "You are far too sweet and sensitive for your own good. Now let's get out of this hell hole."

MAUVE COTTAGE

"SUCH A charming interlude, didn't you think?" The yellow cravat had walked up to them, extending his hand. "Fraicheur," he said. "Augustine Fraicheur." He sidled between them and, as Hermione smiled at him, linked their arms in his. "Don't you find the country rather noisy after London, Miss Tupper? We like it, but to more sensitive ears . . ."

"It's terribly sweet of you to ask. Of course my assistant, Miss Crisp, suffers much more than I do. She is terribly delicate, as you can see." Augustine glanced at the squat and dark-suited figure beside him, as Evangeline went on to say, "How do you know my name, by the way?"

Augustine gave a little shriek. "Our mutual friends, of course! The Hanovers. I dote on them, don't you?"

Evangeline nodded enthusiastically. "I feel so close to them sometimes, it's almost frightening."

"I agree. And they're so fond of you, too. From their description, I would have known you both anywhere."

This did not sound particularly like a compliment to Evangeline, but Hermione was rather touched. In any case, a friend of Floey Hanover was a friend of hers. "Would you care for a fag?" she asked him.

"I beg your pardon?" For some reason he seemed offended by this. "A cigarette?"

"Oh, dear no. I'm afraid in the country we don't have such unspoiled tastes. I envy you, I really do."

"Well," Evangeline replied, "I have been described as a man's man."

"I don't doubt that for a second."

She was growing uneasy with this conversation, and disengaged herself from Augustine's arm. "Do tell," she said, quickly changing the subject, "who was that dog's dinner in the front row? That one over there." She pointed towards Mrs Trout, who was now being carried down the main street as if she were Guy Fawkes being taken to a bonfire.

"That's dearest Lola. Lola Trout. Quite the uncrowned queen of Colcorum, if I do say so myself." The three young men carrying her for a moment wavered under the burden, and he laughed. "We must seem terribly decadent in the country. Almost Roman."

"Do you have many queens in the rural areas?" Evangeline asked, without the trace of a smile.

"They say there's one in every village. But I wouldn't really know, would I?" He laughed more loudly than before. "And I'm not going to say another word about Lola until you come in for a Campari." They had been walking down the main street, and now Augustine stopped at the door of a small cottage. He looked up at the sign above it, 'Mauve Cottage', ornately carved in wood. "Named after a great chum of mine who owned it. Mauve Freedom Hooper. Did you know him?"

Both ladies shook their heads. "Tragic death," he said. "Absolutely tragic. Do come in." They entered what might have been a museum of Regency style – the striped wallpaper in white and rose, the set of elbow chairs in a dark wood, the mahogany side-tables, the sofa covered with blue silk, the footstool with its brocade covering, the polished wooden floor, the damask curtains. "Do sit anywhere," Augustine said. "I always do."

Evangeline looked around for a brief moment and then put up her hands in a little act of homage. "I've never seen anything so beautiful in my *life*. I could perfectly easily die here."

"Yes. That's what happened in Mauve's case." He tried to remain solemn, but he could not suppress a smile. "It is rather special, isn't it?"

"You have a gift. An absolute gift. Let me touch you."

Augustine Fraicheur nervously backed away from Evangeline, although in fact she had no intention of actually putting her hand upon him. "I do deal in antiques, after all," he said, as if warding off a blow. Then he became confidential again. "Actually, my shop is beneath them."

"Them?"

"You know. The Clares. The crippled woman. And your archaeological friend."

"That woman is so brave," Evangeline said. "I was just saying that to my assistant. Wasn't I, Miss Crisp?"

Hermione stared at her but did not reply, and Evangeline turned instantly to Augustine. "I don't want a Campari," she said. "Do you have any real ale?"

"I'm afraid we don't have real ale in the country, Miss Tupper. Our natural tastes have been quite spoiled. Would a malt whisky be too cravenly sophisticated?"

"As long as it's neat," she said.

"Not even a little Perrier?"

"No. As rough as you've got it."

"Snap," he said, "I like it rough too." And with a little giggle he disappeared, only to emerge a few moments later with a silver tray bearing three drinks. He settled down on the sofa. "Don't you think," he said, holding up his gin-and-tonic, "that the chink of glasses must be one of the oldest sounds in the world?"

"I'm sure," Evangeline replied, "that it is in this household."

Augustine was beginning to enjoy this conversation. "Now tell me," he said. "Who were we going to gossip about?"

"You were telling us about the fascinating Lola Trout."

"Do you have a handkerchief?"

Hermione took him literally, and pulled out from the breast pocket of her dark suit a large white cloth. "Here," she said. "Blow on this."

"I only meant," Augustine said, politely declining the proffered article, "that it is a very sad story."

"Don't tell me!" Evangeline exclaimed. "I know I shall cry buckets. I always do."

Augustine took a large gulp of his gin. "Do you remember that very tall man who spoke in the village hall?"

"The one who had the terribly good idea of calling in the army?"

Augustine nodded. "That was Mr Trout."

Evangeline opened her eyes very wide. "You don't mean . . ."

"Lola's son."

"Oh." She sounded disappointed.

"But he hasn't spoken to his mother for twenty-six years." He took another large gulp. "Isn't it divine?"

Evangeline swirled the whisky in her glass, and looked at Augustine through it. "There can't have been anything like it since the Borgias. Do tell."

"It's too ghastly, really." Savouring the suspense, he left the room quite suddenly and returned with bottles of drink. "But as long as it's strictly *entre nous*?"

Evangeline bowed her head for a moment. "No force on earth could drag it from me."

"Well. There were three Trouts. Father. Son. And Lola. Now personally I love difficult women, don't you?"

"I don't think," Evangeline replied, "that I have ever met one. Have you, Miss Crisp?" Hermione shook her head slowly.

"Aren't you the lucky ones?" Despite his firmly creased beige trousers, and his yellow cravat, and his white jacket – he might have passed as an English gentleman of the pre-war years – Evangeline was beginning to suspect that there was in fact something rather vulgar about him. And his watery eyes seemed to gleam as he surveyed the two women above the rim of his glass. "The point is that Lola is an absolute bitch." He uttered the last word with relish. "The late Mr Trout, her husband, was also a bit of a bitch. And so . . ." He took another gulp.

"And so?"

"He passed on."

"He left Colcorum?" Evangeline was becoming impatient with Augustine's somewhat cryptic remarks.

"Oh dear no. Nobody leaves Colcorum." His fingers fluttered towards the ceiling. "He was taken up into a larger bosom than Lola Trout's."

"He kicked the bucket, did he?"

"He positively dented it, dear. Everyone said that it must have been a heart attack. Everyone, that is, apart from the son. Simon Trout. Simon knew what bitches—" again he savoured the word "— what bitches his parents were, and he claimed that the mother had poisoned the father. I don't know what evidence he had, but Lola has always been very good with her herbs. Potions of this. Potions of that. Positively out of the jungle, dear. Anyway, terrible scenes follow. He accuses her. And you know that Joan Crawford gaze she's got?" Augustine Fraicheur opened his eyes very wide, and something close to a basilisk stare swept over the walls of Mauve Cottage. "A bit like that. Then she slaps him. He slaps her. And then she throws him out of the house. And *then* she burns his bed and all of his clothes. I don't know what happened after that – we never pry in the country, have you noticed that? – but I do know that they haven't

232

spoken to each other since. And that was twenty-six years ago. Isn't it a scream?" He leapt up again to pour some more drinks. "We are absolutely wicked in the country, aren't we? It must come as a shock after the primitive innocence of London."

"That is the most ghastly story I have ever heard in my life." Evangeline almost intoned the words. "Just look at me! I can't stop shaking!" She held out her right hand, which seemed only momentarily to tremble. "But tell me this." Disappointed, she withdrew her hand from public examination. "Just tell me this. Why weren't the police informed at once?"

"Oh no." Augustine seemed unsettled. "They don't like Lily Law around here. Pardon my French. The boys in blue are not welcome in Colcorum. Besides, Lola was related."

"I knew it! I knew there was blue blood in her. I was telling Miss Crisp that there was something highly aristocratic about her general bearing."

"No, my darling." The more drunk Augustine became, the more intimacy he assumed. "Nothing to do with Debrett's. Lola Trout is related to the Mints."

"The Mints! But I adore the Mints too!"

"Of course." Augustine did not sound altogether sure of his own feelings. "Aren't they lovely? And so clean, too." In mock horror he clapped his hand over his mouth. "I didn't say that, did I? It must have been someone very large and very outspoken just behind me. Bottoms up." He took another large swallow. "It's not wise to say anything about the Mints," he explained in a lower voice. "Everyone is related around here, you see. They are not what you or I would call normal people." He balanced his empty glass on his knee, as he leaned forward and whispered, "Rituals. Do you know what I mean? And incest. I'm the only one who has stood out against the trend. And Frank, of course. A Belfast boy, actually. *My* assistant."

He glanced at Hermione as he said this, but Evangeline was the one who responded. "Frank? That's a good masculine name."

"You never can tell, can you? But he's very good with fabrics. It's quite a joy to see him running them up."

Evangeline was not particularly interested in Frank's skills. "Tell me more about the Mints."

"Despots, my dear. Absolute despots. This whole village is controlled by them." He poured himself another gin, and forgot to

233

whisper. "That's why they all hate strangers."

"They don't hate me!" Evangeline was adamant about this. "They adore *me*."

"Oh really?" Augustine was deep in his drink. "I suppose you think they're grateful you discovered that ghastly tomb? Or whatever it is."

This was said with unmistakable irony, and Evangeline, who was beginning to slump on the Regency sofa, struggled upright. "Of course they are."

"Think again, darling. They've known about it for years. It was meant to stay a secret, you see. Until you came."

To other ears this news might have been of some significance, but Evangeline was so ill-informed about the nature of the site that it meant nothing to her. "Naturally," was all she could think of saying. "I've always understood that perfectly well."

Even so, Augustine seemed to think that he might have said too much. "By the way," he added quickly, "where did you get that dress? It's a lovely blue."

With a comfortable gesture, Evangeline smoothed it down with her hand. "It's nothing special. Just a country outfit. I wanted something very wintry."

"You certainly found it." He cocked his head to one side, and inspected her thoroughly. "You're about my size, aren't you?" He grew confidential once again. "You know the women in this village dress like sluts. Really they do. It's disgusting." Augustine now seemed genuinely angry; his voice rose an octave, and it was clear that his good humour could turn very quickly to rage. "I think women always ought to be well dressed. They ought to look their best. Not like the tarts around here. I could throttle them sometimes. I could really." Once more his vague, weak eyes gleamed; and the sudden surge of aggression seemed to animate him. "Frank thinks your friends are very noisy," he went on to say with barely concealed annoyance.

"I have so many friends I don't know . . ."

"The Clares. Above my shop. Him and the crippled wife."

"The Clares are, I think, my closest friends in the world." Evangeline tried unsuccessfully to sit upright again. "A noise from them is a noise from me."

"But she clumps around so much. Like Captain Ahab, dear. And she cries, too. She cries all the time. Sobs her little heart out."

"Why?"

"Probably loneliness," he muttered, his anger transformed now to lugubriousness. "Despair. Melancholy. Madness. I really don't know."

These words seemed to depress Evangeline, too, and with a supreme effort she rose to her feet. "We've had an absolutely lovely time," she said. "Lovely to talk to a real country person."

He led them to the door. "We must have a proper talk next time," he said. "All about dresses."

"I can't wait. But my assistant is the real expert, you know. She is the authority on anything feminine. Goodbye."

"You were very quiet," Evangeline said as they walked down the main street of Colcorum.

"Was I? Well, you talked enough for both of us." In fact Hermione, even though she was accustomed to her companion's manner, was beginning to realise how strained and difficult Evangeline had become; in this alien setting, she was beginning to see her clearly. But she said nothing, and they walked in silence for a few moments. "What was all that about the tumulus?" she asked at last. "What secret did he mean?"

"I wasn't following every detail, Baby Doll."

"He said that the Mints have always known about the tomb."

"Did he?" Evangeline was too tired to think about such things. "Just a misunderstanding. Probably just a misunderstanding." And she was too tired to realise also that, as they went back towards the village hall, they were being watched.

·59·

THE RAT KING

DAWN AT the camp-site; a grey-light gusts along the caravans and the old cars and the makeshift tents; a dog barks somewhere in the valley; a flock of wood-pigeons are disturbed and, when they rise up from the beech, it is as if the top of the tree itself has broken apart and ascended into the air. The calls of other creatures also mark the beginning of this winter day but, suddenly, these eternal sounds are broken by a single loud scream. And then another. They were coming from Corona's tent, and the next moment she ran out still screaming. "There's something in there!" she shouted as Spica and Auriga, pale and wide-eyed, hurried out after her. "Something was crawling over me." Corvus and Cetus tumbled out of the van into which they had been consigned. "I could see its eyes!" she screamed at the men, as if somehow they were responsible. Then she became rigid and said in a dry, quiet voice, "Here they are. Look around."

And when they looked down they saw several large rats scampering across the earth; but not so much scampering as hopping away, disturbed by the noise and by the beam of the torch light which Cetus now directed among them. They were scurrying in no one direction – some of them had crawled under the parked cars, some of them had climbed the canvas of the tents, others were picking their way over the bare feet of the sky-children. Corona, unable to move before, now bent over stiffly and was sick upon the ground. Her sisters clung to one another and screamed at the two men, "Do something! Get rid of them!"

Already the other travellers had been woken by the noise and, as they hurried from their beds in alarm, more small dark shapes could be seen leaping or crawling away from them. The camp-site had been invaded by rats. Two of them were swinging on the patchwork curtains within one of the caravans, three had climbed upon the roof

236

of Corona's van and were now standing on their hind-legs sniffing the air, two were clinging to the fur of a cairn terrier while, in the general confusion, three more had hidden under the masks of the Theatre of Peace. And there were still more of them, and more, swarming across the site, their long tails arching over the hard ground.

The more robust travellers began trying to chase them away; at first they did not want to kill them but, as they began banging saucepans or kettles to scare them, and as they began to fan out in a circle to find the ones still concealed, the urge to destroy took possession of them. With large stones and thick sticks they beat down whatever rat they found, leaving heaps of brown skin and pink flesh upon the ground. The surviving rats tried to flee along the Pilgrin stream towards the other end of the valley and, with whoops and yells, the travellers pursued them. But then they stopped. They fell silent. And they began backing away. There was high-pitched screaming of another kind for here, at the edge of the camp, clearly visible now that the sky had brightened, was the rat king.

Seven male rats, with their tails so intertwined with each other that they could not flee but lay squealing on the ground, tugging in different directions and forming the shape of a star. Seven rats caught in a knot: this was the rat king. And the travellers were afraid because the rat king, so rare a thing in nature, is a warning of disaster and the symbol most feared by those who move from place to place. "We can't stay here." This was the young man who had rebuked Evangeline the week before. "We can't touch it. And we can't stay here." One of the travellers' children wanted to know how the rats had got their tails twisted so. "Nobody knows," the young man said. "But you mustn't look at it. You have to come away." The others were glad to turn their backs upon the rat king, too, but they could still hear it squealing when they returned to the others. They were standing in small groups, making sure that they kept away from the battered corpses of the rats, and shivering in the cold winter morning. On this spot where blood had now been shed, a new atmosphere seemed to be rising among them. And it was with genuine fear that the young man spoke first. "We'll be moving on," he said. "We'll be going farther west." They began piling their possessions into two caravans, taking care all the time not to look in the direction of the rat king. Corona and her group were even quicker. It was customary for them to begin each day with a chant to the Great Mother, but on this particular morning they hurried into the blue and white van and drove off. The Theatre of Peace followed, forgetting even to make their farewells to the travellers.

They were the last to leave, but they waited patiently as the young man dug a small pit and threw the corpses of the rats within it. And, as he levelled the ground on top of them, the shrieks of the rat king seemed to rise even higher into the cold morning air. Then the travellers left – they were moving onward, moving across the face of England.

Pilgrin Valley was silent once again: even the rat king made no noise and, now that there were no human beings beside it, it ceased to struggle and waited patiently for its termination. Later that day two men came up to it. They were carrying sacks upon their backs, and they were both still chuckling at the success of their plan to drive out the strangers and so to protect the tomb.

"You showed them, Boy," one of them said as he put down his sack and went up to the rat king with a pair of scissors. "You certainly showed them."

•60•

THE SOUL'S MIDNIGHT

THE WINTER sun was half way across the sky but still so low upon the horizon that it seemed to be just beyond the trees; Mark Clare looked up at the ash upon the ridge above him and it was burning, its branches shimmering in the heat, the sun within it like a cold fire. And the firelight stretched across the sheep in the neighbouring field, who trod not upon grass but upon vivid green shadows. "The circle is the important thing," he suddenly said. "That's where we were wrong. We assumed that the tumulus was the central object, but of course it isn't. The stones form an ellipse more than a mile in circumference, so the actual centre lies over the valley. The tumulus was only the first stage."

Martha Temple looked triumphantly at Julian Hill. "I didn't want to say anything at the time—"

"Naturally." Julian was very grim.

"But I always knew the tomb was never as important as you thought. I loved your theory about an astronomer—" she managed to suggest that the entire explanation of the grave had been Julian's responsibility "—but then why did we only find the body of the hanged man? It didn't make much sense, did it?" Julian remained impassive, if somewhat pale, but Mark was listening to her intently. "And why was the grave so empty?" she was asking now. "It has remained undisturbed for thousands of years, but there were relatively few artefacts. And very few ritual objects. Strange, don't you think?"

Undisturbed: this was the word which worried Mark. There was no evidence of entry – there could have been no entry – and yet the interior of the tomb had the indefinable quality of human presence. Undisturbed. Mark knew the difference between the raw emptiness of a primeval site and the echoic attentive atmosphere of one which

239

had at some stage in recent human history been used or occupied:
the tomb in Pilgrin Valley was just such a place. Undisturbed. And
yet the chambers seemed to have been swept clean, the few remaining objects arranged neatly in accordance with some previous
design. Undisturbed. He was convinced that in the last thousand
years there had been some who had come to pay homage, but how
had they entered the mound? And what were those noises he thought
he had heard behind the wall of the terminal chamber?

"I suppose," Martha was asking Julian, "you will have to correct
your pamphlet. Or article. Whatever it was. Do you think you'll
have to apologise, too? What *am* I saying?" She looked around, as if
she had suddenly become two people and was consulting an image of
herself just behind her shoulder. "It wasn't really your fault, was it?
Any one of us could have made the same silly mistake. I often make a
fool of myself, too."

Far from comforting Julian, however, this little confession seemed
to depress him even further. He shook his head. "The theory is
right," he said without looking up at her. "It is just the evidence
which is wrong."

"What an original idea," Martha exclaimed. "Do tell."

But, without saying anything further, Julian walked away.

There was a sense, however, in which he was right. And that
night, in Crooked Alley, Mark Clare could think of nothing else.
There had been times during this excavation when the evidence
seemed unreliable and capricious – there were even occasions when
it seemed to be assembling itself for his benefit, the tomb itself taking
an appropriate shape in order to please and then to baffle him. And
so he dreaded that inevitable moment when an unexpected discovery was made, a discovery which undermined the construction
placed upon previous finds. For, when the theory fell apart, the
evidence went with it. All the objects were still there, but as soon as
they lost their coherence they lost their identity; they returned at
once to that disassembled and dishevelled state in which they had
first been found. That new discovery, that suddenly revealed artefact
or altered carbon dating, acted as a piece of primal darkness blotting
out all light – it was a contagion which sent everything else spinning
back into the abyss. And these new fragments were always waiting
just beneath the surface, waiting for that unforeseeable moment
when they in their turn would be discovered: as he stared up from the
bed he saw that these fragments of darkness were part of some

general dislocation, some general pain. He looked across at Kathleen, who seemed to be sleeping. But then she opened her eyes and for a moment they stared at one another. "I'm sorry," was all she said.

"I was thinking of the tumulus." He felt a certain shame, his thoughts being so far from her, and he went on in extenuation, "I was thinking that I don't understand it at all. Can't you sleep?"

"The strange thing is, that I can't think of anything to sleep *about*. Does that make any sense?" He said nothing. "What time is it now?" she added in a lower voice.

He leaned across to look at his watch, left by the bed, "Three o'clock."

"The soul's midnight," she said.

"I never heard . . ."

"This is the time when people are most likely to die. That's how it gets its name." She turned restlessly in the bed, so that now she was no longer facing him. "But I think it's a peaceful time. A holy time." He put out his hand towards her, but then she turned once again and spoke directly to him. "Go to the tumulus now. Visit it in the night. In the silence." It was as if she had understood all his previous anxieties and hesitations for it had occurred to him, too, that the darkness of the tomb might well be resolved in the actual darkness – away from the exigencies and the false clarity of the day. "There are some things," she went on, "that you can only see in the night. It's the time when all the secrets of the world are revealed, so why not those in the valley? And perhaps this is the time that he died."

"You mean—"

"The man inside the tomb. This may have been his hour."

"Do you think—"

"Go now." She was urging him forward but, still, he was reluctant to leave her. There was something about her tone that worried him. "I don't mind being alone," she added, again as if in response to his unspoken thoughts. "I feel quite happy now." She was trying to diminish her own role in his life but she could not have guessed that the more unworthy she declared herself to be, the more unworthy he felt of her.

"It might make a difference," Mark replied. "I've never been there at night before. I've never been there by myself. It is possible . . ."

"Find out everything and tell me next time."

"Next time?"

But she had closed her eyes again and, thinking that she wished to sleep, Mark quietly left the room. He dressed and drove slowly towards Pilgrin Valley. It was some time later that Kathleen heard the ticking of the clocks in the antiques collection below her. It was the only sound that could soothe her now and she rose up from her bed so lightly, so lightly, it was as if she had ceased to exist. Leaving the sleeping dog behind her, she went out of the flat and descended the stairs. She knew where Augustine concealed the key which opened the inner door of the shop and very quietly, so as not to disturb the ticking of the clocks, she walked into the dusty room. In the darkness she could see only the glass facings of the clocks, reflecting the streetlamps in Crooked Alley and the moonlight which pierced some ragged clouds; she saw only streaks of light, while the dials remained obscured. But she could hear them all around her; she could hear the whirling of the orrery, the rustling of the hourglass, the clanging of the marine chronometer, the faint ticking of the pocket watches and the darker beat of the grandfather clocks. And she moved among them, putting out her hands to steady herself in the darkness, still feeling very light, still feeling so light that she need not exist at all. And what need was there for her own existence in this cave of time, in this place where the movement of the hours and years was steady, insistent, remorseless? But this was a comfort to her, this sense of continuity, because in the passage of time she could be blotted out, utterly forgotten. There was no need to fear for herself, then, and as the clocks chimed the hour around her she lifted up her arms in celebration.

She climbed the stairs, quietly still, and went back into the flat; she dressed herself, making sure that she put on the clothes she always wore, and then she took the fragment of sea-lily and placed it in the pocket of her red coat. But then she turned around, put her hand through her hair and crept into Mark's study; she took out the sea-lily and placed it on his desk. She was about to leave the house when she went over to the dog and kissed it, as at once it sprang awake. "Goodbye, Jude," she whispered. "Goodbye, old friend. Go back to sleep now." Saying farewell to the dog was like saying farewell to the whole world. Then she left the house, and hurried through the dark streets of Lyme to her destination.

·61·

FOGOU

MARK CLARE stood in front of the tomb but, in this
darkness, it was difficult to see where the stones
ended and the sky began. He held his torch in his
right hand but he did not want to use it, not yet, and
gradually the starlight revealed to him the true outline of the
chamber grave. He had already dismantled the green canvas which
protected it – he wanted to view the structure entire, as it had been
on just such a night as this thousands of years before.

He was trembling in the cold, and even the crackling noise he
made within his anorak seemed too loud; but then the silence
enshrouded him, and he could not move. He had the strangest
sensation of being listened to. With an effort he walked across the
forecourt and put his hands against the markings on the blind entry,
feeling the whorls and spirals with his fingers. He knew no more than
the people who had carved these shapes and, beneath the canopy of
the heavens, on this dark night, they seemed to him to represent true
knowledge. Now, when he looked up, he saw the same stars: there on
the horizon, as Damian Fall had shown him, were the Pleiades. And
there, with its faint red glow, was Aldebaran.

He walked slowly around the tumulus until he reached the small
side entrance between the stones: he knelt down and for a moment
peered into the absolute darkness. Was Kathleen right? Was it now,
in the most silent part of the night, when the tomb was most like its
ancient state, was it now that he would begin to resolve those
problems which the excavations of the day had revealed? What was
her phrase? The soul's midnight? He bowed his head and passed
through the entry.

The side chamber was completely empty now, its artefacts already
collected and removed, yet Mark walked carefully through it: it was
as if the outline of the bowl and dish still remained on the floor, as

243

tenuous as the outline of the dark stone against the dark sky. He lay down on the pavement and then very carefully crawled through the porthole in the septal stone which blocked the chamber; he came out in the central passageway, raised himself slowly and then, crouched beneath the low stone roof, he shuffled towards the terminal chamber. He knew his way in the dark but he had no idea how long it took him to reach the chamber, since in this place he never had any sensation of time. He had already noticed how much warmer it was here than in the valley outside, and now it occurred to him that the stone walls of the chamber grave might keep out more than the winter air. They might also keep out time itself and, for a moment, he had to fight back his panic: he might be trapped here, never able to return to that other dimension from which he came.

He had reached the polygonal chamber but, before he entered it, he looked around in case there were someone hiding here. But he could hear only the sound of his own rapid breathing and now, with arms outstretched, he entered this room of the dead. He could see nothing but, without knowing why and with a low moan he did not understand, he lay down in the attitude of the hanged man whose remains had been found here – the body crouched over, the hands upon the knees, the head thrown back. He could hear the beating of his heart, sounding like a muffled drum through the chamber, and he felt a giddiness in his head. Still he could see nothing but, with his eyes wide open, he knew he was looking at that point where the capstone of the roof was cunningly joined with the upright stones of the wall. And he waited.

Nothing happened. He did not know what he expected – some intimation of the past, perhaps, some alteration in his own being – but, lying on the floor in the posture of the hanged man, he felt nothing. And this was the way it had always been, this bareness, this blankness of stone. So was it with something like resignation that the victim had gone to the sacrifice? Yet who was he to talk of sacrifice?

He repeated these words out loud: "Who? Who am I? Who am I to talk? Who am I to talk of sacrifice?" And now he sensed a presence – the presence behind the words, the presence within his blood, the presence which sustained his own breathing moment by moment. This presence was like a pressure all around him, and he felt it as surely as he felt the hard earth of the floor which bore his weight. And could this be true, after all – that he was as much a part of the earth as the earth was part of him? It was being sustained, too, moment by moment, continually made and remade, held in place by some inconceivable force. And this was something they had known. This was why they had built the mound of stone.

There were voices close to him – no, not voices. Something else. Mutterings or whisperings from which all sense had gone. And his shock was so great that it was as if he had vanished from the tomb, leaving only these sounds in his place. But they were not close to him. They were coming once more from the end wall, the eastern wall built against the slope of the valley. He rose and walked calmly over to it – he displayed no fear because he did not believe himself to be really here. He was playing someone else's part.

For the first time he put on his torch, and in that momentarily dazzling light the surface of the rock seemed to advance, shudder and retreat. And the beam of the light managed to dispel his fear, helping him forward down the bright path of cause and effect. Now he realised that he might have mistaken the sound of an underground stream, or even of a sudden wind entering the tumulus itself. Yes. The noises were clearly coming from behind the eastern wall, from somewhere within the valley. He put his ear against it, not wishing to breathe until he had identified the source of the sound. He could hear those murmurings which were like the distant residue of shouted words. But, if the stones of this end wall were as massive as those in the rest of the grave, then no echo should be able to pass through them. He was quite calm now in the glow of the torchlight. He considered the possibility that certain vibrations from the grave came to a focus at this point but, no, these sounds were coming from somewhere beyond the wall itself. If this were so, then there must be a hollow space behind these stones . . . and at once he knew. He was on the other side of a souterrain. An underground passage. An earth-house. A fogou.

This was why the chamber grave had been built against the side of the valley; its terminal chamber had almost been inserted into the slope so that it would be easier to hollow out a tunnel within the earth itself. And this was why the chamber grave was not at the centre of the stone circle: it was an entrance, an opening into another passage which would – Mark felt certain now – lead to the centre of the stones. This passage grave was not the culmination of some ritual but rather its beginning, with the hanged man marking the way forward. He was the door-keeper to the world beneath the ground.

It was some time later when he looked at his watch. Five o'clock.

But he could not leave this place, now that he had learned its secret. He knew that he would have to remain here until daybreak, until the others came, so that they could then at once begin work on the removal of the stones which concealed the underground passage. The noises now had faded – or perhaps he had become so used to them that, like the casual sounds of the outer world, he no longer needed to hear them.

He must have slept, and dreamed, because his wife was taking him by the hand and leading him through the stones. They were descending steps into the earth, and he knew that she was taking him to the object of his quest. And yet they were not travelling downward into the earth but upward; they were treading the stone steps of Swithin's Column. When they reached its summit they found Damian Fall looking through a telescope at Aldebaran, while Kathleen wrote words in red chalk upon a ruined wall.

The image of these words was still imprinted upon the darkness when Mark opened his eyes. And at once he was filled with a horror of this place: to have slept here, to have dreamed here, was like a kind of death. He turned on his torch and looked at his watch. Seven o'clock.

◆62◆

EIGHT O'CLOCK

SEVEN O'CLOCK. Julian Hill was standing in the large field just beyond Pilgrin Valley. He was close to Damian Fall's cottage, too, so close that he could see a lamp being carried from room to room; two owls called to each other from different sides of the valley, and then the lamp suddenly went out.

He turned on his torch and peered at the map he held in his hand — it was an Ordnance Survey plan of the area but Julian had carefully traced upon it a computer projection of the stone circle which had once dominated this valley region. Its original shape and dimensions had been superimposed upon the existing landscape, and the place where Julian now stood was designated by the computer to be at its centre. But he was standing in a bare and windswept field, nothing beneath his feet except scrub and thistle; there were small white stones scattered over the cold earth, and he kicked out at some of them viciously. He was angry — angry that Martha Temple had derided him and his theory, angry at himself for coming out on such a cold morning with such little result. But if there was one thing more powerful than his anger it was his will. He stared down at the hard earth as if somehow he might penetrate its secrets, scrutinised the map again and, in the glare of the torchlight, noticed for the first time that a track was faintly marked going eastward from this spot. He looked up, turned off his torch and allowed his eyes to become accustomed to the early morning gloom; he could see no path through the field itself but, about three hundred yards to the east, he could see the outlines of some stunted or broken trees. They were no more than a smudge upon the horizon but, in this bare landscape, clearly visible.

He walked towards them, his mouth firmly set, with no other sentiment than one of determination. Nothing mattered to him now

247

except the resolution of this mystery. This was not for the sake of the tumulus itself, for he had no disinterested curiosity: he knew that, as soon as he explained it satisfactorily, he would rapidly move on. It was for the sake of his own pride. And he kicked the stones out of his path as he approached the ancient trees.

They must once have formed a copse but they had been cut down many years before – or, rather, they must have been blown down by some strong wind since there still remained the shattered and useless trunks, some of them five or six feet in height and covered by moss, bramble, and trailing creeper. Julian looked down at his map again and realised at once that this spot marked part of the outer perimeter where the stones had once been set; but it was unvisited now, and had the savage odour of quiet unchecked decay. He brushed away some ferns growing among the trees, each frond stiffened with a thin patina of frost, but all around him was layer upon layer of rank vegetation. And this angered him, too: he had been looking for stone, and had found only putrefaction. He wiped his forehead and then leaned one hand against a ruined tree, its bark flaking off beneath his palm, while he considered his next move.

The first rays of the rising sun had already reached the copse; the top of the trunk against which he leaned was still in shadow but a large cobweb, strung across the opening of its hollow, glistened as the pale light moved upward. The early frost was melting, and a drop quivered and shone beside the cobweb before falling from the bark onto the mossy floor. This might have been a tree he had climbed as a child, and for a moment it seemed to Julian that it was the beginning of some bright path into an enchanted place. To pass through the tree and to find protection against the wind of the world – how strange for him to remember the sensations of his childhood. On a sudden instinct he bent down and ducked within the hollow of the tree.

It was curious: he had expected the ground beneath his feet to be soft and yielding, but it was quite hard. And, when he stamped his foot upon the spot, something rang like stone. He crouched down and with both hands scraped away the detritus which had been blown here and, as he did so, he could feel the hardness of stone beneath his fingers. With a fresh access of energy he scraped away the dead branches, the leaves and the moss until he could see, at the bottom of the hollow, a slab of stone which exactly matched the interior shape of the trunk itself. Julian knew what kind of stone it was: it was the same dark flint which had been used to erect the chamber-grave itself. But how could this be? How could the stone be here? No tree could have grown around it to ensure such a perfect fit. But, if it had been so neatly carved and placed here, then surely it must act as a concealed cover or perhaps even as an entrance.

Julian stamped upon it, and thought that he heard some dull muffled echo. Then he went back into the field, found a large rock, and carried it to the copse in triumph; he went up to the hollow trunk and with all his strength hurled the rock down upon the covering of stone, sensing almost at the same moment the faintest of reverberations. But it was enough, and he knew now that beneath this stone was an empty space or even a passageway. And he used the same words as Mark Clare. "A souterrain," he said out loud, his words muffled by the dead trees. "An earth-house. A fogou."

He knelt down and put his hands on either side of the stone. But he could not lift it, and he gave up the attempt readily enough. It was not that he experienced any fear at the prospect of going beneath the ground – at least no fear which he would have cared to recognise; but he had seen enough. His theory had been proved, and the triumph he felt was less at the discovery than at his own vindication. The business of excavation could be left to others.

So it was with the exhilaration of a labour completed, of a speculation proved, that he left the copse and hurried back across the field towards Pilgrin Valley. And as soon as he crossed the ridge he saw Mark Clare standing by the chamber-grave, waving his arms in the air and shouting something which Julian could not hear. But as he rushed down the eastern slope he heard him shouting, "Great news! Astonishing!"

And Julian was shouting. "Yes!" as he came towards him.

Both of them became quieter as soon as they were close to each other. "Have you guessed it?" Mark asked him.

"Guess? Guessed what? Not at all. You see, I have something to tell you." He took hold of Mark's arm, and in the action dropped his torch. "I've found it."

"But—" Mark bent down to pick up the torch, making sure that it was turned off.

"I was right all along. I've solved the mystery."

"Yes," Mark said. "There is a passage."

"What?" Julian stepped back, astonished and not at all pleased by his interruption. "How did you know?"

Now it was Mark's turn to be surprised and he said, slowly, "The stones in the terminal chamber conceal a hollow space. But you don't mean that—"

"Yes. I've found one, too." And as they compared their discoveries they realised that each of them had found separate entrances for an underground tunnel, which ran for at least seven hundred yards between the chamber grave and the copse of ruined trees. There was no doubt that these entrances had been carefully or even cunningly concealed, and yet this was not a secret that could have remained undiscovered since the building of the tomb: if that had been the case, and if the entrances had been neglected for so many thousands of years, they would by now have been quite destroyed or altered beyond recognition. They would have been folded back into the earth and the underground passage itself would have become no more than a fault-line, to be revealed only when the earth itself was torn open. The passage must have been built more recently, therefore, or it had been continually preserved over a long period.

Yet Mark did not mention the noises which he had heard when he was standing in the polygonal chamber. He said only, "We will have to go forward very carefully. There may be underground streams or chasms, or—"

"Yes. Of course." Julian was scarcely listening to him. "But the important thing is that we can reach the absolute centre of the stone circle. The dead centre."

There was a sense of danger or menace here, which Mark could not dispel. "I wonder," he said, "what the hanged man means . . ." Then he felt as if all the energy had been taken out of him, and he experienced a sense of loss so strong that his life seemed to have been snatched away. He opened and closed his mouth, attempted to swallow, and then had to fight back a rising sickness. "What time is it?" he asked very weakly.

"Eight o'clock."

"Martha will soon be here—" He was trying desperately to regain his sense of the world, but he could not say any more. He no longer knew who he was and so great was his fear of himself that he did not want to stay close to Julian Hill. He staggered back and, to Julian's astonishment, walked away from him until he could lean against the side wall of the tomb.

"What is it?" Julian called to him. "What on earth is the matter?"

Mark had his eyes closed, and when consciousness returned it was with a sense of terror. He looked down at his hands, and then intertwined them. Then he thought of Kathleen. "I have to go," he said. "Something is wrong. Something is happening."

·63·

THE FOX

MARK RAN up the stairs of the house in Crooked Alley, calling out "Kathleen! Kathleen!"; and his dread ran up the stairs beside him. As soon as he entered the flat he knew that it was empty; it had an especial quality of emptiness, too, as if nothing could ever have breathed here. But still he went from room to room, whispering her name. Jude ran after him, not letting Mark out of its sight, and, when he stood in his study, it looked at him anxiously. He picked the small dog up and for a moment buried his face in its fur; then gently he let it down.

Kathleen had placed all his books and magazines neatly upon his desk; she had wanted him to carry on working, he understood this at once, and when he went over to his papers he saw that she had put the fragment of sea-lily upon them. To keep them from blowing away. But there was no other sign of her presence here and once again, calling out her name, he walked from room to room. His mouth was very dry now. He went into the kitchen for some water, but everything here seemed unfamiliar to him: the plates, the cups, the spoons, the glasses, the refrigerator. These things were part of their life together, but they might have been the tokens of any life. All lives were the same. The plates rattled slightly as he ran his fingers along them. In Pilgrin Valley they had once eaten their food around the fire, and then beaten the ashes back into the earth. Another time. But everything here was being sluiced away, all the lives around him ebbing with it. He picked up a glass and noticed that there was a hairline crack in it, running from its rim down to its moulded base.

Swithin's Column. Suddenly he knew the place where he would find her. She had got up before dawn and gone to the empty tower. But before he could act upon this knowledge he felt himself invaded by some kind of fever, or sickness. He dropped the glass and, as he leaned over the sink, he saw the sweat dripping from him like melted fat. Then he managed to break free.

He drove to Colcorum, but it seemed to him that he was not going forward at all; that, somehow, the world was moving past him: so great was his fear that he had no sense of himself as capable of action. It was raining by the time he reached the forest which stood before Swithin's Column; the beech and the oak remained quite still in the downpour, mutely accepting the rain which had always fallen upon them. He plunged into the undergrowth, not certain of his direction but following the secret tracks which crossed the forest, and he felt no pain as the low branches whipped across his face. He just wanted to see her again, and in his panic he thought that he had returned to the rain forest of so many years ago – the rain forest from which he had emerged onto a dazzling plateau, and from which he had seen the place where men once flew. He was praying, but he did not know what his words meant. Now his sweat, his tears and the rain mingled on his face as he rushed desperately forward.

He stopped when he reached the edge of the forest and, across the ploughed field, saw Swithin's Column rising up among the fir trees on the isolated hill. He looked down and noticed that there were tracks in the muddy earth which led that way, and with a cry he followed them. He might have been running for ever. By the time he reached the foot of the hill he saw two men standing at the base of the tower, and in his extremity he wanted to call to them, to hold onto them, to be comforted, to be forgiven. Then he saw that they were looking down at something lying upon the ground. He knew who it was. He bent down and was sick in the undergrowth. When he stood up again he put his hand above his eyes, as if he were trying to peer into the distance, and looked at his wife lying between the two men. Now for the first time that day his fear was displaced by his pity – pity that she had become what she had always feared to be, the object of others' scrutiny.

Slowly he climbed up the path towards the tower but, as soon as they saw him, the two men instinctively stepped back. "I know," he said, trying to reassure them. "I know who she is." He wanted to keep on watching them; he wanted to divert them from his wife; he wanted to protect her from their curious gaze. And yet, also, he wanted to be sure that he himself was not an object of horror.

One of the men must have taken off his overcoat and placed it over the body but, for some reason, he had left Kathleen's face uncovered;

Mark smiled as he looked at her for the last time, because he saw how all the suffering had left her. This was how he would remember her, in the years that followed. And the rain fell upon her mouth and forehead just as it fell down upon the quiet trees. "I have to," he said. "May I?" And very gently he took off his jacket, knelt down, and placed it over her face.

He could look away now, and he stared at the edge of the forest across the field. There passed across his line of sight a red fox slowly making its way against the misty trees; it moved without fear, but before leaping back into the forest it turned once and seemed to look directly at Mark. In his bewildered state he believed that some kind of understanding had passed between them; the animal and the human were in the same frame. The frame of origin.

"This gentleman found him," someone was saying. Mark stood up awkwardly, wiping his eyes with the sleeve of his shirt, and for the first time realised that the woodlander was here – the vagrant whom Kathleen had seen feeding the birds of the forest, and whose story Mark had told. Now, standing by her body in his ragged clothes, he added a new solemnity to her death. For a moment Mark felt ashamed – ashamed to have accepted this as his private calamity, to have stolen her death from the world. The woodlander's eyes were very bright; and yet he had that attentive but tremulous look which is sometimes to be observed on the faces of the blind. "She weren't moving when I came up to her," he said gently. "She were already gone."

"Did you see—"

"She just sort of fell. From the tower."

He had a slight but noticeable stutter, and Mark realised how it was that he had fled from the world and become an inhabitant of the woods; but it seemed strange to him that, at this moment of calamity, he should understand this man's life better than his own. He knew that he would soon feel a sense of loss and of grief so great that they could hardly be endured but, for the time being, he was able to stand upright in the world. Only she had fallen. He had an image of a dead bird falling upon water, sending its ripples to the furthest edges of the pool; so it was that the earth shook at the moment of Kathleen's death, sending out waves into the past and into the future.

"Here they are," the other man said. He was the farmer whose field surrounded Swithin's Column. "I had to call them." Two policemen were walking slowly, apparently studying the furrows as they went. And, as he watched them coming across the field in silence, Mark knew how she had crossed it – Kathleen had moved across it slowly at first, not sure if she could carry out her intention, but then she had looked up at the summit of the tower and walked much more quickly.

"This is the deceased," he said when they eventually came up to him. Still nothing moved him, nothing but the effort to ward off the pain. "The deceased was my wife."

A few awkward preliminary questions were asked, but it was clear to all of them that she had killed herself. The atmosphere of this place had told them at once; there had been no violence here. Only the ending of some great sorrow, which had passed into the earth itself.

"Is there a note?" one of the policemen asked him. All of them looked away, not wanting to add to Mark's misery.

"No. I don't know . . ."

"No one has been up—" the farmer began to say, and then looked at the tower. The two policemen walked over to the small wooden door at its base; it was already ajar, and cautiously they opened it further before beginning their ascent of the circular staircase. Mark did not want to follow them. He did not want to see that room which he and Kathleen had once visited together, and from which she had flung herself. And had she known even then? Had she known that this would be her last place on earth? Had she chosen it that day? And he remembered how Jude had not wanted to enter it; it had known, too. And the woodlander had known, when he rose to greet her. All the world had known, except him. On a sudden impulse he went after the policemen, hurrying up the stairs just as she had done a few hours before – hearing the echo of his own footsteps against the ancient stone as he climbed to the summit.

When he arrived at the small circular room, with its bare arched windows, they were leaning over a ledge. But they heard him enter, and turned around quickly. "There's nothing here, sir," one of them said. "Your wife must have—"

"I know. I understand." He felt the urine running down the side of his trouser leg and into his sock. "I'm sorry," he said. "I'm very sorry."

They helped him down the stairs; they drove him back to Crooked Alley; they interviewed him as gently as possible; and then they were gone.

It was as if they had never been. The events of that morning had passed so quickly that Mark had difficulty in believing that anything had happened. Now he was alone. Perhaps nothing had happened. Of course. He must insist that nothing had changed. Kathleen would open the door and they would be happy again. He went into their bedroom and opened the wardrobe. One of her hats was hanging here, so Mark took it out and put it on. And then he began talking to himself and to Kathleen, all the time fingering the edge of the blue hat. No. This should not be happening. This is madness. He took it off, and was about to fling it into a corner of the room when he checked himself. He kissed it and put it carefully away. And it was only now, when he put his hand up to his face, that he realised he was still crying.

There was a scratching at the door, and for a moment he believed that it was the red fox he had seen in the wood. The fox had seen his sorrow and had come to comfort him, to let him ride upon its back and fly to the woods. He opened the door. It was Jude, crying to be let in. So he picked up the little dog and cradled it in his arms, smelling Kathleen's perfume as he held it close to him.

·64·

LUD MOUTH

"HAD OUR beauty sleep, have we?" Augustine Fraicheur was sitting on an ebony stool in the antiques shop, polishing a silver pocket watch with a small cloth. He seemed to register no surprise at Mark's dishevelled appearance, or the fact that he was holding Jude in his arms. "Had a nice lie in?"

Mark now felt very calm but for some reason he found it difficult to speak; he tried once, coughed, and then tried again. "Can you take care of the dog for me?" This was the first favour he had ever asked of Augustine, and with embarrassed impulsiveness he went over and put the dog in his lap. A clock struck the hour behind him. "It will only be for a little while."

Augustine held the dog with his free hand, although in fact it made no effort to struggle or to escape: it seemed that Jude was resigned to this further separation. "Is it a bitch?" he asked Mark. "I hate bitches."

But Mark had already gone. He had started walking through the town and, although he did not care in which direction he went, he found himself fleeing from the narrow streets and hastening towards the sea. Without thought or purpose he made his way to the coastal path between Lyme and Lud Mouth, a barren stretch of the coast which fault lines and frequent slippages had rendered dangerous; there were signs warning the casual traveller of the risks involved in walking here, but Mark did not see them.

The rain lifted as he walked on, but it was only when the mist cleared that he stopped and looked down from the height which he had already reached; he was on the grey cliff of St Gabriel's Point, with the sea and rocks some hundred feet below. He could see the twelve stones about which so many stories had been told, but he felt no fear. He merely looked down with interest, since the ground

257

beneath his feet seemed to him to be no less distant than the strand against which he could hear the waves beating. So why should he not hurl himself down upon it? At his back he could hear the birds singing in the ruined village of St Gabriel's, long since abandoned, and in that moment of choice they sang to him. He stepped back from the edge of the cliff, and walked on.

The decision whether to live or die did not, in truth, seem to him to be an important one: if he felt anything at all it was only that, without substance, even without identity, he had no right to jump. And yet he realised how, in that instant, he had felt free. This was the choice which Kathleen had exercised, and he felt a certain exhilaration. If she had made her own choice, then there was no need to pity or to mourn her. And yet only in that instant of decision had there been any freedom: as soon as Kathleen had fallen from the arched window of Swithin's Column she had ceased to be free just as now, somehow, he had made his own judgement and consigned himself to his life. There was no freedom in life, and certainly there was none in death: only in that moment of uncertainty had he known it. But if that choice between life and death could be prolonged by some other means, so that the individual decision no longer really mattered, then the real nature of the world might be disclosed. Now he remembered the passageway in Pilgrin Valley, which ran under the earth; the passage of stone was also the passage of time, and perhaps it was only there that true freedom could be found. Was it at the moment of his discovery of the souterrain that Kathleen had plunged to her death?

He had walked as far as Lud Mouth, a shallow curve in the cliff where the limestone and clay of the region are displaced by orange greensand; there was a path from the clifftop here down to a stretch of sand and shingle at the sea's edge. Yes. He hurried down the face of the cliff to the shore. He did not take off his shoes and socks, but walked out into the water until it lapped around his ankles. This was where Kathleen had come as a child, where he had first seen her. In time. Another time. "There is always one left behind on the shore." That was what she had heard as a child. But now it was he who had been left behind. She was safe now.

The sky had cleared and, in the winter sun, the waves themselves seemed to be emitting light. Or was it just the light on his face? He turned around and looked at the orange cliff behind him. Orange rock, with the light blue sky soaring above it. And the orange and the blue calmed him, for this was what the world had been before there were people in it. Orange stone and blue air. The peacefulness here was a relic of lost time and, when he considered this, he realised also that his own life was simply borrowed from time. It was not his to throw away.

He waded out of the water and started walking towards the cliff-face. When he came up to it, he stretched out his arms and put his face and hands against the orange stone. It felt warm to his touch, warmer than the surrounding air, or was it the heat of his own body returning? With his palms spread out against the stone, he seemed to sleep. And, as he slept, he took in the warmth of the landscape. The orange stone absorbed his salt tears. When he opened his eyes he saw that a flock of gulls had descended upon the cliff-face, and were now perched on the strange knobs and outcrops carved in it. They looked down at him with interest and, as Mark walked away from Lud Mouth, he knew that grief and guilt would follow soon. But he understood, also, that he must re-enter the world.

·65·

CONNECTIONS

THREE DAYS later Mark Clare, contemplating the coming inquest and funeral, received a letter from Damian Fall. It read, simply: "Let us look at the stars together. Come to Holblack Moor on Monday night." Which was, Mark realised, that very night. He was not sure if Damian had heard the news of Kathleen's suicide, but the prospect of visiting the observatory somehow comforted him. He might, as he said to himself, see things in a different light.

And so that night he drove along the dirt track which led onto the moor and the vicinity of the domed building. It was only when he had switched off his engine, and allowed the darkness of this place to envelop him, that he realised with horror how he had left on his headlights as he swept across the moor. It was possible, after all, that these stray beams had affected Damian's observations of the sky – but, at the same time, he recognised how strange it was that he should be worried about such things so soon after the death of his wife.

He walked up to the small office alongside the dome itself and knocked softly on the metal door. It was opened very quickly but, in the darkness, he could not see who was standing in front of him.

"Oh, hello." It was Brenda's voice. "Come in quick. I don't like standing in the dark." She gave a giggle and closed the door as soon as he entered. "You never know, do you?"

"Know what?" Mark was puzzled.

Brenda chose not to hear this; she was still making her way to the light-switch, with a number of little groans and squeals as she brushed against various objects. "I have to do it, you see," she went on. "We don't like any light outside. Was that you who just touched me?"

"No. I'm over here."

260

"Never mind." She sounded disappointed, but she did now manage to switch on the light. "Oh hello," she said again, as if they had just met. "It's you, isn't it?"

"Who did you think . . ."

"I didn't know, did I? I just knew it was a man." Her hair was ruffled, as if she had just woken from sleep, and she tossed her head back. "Have you come to see His Highness?"

Mark presumed that she meant Damian, and nodded. "I think," he said, "that he's expecting me."

Brenda allowed herself a little smile. "Don't go away," she said. "I'll be right back." She opened the sliding door and entered the small passage which led into the observatory, and did not return for several minutes. "He says he can't see you," she said very flatly. "He says he's very sorry. But he can't." She sounded so resentful that it was clear that Damian had in some way upset or unnerved her.

Mark was astonished. "But he sent me a note." He took it out of his pocket, and held it towards her. "He wanted to see me." He felt isolated once again, this sudden and unanticipated rejection somehow bringing back memories of Kathleen's death; and he felt afraid, as if there were no one on earth willing to help him.

But at this moment the sliding door was opened again and Alec, Damian's assistant, emerged; he glanced quickly at Brenda and then went over to Mark. "Shall we go outside," he asked him. "It's a beautiful night." He put his arm around Mark's shoulder and steered him gently towards the door, closing it softly behind him as the two men walked out upon the moor. They were silent for a few moments. "I was sorry to hear—" Alec began.

"No. Don't be sorry. There's nothing to be sorry about."

This seemed to relieve him. He took the older man's arm and said, more cheerfully, "Shall we take a walk beneath the stars?" All the time he was glancing surreptitiously at his face, but Mark was looking up now and Alec could not see his expression.

"So far away," Mark said at last.

"And getting further. The galaxies are moving away from us at forty-four thousand miles a second. Serious speed."

"It's so hard to understand." Mark kept on looking upward as they walked further away from the dome, onto the open moor. "So hard to believe."

"Seeing is believing. Isn't that what they say?"

"And how far does the universe extend?"

It was clear to Alec that Mark was drawing some comfort from the meditation of this vastness. "We can see for ever," he said, more softly, "We can detect quasars which are thousands of millions of light years away."

Mark put out his hand, as if holding onto the sky. "And what else is there?"

"Pulsars. Neutron stars. Red giants. Interstellar gases. Clouds of stars. Constellations. Galaxies. Thousands and thousands of millions of galaxies distributed evenly through space. And our own galaxy contains one hundred thousand million stars. Far out, right?" He laughed at his own joke.

"Then why," Mark asked, "is the sky not covered with stars? Why is there so much darkness still?"

"If you wanted to see the universe filled with light, you would have to look back into some inconceivably remote time." Alec's seriousness was that of a young man not quite certain how far he could take it, not quite certain that he might not be ridiculed; he was a romantic about his work, but one still hovering on the edge of self-conscious laughter. "We would have to see into the time of origin. We can look back thousands of millions of years, but not that far back. Not yet. And if we did—"

"What then?"

"Then," Alec replied gravely, "in my opinion we would cease to exist. To see the beginning is also to see the end."

Mark marvelled how this young man could entertain such thoughts; he had seemed so high-spirited, so full of energy. But perhaps this darkness above them was the reason for his cheerfulness. "Is there such a moment," he asked him. "Is there a moment of origin?"

"Oh yes." Suddenly Alec did a little dance on the moor, making whooping noises as he did so. "Oh yes. We still get the cosmic radiation from it. You can see it on your television screen."

"You mean we can see the evidence for the origin of the universe?"

"No doubt about it. It's everywhere. It will always be with us." There was a gust of wind which swept across the moor, but it dropped as suddenly as it had arisen. "Everything is related, you see," Alec went on. "The earth was formed from the solar nebula, the solar nebula from the galactic gases. Everything is part of everything else. Even the most distant stars may be affecting us." Again he was embarrassed by his own tone, and he executed a few dance steps on the ground. "I can't help it," he said. "I've got to keep moving." They had walked some distance now from the dome, and the young man turned his head to watch it gleaming in the starlight. "You must forgive Damian," he said. It was clear that for some reason he was anxious about him; in fact Damian had been behaving very oddly that evening. He had been talking loudly, and then had withdrawn into his own thoughts. He had asked Alec if he had seen any microphones and then, just a few minutes before, he had refused to see Mark. "Sometimes he shuts himself away," Alec was explaining. "I've always thought he must be a very disappointed man. You know sometimes he is so clear, sometimes he has so much vision. And to end up here—"

"Most people are disappointed," Mark replied. "Perhaps that's why he likes to look up at the stars. You know," he went on, his voice dropping a little, "Kathleen used to watch the stars, too. From our bedroom window. And until now I never understood why."

"I'm sorry," Alec was embarrassed. "I didn't mean—"

"No. Don't be sorry. What is that story, you know, the one which says that every soul is turned into a star at the moment of death? Have you heard it?"

"No." For some reason Alec felt exhilarated by what Mark had said. "But perhaps there is some truth in it. Perhaps souls are made of the same material."

Mark laughed. "How could that be?" And then he realised that this was the first time he had laughed since Kathleen's suicide.

"I told you everything was related, didn't I? Well, even our bodies are built with the fossilised debris of dead stars. Stars which ceased to exist millions of years before the earth was formed."

"I don't understand."

"But didn't you know that we were made from the ashes of dead stars? All the materials of life come from the cosmic trace elements." Alec put his hand upon Mark's shoulder. "You have a universe inside you, my friend. The real thing."

"So perhaps the story is right, after all. Perhaps our souls do become stars."

"And there's something else, too." Alec sounded as if he had discovered all of these things for the first time, and was eager to share his knowledge. "If you ever put blood plasma under a microscope, do you know what it looks like?"

"No."

Alec was triumphant. "It looks exactly like a star field."

And once more Mark felt a sudden rush of happiness. "So everything connects," he said. "Everything is part of the pattern."

"Yes. If only we knew what it was. But I suppose – I suppose—" he was trying to put his own thoughts in order – "I suppose that we could only see the pattern if we were outside it. And in that case we would have ceased to exist. So all we can do is make up our stories. That's what Damian once told me." For some reason, he sounded anxious again. "He said that we don't know more than ancient astronomers. We just know different things, just as we wear different clothes and speak different languages."

Mark was only half-listening to this since he, too, had been trying to order his thoughts. "But if we are all part of the same pattern," he said, "then nothing is destroyed. Things just change their form, and take up another place in the pattern. No one really dies." He put his hand up to his face, feeling a happiness that was also unhappiness, and both were mingled, and both were the same.

There was a noise which, in the stillness of the moor, sounded like a long sigh. But Alec knew what it was: he turned around at once, and saw the great white dome of the observatory slowly opening. "I must get back," he said. And then he added, almost to himself, "I don't know what he's doing in there."

"Of course. Go back. I know my way." Alec simply touched Mark's arm before hurrying away, and Mark smiled at him. Then he stood quietly and looked up at the heavens.

·66·

LETTERS

"IS THIS the opening?" Evangeline Tupper was standing in the copse beyond Pilgrin Valley, where Julian Hill had discovered the second entrance into the ground.

"Actually," Martha Temple said, very sweetly, "there is a bigger orifice elsewhere."

Evangeline ignored this. "Will you be crawling down it yourself, Miss Temple?"

"No. Mark and I will be leading the excavations at the other end." She watched with disapproval as Evangeline stifled a yawn, and began walking into the field. "But I'm boring you with the trivial details—"

"Not at all. Nothing is too trivial for me."

"Would you like to join us? The passage does seem to be quite wide."

"I would adore to. As you know. But unfortunately I have to see my favourite people in the whole world."

"You don't mean—" Martha had no idea what she meant.

"Of course! The Mints!" In fact hers was rather a delicate mission; since the passage ran beneath the Mints' fields, even more of their land would be disturbed by the archaeologists. "That's why I'm dressed to the absolute gills. Couldn't you tell?"

Martha smiled. "I thought," she said, "you were in mourning for dear Mrs Clare."

It was a week after Kathleen's death, but it was clear to everyone that the exploration of the underground passage should no longer be delayed; too much excitement had been aroused. Mark himself had returned to work four days ago, just after his visit to the observatory. The conversation with Alec on Holblack Moor had changed him but, as yet, he did not know to what purpose. He felt that, if he had looked at the stars long enough that night, he would have understood

265

everything. He would have seen the pattern. But they had led him forward only to leave him in the dark; however avidly he gazed at the sky he was still held down by the earth, and in that disparity was the puzzle which he could not yet solve. He had seen the light but he was controlled by gravity – even though, as Alec had told him, they were both part of the same force. The newly discovered passage, the blind entrance with its pattern of the constellations, the hanged man, the fact that the stone itself was the debris of dead stars, even Kathleen's suicide – all of these things were somehow connected, but the nature of the connection was not yet clear to him. He no longer believed that he had 'lost' Kathleen, but he did not know in what sense he might find her again. This was why he had returned to Pilgrin Valley so soon, and why he was eager to pursue his journey into the souterrain or earth-house.

If it was a house. Over the last few days Julian had conducted a number of electronic surveys to detect all the hollows and anomalies in the area between the two stone entrances, but the picture which emerged from the computer was in some ways incomplete. A long passage could be traced but there were sections where it seemed to break off or to fade, and there were other areas where it made blind divergences to the side. At that most significant point, precisely in the centre of the standing stones, there was activity which suggested a vast recess somewhere beneath the earth; and yet even this was not entirely clear, since certain magnetic anomalies here scattered the echoes and signals in every direction.

There was no choice but to descend into the passage itself and, with a team at each end, methodically to move towards the centre. This journey would not be without danger, however. The passage itself might not have been entered for hundreds, if not thousands, of years; they might encounter crevasses, rock falls, or some more general subsidence. Mark was aware of these difficulties, but he had to go on. And it was as if Kathleen herself were leading him forward.

So now he was standing within the polygonal chamber. The entry stone had been removed, without damage to the fabric of the tomb itself, and even before an arc-light had been brought to the mouth of the passage Mark sensed that there was no other obstruction in front of him – the way into the ground was open. And, after her brief conversation with Evangeline, Martha was now ready to join him. "What's that lovely old saying?" she said as she put on her yellow hard-hat. "Abandon hope all you who enter here? You lead and I'll follow." He ducked his head and, saying nothing, went into the passage.

It was no colder than the tomb itself but it seemed to him to have a much damper atmosphere; as soon as he put his hand against the wall, he realised that it was wet and slightly powdery to his touch. "Limestone." For some reason he was whispering. "This is a limestone passage." They walked forward slowly, stumbling over the uneven ground, and as soon as they had gone beyond the range of the arc-light Mark switched on his torch. Something glistened in its beam and, on the ceiling no more than a foot above his head, he glimpsed sparkling deposits of black and silver ore. He put out his hand, and both of them stopped to survey the beginning of this souterrain. The limestone itself seemed grey, almost unhealthy, in the unaccustomed light; slender trickles of water ran down the walls, giving them a striated appearance, and there were clusters of green moss on the surface of the stone. Further down the passage, just at the point where the light faded and where the darkness under ground began, Mark could see bands of red and brown clay like fissures in the limestone. At his feet a narrow stream of water followed the slope of the passage further down into the earth.

Perhaps it had been the sound of this water that he had heard from within the chamber; perhaps there had been no voices, after all. But it was already clear to him that this was not a natural passage: it had been fashioned deliberately, carved out of the stone, and as he walked forward it seemed to him that he was in some sense trespassing upon ground that did not belong to him, that did not belong to anyone still living. He stopped suddenly when in the beam of the torchlight he saw two smaller tunnels branching off from the main passage in opposite directions. "Oh dear." He had forgotten that Martha was behind him, and he was startled by her voice. "Oh dear," she repeated. "We are in a maze, aren't we?" She seemed to be relishing the situation.

"A labyrinth perhaps." Mark looked from one opening to the other, uncertain how to proceed. And then he caught a slight scent in the air, something like a perfume, coming from the right-hand tunnel. It reminded him of Kathleen, and in that instant all the details of her death returned to him. For a moment he felt faint, and leaned against the wall of the passage. How strange it is, he thought, to remember such things here. But then perhaps not so strange. In this place time might not simply go forward, forgetting and forgotten; it might move in other directions also.

"Is there anything wrong?" Martha had put one hand against the limestone, and was scrutinising the grey powder on her palm. "Anything the matter?"

"No. Nothing." He made an effort to stand upright again. "Except that we may have been mistaken about the site all the time."

Martha laughed, but her laughter sounded so odd in the tunnel that she stopped at once. "Of course I didn't like to say anything at the time. But I did think that Julian's theory was preposterous."

"No. We may all have been wrong. The builders of the tomb may not have worshipped the stars, after all." He was looking into the mouth of the tunnel where he had sensed Kathleen's presence. "They may have worshipped the subterranean powers. There is something strange about this place. Don't you feel it?" Martha looked into the mouth of the tunnel, too, but she said nothing. "Let's go on," he said. "Let's go deeper."

"Do you really think—"

But he had already moved forward. Yes. There was something strange here, the strangeness of being under the earth. Some weight, no less onerous for being invisible, was pressing down upon them; and, although they could have stood upright in the passage, they bowed their heads as they made their way. Their footsteps and their whispered voices did not echo here, but seemed to eddy away into the soft stone which surrounded them.

Something glinted in the torch light, something to Mark's right. He paused and to his astonishment saw, on a small shelf carved into the limestone wall, three small coins. He shone the torch full upon them. But he did not want to touch them. "I hope you're not going to tell me," Martha whispered to him, "that our neolithic friends invented coinage, too."

He smiled, but it was a nervous smile. It was as if they had discovered some private joke, the perpetrator of which might be hiding around the next corner. "No," Mark replied. "Obviously the coins are of a later date. So there must have been people here after the tomb was sealed. Long after."

He swung the torch around and in that sudden movement he thought he saw something on the ceiling. He held the torch up and there, scrawled upon the stone roof in red ochre, were some letters. And, in the tremulous light, he was able to read 'L.M. 1586'. He swallowed back his fear. "I think," he said in a loud voice, "I think we ought to call in the others."

And so slowly they retreated, saying nothing to one another. He was not sure if Martha had seen the writing, too, but he did not want to talk about it. Not yet. This discovery was so odd, so unexpected, that he wanted to consider it quietly in the daylight. Not here. Not in this place. Not in the fogou where it seemed that the centuries were collapsing together.

·67·

YOU NEVER KNOW

"IT'S GOOD news week!" Evangeline Tupper stood on the Mints' threshold. "And I'm the good news bear!"

"Good news, then, is it?" Farmer Mint was out of breath, and his hair was streaked with some kind of grey powder; it seemed to Evangeline that he must have run very quickly all over the house and scraped his head on the ceiling before answering the door. "Boy Mint is out in the fields," he added.

"Preparing something delicious for lunch, I'm sure." Evangeline was by now used to the farmer's ways, and without further invitation walked into the living room. "Everything is looking as lovely as ever," she said, resisting the impulse to retch at some strange smell coming from a corner of the room. She gazed instead with apparent enthusiasm at the familiar bric-a-brac of the Mint household – recently increased by a collection of old buckets and radios which were mingled promiscuously together in front of the ancient stove. "And whenever I see your ancestors," she added as she went over to the collection of paintings and miniatures above the fireplace, "I think of England which never, never will be a slave."

"I wouldn't know anything about England, Miss Tupper. We don't discuss it here."

It was clear to Evangeline that Farmer Mint was not to be diverted by her pleasantries, and was waiting for the news she had to bring him. "Aren't you the lucky one," she said, still pretending to look at the portraits. "Having an absolute tunnel running right under your land." She had decided to put this matter in the best possible light. "Dame Nature really seems to have dealt you a winning hand."

"Is that the good news?" He did not seem particularly surprised by her revelation.

"Of course it is! My dear, it might be another Cheddar Gorge.

270

Pictures of bison and so forth."

"Is that right?" Farmer Mint put his head on one side, and flashed an almost toothless smile. "We don't know nothing about no tunnels."

"This one is positively dank with age." She tried not to look at his mouth. "Really primitive." Then she remembered the need to be positive. "But primitive in a very nice way. I'm sure you could grow something down it eventually."

"We don't go poking about in no holes."

"Not even a nice big one?"

"No holes. No bison. No tunnels."

Evangeline was not sure how to continue this conversation: far from being dismayed by the further encroachment upon his land, the farmer seemed quite uninterested in the discovery. But at this moment Boy Mint burst into the room, and Evangeline welcomed the interruption literally with open arms. "Here he is," she cried. "My gorgeous boy-friend. Tell me your secret."

"Secret?" He stepped away from her and glanced across at his father. "What secret?"

"The secret of eternal youth, of course. Has it got something to do with sheep's glands?"

Farmer Mint answered for him. "He don't know no secrets."

"One more double negative and I shall *faint*."

"And he don't know nothing about no tunnels."

"Catch me." She pretended to stagger back but, since neither of the men made any effort to move towards her, she sat down very suddenly on a somewhat damp chair.

"That's the pig's seat," Farmer Mint said. "When he's at home."

She got up quickly, not without a suspicion that they were making a fool of her. "I take it then," she said, "that the archaeologists can carry on? Just go on as before?"

"That's a tautology," Farmer Mint replied. "Almost as bad as a double negative."

Evangeline realised that no more helpful answer was likely to be volunteered, and began walking to the door. "We must keep in touch. You never know—"

"No. You never know, do you?" Farmer Mint opened it for her. "You never do know."

"—what may come out of the tunnel."

He laughed at this. "What goes in must come out. I'll agree with you there."

"I'm so glad that we can agree upon something." Evangeline blew a kiss at both of them. "It puts me in a much happier frame of mind."

As soon as she had walked down the path, Farmer Mint slammed the door and bolted it. "The old cow is right," he said, chuckling. "What goes in must come out."

Boy Mint walked over to the portraits, and took off his cap. "Shall we discuss it with the others tonight?"

"It don't matter what any of us say. It's what we do. And we don't do anything. Not just yet." He joined his son, and gazed with him at the long line of Mints. "They can wait a little longer," he said. "Just a little longer."

·68·

ON THE TELEPHONE

"MY DEAR. You should have seen them trooping into the village hall, with Lola Trout in the lead." Augustine Fraicheur was talking to Evangeline Tupper that night on the telephone, one of the many conversations since their first meeting in Colcorum.

"I'm dying to know what she's wearing."

"Well." There was a little slurp of gin. "Do you know those old stained things the Salvation Army practically have to give away?"

"Which look as if they've been to hell and back?"

"She's got a dress exactly like that. A sort of mouldy snuff colour. She was being carried by two strong boys, as usual, but the skirt was so long she kept on tripping over it. She was tripping all the way down the street."

"I don't believe it!"

"Literally tripping. And then she stops at my door, bangs on it like the porter in *Macbeth* and starts screaming out 'Piss! Piss!' Honestly. It turns out that being carried excites her bladder, and she had to spend a penny. In my loo, too. And I just had it carpeted."

"Regency striped?"

"It is now."

"This is horrible!" Evangeline squeezed her legs together in delight. "This is like something out of the Sixties!"

"And then, when she's *quite* finished, they all follow her into the village hall. With the Mints in the lead. They're not the Sixties, my dear. They're the Dark Ages."

"I just saw them this morning. Aren't they ghastly?" Since she now suspected them of making fun of her, her opinion of them had altogether changed. "All that terrible facial hair."

"—and then your friend, the comic, goes in after them."

"Joey Hanover? Isn't he priceless?"

273

"I could put a price on him."

It was clear that Augustine was no longer impressed by Joey, so Evangeline added quickly. "He's not my friend, actually. My assistant knows his wife. And you know how innocent Hermione is."

"Blissfully. She should still be sucking at the breast."

"Well. Let's not go into that now."

Augustine giggled. "So they all literally sweep into the hall. Have you ever read Thomas Hardy?"

"Not as far as I know. But I gather he's absolutely divine about Dorset."

"He has this marvellous scene at a country dinner. Pass the turnip, and so forth. Tonight is exactly like that."

"And you say they meet once a year?"

"Like the Queen's birthday, dear. All the Mints and their relations put on their warpaint, and stamp their little rustic feet. I can hear them now—"

"Don't tell me that. That would be too marvellous."

"I *can*." Augustine's voice rose a little in emphasis. "When they leave the window open, I can hear every word. After all, I'm only a stone's throw—"

"I'm sure they make good use of it."

"—a stone's throw from the hall. Listen." At this point Augustine put the telephone receiver close to his own open window, but all Evangeline could hear was the sound of the ice clattering around in his glass as he took another large swallow. "Did you hear that?"

"I certainly heard something very strange."

"That was Farmer Mint. He's giving his annual report."

"What on earth is there to say about cows? Or whatever those things are."

"So far he's been talking about rats."

"Don't."

"He said something about rats being in short supply this year, and then I distinctly heard La Trout laugh. Not an attractive sound, I can assure you. Hold on." There was a silence during which Evangeline grew more and more impatient; she was just about to put down the receiver, when Augustine returned. "He's just been introducing *your* friend, Joey. A late arrival, he said, but long expected. Now he's explaining something about him."

It was clear that Augustine was about to go back to the open window, and Evangeline interrupted. "By the way, do you have any idea what they're eating?" She was always fascinated by the food of others.

"Just the usual coarse country fare, I imagine. Pizzas and so forth." There was silence again as Augustine listened.

"Now what's happening?"

"Joey Hanover is making a little speech. Speechette. He's saying what a privilege it is to meet them all. After such a long time without knowing anything about them. And now La Trout has shouted something."

"This calls for a stiff drink," Evangeline said. Augustine continued with his commentary, not realising that she had left the telephone and gone over to the small refrigerator in her hotel room. When she came back she gave an audible gasp of excitement, just for Augustine's benefit.

"I *know*," he exclaimed in response. "And now the little Mint has started. He's talking about some tunnel or other. Some underground passage."

"Of course. I was the first to tell them. They were utterly astonished."

"And now he's shouting something about Old Barren or Barren One."

"Really?"

"And now they've closed the window."

"Damn."

Augustine was already so bored by the Mints that he no longer cared whether he heard any more of their dinner conversation. "Tell me," he added, more comfortably, "what are you drinking?"

"Gin and it."

"Oh snap. So am I. Isn't it lovely?"

"Nothing lovelier." At this moment Hermione came into the room. "I really have to go now, darling." Evangeline became more formal, almost pert, with him. "You know what it's like for us working women."

Augustine was annoyed by her sudden change of tone, although he had already become accustomed to it. "Join the club, dear. I suppose I'll hear from you when you need more information?"

"Of course you will. But now I really must fly."

Evangeline put down the telephone as Hermione stared at her. "What was all that about?"

"Nothing, Baby Doll. Nothing at all."

·69·

THE DINNER

IT WAS getting late at the Mint dinner. Under the festive moss and bracken, which had been draped over the dark exposed beams of the ceiling, several relations looked glumly at one another or yawned quietly in the corners of the village hall. Farmer Mint and Boy Mint were enjoying themselves, however. They had both drunk large amounts of their own special Mint cider, so strong that clumps of what looked like cow dung were floating in it; they were now clutching each other, heads close together, whispering something which sent them into roars of laughter.

Joey Hanover was beside them, dressed for the occasion in a light blue velvet suit. He was talking to Lola Trout, sitting across from him along a narrow wooden table which ran almost the whole length of the hall, but he was now so drunk that he seemed to be quoting the words of one of his old songs without realising the fact. "You know, Lo," he was saying. "I knew by the smoke that so gracefully curled. Above the green elms. That a cottage was near."

"Get off!" She kept on running her tongue across her upper lip which, to those who knew her well, meant that she was enjoying this conversation.

"I know what you mean. I respect your opinion. But can I just add that a cottage was near? And I said if there's peace to be found in the world, Lo, a heart—"

"Eat shit." She drained off her own glass, and now waved it wildly in front of her.

"A heart, Lo, that was humble might hope for it here. And that's when I saw my guardian angels. Hello. What's this?" Farmer Mint was holding over Joey's head a pair of antlers, stuck on what looked like a wooden helmet. "Unless I am very much mistaken, something's been mounted."

276

Farmer Mint was chuckling. "Go on, Boy. Tell him what to do."

"You have to put them on. That's what *you* have to do."

"Me? Par excellence the idol of the day?"

"Uncle, it's a family custom."

"Well, I'm game." Joey rose and took the horns from Farmer Mint; there was a leather strap beneath the wooden helmet, and it took him only a few moments to fasten the whole apparatus to his head. He put up his hands to touch the horns, and suddenly he was filled with a wild exhilaration. "You never expected to see me stuffed, did you?" he said to Lola, and then jumped onto his chair. "And here's another funny thing." He looked at the assembled company as if they had become just like the audiences he had once known. "My wife. God rest her soul." The antlers felt heavy on his head, and he swayed a little in the chair. "She's still alive, you know, but I'm hoping." At this Lola screamed with laughter. "Have you got knickers on, lady?" He gave her the famous Joey look. "I'm coming down in a minute. Anyway my wife, my wife—" He was now deep into his old act. The sweat was pouring down his forehead and face, but he wiped it off with the sleeve of his blue velvet jacket. "I won't say that she's ugly, but a man has to walk in front of her with a red flag. He does. And she's that mean, she . . ."

As Joey continued with his act, Farmer Mint sat down next to Simon Trout. "Your old mother seems to be enjoying herself," he said. It had been one of his self-imposed tasks, over the last twenty years, to arrange a reconciliation between mother and son.

"I hadn't noticed. I wasn't looking in her direction."

"She's looking good for her age, isn't she?"

"Withered, I would say."

"Withered, yes. But firm with it. Nice and firm."

"She never changes. She never will change. And what's more—" he looked Farmer Mint defiantly in the face – "neither will I."

Drunk though he was, Farmer Mint realised that no effort in this direction was likely to succeed; so he changed the subject. "You know," he said, in a much lower voice, "that they discovered the tunnel?"

"I heard."

"They're getting very close."

"Have they found—"

"No. Not yet. But they'll get there in a week or so." He looked at Joey Hanover for a moment, still sweating and swaying on the wooden chair. Farmer Mint laughed and clapped his hands before turning back to Simon Trout. "We're going to have to do something," he went on. "We're going to have to take some action, we are. Before they find—"

"Has Joey been told yet?"

"Me and the Boy are waiting for the right time. He has to be told. Now that he's one of us."

"She hates me, you see." Joey was continuing with his performance. "Yes she does. She must do. She's lived with me for twenty years. And fat." Joey passed a hand over his face. "She's so fat that." He stopped quite suddenly. "I'm sorry," he said. "I just can't remember the next line." He got down from the chair on which he had been standing and sat down heavily, his head dipping under the weight of the antlers. Clumsily he unstrapped them and placed them on the table in front of him. Boy Mint was watching him closely and was surprised to see him shaking not with disappointment, or embarrassment, but with laughter. He thought he was laughing at the helmet itself, and indignantly he stretched across him to remove it. "This is precious," he said. "This is our heirloom."

Joey looked at the antlers more closely now, seeing how ancient the carved and polished bones must be. "I'm honoured. Honestly. I am. I was just laughing at myself for not remembering my lines. It doesn't matter any more, you see. It just doesn't matter. I'm free."

"Joey!" He flinched at the loud squawk which came from somewhere above his right shoulder. It was Lola Trout, who had somehow managed to rise unaided from her chair and walk around the table. "You know what you can do, Joey, don't you?" He shook his head, expecting some terrible insult. "You can carry me around the room!" There was a general murmur of surprised approval: clearly it was a great honour to be so invited, and with a smile Joey Hanover stood up to take Lola in his arms. He staggered under the unexpected weight, but soon stood upright and with a great drunken effort managed to carry her from one end of the hall to the other, his face buried in the folds of her snuff-coloured gown. "There," he said when he eventually put her back in her seat. "Was that nice?" He was panting for breath.

"That was pathetic!" But she was obviously pleased by her excursion. "You need a few lessons," she added. "Then you can carry me anywhere."

Joey bowed to her after this kind offer, and was just about to return to his seat when Farmer Mint grabbed his arm and led him to a corner of the hall. "Walk this way," he said. "Something to tell you." He spat on his hands, rubbed them through his hair and then began to explain something to Joey very seriously and very slowly. But by now both men were so drunk that, although they agreed with each other very fiercely, neither had the faintest idea what they were discussing. "I'm with you!" Joey shouted. "I'll never, never leave you!"

"That's a good boy," Farmer Mint shouted back. He might have been talking to his dog. "That's a very good boy!" With a supreme effort he grabbed a piece of old moss which was hanging from the rafter above him, pulled it down onto his face and shoulders, and then collapsed into a drunken stupor. Boy Mint had been watching this exchange and as soon as his father had fallen he got up, put on his cap, walked over to him and hauled him across his shoulders with no more effort than if he had been a bag of peat compost. "It's all true," he said to Joey as he carried him away. "What he told you is all true."

"Of course it's true!" Joey was very insistent, although he had no idea what was meant. "It's very true!"

The departure of the Mints was the signal for a general exodus by the guests, but it was only when Joey staggered outside and saw his car that he remembered he was being met by Floey. She was waiting for him, her fingers drumming on the rim of the steering wheel, but as he approached the car he kicked one leg in the air and began to sing very loudly, "We won't go home till morning, dearest Floey. "No, we *won't* go home till morning. We won't go home till morning. Till something-or-other doth appear."

"I'll appear in a minute," she said, opening the door for him. "I'll appear behind you with an axe."

"Family occasion, dearest Floey."

"Do you know how long I've been waiting here? My tiny mind is frozen."

"Very lovely lovely family occasion."

"Oh yes." She watched him as he fell into the back seat. "Let's hope you don't sell your birthright for a mess of porridge."

There was a faint cry of "pottage" but Floey did not hear and, with a grim smile of satisfaction, she began to drive her husband through the dark street of Colcorum.

Augustine Fraicheur had been watching this scene through a gap

279

in his striped curtains. "What a performance," he said out loud to no one in particular. "I can't wait to tell Evangeline. She is going to *scream*."

As the Hanovers travelled past Pilgrin Valley Joey lay in the back seat and crooned, "One little kiss for Mother. Kiss me, Mother, ere I die." Suddenly he sat up. "Flo," he said. "He told me that there's something in the tunnel."

·70·

AT THE CENTRE

THEY HAD been working in the underground passage for three weeks, two teams moving slowly from each entrance towards that central point where all their hopes rested: hopes raised by the discovery of the three coins and of the red markings on the limestone roof of the tunnel, and then further increased by other 'finds' in the course of their slow journey. They had already located and removed part of a leaf-shaped sword from the early bronze age; two undecorated bowls from the early neolithic period; some grooved ware from the late neolithic; a globular urn from the middle bronze age, dress pins and bone tweezers from the early bronze age. So, to their astonishment, there was evidence of a continuity stretching for many thousands of years; either all of these artefacts had been collected and at some late stage taken into the tunnel, or the passage itself had been considered a sacred place over many generations with the tumulus acting as a landmark for its entrance.

But there was something more puzzling still. The red markings which Mark had seen were soon found elsewhere – sometimes daubed in red ochre, sometimes scrawled with black slate. Mark had read "L.M. 1586" but now others had come across "T.M. 1750", "O.M. 1690", "J.M. 1827" and a crudely written "George. 1894". The meaning of these letters was not at first clear but their significance was not difficult to determine: the passage had been known and used as late as the nineteenth century, during a period when the tumulus itself was completely covered by the ash forest. But, if that were so, why had nothing in the tomb itself been moved? Why had the hanged man, the guardian of the secret entrance, remained quite undisturbed?

These were the questions which they were still debating with one another as they met on a cold February morning. All the instruments agreed that on this day they would be able to break through to the central area; they might need literally to break through, in fact, since as they came closer and closer to their destination they had discovered various impediments – heaps of limestone rubble, false turnings, large boulders – blocking their path. But they had gone forward steadily, and now they were ready for the final move.

They were huddled together in small groups, their breath like splinters in the freezing air. "So what is this M?" Julian Hill was asking. "Does anyone know? Of course," he went on hurriedly, not listening for any response to his question, "it may not be an initial at all. It may be some ritualised sign."

"Could it mean misguided?" Martha asked sweetly. "Or moron?"

"What is the sacred name for God?" Mark had thought of this before, but only now mentioned it. "The one which, when uttered, will bring about the end of the world?"

"If I knew," Martha replied, "I certainly wouldn't tell you in public."

Owen Chard had been biting the end of his unlit pipe and now removed it very slowly from his mouth. "I'll tell you what M means," he said. "It stands for Mint."

"I think," Mark said, in the sudden silence, "it's time that we began."

And so they made their way. Owen and Julian went to the entrance hidden in the copse, while Mark and Martha continued their journey from the terminal chamber of the tumulus. The various assistants, who had been working on this excavation since its beginning so many months before, would wait for them at the respective entrances. At some time in the course of that day, they would meet and shake hands beneath the earth.

Mark moved forward cautiously still; even in those sections of the passage which they had already explored there was still the danger of slippage or rockfalls, and he did not speak as he walked in front of Martha. Only the sound of their boots scraping the limestone floor could be heard as they descended further into the earth; but, although the passage seemed to be sloping downward all the time, its roof became higher, and soon they were able to go forward quite easily without bending or crouching. And it occurred to Mark that this was part of the design: the builders had determined that, as the worshippers moved further from the surface of the earth and came closer to the centre of this ritual way, they would be able to walk freely for the first time.

They had arrived now at the final section, the central area still hidden from them by a wall of limestone boulders which might have lain there for centuries but which seemed to Mark, for reasons he could not properly explain, to have been recently or hastily erected. But he said nothing of this to the others. A similar wall blocked the passage on the other side and now, in a final effort, they worked together to remove the boulders one by one. Neither party could hear the other, since the central area seemed to prevent any sound from passing through, but they progressed at a similar rate. It was hard and uncomfortable work but their enthusiasm invigorated them, even if that enthusiasm was tinged with fear at what they might find when they removed these barriers. They were deep beneath the earth, in a place no person was meant to come, and the stone boulders themselves seemed to them heavier than they should be, unwieldy, alien. Once they stopped, both parties hearing the echo of movement somewhere above their heads; but it faded away, and they continued with their work even more swiftly. Until finally they broke through.

At the same moment they stepped into the central area. They found themselves in a round space, cleared of all objects but with one small tunnel cut into the side of the rock. The roof was higher here and they could look up into the gleaming recesses of the limestone; it appeared to them that they were at the base of a giant cone and, when they peered into the abyss above their heads, the ground on which they stood no longer seemed so firm. They were in a cavern beneath the earth but they might have been floating away, the stone turned to water and cloud around them; and, although no one spoke, they knew that they all felt this. Some fragments of rock were scattered across the floor of this place, and a thin stream of water ran down one wall before passing off at an angle into the depths below them. The four of them stood silently, instinctively forming a circle, hearing only the faint echo of water steadily dripping somewhere close to them.

They might have stood there for ever, but then Mark broke away. "Hold on," he said. "I have an idea." He walked over to the small opening carved into the side, and crouched down beside it. It was as if he were listening to something but the others, perhaps dispirited by the emptiness of this place, made no effort to follow him. "I shan't be a minute," he said. Then he ducked down and crawled into the side tunnel. He had taken one of the portable lamps with him, and in the suddenly attenuated light Martha switched on her torch and swung it towards the opening through which Mark had disappeared. The damp walls glistened around her but after a few moments the torchlight began to flicker, and to fade; then it went out.

It could only have been a few seconds later that they heard a cry – or a call – which spun out from the small tunnel and whirled upwards into the cavern above their heads. And at the sudden sound of Mark's voice Julian dropped the portable light he had been holding and it, too, went out. For a moment they were all silenced by the darkness around them for it was a darkness like no other, a darkness more intense than that of night. They could smell it, dank, ponderous, threatening; they could even taste it.

"Oh my God!" Martha said at last. "Whose fault is this?"

"It's nobody's fault," Julian snapped back at her, his fear adding to his anger. He reached down to feel for the light he had dropped but he touched Martha's leg, and she cried out in alarm. "Don't panic," he whispered, appalled by her scream which, in his nervous state, he thought might send rocks tumbling down on their heads. "It's just me."

"I didn't panic. Just don't touch me."

"Stay calm." Owen sounded some distance away; but this was just a trick of the echo, since he was next to them. "Julian and I still have our torches." For a moment they could not find them, although they were strapped to their waists: the intense darkness had so disoriented them that they were not sure of the precise alignment of their own bodies. Eventually they switched them on but, in the twin beams, they seemed only to be lost in a sea of blackness. They moved cautiously, as if there were caverns into which they might fall, the darkness billowing around them. Even when they found the outline of the tunnel which Mark had entered, they could not see into the blackness beyond. "That was definitely his voice," Owen said. "We're going to need ropes. And proper lights. I'll stay here in case he gets back. You two go and get help."

Julian Hill needed no persuasion to turn back, but Martha was annoyed by this sudden assumption of authority by Owen. "I hate to intrude," she said. "But don't you think we should try and find him now?" She moved her feet as she spoke; she did not like to stand still since then, she feared, she might be sucked further into the earth.

"Look." Owen shone his torch into the tunnel, but its beam

penetrated only a few inches before being snuffed out by the darkness. "There may be pot-holes here. There may be other passages. We could be lost for ever."

"I suppose," she replied, "that for once you may be right." So she and Julian returned, hurrying back to the main entrance where the others were expecting them. Owen sat down in the central circle, took out his pipe, clenched it firmly between his teeth, and waited for them to return.

And what of Mark Clare? He had entered the tunnel without any thought of the consequences. He had just wanted to leave the others for a little while. In this sacred place, he needed no company. As soon as he crawled through the entrance their voices were blocked out, and at once he felt at peace. So he went forward in confidence – he trained the beam of the portable light on the ground in front of him, bending forward as he crept along. This was a narrow passage, no more than three feet in width, and when he put his hands against its side he realised at once that it was made of drier and firmer stone than any used in the main tunnel. The rock itself had changed; this had the hardness of granite.

There seemed to be no recesses or passages to either side of him, and so he continued going forward. "This is the way," he said out loud. And indeed it seemed to him that he was moving down some sacred avenue, away from the circle in which the others still stood. "This is the way," he repeated after a few minutes. "This is the way, the truth and the light." He sensed a shape in front of him, stopped, and tried to stand upright. But then something hit him on the back of his head; he stumbled forward, and he fell.

•71•

SILHOUETTE

IN THE after-shock Mark dreamed that he was still falling but, when he put out his hand, he realised that he was sprawled upon flat ground. He did not know how long he had lain here but, reluctantly and cautiously, he began to rise. Not because he had any desire to move, only to make sure that he could still do so – that the sudden feeling of exhilaration which now possessed him was not some recompense for injury. But he knew at once that he was unharmed. "I might have been lowered by angels," he said out loud. And then he thought of Kathleen.

The light he had been carrying before his fall was lying some feet away from him, lodged between two large stones, its beam travelling upward and slightly aslant so that it resembled a ladder of light. Mark followed it with his eyes until it reached that point above his head from which he must have fallen: he could see the broken edge of the passage on which he had stumbled, the low ridge against which he had hit his head and, on the other side, he could see how the passage continued. So this hollow, or crater, cut the passage in two; it might almost, if such a thing were possible in this subterranean world, be some kind of trap. And yet he knew that any rescuers would find him easily: they would come with their voices, their lights and their ropes; they would raise him from this place and take him back to the surface and to the outer air. But he was not sure, yet, that he wanted to leave.

Their lights. Suddenly the electric beam of his own light disgusted him and he walked over to switch it off; the ladder disappeared, leaving an after-image which hovered for a few moments like an hallucination. He sat down again, in the same spot where he had fallen, and leaned against the stone. Welcoming the darkness which seemed like a companion sitting beside him. But he could not remain in the dark: even as he sat here scenes and images from the outer world emerged from him, staining the air before him in dumb show. Colours, movements, pictures, all of them creating stories in front of him. There were figures walking silently – not figures, but shadows with faces which merged indistinctly with one another. And then there were wheels of light. Spirals. Strands of brightness. Pulses of colour. Even this place was filled with ghosts but when he tried to track them down, to exorcise them, he did not know from where they had come. They must have issued from the deepest part of himself, and yet they were quite impersonal; they seemed to have no real origin.

Other images rose up silently in front of him – children playing in a field, the broken statues in Augustine's yard, the slope of the Pilgrin Valley itself. Even now he knew that he could leave all these things behind for ever; but then, out of the darkness, sprang Jude. The dog, yes, was another living thing that had depended upon Kathleen. But it was just an involuntary memory; Jude faded into oblivion, like the after-image of light. Everything was so frail, as frail as the images forming and then dissolving, as frail as the electrical activity within Mark's head. Yet this frailty was all there was. It was life itself, and he understood how the little dog was an emblem of some general helplessness which he shared. Perhaps it would be easy to leave that frailty behind, but would not a kind of pity – a pity for the human state – always stop him?

And now, for the first time, he began to think of Kathleen's funeral without dread. It had been arranged for next week, but the whole slow process of the investigation and the inquest had seemed to him to be taking place outside the current of time, for it had been a prolongation not of his own misery but that of Kathleen. During all this period he had not thought of the funeral as some laying to rest, some accommodation with eternity, but an ending no less abrupt and arbitrary than her death. Everything had been incomplete, irreconcilable, inconsolable. But now, sitting in the darkness under the earth, this incompleteness, this frailty, was no longer a thing to be feared or even regretted. It was to be accepted, and he no longer felt afraid. He became quiet – or, rather, he began to feel the presence of the earth around him, enfolding him, obliterating the gleams and slivers of his private consciousness. It was as if these were porous stones which could draw off human images as easily as they absorbed water.

He must have slept since, when he raised his head again, he found that he had changed position and was lying curled upon the ground. But, if that were so, then he must have slept with his eyes wide open because he had become accustomed to the darkness: it was no longer an opaque resisting medium but seemed to sink and drift, to billow out or fade in response to some internal pressure. And, when he shook himself awake, he noticed in the distance a band of paler darkness like dying firelight, like the phosphorescence of ruined stones, like the ghost of light. There was an arch cut into the rock in front of him, and beyond that arch he could see an alcove where this barest perceptible haze on the surface of the darkness seemed to hover; he rose and began walking towards it. He stepped beneath the arch and then quite suddenly he stopped; he stopped because he sensed that he had reached the end of his subterranean pilgrimage. This alcove was the house under the ground.

There was an oblong slab of stone about seven feet in front of him which, in the paler darkness, seemed to him to resemble an altar. And there was something lying upon it. He stepped uncertainly towards it, hands outstretched, but drew back with a gasp when he realised that this thing was not itself made of stone. It was something else. Tentatively he touched it again, and felt the wood beneath his trembling fingers. This was a wooden box, some four or five feet in length. A wooden coffin. He put his hands against the side closest to him, and with his fingers he could trace notches or grooves carved into the wood. They seemed to be forming letters even as he touched them.

He took two steps back, stared wildly at the altar for a moment as if he were trying to reach some decision, and went back for the light he had left propped between the stones. Then he returned to the small square room and, when he turned on the light, he saw that this wooden box or coffin was so cunningly sealed that it might have been constructed out of one single piece of wood. There was only a worn groove to mark the position of the lid, and there were tight wooden bands encircling it – just as if something had been locked in. And when he stepped up to the altar Mark realised that, on the top surface of this coffin, there had been drawn, in red ochre, the silhouette of a figure lying crouched with its knees drawn up against its chest. And what of the words he had touched? The carved words. He knelt down and shone his light against the side of the coffin and saw there, clearly marked, 'Old Barren One'. He had no way of knowing how long those words had been inscribed there, but Mark knew at least that he had reached the centre – the origin – for which he had been searching. This was the body for which the tumulus had been built some four and a half thousand years ago, the silhouette in red ochre representing the shape inside – if, indeed, any recognisable shape still remained. He knew that, encased like this, organic remains could be preserved for many, many centuries. But for precisely how long?

And why had it been concealed for so long? Why was it being concealed even now? He had reached the end of his quest, but he could see neither backward nor forward. He switched off his torch, and with bowed head placed his hands once again upon the wooden casket. Alec had told him that the human body contained cosmic debris, and was the relic of dead stars. Surely here, if anywhere, this was true: there was starlight above and beneath the earth. Those who had come to Pilgrin Valley had come to venerate the body but also to worship the stars; and in so doing they had created a circle of light, like the circle of stones above his head. He had seen eternity, too, for here there was no beginning and no end. "Kathleen," he said.

He had entered another time, a time where his wife continued to exist. He could remain here always, and in this moment of acceptance he felt at peace not only with Kathleen but with all the dead. And when he thought of them, when he thought of the past, he saw only the perpetually mined movement of starlight drifting through space in a silence like the silence of this place. And, yes, the silence here was the silence of the dead, the silence of those who had come before him and who had led him under ground just as surely as if they had taken him by the hand. They were the stone against which he leaned, the rock upon which he stood. They had become the world. He knew what time was now: it was the word for that which no living thing could understand, because to understand it would be to exist outside it. Only those who had died could comprehend time, for time was God. And in the house under ground he no longer felt any fear.

Then he heard the murmur of voices. These were his rescuers and, reluctantly, he went back into the pit and waited to be escorted into the upper world.

PART SIX

It is therefore a truism, almost a tautology, to say that all magic is necessarily false and barren; for were it ever to become true and fruitful, it would no longer be magic but science.

The Golden Bough
J. G. FRAZER.

•72•

ALDEBARAN

ALDEBARAN. OLD. BARREN. These were the words that came into Damian Fall's head as he looked out of the window of his cottage at the setting sun. And this was how his own life was setting, too. He watched it as it trembled on the horizon, so close that it seemed to be descending into Pilgrin Valley itself. Then he licked his forefinger gently, and held it up towards the dying star.

He had heard every sound in the valley tonight. He had heard the shouts and laughter as Mark Clare was rescued from the cave under the earth; then, much later, he had heard the Mints arguing loudly beside the tumulus; but it was quiet now, and he was alone. And as he watched the dusk thicken the air in front of him there was a familiar disquiet, a stirring, beneath his scalp; it was as if something there had swerved and changed direction.

There were noises in his head — no, not noises, voices, and they were rising like a wind which brings sickness. And it occurred to him that this cottage was a tumulus, too, but one in which others beside himself were housed. Shadows stirred in the room around him, and they were the shadows of the people who had once lived here, crossing and recrossing in front of him. There was a sudden harsh laugh: Damian put his hand over his mouth, and stared wildly around.

But the shadows had not heard him. They had gone now and, in their place, had come a greater darkness when he realised with horror that the windows themselves had darkened — that they had come alive. They were trembling with life, and when he took a step forward he saw that there were swarms of large flies blocking the light. And then Damian realised that they were trying to reach him; their eyes were upon him, even in the darkness. He swung his arms savagely around as if the flies had already eaten through the glass and had entered the room. He turned a full circle, swaying slightly, and when he looked around the flies had gone. The windows were quite clear again, letting in the last fading light of the day.

It was in this grey light that he watched the engravings upon his wall; they were no longer still, but seemed to have been infused with life. The chart of the Pleiades began to move and shimmer; Ptolemy looked across at Damian before raising in triumph a burnished image of the sun; Copernicus turned the astrolabe with the forefinger of his right hand, and then licked the dust from it; Tycho Brahe reached up to the artificial stars he had placed upon a velvet curtain, and at the same moment the old man in monk's habit peered with wonder through a wooden tube. There were two men in short wigs, walking upon a wooden floor in the dark, and Damian could hear the beating of two large clocks inside cases which were fastened to the wall. As his eyes grew used to the starlight he saw that they were standing within an octagonal room, and now one man walked over to a large brass quadrant beside an open window. "You see," he was saying to his companion, "how the angle of the equinoctial gradient has changed?" Damian knew that the words were his own and yet not his own. He walked backwards, and he could hear his shoes upon a wooden floor. "Yes," he said. "It has changed." But all he sensed now was the ticking of the clocks.

It was time to leave the cottage. Perhaps there would be safety in the night. In the darkness he could hide from his attackers. For, after all, was he not worthy of attack – he who had achieved nothing, who had no reason to exist? He could not stay here, not in this house above the ground where he was so much exposed. He was about to close the curtains but then he put a hand on his arm to check himself; no, for that might be to close something in. And no lights, no electric lights; they were the lights of prison. If he switched them on he might glimpse his own shadow – he was afraid, literally afraid, of his own Shadow. He took up his jacket and ran out of the cottage, making sure that the door was still open after he had left. Let it be open to the valley tonight.

He climbed into his car and travelled through the gathering darkness to the observatory on Holblack Moor, where he knew he could find rest. He would soon be safe under the dome and, as he drove out of Pilgrin Valley, he amused himself by wondering how he might seem to anyone who was sitting beside him. He turned his head and smiled at his invisible companion, his dark face in profile against the dark window. I am not like this at all, he said. This is not really me at all.

There was no one at the observatory when he arrived; it was still too early for Brenda or Alec, who came at ten in order to work through the night. So he made his own way into the office, humming a little tune, and quickly passed through the passage into the observatory itself. He pushed a button and was bathed in red light as he turned to slam and lock the connecting door. Then he stood with his back against the wall. He was standing on the cliff of himself, looking down and frightened of falling.

Aldebaran. The giant star was waiting for him, as it had always done. It was the star which controlled all the sighs and tears of the earth, just as the moon controlled its tides. He must have known this from the beginning, but why was it now so important? He must watch red Aldebaran, in case time ran out. But how could time run out? Where could it run? It was the shape of the universe itself.

He descended the metal stairs to the control room beneath the floor of the observatory, where he was greeted by the murmur of the faint object spectrograph. The red light from the observatory penetrated this dim recess and he watched the spectral lines as they emerged from the printer, issuing from the immensity above his head; this starlight was thousands of years old but was now converted into lines and bands of colour, restored, changed into a different pattern, lost colours revived, impulses turned into form. Where others might look up at the night sky and glimpse only a faint light, blown by the gusts of the thermal currents and obscured by the giddy atmosphere, Damian could see the true identity of Aldebaran as it emerged in these lines which were like the spectral handwriting of one long since dead. Yes, that was it. He was haunted by the ghost of Aldebaran. The ghost was in the room with him. His eyes ached, and he passed his hand across his face.

But what was this? This could not be happening. As he watched, the spectral lines began shifting towards the shorter blue wavelengths at the end of the spectrum; the lines were coming together, they were being compressed by some enormous force. And he knew why this was so. The blue-shift meant that the giant star was no longer moving away; its passage from the red to the blue end of the spectrum meant that it was now moving towards the earth. It was approaching at enormous speed. In his agony he rushed over to the photon counting detector, which seemed to spring into chattering life even as he approached it and there, on its monitor, the figures which measured the background heat radiation of the universe were moving too rapidly. The numbers rose as he watched, numbers merging into one another so fast that they seemed like a series of faces entwined with one another.

He might have watched them for hours, seeing faces he recognised in the bewildering spirals. But he knew now. At last the long agony of the universe was over. The flight from its moment of origin had come to an end. It had ceased to expand and was now rushing towards him. Damian. He held onto the equipment, as if he were in danger of being blown away. This was the time he had always anticipated and had always feared.

He broke away from the photon detector and climbed back up to the dome, where he stopped suddenly, thinking he could hear the groaning of the night sky. So this was why he had seen the trembling flies. This was why he had heard the old voices in the cottage: the heat of the encroaching universe had woken them, and they had begun to celebrate the death of the cosmos which had imprisoned them for so long. The ground trembled beneath his feet: yes, they had come from beneath the earth, greeting the livid sky from which they had been formed. They were the shadows he had seen in front of him. And when he closed his eyes he could see the trees in Pilgrin Valley, ringed with fire and still burning.

But why had the ending not yet come? If the universe were contracting, returning to its unimaginable moment of birth, then surely it would have happened instantaneously? Once the pressures of time and space were reversed, and the universe doubled back upon itself, surely this unravelling would occur outside time – would occur, in a sense, after time had ceased to exist? So perhaps it had already happened. Perhaps the collapse of the universe had taken place, had reached past the moment of origin to be transformed into some other shape.

No. This could not be so. There was a world around him still. He lived and moved. He still existed, or else why should he be suffering so? No. It was only Aldebaran. Only the red star had been shaken from its accustomed place. Somehow Aldebaran had fallen from its sphere and, with the clairvoyance of one who has seen into extremity, Damian connected its fall with the disturbances in Pilgrin Valley. The shadows and the voices had been real, after all; they had come to warn him. Barren. Old. He went over to the monitor which interpreted the faint impulses caught by the electronic camera: here on the screen was the image of the great star itself, its light and dark patches suggesting that it was no longer of uniform brightness but was being twisted apart in some giant convulsion. All these images were growing paler, too, which meant that the star was becoming steadily hotter, coming much closer to the earth. The universe was not falling, just the one red giant star which had slipped out of its constellation and was now moving towards him. Damian felt his stomach melting in the heat. He looked down at the monitor again, and saw how the computer-generated squares of light were breaking up and shuddering at the edges of the screen. And he caught his own face reflected in that screen, bathed in red but with the mouth and eyes quite dark.

He moved to the other side of the observatory and, with a deep sigh, opened the dome. Slowly the two hemispheres of the roof parted, and starlight flooded the chamber, as it had always done. Damian wanted to look up with his usual calm eye and to recognise the familiar constellations shining down upon him; but he saw only random points of light swaying above his head and ready to fall. And he looked into the abysses between them, the gulfs of darkness which were not of this time, not of this time in which he had his being. And there were no stars, there were only words with which we choose to decorate the sky. These points of brightness were travelling from objects already long dead and the visible firmament was no more than a wave of dying energy, eddying through unimaginable spaces to some unknown destination. The universe was a structure established upon . . . established upon what? Nothing. And as he looked up he was filled with the fear of emptiness, the fear of non-being. And he became nothing. He crept into a corner of the observatory and sat down with his knees drawn up against his chest, crouched under the vast emptiness of the universe.

·73·

RESURRECTION MEN

"BE CAREFUL with him. Don't shake him up." There were three men in the subterranean passage, two of them carrying a large object wrapped in black plastic sheeting while the third walked ahead of them with a lamp. But they did not really need the light: the two carriers seemed to know their way so well that, despite their burden, they were able to anticipate every curve and declination in the tunnel. They were accustomed, also, to the changes they felt within themselves whenever they journeyed under the ground: they left the domain of ordinary time, and the echoes of their voices were like the other echoes which they sensed all around them. Time was curving back upon them, encircling them and also protecting them. It was as if they lost their ordinary selves and became the servants of this force – no different, perhaps, from those who first built this passage and from whom they believed themselves to be descended.

"He's in safe hands. None could be safer. Not on this earth." The first carrier stopped for a moment, and looked back at his companion. "What do you say, Boy?"

"As safe as houses. Isn't that what those fools call it? The house under ground?"

"Don't talk too loud." Simon Trout, who was carrying the lamp in front of the Mints, put his finger up to his lips. "They may be listening."

"The only ones listening here know all about us." Farmer Mint said. "They know our voices." And indeed only the dead could have heard them: it was into the round space of the souterrain, beneath the centre of the stone circle, that the bodies of the villagers were always brought; in this hollow within the rock, where the archaeologists had lost their lights, the corpses were prepared for burning and the smoke of their funeral fires ascended into those shafts and fissures which so resembled a cone.

"I'm talking about the ones still living," Simon Trout explained impatiently. "They might be listening. I'm talking about them above ground who may still be on the watch."

"There's no one watching. Don't you worry." Farmer Mint gave the signal to his son, and they picked up their burden again. "They've all gone home by now."

It was the night of Mark Clare's rescue from the hidden chamber, where he had found the wooden casket with the words 'Old Barren One' carved upon its side. This was the discovery which his colleagues had hoped for and, as soon as Mark was lifted out of the pit and taken into the upper air, they began to organise their excavation of this area. The pit itself would have to be thoroughly cleared, but the archaeologists had noticed that, although the central area had been swept clean of objects, there were traces of ash against the side of the rocks there; and the roof of the cavern above seemed, on first inspection, to be scorched or blackened. There must have been fires here, just at the point where the passages came together. But the prime object was the coffin which Mark Clare had found; this wooden casket would have to be removed, opened, and its contents examined. So it was true that Damian Fall had heard laughter as he sat in his cottage: it had been the laughter of the archaeologists who realised that, at last, their quest was over and that the secret of the tumulus had been resolved. Whoever was within the coffin – king, astronomer, or sorcerer – was clearly the object of the cult which existed in Pilgrin Valley; the tumulus was the entry to his mystery, the stone circle the emblem of his power.

It was long past midnight now and, under the cover of the darkest part of the night, the three men began to climb out of the passage which they knew so well. But they need not have feared discovery: as Farmer Mint had guessed, the others had gone home hours before. Simon Trout emerged cautiously from the entrance hidden in the copse, making sure to shield the lamp with his hands before he ventured into the cold night air. Farmer Mint and Boy Mint followed, alternately heaving and pushing the wooden coffin until it, too, re-emerged in the outer world. They kept it wrapped in the thick plastic sheeting, and laid it carefully on the hard ground. "Let him down gently," Farmer Mint whispered. "Lay him down gently on his own ground."

"He shouldn't have to leave," his son whispered back. "He

shouldn't have to be taken out in the night. Not like this.'' His companions understood what he meant – the wooden casket and its occupant were in the wrong place, almost in the wrong dimension. The wrong time. And for a moment Boy Mint thought he heard noises coming from within the coffin.

"He'll be back. Boy. He'll be back in good time. He understands."

Simon Trout glanced nervously around, and saw Damian Fall's cottage across the field. "Who lives there now?" he asked, pointing towards it. "Who is it?"

Boy Mint chuckled. "He won't be any trouble, he won't. I saw him go off hours ago. Like a lamb to the slaughter. There's only the angels left there now. The guardian angels."

As his son spoke Farmer Mint bent down and reverently passed his hand across the coffin. "We can't take him home," he said, as if anticipating their thoughts. "Because they might look for him there. And we can't take him into Colcorum. Too many foreigners. Begging your pardon," he added, lifting his cap to Simon, who lived in the village, "but there *are* strangers there. So the Boy and I have come up with a beautiful plan."

Simon Trout could hardly contain his impatience and anxiety. "What plan is this?"

Boy Mint put out his palm and then slapped it with his other hand. "We take him to Uncle Joey," he said. "Joey Hanover, as was."

"But—"

Farmer Mint took up the narrative. "He's family, isn't he? He's one of us. He's worn the stag." He chuckled. "And no one would suspect him would they? No one knows that there's a connection, do they?"

"They do *not!*" Boy Mint clapped his father on the shoulder. "They'd as soon suspect Uncle Joey as – as—" He searched for an appropriate name. "As Miss Evangeline Tupper herself."

"Have you told him?" Simon Trout seemed somewhat doubtful. "Have you warned him?"

"Not in so many words. But he's a good boy. He'll understand." He gestured to Boy Mint and together they took up the coffin again. "Be careful," he said. "We don't want to wake him. Not yet."

·74·

MY OLD MAN

DAY WAS breaking as they drove up to the Hanovers' house near the Cobb, but Joey was already awake; he was standing in his small front garden, wearing a scarlet dressing-gown despite the cold, and poking the frost-hardened soil with a stick. And as he did so he was singing:

> "Oh I do like to be beside the seaside—
> Even when it *is* very cold—
> Oh I do like to be beside the sea."

"Hello there," he said as Simon Trout and the two Mints opened the garden gate. "Who's the early bird and who's the worm?"

"We've got a little bit of a surprise for you, Joey." Farmer Mint looked very seriously towards him. "That's what we've got."

"Don't tell me." Joey closed his eyes. "It's my mother-in-law. You've had her stuffed."

"Close. But not close enough. You tell him, Boy."

"It's a member of the family, Uncle. You're right about that."

Joey suddenly turned pale, and dropped his stick upon the frosty ground. "It's nothing to do—" He coughed, shook his head, and started again. "It's nothing to do with my mother, is it?"

"Oh no." Farmer Mint did not take his eyes off him. "Further and further back than that. Deeper and deeper than that."

Joey was curiously relieved. "So what's the surprise, then?"

"He's in the back." Boy Mint said, indicating the scruffy green van in which they had arrived. "He needs a good home, he does."

Joey looked in the direction he was pointing, and laughed. "My old man said follow the van. Do you know that one?"

Now it was Farmer Mint's turn to laugh. "The old man is *in* the van this time."

"Not my fath—"

"No. I told you. Go further down. Further and further down."

"Should I invite him in then?" Joey Hanover was smiling. 'It's terribly chilly here, don't you think? When the wind blows?"

"He don't worry about the cold. Not him. What do they call him, Boy, when he don't notice the cold?"

"Impervious, father."

"That's the one. He's impervious, he is."

"He's dead," Simon Trout said in a lugubrious voice. "And he's been dead for rather a long time."

Joey Hanover looked at them in surprise, and then he started laughing. "I know," he said. "This is one of your routines, isn't it?" He assumed that this was another ritual 'testing', just like the pair of antlers he had worn at the dinner in Colcorum. "Bring him in then. What do you want me to do with him? Put him on my head?" And Joey led the way into the house.

"He's taking it very well," Simon whispered to Farmer Mint.

"He's not taken it at all. Not yet. But we'll do what Joey says. We'll bring him in. I've got a feeling he's going to like it here."

The three of them went back to the van and then brought the coffin, still wrapped in its black sheeting, up the garden path and into the house. They carried their burden slowly, and a silence seemed to descend upon the immediate neighbourhood; no birds sang as they lifted him across the threshold. Floey Hanover, wearing a vivid blue dressing-gown, was waiting in the front room. She glared at them as they lowered the coffin onto the floor. "Was it the cough that carried him off?" But she did not sound very amused.

Joey, now appreciating the joke, studied the bundle with a practised eye. "It looks like the old carpet trick, Flo," he said. "Do you remember the Human Hairpin?"

Farmer Mint began carefully to unwrap the plastic sheeting, and Floey sniffed the air. "It smells," she said, "like one of those things you find in telephone exchanges. You know. It rhymes with tulip." Joey was not listening to her. He was watching, fascinated, as the wooden casket was slowly revealed. Floey stopped talking, and also stared in amazement at the coffin. There was a change of atmosphere in the room; it seemed to the Hanovers to become wider or darker, and to be rocking gently from side to side as if it were balanced upon a slender pillar.

"Now this," Farmer Mint said proudly, "is the head of the family. This is the original Mint, Joey. The old one. Tell him, Boy."

"Yes. Tell me." Joey was staring at the silhouette in red ochre, of the figure with its knees up against its chest.

"We don't know how old he is," Boy Mint began. "Not to the exact year."

"Or century, Boy. Don't forget we don't know the century neither." Farmer Mint added this triumphantly, as if the further confusion only increased the importance of the object which they all now encircled. As if chaos were part of the pattern.

"But we do know he's as old as the burial ground. As old as the stones. He's always been with us. He's always been under the ground."

"Always looking after us, Joey."

"He's a Mint. That's what he is. And the Mints have taken good care of him."

Joey recalled the portraits of his ancestors which had been fixed above his cousin's fireplace. "Did you say you kept him under ground?"

"His ground. Under his ground." Farmer Mint put his hands in his pockets with a very deliberate gesture. And then he began explaining to Joey how the ancient coffin had always been concealed within the underground chamber; how generation after generation had come to venerate or to placate their ancestor. He did not know precisely when the souterrain had been discovered, and there was always the possibility that it had *not* been discovered but continually used. Used from the time when their original ancestor was carried through the valley and buried there. And he told Joey that there were stories – histories – connected with the resting place. Stories of human sacrifice, of blood poured into a small pit at the centre of the standing stones, of divination at the time of ritual killing.

"We don't do such things now, Uncle." Boy Mint wanted to reassure him. "This was ages and ages back."

"Not that far back," Farmer Mint added quickly. Joey said nothing, but continued to listen to his narrative. How, at the death of any relative, the body was taken under ground and burnt in the central area of the souterrain; how the ashes of the dead were then sprinkled over the fields around Colcorum and Pilgrin Valley. And how, every five years, the villagers made a ritual descent into the passage, crossed the round central area in solemn procession, and then journeyed down the small tunnel into the sacred enclosure – how they congregated around the coffin there and prayed to the spirit within it. Of course they had known all about the tumulus, hidden by the ash forest until the recent fire. But it had always been considered outside their bounds. It had never been touched or opened because there were other stories – stories how, at certain times, the original inhabitants could be seen clambering over the valley towards the tumulus; how it was an unlucky spot where the dead could take hold of the living.

"My own parents," Joey said. "My own parents died there."

And there was another story, too – that, if ever this coffin were opened, the dead would arise again and take over Pilgrin Valley. "That's why we had to take him away," Farmer Mint was saying. "From *his* land. From *his* tunnel. To protect him. From them."

"You mean?"

"Them. The experts, or whatever they call themselves. They were disturbing the peace. That's all they were doing." There was the sound of Floey Hanover trying to stifle a laugh, or groan; she had taken a handkerchief out of the pocket of her dressing-gown as Farmer Mint had been talking, and had now stuffed it in her mouth. "That's why," he added slowly, "we had to take him away."

"How old did you say it was?" Joey was staring once again at the silhouette in red ochre.

"Ages and ages back." Farmer Mint went over to the coffin and looked down at it, almost with the pride of ownership. "Right back to the beginning."

"The beginning?"

"I can't put it into words exactly. When things began. Started. You know—" He hesitated and then stopped.

"But how do you know," Joey asked, "that there's anyone still in there?"

"We feel the weight. We can still feel the weight of him. Don't you worry about that."

This was too much for Floey, who removed the handkerchief from her mouth and burst out in laughter. "Open the box!" she shouted. There was a note of hysteria in her voice. "Take the money or open the box!" She got up hurriedly, and started to leave the room. "Excuse me," she said. "I have to spend a penny."

The four men were silent for a few moments. "So what do you want me to do?" Joey picked up the handkerchief which his wife had dropped, and wiped his own forehead with it.

Boy Mint looked at his father, as if for permission to speak. "We want you to keep him."

"Keep him!"

"Just for a while. Just till they give up searching for him. And then we'll come and take him off your hands."

"I don't have to touch him, do I?"

"Just a figure of speech, Uncle. Just a figure."

"But where am I going to put it? Him."

Simon Trout, who had wanted to speak ever since he entered the house, now saw his opportunity. "Somewhere cold," he said. "And dark."

Farmer Mint took over. "It's winter, isn't it? That's cold enough. Have you got such a thing as a garden shed?"

"I have."

"Put him in that. He'll be happy there. Quite happy."

Floey had come back into the room. "It's the first time," she said, "that I've had a corpse in the garden." She went up to her husband, and gripped his arm very tightly.

"This is family," Farmer Mint said softly to Joey. "He's your family. He's one of us." And Joey, thinking of his lost parents, thinking of his origins, thinking of the remote time from which he had come, thinking of the peace he felt here, nodded.

GREEN FINGERS

"DON'T TELL me. Let me guess." Evangeline Tupper was sitting in the Hanovers' front room. "I love games." She was holding up the large ammonite which, several months before, Floey had picked out of the blue lias clay on St Gabriel's Shore. "It's on the tip of my tongue."

Hermione took it from her, and put it up to her ear. "I think," she said, "that's its something to do with Amazons—"

"But it's pink!"

"—or with a religious order."

"It's an ammonite." Joey came in from the garden, but stopped at the threshold of the front room in order to take off his thick gardening gloves.

Evangeline watched this ceremony with something like distaste. "Dear Joey," she said. "I suppose you have very green fingers?"

"I've only been in the shed," he said; and instantly regretted it.

"Bulbs and things?"

"And things."

"Joey is a great herbivore," Floey said. "He's ever so well known for it." But it was clear from her tone that she did not want to dwell on the subject of gardens or garden sheds, and almost at once she turned to Evangeline. "Tell Joey what happened in the observatory."

"Oh no." Evangeline pressed her hands between her knees. "You know that I never gossip." In fact she had talked about little else for the last ten minutes. "Really, it's too ghastly even to mention." The Hanovers waited patiently for her resolve to collapse. "All right then. You win. Well—" She gave Joey the full benefit of her innocent expression. "You know that strange little human being who lives in Pilgrim Valley?"

"Farmer Mint?" There was a certain cautiousness in Joey's voice.

"No. Not the grim reaper." Hermione had never told Evangeline about the family ties between Joey and the Mints; hence her relatively plain expression of distaste. "Revolting though he is. The other one. You know. The one who lives in the ugly little cottage. The astronomer."

"I never met him."

"Haven't you really? Well. It's too late now."

"Get on with it." Hermione had heard this story several times, and was growing impatient.

"That astronomer." Evangeline took out a Woodbine and knocked its tip on the palm of her hand before continuing with her sentence. "That astronomer went quite mad in the observatory. Barking, dear Joey. Absolutely barking. They found him curled up in a little ball, screaming that the sky was about to fall in. Just like that character in the fairy tale. And he kept on talking about Old Barren or Old Ones."

Joey suddenly became very attentive. "What was that?"

"You know. Old things."

"Do get your story straight," Hermione said, not without asperity. "He was talking about a star. Aldebaran."

"Quite. Some nonsense or other like that." Evangeline's cigarette was not yet lit, and she fumbled in her handbag for a small gold Rolex lighter. "Eventually he had to be injected with something. Isn't it too awful for words?"

"Poor man," Joey said. He looked across at Floey who all the time had been examining her hands, having placed them firmly in her lap.

"I know." Evangeline sighed, and let out a ring of cigarette smoke which ascended to the ceiling. "In the old days they would have taken a whip to him. But I suppose progress is inevitable. Now. Tell me your news."

Floey was still looking down at her hands. "Nothing. Nothing ever seems to happen to us."

"And then of course," Evangeline went on, pausing only for breath, "there is the other huge drama. At the excavations." Floey and Joey looked at each other very briefly, but she had noticed their momentary glance of complicity. "I suppose some gossiping bitch has already told you about it? People can be so vile."

"Told us? Told us what?" Joey was humming a little tune, but Evangeline noticed at once that he was blushing.

Hermione saw this, too. "Forget it," she said to Evangeline. "Put a sock in it."

"You naughty thing. You should never say sock. You should say stocking." She pronounced the word very slowly, but all the time she was looking at the Hanovers. "Or, at a pinch, tights. But not socks. Never socks. Now. Where was I?" She took another long drag of her Woodbine, while the others said nothing. "Oh yes. Something's been stolen. Some ghastly old object has been taken away." And she noticed how Floey was blushing now, too, and how Joey gave an almost subliminal glance towards the gardening gloves which he had dropped outside the door. "We all suspect the Mints, of course, ever since we found some funny little letters in the tomb. And that reminds me." She put her head to one side and smiled at Joey. "I *knew* there was something. Weren't you seen at the famous Mint dinner in the village?"

"Yes," he replied, somewhat desperately. "They wanted an act for the night."

"How sophisticated of them." She looked at him for several seconds. "Of course this object is of enormous value. I'm not accusing the Mints for an instant, but the robbers are bound to be thrown into jail. For ever, probably."

Floey rose to her feet. "I must go upstairs," she said. "I've got a slight pain in my clavicle."

"Do be careful with it." Evangeline was almost cheerful. "It's the only clavicle you've got."

There was a silence as she left the room, which her husband finally broke. "Talking of coffins," he said, "reminds me of a joke—"

"I didn't mention coffins." Evangeline was very stern. "Whatever gave you that idea?"

Joey was becoming flustered. "Yes you did. You said coffins. I heard you. Definitely coffins."

Hermione knew all about his connection with the Mints, and now guessed that he might somehow be involved in the theft. "I hate to throw a spanner in the works, Evangeline—" Her friend shuddered at the phrase. "But you mentioned coffins at least twice."

"Did I really? How extraordinary. I must be raving. Like that astronomer. Absolutely raving." She saw how Joey was biting his lower lip. "I must just go and see Floey," she added, getting up very quickly. "I'm terribly worried about her clavicle." She left the room but, instead of going upstairs to Floey, she tiptoed through the small kitchen and opened the back door to the garden: there was something wrong here. She sensed it. Something to do with the ghastly Mints. She walked out into the garden and, ducking down beneath the window, scurried over to the garden shed. But as she approached it she felt very faint, and for a moment leaned against its mouldering door; she had had a sudden vision of her father, dead. She passed a hand across her face and turned around; she did not want to open the door of the shed – something held her back – and instead she peered through its cracked and smeared window. At first she could see nothing but two green bags of compost, some flower pots, an old rake and the broken engine of a lawnmower. But then, beneath a low shelf and lying upon the ground, she saw a large object half-covered by empty potato sacks. At once she knew what it was. And she felt afraid. She ran back into the kitchen, only to find Floey standing in front of her with a knife raised in her hand. "Don't do it!" Evangeline screamed.

"Don't do what?" Floey screamed back. Both women were in fact equally startled. "Don't cut the cake?" There was a Scotch seed cake in her other hand.

"Don't—" Evangeline tried to recover from her fright. "Don't ever cut down those rose bushes. They'll be absolutely lovely next year." And both women looked at each other, uncertain what the other knew or guessed.

Alarmed by the noise, Joey now came into the kitchen. "Did somebody drop something?"

"I dropped a hint," Evangeline said, moving towards the door. "About your divine blooms." For some reason she did not want to be left alone with them any more, and she called out to Hermione. "Miss Crisp." She looked quickly at her watch. "Miss Crisp! It's time to be on our way!" She glanced back at the Hanovers, who were standing together now. "It gets dark here so early, don't you think? And cold, too. So cold."

·76·

THINK PINK

THE TELEPHONE was ringing as they returned to their room in the Blue Dog, and Evangeline rushed to answer it. "It's me," she shouted. "Miss Tupper!"

"Is it really? It sounded like Winston Churchill." Augustine Fraicheur, enjoying a pre-lunch drink, was in playful mood. "Voices can be so deceptive, can't they?"

"Along with everything else."

He smiled at his gin. "Any *news*?" Augustine accentuated the last word, as if he were anticipating something very shocking indeed.

"Actually," she replied, automatically delving into her handbag for another Woodbine, "I have the most fabulous piece of gossip." She paused to light it. "But I don't know if I should tell you."

"Torturer!" He screamed with pleasure.

"Honestly. You'll have to wait."

"I can't *bear* it."

"But I promise that you'll be among the first to know."

"I think I'm beginning to go mad."

"Like poor Damian Fall?"

"Fall was an astronomer. I am an antiques dealer. A much tougher breed. Now come on and tell me before I call the police."

"Actually the police are very apropos. Is that the expression?"

"Yes, that's the expression." Augustine was becoming impatient.

"Well." She took a long drag of her cigarette. "Do you remember that coffin which was stolen from the valley?"

"That ghastly old thing your friends dug up?"

"We didn't dig it up. We knew where it was to be found." From her tone it was clear that she had organised the entire excavation herself. "But the gorgeous thing is that now I've found it again. And you'll never guess where."

"The hotel kitchen?"

310

"In the Hanovers' garden shed." At this moment Hermione Crisp took a step towards her, put out her hand, but then hesitated. "In their absolute shed. Doesn't it remind you of one of Saki's short stories?"

"I thought sake was a drink."

"To you, my darling, anything could be a drink." Augustine's reaction was less fulsome than she expected, and at once she became bored with him. "Listen. I have to go now. I have to telephone Mark Clare and tell him the good news about the coffin."

She put down the receiver without waiting for Augustine's farewell, and was about to dial Mark's number when Hermione put her hand on top of the telephone. "Don't," she said.

"Why, Baby Doll, what lovely red nails you have today."

"Don't do it. Don't tell him about Joey." As soon as they had left the Hanovers, Evangeline had vividly recounted her discovery of the old coffin in the garden-shed; Hermione was not particularly surprised, but she was alarmed for her new friends. Flocy's revelation that her husband had found his family once more had delighted her, and she saw no reason why that reunion should be injured by Evangeline. And, even as she listened to this conversation with Augustine, she had decided to tell Flocy to remove the coffin. Before it was too late. "Don't ring Mark Clare," she said.

"I have to tell him, Baby Doll. These silly men love a good drama." Hermione shook her head, looked up at the ceiling, sighed, and then came to a decision: she went over to the door, locked it, and put the key down the front of her starched white shirt-front. Then she went over to a suitcase left in a corner of the room, and took from it two thick pieces of rope which were generally used to fasten it. She walked over to Evangeline, grabbed hold of her wrists and pinioned them together. Evangeline watched all this with astonishment, as if it were happening to somebody else. "Baby," she whispered. "This isn't a very feminine thing to do."

"There are times when a woman's got to do what a woman's got to do." She tied Evangeline's wrists with one piece of rope.

"Is this some lovely new game, Baby Doll? In which case, you had better tell me the rules."

"This is no game." Now she was tying Evangeline's ankles to the chair. "You have to leave the Hanovers alone for a while. They need time."

"Baby." Evangeline began to sound stern. "Unless I am very

much mistaken, I am being tied up. Like some Mormon woman.''

"Do be quiet. Just for once."

She went into the bathroom and returned with a roll of Elastoplast. "Hermione darling." Evangeline was horrified by this new development. "Remember what I always tell you. Think pink." Hermione cut off a strip of the Elastoplast. "Think pink!" And she put it over Evangeline's mouth.

After a few moments Hermione picked up the telephone and rang the Hanovers, but there was no answer. So she sat down and waited, stonily watching Evangeline as her companion rolled her eyes dramatically and issued a few moans of muffled protest.

It was at this moment that Augustine Fraicheur was leaving the antiques shop on his way to the Hungry Donkey; his straw hat was tipped rakishly at an angle, and it fell off as he tried to lock the outside door. He had just retrieved it when Mark Clare and Martha Temple walked up beside him. "Hello," he said, his speech slightly blurred. They were both dressed in black, and he giggled. "My dears, you look as if you've just come from . . . Oh. I am sorry." He suddenly remembered that this had been the morning of Kathleen's funeral. "I'm terribly sorry. I forgot."

"We don't mind, Mr Fraicheur." Martha Temple seemed to have assumed the role of chief mourner. She had announced after the funeral that she would "look after" Mark; he had wanted to leave alone and, as far as possible, unnoticed but she had solemnly marched back with him to the waiting car and, on the slow drive back into Lyme Regis, she had been recalling all those colleagues who had not attended the ceremony. "A little thing like that," she added to Augustine, "could slip anybody's mind."

He was eager to change the subject. "As it happens," he said very quickly. "I was rather *préoccupé*. Our dear friend Miss Tupper just called."

"Oh yes?" Martha Temple looked at him with fresh animosity. "We were expecting to see her today, too."

"—and she had the most extraordinary piece of news." His eyes glistened from the effect of the gin, and he dabbed them with his pocket handkerchief. "Most extraordinary."

Mark was waiting, head bowed, to walk past him and enter his flat. But Martha was now interested. "What news?"

"I should really leave it to her, of course." Augustine hesitated, but he could not resist. "It was about that coffin you lost. She's found it."

Mark looked at him for the first time, and Augustine flinched. "Found it?"

"She says she found it with the Hanovers. She found it in their garden shed."

"I knew it!" In fact Martha Temple had only the faintest recollection of the Hanovers, and had spent the last few days throwing dark suspicions upon everybody else. "And in a shed, too."

Mark remained calm. "When did she tell you this?"

"Minutes ago. I was just pouring myself a large gin. You know the way one does? And then she 'phoned. She was ever so excited."

Mark walked past and climbed the stairs, followed by the others. When he entered his flat Jude was waiting to greet him, and the sight of the little dog awakened all of the sorrow he had felt at the funeral. He picked him up, and buried his face in the dog's fur.

"Don't you think," Martha said, "you should call Evangeline at once? There are several people who ought to be in jail by now."

Reluctantly he put down the dog and went over to the telephone. He spoke in a low voice for a few moments, as Martha strained impatiently to hear. "That was Miss Crisp," he said. Martha gave a little shake of disapproval. "She says that Evangeline has gone back to London."

Augustine, already convinced that he was responsible for the whole development of this mystery, was irate. "Evangeline always confides in me, and she didn't even mention London! Not a syllable."

"The police." Martha was very firm. "We must call the police at once. I have a great many things I wish to tell them."

"No. Not yet. Let me think." Already the images of the funeral re-emerged as Mark tried to consider his next move. He was once again beside the open grave, watching as his wife's coffin was lowered into the ground; now he could see the earth being tossed upon it. And for a moment, in his perplexity, it seemed to him that the Hanovers had taken his wife's coffin. "Martha. You and I will go to the Hanovers now. Evangeline may have misunderstood. I just don't know—" He was rubbing his forehead savagely with his hand. "Mr Fraicheur, would you mind—"

"I'll do anything. Anything."

"Would you mind telephoning two of my colleagues, to tell them what has happened?" Yet it all seemed so pointless to him. And, as Mark talked, the dog lay still at his feet.

·77·

AMMONITE

THE HANOVERS had just returned from a walk along the Cobb when Mark Clare and Martha Temple called upon them; and, as the archaeologists were shown into the small back room, it occurred to both of them that Evangeline Tupper might have been quite mistaken – or, more probably, that Augustine Fraicheur had exaggerated her suspicions. Certainly nothing could have been calmer than Floey's demeanour as she poured them coffee. The Hanovers did not seem even to be particularly surprised by this unexpected visit, but it was clear that they were waiting for some explanation. And yet neither Mark nor Martha really knew how to begin – until, that is, Martha remembered the shed. Slowly she went over to the window which overlooked the garden. "How lovely this must look in the spring. When everything is reborn." She paused. "Will you have ladies' fingers?"

"I hope so." Floey looked down at her own, which were now trembling slightly. "We have champions and acrimony, too."

"Campions," Joey interpreted. "And agrimony."

Martha smiled sympathetically at Floey. "I do envy people with time on their hands."

"Joey is very keen on his contagious borders."

"I would love to see them. Can I go outside?" She noticed how furtive the Hanovers suddenly became, but at this moment the telephone rang in the next room. Joey went out to answer it: it was Hermione, rapidly explaining how Evangeline had found the coffin and had then telephoned Augustine. "Evangeline will keep her mouth shut for a while," she was saying. "But not for long."

"That is nice to know," Joey replied, without thinking. "Ta very much." But, by the time he put down the receiver, he had gone quite pale. He stood for a moment, vacantly staring out of the window and stroking his cheek. Then he telephoned the Mints and, as he outlined

315

the situation, Farmer Mint signalled to his son who was feeding the chickens in the yard. They would, he said, arrive in fifteen minutes. Joey came back into the room, humming a vague tune.

"We were just saying," Martha announced very brightly, "that we would love to see your garden. Weren't we, Mark?"

Mark had said nothing; he was hardly looking up at all. "Yes," he said. He had been thinking of the flowers at Kathleen's funeral – flowers cut or uprooted, as if in killing them the mourners were re-enacting a symbolic death in homage to the human one. "Yes. Of course."

"The garden is not at its best this time of year," Joey closed the door firmly behind him. He knew that he had to detain them here until the Mints arrived and had removed the coffin. "But it does remind me of a song I used to know. Years ago now. Would you like to hear it?" He put out his arms and went down on one knee, but then froze in this striking posture. He could no longer remember any words. "La la la," he sang, "something, la la, to do with a little plot. Silly me. And there was a body in it somewhere." Then he stopped, very suddenly, and awkwardly rose to his feet.

"That was lovely," Martha exclaimed, clapping her hands. "And with a real moral there, too. For all of us."

"More coffee?" Floey became very attentive to the others.

"I'd love some." Martha looked across at Mark, as if urging him to talk, but still he said nothing. So in turn she became very cheerful. "It's so nice," she said, "to have a rest from the excavations. I suppose you've heard all about our trouble there?"

Floey perceptibly tightened her grip on the coffee-pot. "Oh. Just rumours. You know how it is."

"Of course I do. So you must have heard that an ancient artefact was stolen?"

"Stolen?"

"Taken. Removed in the night. It was one of the most valuable objects ever found in this country."

Joey began to say, "How do you know how valuable—"

His wife stopped him with a glance. "We never heard anything about that, did we, Joey?"

"Not a dicky bird, Floey."

"Really?" Martha was now certain that something was wrong here, and began to enjoy herself. "Not even a little bit of a birdy here and there?"

"No," Joey was very stern. "We know nothing."

Martha turned to Mark. "I think," she said, "that you ought to tell them. It's only fair." She already realised that, if Evangeline's suspicions proved false, no blame could be attached to herself; so she relaxed a little. "They have a right to know."

"To know what?" Floey seemed indignant.

Mark really did not know what to say; his head was bowed, and he was picking at a thread in the armchair as he spoke. "There's just a chance," he said. "Just a possibility—"

He was too slow for Martha. "Evangeline Tupper tells us that you have a coffin in the garden shed. Strange as it may seem."

"Now there's a funny thing," Joey was quite at a loss.

"Isn't that a funny thing?" his wife echoed.

"Very funny indeed," Martha replied. "But I'm sure there's a perfectly rational explanation for it. Why on earth would you want to keep a coffin in the garden?"

Joey swallowed very hard. "I don't think—"

Martha forestalled him by rising to her feet. "So if you would just allow us to take a tiny peek, we can all be satisfied."

"You can't," Floey replied, also rising to her feet. "The garden door is locked. And I've lost the key."

"How curious." Martha walked over to the window. "But that pile of, of—"

"Sticks," Joey said in a low voice.

"But that pile of sticks looks as if it has just been put there." She craned her head, and noticed that in fact the door to the garden was ajar. "I wonder," she added, sweetly, "if I could just go and powder my nose?" She left the room without waiting for an answer but after a few seconds Floey, taking something from the mantelpiece, followed her.

So the two men were left alone together, neither really knowing what to say to the other. And Joey could not bear the silence. "You know, don't you?" he asked.

Mark sighed, and smiled at him. "Sometimes," he said, "I don't think I *know* anything at all."

Joey looked at him carefully, and for the first time noticed that he was wearing an arm-band on his dark suit. "I'm sorry," he said. "I didn't realise—" He had heard about Kathleen's suicide, but had not really thought of it since the Mints' arrival with the coffin.

Mark put up his hand. "No. Don't be sorry. It's all over." Now he began to find the words which had been eluding him since the funeral. "As long as I can think of it as a natural thing, as an inevitable thing, I can go on. Did you hear how I was caught in the underground passage for a while?" Joey nodded. "It was there I first realised it. That I first understood how nothing really dies. Just because we are trapped in time, we assume that there is only one direction to go. But when we are dead, when we are out of time, everything returns." Joey was listening to him intently. "Everything is part of everything else—" Mark broke off. "—I don't know. Am I making any sense?"

"Of course. How could it not make sense? After what has happened to all of us?"

Mark hardly understood this. He wanted to complete his thought. "And do you know," he went on, "someone once told me a wonderful thing. He told me that our bodies are made out of dead stars. We carry their light inside us. So everything goes back. Everything is part of the pattern. We carry our origin within us, and we can never rest until we have returned."

Joey Hanover had put his hands together, as if he were praying. "Yes. I know that, too. Why do you think I came back here? I was looking for my own past." He stopped for a moment. "And why do you think it was that we had to take him from you?"

"Him?"

"The old one in the coffin. He's part of us, too, you see."

There was a scuffle and a sudden noise outside; both men looked at each other in alarm, and rushed out into the hallway. Martha Temple was lying upon the floor and Floey Hanover stood over her, brandishing the ammonite in her hand. "She tried to get into the garden," she said. "So I gave her a little – what's that word, Joey, which rhymes with rash?"

·78·

AT LAST

FLOEY SOLEMNLY handed the ammonite to Mark Clare. "You can use it," she said, "in the evidence against me." Then the doorbell rang and Mark was so startled that at once he dropped the fossil, which fell with a thud onto the hall carpet. Floey expected the police somehow to have arrived already and she marched towards the door, opening it with a great flourish. The Mints were standing there, both of them twisting their caps in their hands. "Where is he?" Farmer Mint asked her.

"He's right in front of you."

"No. Not Joey. Where is *he*? The old one?"

"He's in the garden shed." She stepped to one side in order to let them in. "But it's too late now."

The Mints were just about to rush into the house, and remove the coffin to some new place of safety, when two cars drew up in the street: Owen Chard and Julian Hill, alerted by Augustine Fraicheur's somewhat hysterical telephone calls, had come to assist Mark Clare. They were still wearing black suits from the funeral. Farmer Mint turned to face them and whispered to his son, "Get out the pitchforks." Boy rushed to the van, dived into the back, re-emerged with the implements and, just as Julian and Owen were about to open the garden gate, burst through them and stood with his father on the threshold of the Hanovers' house.

"Oh dear. Oh dear." Owen shook his head at the two men facing them. "We are back in the seventeenth century, aren't we?"

"I don't care what century it is," Farmer Mint replied. "You don't come no nearer. Not a step nearer."

"Not *you*," Boy echoed. At this point Floey, overwhelmed by the events of the last few minutes, gave a little scream and slammed the front door.

Julian Hill tried to advance, but Boy Mint brandished his pitch-

319

fork and he retreated. "We are only archaeologists," he said. "We only want to examine a find."

"He's not a find." Farmer Mint shouted. "He's a Mint. He's one of us. Joey! Joey!" Joey heard the call, and opened the front door to hear what his cousin had to say. "Joey! Burn him. Burn the old one before they get him. Let him go back."

"Burn him?" Joey was incredulous.

"No!" Julian shouted. "Leave it to us. We need to study it!"

"You know what you have to do, Joey." Farmer Mint spoke very slowly. "He can't be taken away from us. Send him home."

Joey closed the door, and turned to face Mark who had heard this conversation. "Are you going to try and stop me?" he said softly.

Mark stepped back. "I don't know." For some reason it was he who was imploring Joey. "I just don't know."

"It's my family. Like yours."

Mark put his hand on Joey's arm, but not as a gesture of restraint. "It must be your decision," he said. "We have to bury our own dead."

Joey smiled. "Yes. That's right. What was it you said about the stars?" He walked into the kitchen, stepped over Martha Temple who was now moaning as she began to regain consciousness, and went out into the garden.

He opened the shed and knelt down beside the old wooden coffin. He traced the carved words on its side with his finger and then he said out loud, "I am the last person. I am the last person on earth to talk to you. Your presence is coming to an end."

The coffin was too cumbersome to lift and so he dragged it along the floor of the shed into the garden; then he stood up, panting, and examined the red silhouette of the crouched figure. "I have to see you," he said. "After thousands of years, someone has to see your face. You can't leave us without being seen." With a deep sigh he went back into the shed, and came out with a hammer and chisel. He looked over his shoulder at the house, almost in embarrassment, but then he saw with relief that Floey had drawn the curtains. Very carefully he put the chisel into the worn groove of the coffin and hammered it home, drawing it upwards and creating a small chink or cavity in the wood. There was no noise. He had expected a sound like some vast intake of breath, but the coffin was silent: he had the strangest feeling that someone was waiting for him. He worked around the edge of the coffin, prising it open very gently wherever he could. And at last it was free.

For a moment he could not open it. He knelt upon the hard ground and, with bowed head, put his hands upon it. "Forgive me," he said. Then he raised the lid.

He saw him. The body was not lying crouched, as the silhouette had depicted. A small human form was lying upon its back, the thin arms and hands crossed upon the breast. And, when Joey felt able to look at the face, the hollowed eyes seemed to be gazing out at him almost in pity. Then something began. Joey stared in surprise at the withered face and limbs because they were being joined by some other force – as he might have stared at a radio which suddenly began to transmit music. There were voices. Joey turned and turned about, his hand over his mouth. They were human voices but they had some different note within them, and at this moment it seemed to Joey that these were the original voices – voices which had known speech but not writing. Like sky without cloud. And as he gazed at the small figure other sounds began to encircle him or, rather, thoughts raised into sound as a sleeper rises after a dream and talks.

Time. Another time. He lifts up his hands to the sky and his voice rises above the valley, calling the animals with their own notes, making the noise of water and the sound of trees in the wind. For in this world sound is the soul of all things, and it rises through him. The leader. In delirium he makes the sound of stone which is the sound of prophecy. He tells them of their dreams: he raises his hands and speaks to them. We are so close to the beginning that we have dreams of origin and of the darkness from which we come. That is why we try to reach the light above our heads. He tells them of the sky. He raises his hands and tells them of the night. They are not fires above us but souls, the souls of those who came before us and light our way. They are the eyes of the dead, always watching. They are our hopes: that is why they are so distant and why there is darkness amongst them. They are the word for far. They are the word for dream. You must make your own fires in the same pattern. Place your fires here, in the valley, in the pattern of the sky. And so make the stars your home.

Joey hears all this and weeps. He turns about and time turns about him; he puts out his hand, bewildered, towards the coffin. But the coffin is no longer there. Time turning. There is a time, he says, there is a time when the seven blue fires rise above the horizon and the red eye watches over them. They mark the time of warmth, and to make this time return you must carve them into the stone. Carve their pattern into the stone. Sky stone. In the valley of the seven stars. I have chosen this place. I have listened to the earth and chosen it. I have chosen the powerful green glowing upon the hilltop, and I have chosen the sacred avenue beneath the earth. Build here. Purify the ground with fire and walk out the circle. Measure the ground which brings on trance and prophecy. Build the house of stone within the circle. And bring me to this place when I am called away from you. So the stones were carved from the sea's edge, lifted and carried along the wooden ways, a passage burnt before them through the vagrant paths of stream and forest and hillside. Shuffling of feet and singing. They build the house of stone. Pointing one way. Only one way. Beneath. And only he may walk the avenue under the earth.

Time. More time. The indivisible moment of his parting from us. He died and we changed the silence with our cries. Lamentation on the brow of the hill. An absence. A curving inwards. And so we carried him along the valley, in a casket of carved wood. Smoke in the far distance to greet the procession, and the animals bow their heads towards the earth in homage. The birds rise from their trees, wings upon wings. He is led to his last home, miraculous journey under the ground in which the guide must die.

He who led us touches hands with the one before him, and touches hands with the one who follows. Like the circling stars and the circling generations of the earth. Locked within the circle. A testament. We lift our hands high, palms outward, facing the sun in honour of him who goes down.

Time. Another time. Joey is turning and turning, his features blurred by the wind from the valley. He hears them there, but he cannot speak. He cannot answer the voices coming out of time. Ancient voices.

Wind sound. Air sound. What turns the light to darkness, and causes the river to run one way? We speak softly to one another, for this is the law, and our voices mingle with the animals who move among us. We know only what they know: we know only the weight of the world, and the innumerable odours around us. Skin. Fur. The sea. The river. The smell of those who sleep upon the ground, and those who shelter in caves. Those who lie among the animals and those who lie among their own kind. Blood. The smell of those who have just come to us, screaming at the light, and of those about to leave us. This is the sum of our knowledge.

Everything falls. Struck by the stone, the beast falls. And then the stone falls from the hand. Death coming and going. Herding us as a dog herds cattle, rushing down the hills, creeping along the bank of the stream, knocking us down with the palm of his hand. Hand across the neck. Why have we been left here, unknown, walking a few short paces over the earth? The earth is still strange to us, each horizon a line of danger. Consider each man in his days: the sun behind him, the sun in front of him. Forced to walk between, to walk through the changing light until he falls into the dark. No more than that. No more. Tied to the world as a dead bird is tied to a tree.

This is the time of change, the strange time foretold by his death. We stare at the giant mound, at the horror of the stone and the dark world beneath it. Our despair is like a stone. We move from side to side, lamenting. Time. Another time. Another dawn. Great sun. Red sun rising. Touching the white frost with flame, turning the hills to purple. Across the fields falls the shadows of the stone, the shadows of the animals, the thin shadows of our bodies. As the sun rises and floods this valley with its light. This, our home. There is no other.

Joey is still watching the face when he seems to awake from his own dream. He has returned to his garden, and is bending over the coffin once more. And in this old face, now, he sees other faces – he sees the features of his mother and, extending his hand, he cries out to her. He sees his father, lifting him from a bed of purple flowers. He sees in this face, too, the faces of all those who had come before him. And the faces of all those he has known. This is the human face he recognised in all those he has loved. Joey is crying, his tears falling upon the ancient human form.

And, as he watched the face within the coffin, he saw a landscape with figures moving across it. But it was the face itself changing, being transformed. The old face began to stir and fade, just as a wind passes across sand and dissolves its features. Entering another time. "So you saw us, too," Joey said. "You saw us at last."

·79·

LIGHT

AT THIS moment Evangeline Tupper pulled up outside the house in a taxi and emerged, triumphant, with Hermione. "Now," she said, "aren't you glad you let me go? Just look at all these silly men." She walked up the garden path. "She had to untie me." She seemed to be addressing no one in particular. "Women's Lib!" She stopped when she saw the Mints brandishing their pitchforks. "What on earth is going on here?"

Julian turned to her viciously. "Can't you see? They won't let us in. They've got the coffin inside."

"I could have told you that," she said, with a laugh. "Hours ago." She walked up to the Mints and put her hands on top of their pitchforks. "I love your style," she said. "But there have to be limits. Even to rural life." She walked past them, knocked on the Hanovers' door, and then turned to wave at the others.

As soon as Floey had unlocked the door Evangeline pushed it open and, paying no attention to her, walked into the kitchen where Mark was bending over Martha. When she saw her lying there Evangeline smiled. "Is she drunk?" she asked him.

Martha, who had been whimpering slightly, made a very quick recovery. "If you must know, I have just been hit on the head with something extremely large."

"Seeing stars, are we? Pity." She examined the bruise on Martha's forehead with almost clinical detachment, and was about to touch it with her finger when Martha jerked away her head. "But at a time like this," she went on, disappointed, "even the most terrible personal tragedies have to be put to one side." She looked at Mark, as if she were trying to remember something. "Where's the body? The real body, I mean."

"Outside."

Evangeline scurried over to the kitchen door, but it was locked.

She turned around, to find that Floey was standing behind her with her arms folded. "So far, Miss Evangeline Tupper," she said. "And no further."

"I wouldn't be too sure of that if I were you." She walked past her and went into the back room which overlooked the garden. She opened the heavy curtains which Floey had drawn, and was in time to see Joey dragging the coffin onto a large pile of sticks. "This is absolute—" She could not think of a word. "—I have to stop him." But she was too late; even as she watched, Joey set fire to the sticks. She rushed into the kitchen and with a loud shout hurled herself against the door; but it did not move and she staggered backward upon Martha Temple who gave an equally loud scream of pain. "This is no time to think of your personal comfort," Evangeline said. "I have a job to do."

She looked wildly around and picked up a toaster from the kitchen table; she was just about to throw it through the window of the garden door when Mark Clare stopped her. "No," he said. "Not now. It's too late."

Together they returned to the back room and looked out of the window. Already the flames were licking the side of the coffin. They could see the pale breath issuing from Joey's mouth; he was singing as the coffin and the ancient body were consumed in the fire. Floey helped Martha into the room, and all of them watched as the smoke rose into the sky. The Mints saw it, too. They put down their pitchforks and stood in the middle of the garden. Hermione joined them, alongside Owen and Julian. All of them watching the smoke flowing into the air.

And suddenly Evangeline knew that her father was standing beside her; smiling, she turned to him. She talked to him, but she made no sound. Mark was with Kathleen again, as he knew he always would be. Joey put his arms around his parents who had returned to him at last. And Hermione was surrounded by the children of St Gabriel, the children who had once tried to fly. The Mints did not need to turn around to know that there were others with them, too, a whole concourse of people who stood and watched silently. But they felt no fear. It was as they had always been told. No one is ever dead, and at this moment of communion a deep sigh arose from the earth and travelled upward to the stars.

Now they were alone again. And now they are children, their parents standing behind them and resting their hands lightly on

them. And now they are also old, tired of the earth and longing for
sleep. The years brushed past them lightly, like the wings of wings.
All this happened in a moment out of time, and out of time it was
gone. "It's all over," Farmer Mint said to his son, as he watched the
smoke growing paler and paler. "He's safe now."

They fell silent as the ancient form flew upwards into the air – high
above Lud Mouth, where Mark Clare had re-entered the world,
above St Gabriel's Cliff, where the lost children had fallen, above
Swithin's Column, where Kathleen Clare had died, above Pilgrin
Valley and his old resting place there. He had been released at last.
He had returned to the frame of origin. The ashes rose into the sky,
higher and higher, rising towards Aldebaran and the other stars,
until eventually they faded into the light.

◆ 80 ◆

THE UNCERTAINTY PRINCIPLE

LET ME be drawn up into the immensity. Into the darkness, where nothing can be known. Once there were creatures of light leaping across the firmament, and the pattern of their movement filled the heavens. But the creatures soon fled and in their place appeared great spheres of crystal which turned within each other, their song vibrating through all the strings of the world. These harmonies were too lovely to last. A clock was ticking in the pale hands of God, and already it was too late. Yes. The wheels of the mechanism began to turn. What was that painting by Joseph Wright of Derby? I saw it once. Was it called 'The Experiment'? I remember how the light, glancing through a bell-jar, swerved upwards and covered the whole sky. But this too went out: the candle flame was blown away by the wind from vast furnaces, when the electrical powers swept across the firmament.

But there were always fields, fields of even time beyond the fires. Empty space reaching into the everlasting. At least I thought that as a child. Then there came a tremor of uncertainty. There was no time left. No space to float in. And everything began moving away. Nothing but waves now, their furrows tracking the path of objects which do not exist. Here is a star called Strange. Here is a star called Charmed. And after this, after this dream has passed, what then? What shape will the darkness take then? I . . . Damian Fall turned to his shadow. Of course you know what we will be observing? Yes, Aldebaran. One hundred and twenty times brighter than the sun.

Burning star. Seeming to be red, but the colours shifting like an hallucination. In this same area of the sky he saw small cones of light, known as the Hyades and believed to be at a greater distance from the earth – cool red stars glowing within the clouds of gas which swirled about them. And close to them the lights known as the Pleiades, involved in a blue nebulosity which seemed to stick against

327

each star, the strands and filaments of its blue light smeared across the endless darkness. Behind these clusters he could see the vast Crab Nebula, so far from the earth that from this distance it was no more than a mist or a cloud, a haziness in the eye like the after-image of an explosion. And yet Damian could see further still. He looked up and could see. Galaxies. Nebulae. Wandering planets. Rotating discs. Glowing interstellar debris. Spirals. Strands of brightness that contained millions of suns. Darkness like thick brush-strokes across a painted surface. Pale moons. Pulses of light. All of these coming from the past, ghost images wreathed in mist which confounded Damian. I am on a storm-tossed boat out at sea, the dark waves around me. This was what the earliest men saw in the skies above them – an unfathomable sea upon which they were drifting. Now we, too, talk of a universe filled with waves. We have returned to the first myth. And what if the stars are really torches, held up to light me on my way? I see what they saw in the beginning, even before the creatures of light appeared across the heavens. I can see the first human sky.

Yes, Aldebaran. Once this region was thought to form the outline of a face in the constellation of Taurus. He smiled at his shadow. But the Pleiades contains three hundred stars in no real pattern. Just burning, being destroyed, rushing outward. The last vestiges of cloud had now drifted away and the entire night sky had reappeared, so bright and so clear that Damian Fall put out his hand to it; then he turned his wrist, as if somehow he could turn the sky on a great wheel. And for a moment, as he moved his head, it did seem that the stars moved with him. Why is it that we think of a circular motion as the most perfect? Is it because it has no beginning and no end?

Time. Another time. He looks out of the window, from the confines of his bed. But he can see nothing now. Only the sky filled with light.

ABOUT THE AUTHOR

Born in London in 1949, Peter Ackroyd is the author of the novels *The Great Fire of London; The Last Testament of Oscar Wilde; Hawksmoor;* and *Chatterton,* the last of which was published by Ballantine Books. He has also written an acclaimed biography of T.S. Eliot; and has just completed his monumental biography of Dickens.